COMES
TROUBLE

Also by Erin Kern

Looking for Trouble

ATTENTION CORPORATIONS AND ORGANIZATIONS:
MOST HACHETTE BOOK GROUP books are available
at quantity discounts with bulk purchase for educational,
business, or sales promotional use. For information,
please call or write:

**Special Markets Department, Hachette Book Group
237 Park Avenue, New York, NY 10017
Telephone: 1-800-222-6747 Fax: 1-800-477-5925**

HERE COMES TROUBLE

ERIN KERN

FOREVER

NEW YORK   BOSTON

Copyright © 2011 by Erin Kern
Excerpt from *Along Came Trouble* copyright © 2013 by Erin Kern
All rights reserved. In accordance with the U.S. Copyright Act of 1976, the scanning, uploading, and electronic sharing of any part of this book without the permission of the publisher is unlawful piracy and theft of the author's intellectual property. If you would like to use material from the book (other than for review purposes), prior written permission must be obtained by contacting the publisher at permissions@hbgusa.com. Thank you for your support of the author's rights.

Forever
Hachette Book Group
237 Park Avenue
New York, NY 10017

www.HachetteBookGroup.com

Printed in the United States of America

OPM

Originally published as an ebook

First Mass Market Edition: September 2013
10 9 8 7 6 5 4 3 2 1

Forever is an imprint of Grand Central Publishing.
The Forever name and logo are trademarks of Hachette Book Group, Inc.

The Hachette Speakers Bureau provides a wide range of authors for speaking events. To find out more, go to www.hachettespeakersbureau.com or call (866) 376-6591.

The publisher is not responsible for websites (or their content) that are not owned by the publisher.

For my kids.
And my other three "kids" for
unknowingly inspiring Lacy.

ACKNOWLEDGMENTS

As always, thank you to my husband, who never tires of bragging about me to everybody he meets. For the two best parents a girl could have, and my sister, also known as my first best friend. To the hardest working agent in the biz, Kristyn Keene. You never lose hope and always tell me what I need to hear. And to super ladies at Grand Central, Lauren Plude and Amy Peirpont. You helped a long-time dream come true. Thank you.

Dear Readers,

Welcome back to Trouble, where the outrageous and unpredictable McDermott family lives. In the last book we watched the oldest of the McDermott brothers, Noah, find his other half in Avery and how they brought balance to each other's lives.

We also met the yummy, playboy younger brother Chase. The carefree member of the family is content in his ways and has no intention of letting any woman get under his skin. So, of course, I knew just the woman who could bring him down a notch.

Lacy Taylor hasn't had an easy life. Her struggles have carved a special place in my heart, struggles that derived from experiences in my own life. I knew she needed to have her happy ending. At the same time, she also needs Chase and his own brand of heroism. Even if it isn't what she thinks she needs.

ONE

THE SECOND LACY TAYLOR opened her front door, she knew the two men standing outside weren't members of the Publisher's Clearing House Prize Patrol. She'd watched enough *FBI Files* to know a federal agent when she saw one. Remarkably bland, dark suits, crisp white shirts, and cheap ties could only be an ensemble put together by an officer of the government.

Lacy stood with her hand on the door frame, not bothering to invite them in for drinks. They probably wouldn't accept, anyway.

"Miss Lacy Taylor?"

He'd called her *Miss*. How polite.

The taller man who addressed her, roughly the size of Santa Claus with thick sandy hair, looked at her with amber-colored eyes and a bored expression.

The other man, whose skin was as dark as the coffee beans she'd ground up that morning, also looked at her with a bland expression. Was that something they were taught in FBI school, or wherever these two exciting gentlemen were from?

"Yeah, I'm Lacy," she answered after holding them in

suspense long enough. They were probably the type of men who didn't appreciate being held in suspense.

The larger man who'd been so patiently awaiting her answer pulled a black wallet-looking thing from inside his suit coat. "I'm Detective Whistler and this," he said with a jerk of his head at the shorter, wiry man, "is my partner, Detective Parks."

Detective Whistler held his impressive-looking identification in front of her face. To appease him, she leaned forward and read the ID. Yep, according to the miniscule piece of paper, he was indeed Detective Paul Whistler, from the St. Helena Police Department. But then again, what did she know about government IDs? She could be staring at a forgery and not even know.

Detective Parks also held out his ID, like the good little partner he was.

Detective Jon Parks, St. Helena Police Department.

"You two are an awfully long way from St. Helena." Okay, so it wasn't the most cheerful way to greet two men who'd traveled so far to see little ol' her. Call her suspicious, but no good could come of two police officers coming to visit.

"Do you mind if we come in, Miss Taylor? We have a few questions to ask you."

So Detective Parks really *did* have a voice. The deep timbre, like Darth Vader's, didn't match his thin, lanky frame at all. Maybe that's why he waited so long to speak: shock factor.

"Questions about what?" she asked instead of inviting them in. Sweat, which had nothing to do with the lack of air-conditioning in her ancient house, beaded on her upper lip and started to trickle down her back. A warm breeze ruffled the thick, overgrown trees in the front yard but only made her swelter even more.

She waited for them to hit her with the words she knew were coming.

"We're looking for Dennis Taylor. Your father."

I just knew it!

Lacy never referred to Dennis Taylor as *Father*. That was a term a man had to earn. Someone who showed more devotion to his cheap whiskey and the hard cement floor of a jail cell was a man who definitely hadn't earned that name. The mention of him still played hell with her emotions, and the emptiness his absence had created inside her had yet to be filled. For years, Lacy had searched for a way to fill it, but she'd lost hope. But she didn't tell them that. They didn't need to know the sordid details of her depressing childhood.

"He's wanted for questioning in a series of robberies. We have reason to believe he may be in this area," Detective Parks continued in his deep, Darth Vader voice.

Robberies? It seemed good old Dennis had not progressed past petty thefts.

Lacy shifted from one bare foot to the other, the wooden floor slick beneath her sweaty feet. "What makes you think he'd be here?"

Detective Whistler withdrew a handkerchief from his pocket and blotted his forehead. "For one thing, an eyewitness spotted him about a mile from here."

"And the other thing?"

"*You're* here, Miss Taylor," Detective Parks said.

Lacy shifted her attention to him. "I'm not on speaking terms with Dennis. I haven't seen him in almost five years." Lacy had filed that day away in the part of her brain called *Never Think About Again*. Showing up at her place of employment with broken handcuffs attached to one wrist and demanding money was not a good way to get back in her good graces. She remembered reading somewhere that he'd been arrested—yet again—shortly after she'd sent him away empty-handed. That was the last time she'd heard anything about him. Five years later, she'd assumed he was still rotting in jail with the rest of society's losers.

"Really?" Detective Whistler and his partner exchanged curious glances. She couldn't fault them for being skeptical. She resisted the urge to stomp her feet like a child and demand they believe her.

"Did you know this is listed as his home address?" asked Detective Whistler.

Lacy resisted the urge to sigh. "I'm sure it is," she said with great patience. "But like I said, it's been a long time since I've seen him." Her hair brushed along her back when she shook her head. "That's all I can tell you." When the men exchanged yet another doubtful glance, she reiterated, "Look, I would love nothing more than for Dennis to slip into a dark hole somewhere and never emerge again. I don't know where he is."

The muscles in Detective Park's jaw clenched as he pulled a business card out of a shiny silver card holder. "Here's my card. It has both our cell numbers on it. If you hear anything or if he contacts you in any way, call either of us immediately. Doesn't matter what time."

Oh, she would definitely do that. For nothing more than to see the look on Dennis's face at being ratted out by his own daughter. Again.

Lacy took the plain white card with their information printed on it in basic black letters.

"Thank you," was all she could think to say.

Detective Whistler gave a nod. "Have a nice day." And the two of them walked down the cracked sidewalk to their unsurprisingly boring black sedan, got in, and drove away.

Lacy stared down the street long after the detectives had disappeared. So Dennis had returned to his old haunts, had he? She hoped to hell he didn't think he'd find help here. *Except maybe help back to jail.*

She shut the door on the heat outside and walked through her even hotter house. Middle of summer was such an inconvenient time for a broken air conditioner, especially since she couldn't afford to fix the stupid thing.

Boris, her late Grandpa Ray's beloved English mastiff, lay snoring on the threadbare area rug in the living room. The dummy hadn't even flinched when the doorbell rang.

"Some watchdog you are."

His response was another loud snore and a twitch of his leg. Boris was a very twitchy sleeper.

Ray had purchased the mastiff as a pup about eight years ago and affectionately named him after the famous old-time actor Boris Karloff. Boris wasn't too bright and refused to sleep on the bed Lacy had purchased for him.

She took the hair tie out of her jean shorts' pocket and pulled her hair into a ponytail. Hell, she couldn't even afford a haircut. Waitressing didn't exactly afford her to enjoy the lap of luxury.

That was another thing she'd inherited from Ray: a mountain of debt.

Something licked Chase's face. Something with a very small, warm, and prickly tongue. It moved from his chin up to his nose. Unless a stray animal had somehow meandered into his house during the night, Chase would say he was in someone else's room.

He opened one bleary eye and was greeted by blinding sunlight.

Son of a bitch.

The bright, cheery light pierced his skull like a thousand nails hammering into his brain. The pressure made every part of his head throb. He recognized the symptoms for what they were: a hangover.

Now, if he could figure out where the hell he was, all would be right with the world.

The thing licking his face moved to his ear. Chase struggled to lift his arm, which had turned leaden along with his pounding head, and swatted the creature away. His hand came in contact with coarse fur and a deep growling meow sounded in his ear. His brain just about pounded through his skull. He groaned and rolled over onto his stomach.

Maybe Garfield had a shotgun and could put him out of his misery. The arms of sleep wrapped around him once again but retreated when a soft, warm, bare leg rubbed along his.

Dark, curly hair came into fuzzy view when Chase managed to open both his eyes. He thought he recognized her, but...no. Who did he know with dark, curly hair? Hell, he knew a dozen women who fit that description.

Great.

"Hello, lover." The husky, sleep-riddled voice was like ants crawling down his legs.

"Why are you shouting?" he mumbled into the pillow. "No shouting. Must be quiet."

The nameless woman next to him cackled like a witch and her leg slid farther over his. "I think someone had too much to drink last night."

Chase's only response was a grunt. Maybe if he ignored her, she'd shut up and go away so he could go to sleep.

The persistent woman didn't get his hint. "Come on, Chase. You promised me one more time," she whined. Chase hated it when women whined.

One more time his ass. He had no clear memory of last night, of even the first time, never mind one more time. He couldn't even keep his eyes open long enough to get a clear picture of her face. Maybe if she closed her curtains at night like a normal person, he could wake up without staring straight into the sun until his eyes boiled in his skull.

Slowly, images from the last twelve hours or so formed in his mind. He remembered closing up the restaurant after work and walking to his truck. It had been late, around midnight, the parking lot mostly empty. Chase squeezed his eyes tighter as the mystery woman next to him scraped her fingernails over his ass. What the hell was her name? She had been leaning against his truck when he walked out of the restaurant. She'd held a six-pack of beer in one hand and a bottle of Jack in the other. That would explain the hangover.

"Chasey . . ." She placed a kiss on his shoulder blade.

Ah, hell. Only one woman had the balls to call him *Chasey*.

Sonja Hartley, a woman with more beauty than brains. Her hair had been straight the last time he'd seen her; that's why he hadn't recognized her. They'd gone on a few dates about a year ago, but their relationship had never progressed past casual dinner and inventive sex. He remembered driving her to her house. His elementary detective skills deduced they had gotten shit-faced, then tumbled into bed. Great. It was like being back in college.

He groaned again and rolled over, if only to stop her from groping his ass. No way was he going another round with this woman. Had he been sober, he probably never would have gone the first round.

"You promised me, Chase." Her tone had gone from sweet and pleading to more demanding.

He tried one more time to open his eyes. The light was still blinding, but this time he managed to hold them open and blink the room into focus.

Holy hell! It was like Walt Disney had thrown up in here. What was the name of the princess who had her own castle at Disneyland? Cinderella? Chase imagined her room looking something like this. The bed was one of those four-poster canopy things with a sheer, gauzy curtain draped across the top. The rest of the room had white furniture and pink, girly shit strewn about on every available surface. If he had to wake up in this room every day, he'd throw himself in front of a truck.

"Chase, I'm serious. I have to be at work in an hour, and I know how you like to take your time."

Work. Shit.

"What the hell time is it?" he rasped, his throat sore and dry, as though he'd spent the night swallowing pinecones.

Sonja leaned across him to check her watch, which she'd discarded on the nightstand. Her breasts scraped against his chest. He had to get away from this woman. His mind was pretty logical about these things, but his manly parts weren't. They tended to respond whenever seeing a remotely attractive woman.

"It's eight o'clock," she responded.

Fabulous. He should have been at work an hour ago. He hoped his father had had a late morning, too, and wouldn't notice his tardiness. *Not likely.*

He kicked off the hideous, flowery, girly comforter and stood on weak legs. Not a great morning to skip his customary jog. He could really use the opportunity to regain his strength. Hell, he didn't even have time for a shower.

"Where're you going? I have a whole hour."

"I don't." He heard her moving underneath the sheets

and avoided looking at her. "Where the hell are my clothes?" He'd spotted his jeans on the other side of the room, but the rest were nowhere to be seen.

"I think your shirt and shoes are still in the living room."

He swiped his jeans off the floor and was about to pull them on when he remembered he was still buck-naked. "Where's my underwear?"

"I don't know." Fake innocence laced the morning huskiness of her voice. She'd pulled herself upright and held the lavender sheet around her breasts. She watched him with deep blue eyes while nibbling on a baby-pink nail.

The last time they'd been together, she'd somehow gotten hold of his watch. Reluctantly he'd driven back here to retrieve it, at which time she'd tried to get him into bed. Heck, maybe she did have brains after all.

"What'd you do with it?" He was starting to feel foolish, standing bare-ass naked in the middle of her room.

She pulled her knees up to her chest. "I swear I didn't do anything with it. Maybe it got kicked under the bed. You were kind of in a hurry," she said with a wicked and knowing smile.

He regarded her with suspicion; she only returned his stare with the same naughty tilt of her unpainted lips. His underwear wasn't under the bed. It could be anywhere, considering he couldn't remember taking it off.

"Screw it," he said, pulling the jeans on. "I'm going commando."

Naked, Sonja walked on her knees to the edge of the bed and ran her index finger over his chest. "Why are you in such a hurry? I'm offering you more sex." Her finger continued its journey down his stomach and into his pants, along with the rest of her hand.

Damn persistent woman. He managed to tear her hand away right before it wrapped around his not-so-sensible parts. "Will you stop molesting me? I'm late for work."

She sat on her heels and crossed her arms under her breasts, completely unconcerned by her nudity. "I see you still live by the same bang-and-run motto."

"You got that right." He tossed the words over his shoulder as he walked out of her room. Sure enough, his shirt lay by the front door, along with his socks and shoes. He gathered them up and walked outside to his truck.

The early morning air was already warm, promising another unbearably hot day. Chase left his shirt off and tossed it onto the passenger seat as he climbed into the vehicle. His phone, which had been left in the cup holder all night, beeped annoyingly at him from the second he sat down. The leather seat burned his backside, one spot in particular on his left shoulder blade. He ignored the pain and picked up his phone.

One voice message. Probably his father ripping him a new one for being late.

"Where the hell are you? There's food missing from the refrigerator. Drag yourself out of whoever's bed you're in and get your ass here."

Yep, his father definitely didn't sound happy. Maybe he'd just say his alarm clock broke.

What a morning to have a hangover.

Twenty minutes later, with combed hair and fresh clothes, Chase walked into McDermott's to face a less-than-pleased Martin. At eight-thirty in the morning, the restaurant was empty except for his father and the head chef, who were gathered in the kitchen. Like every morning, sous-chefs were at work pressing fresh pasta and cutting vegetables for the day's meals.

"What happened?" Chase walked across the large room and came to a stop in front of the two men.

His father turned to acknowledge him. "You're an hour and a half late."

"Sorry. I overslept." That was as close to the truth as he'd get. "Your message said there's food missing from the fridge."

"Five pounds of halibut are missing." A muscle in his father's jaw tensed.

"How do you know?"

"I did a supply check last night when I left. I counted fifteen pounds of halibut. When I got here this morning, there were only ten pounds," Henry said. Unlike most chefs, Henry's demeanor was calm. He was one of those men with very unremarkable looks, except for the russet-colored Fu Manchu and the sideburns that grew all the way down to his jawbone. Other than that, his five-foot-nine height made it hard for him to intimidate anyone. But the man could cook anything.

"What were we doing with fifteen pounds of leftover halibut?" Chase asked. They rarely had leftover food. Extra food equaled money loss, unless it was something they could puree or add as a side dish. Neither could be done with halibut.

"That's not the point," his father interjected. "We have over a hundred dollars' worth of seafood missing and no explanation. Where do you think they went, Mr. GM?" Martin directed his question to Chase.

"What're you asking me for? We shouldn't have had any leftover seafood anyway."

Henry threw a cautious glance at Martin. His throat worked before he answered. "We had a slow night."

Chase slid his hands into his pockets and jingled the change. "Have you asked Meryl and Phil?" Meryl and Phil, the sous-chefs, were the backbone of Henry's operation, and nothing went on in the kitchen they didn't know about.

"Meryl wasn't here last night. And Phil doesn't know what happened to them." Henry's thick fingers pulled at one of the buttons on his pristine white jacket.

"Seems to me we have a dishonest employee on our hands."

"Wait a minute, Dad." Chase knew exactly where his father's thoughts were heading. "Those fish would have been thrown away anyway. And you don't know that someone stole them. There could be a dozen explanations for this."

"Such as?"

Well, shit. He didn't have any ideas off the top of his head. His brain was still beer-foggy.

"I didn't think so. I have some paperwork to go over in my office. But I want you," Martin said with a glance at Chase, "to start going over the security tapes. Have something ready to show me by the end of the day. In the meantime, I don't care for tonight's specials. You and Henry need to come up with some new ones." With that, he disappeared through the heavy metal door that led to the offices upstairs.

That was his father for you, ever the consummate order-giver. Why was the man even here? He should be at the new restaurant that opened a few months ago. Hadn't Chase proven he could handle things here without the need for a babysitter? His father was such a control freak. Chase tried not to resent the particular trait that ran strong in his own blood. In fact, it was what made his father so successful. He just knew now Martin would use this whole someone-is-stealing-from-me thing to breathe even further down Chase's neck. Like he was some teenager in training who didn't know shit about restaurants.

As Henry walked away, Chase stood in the empty kitchen and couldn't ignore the burning on his back. Had Sonja held a lighter to his skin last night while he slept? The same small spot had burned all the way to work. It almost felt like someone had seared off his flesh. He rolled his shoulder to try easing the burning. It didn't help.

A heavy sigh flowed out of his sleep-deprived body. Might as well start watching those tapes. As if he didn't have anything better to do.

"Rough morning?"

The light bedroom voice floated over his skin and washed away any fatigue he'd been feeling. His senses went on instant alert. Funny how Lacy Taylor, a woman he hadn't given a passing thought to in his youth, managed to do that to him.

He turned and let his gaze meander down her body. A thin cotton shirt, draped loosely over small but perky breasts, fell almost to the hem of some frayed denim shorts. The cutoffs did a piss-poor job of covering creamy, slender thighs, thighs that were built to be wrapped around a man's hips. Chase's MO was usually a busty brunette. He didn't make a habit of going after skinny blondes who cut their jeans into shorts and were always ready to verbally spar with him. Lacy had a way of making his body rebel against his own mind.

"You're brooding," she added when he didn't respond to her.

"I don't brood."

She flipped a strand of long blond hair over her

shoulder. "All men brood. It's an occupational hazard. Plus I could hear your teeth grinding together when I walked in."

One corner of his mouth kicked up. "You think you're cute, don't you?"

"Noticed that, did you?"

He crossed his arms over his chest and ignored her comment. "You're here a little early."

Her teasing smile fell a fraction. "I need next week's schedule."

"You know Anita doesn't post those until Wednesdays."

"I was hoping she'd be here working on it."

"Sorry to disappoint."

Her teeth sank into her full lower lip as she gazed around the empty restaurant. The mischief lighting up her green irises faded. Chase wanted to coax that light back into her eyes. Getting her all riled up had become a favorite pastime of his. Lacy wasn't one to take flak from anyone, least of all him. She met him head-on every single time.

"She'll be here later, if you want to come back," he suggested when Lacy continued to gnaw on her lower lip.

She glanced at him but didn't say anything.

"Or she might already have it started in her office. I could take you back there." *Okay, now you just sound creepy.*

Her emerald eyes narrowed at him as though she'd just read his thoughts. "I'll just get it tomorrow night when I come to work."

"Is something wrong?" he found himself asking.

Her steady gaze dropped down to his midsection for the dozenth time in the past few minutes. He forced himself not to react.

"Nothing's wrong," she replied.

"You really can't lie worth a damn, can you?" he countered as he took a step toward her.

She didn't bother backing up. "I can lie a lot better than you think."

He lifted his brows and took another step until he was a whisper away from her. Lacy stood her ground and for once didn't have some smart-ass comment. Chase prided himself on being excellent at reading people. Lacy always pretended indifference around him, but her eyes gave her away. All he had to do was look into their depths to see through her.

"Really?" He bent over and whispered in her ear, "Because your attention is focused on things it probably shouldn't be."

Her jaw just about hit the floor as he brushed past her. One point for Chase.

TWO

Tonight was supposed to be Lacy's night off. An hour earlier, Becky-Lynn, one of the other servers, called begging Lacy to fill in for her. Lacy, being the gosh-darn nice person she was, couldn't say no. Instead of spending an evening at home, listening to Boris's snoring, here she was, waiting tables for people who couldn't decide if they wanted their steak rare or medium. *The tips tonight had better be good.*

Not that McDermott's wasn't a fine place to work, because it was. She'd been working there for two years now. What was supposed to have been temporary until she found something better ended up being a full-time career waiting tables. Over time, McDermott's had sort of grown on her. Kind of like a bad haircut where you say to yourself, *Eh, what the heck. I'll keep it,* because you know there's no other choice.

Plus she was good at her job. Probably one of the best servers there, if she did say so herself. The other waitstaff was friendly, and Henry was a doll. He didn't yell at his kitchen staff the way some chefs on those reality shows did. Lacy could deal with that.

There was one teeny, tiny thing she could do without, though. Most women probably wouldn't share the same complaint. But *most* women didn't have to deal with Chase McDermott the way she did. The man had been the bane of her existence as a teenager. He'd single-handedly coined the phrases *Twiggy Taylor* and *Lanky Lacy*. What surely was meant to be a joke had stuck with her all the way to college. So what if she'd been a little on the thin side in high school? Was that a reason to make someone's life miserable? She couldn't go hang out with his brother Brody without Chase answering the door and saying, "Well hello there, Miss Twiggy." Even now the phrase made her want to snarl like a rabid animal. Brody had never said those things to her because he was such a swell guy. Why couldn't she have had a crush on him instead of his mean older brother?

Okay, so she really didn't hate working for Chase. He was a good boss. And kind of, sort of, easy on the eyes. Well, more than that. She was adult enough to admit Chase McDermott had grown into a fine-looking man. Her heart fluttered a little whenever he was within sniffing distance. Not even under the pain of death would she admit that to anyone. Especially to the man in question, who had an ego the size of Saturn.

She fed her latest order into the computer and decided to use her upcoming break to her advantage. She got Matt, one of the other servers, to cover her tables while she took thirty minutes to herself. After eating a barely satisfying ham and cheese sandwich with stale chips, Lacy went upstairs to do something she'd been dreading all night: speak to Chase.

While she might not hate working for him, she *hated* asking him for favors. Yes, he'd given her a job when most of the other places in town hadn't been hiring. But at an early age, Lacy discovered Chase had an uncanny ability to make her feel like she always owed him something. She couldn't fault that as a family trait, because Brody had never been like that. It had to be a unique Chase trait.

She knocked on the office door. After hearing a muffled response, she opened it. She had no idea if he had said "come in" or not, but what the hell? She went in anyway.

The man who'd made her heart constantly do its own love/hate tug-of-war didn't acknowledge her when she entered. He sat perched on the edge of his desk, remote control in one large hand pointed at the small television on the credenza.

"I need to talk to you about next week's schedule."

His attention stayed on the black-and-white image on the television. "You know I don't deal with scheduling."

"I know but Anita isn't here, and this can't wait."

He pushed a button on the remote and the image on the screen froze. His blue eyes zeroed in on her. Lacy had never been able to fully prepare herself for his eyes, which were the same color as a cloudless sky. They were one of the first things that had drawn her to him and influenced her stupid teenage crush. Now was no different. Only she didn't have a crush on him. Really, she didn't. In fact, she did her best to ignore him and the way he made her insides feel like cottage cheese.

His gaze lowered to her button-up white shirt, which was the customary McDermott's uniform. "What's so important it can't wait?"

"I need a few days off next week."

"Find someone to fill in for you."

She took a deep breath and caught a hint of his scent. It was a manly soap that reminded Lacy of Irish Spring.

Chase wasn't really a cologne kind of guy. Her eyes almost rolled back into her head. From now on she'd always associate Chase with that distinctive bar soap scent. "I've tried that already. No one can do it."

He crossed his arms over his chest, which looked hard and sculpted beneath his light blue shirt.

"What do you expect me to do about it?" A mischievous glint lit his eyes, making them even bluer. Why did she still have to be affected by him?

"Find someone and make them do it." Yes, she knew that sounded childish, but he was the boss. He could do it easily.

A slow smile graced his boyish face and developed into a laugh. The kind of laugh that rolled over her and felt like a caress of very talented hands.

His laughter died but the smile lingered. "Why do you need these days off?"

She shifted from foot to foot and tucked a strand of hair that had come loose from her ponytail behind one ear. "That's not really any of your business, Chase."

Again his gaze lingered on parts that weren't her face; this time her hips drew his attention. "If I have to rearrange the schedule, it is."

She heaved a sigh. He had her on that one. "I have some things of Ray's I need to work on." A bit of an understatement but still the truth. After being abandoned by her mother at the age of four and having a father who spent more time in jail than out, she'd relied on Ray as the only person who wouldn't abandon her.

Chase slowly shook his head. "That doesn't sound like a good enough reason to take time off work."

They stared at each other a few tense moments. She really didn't want to go into details. But Chase was going to stare at her in that unnerving way of his until she blurted it all out.

"What's really going on, Lace?"

He and Brody had been the only ones to ever call her Lace. It was not a nickname she'd been particularly fond of. On the other hand, anything was better than Lanky Lacy.

He remained on the corner of the desk, his massive forearms crossed over his chest. He kept rolling his left shoulder, like he had an itch he couldn't reach. She'd noticed him doing that earlier, accompanied by a wince of pain.

"Why do you keep moving your shoulder like that?"

His eyes narrowed. "What do you mean?"

She motioned to his left shoulder. "You haven't stopped flexing it all night."

His disarming smile returned. "Can't keep your eyes off me, can you?"

Her eyes lifted heavenward. Lord help her with egotistical men. "What'd you do to it?"

"Nothing," he answered a little too quickly.

"Nothing?" she answered with a mocking tone of her own. "Let me take a look at it."

"That's not necessary," he said with a shake of his head.

She offered him one of her sweet smiles, which probably came off more condescending than genuine. "I'll make a deal with you. You let me look at whatever's bothering your shoulder and I'll tell you what's really going on."

"Boy, you really want to get my clothes off, don't you?"

"Forget it." She turned toward the door. It was impossible to have a serious conversation with a man who thought every woman wanted to get in his pants.

"Lacy," he started with that chuckle she always

found way too sexy. "I'm kidding. Come on, don't walk away mad."

When she turned back around, he'd stood from the desk. He towered over her at six-three . . . Well, she didn't know exactly how tall he was. But he was *really* tall. Lacy stood at an average five-seven and Chase had to be a good six or seven inches taller than she was.

"You never did take a joke very well."

She planted her hands on her hips. "I don't appreciate being teased when I'm trying to help someone."

He held his hands up in defense. "All right, calm down. If you're that worried, you can look at it. But don't forget your end of the deal."

"Yes, Daddy."

That remark earned another teasing smile. When she stopped in front of him, he flicked the end of her nose with his index finger. "You're so cute when you get riled."

"Oh, is that why you do it? Turn around," she said before he had a chance to reply. "On second thought, you need to sit down."

He glanced over his shoulder at her. "Why?"

"You're too tall. It'll be easier for me to check your shoulder if you're sitting."

A pregnant pause filled the air before he answered. "I don't think it's my shoulder. The burning feels like it's in the middle of my back."

"Burning? What kind of burning?"

His wide shoulders moved in a shrug. "I don't know, just burning."

"When did this burning start?"

Another pause. "This morning."

"Okay," she said, unsure of what to say next. "You have to take off your shirt."

In one fluid motion, he pulled the shirt out of his pants and drew it over his head. The whole time, Lacy watched, fascinated with the way each muscle moved beneath his tanned skin. She'd seen him without his shirt before, years ago at the local lake. He'd been a boy then, somewhere around seventeen or eighteen. Years had made him bigger, taller and wider. She could count each defined muscle in his back just from watching him move. But she wouldn't. That would be too . . . well, she just wouldn't.

His skin looked like satin over muscle, and she wanted to run her hands all over so her fingers could feel each and every ridge.

When she focused her attention on her task and not how delicious he was, she noticed four thin, long, bloody scratches. Right where he'd described them.

They looked painful. Lacy also knew exactly what they were the second she looked at them. Fingernail scratches.

"Um . . ." She cleared her throat and touched her index finger to one of them. "How'd you get these?" Her finger came away clean, as the blood had long since dried. But they had bled.

"I'm not sure." This time he cleared his throat. "Exactly."

Okay, liar.

"Do you have any rubbing alcohol in here?"

He threw an alarmed glance over one thick shoulder. "Why?"

"Chase, these have to be cleaned. Do you know how much bacteria is underneath a human fingernail?"

When he turned, she had to back up so he wouldn't consume her personal space. "What makes you think these were done by fingernails?"

She held up one hand. "Look at my nails. They're almost the exact size of those scratches."

"So?"

A rude noise popped out of her mouth. She placed her hands on his hard shoulders and turned him around. "I know what fingernail scratches look like. So do you have any alcohol or not?"

"I think there's a first-aid kit underneath the sink in the bathroom."

The bathroom adjoining his office was no bigger than a coat closet. Done in bland white tile and industrial, blinding light, she felt as though she'd entered a sardine can. There was a little black pouch with a red cross on top, right where he'd said it would be. Lacy opened it, found the rubbing alcohol and some cotton swabs. She walked to Chase's fine backside and tried not to laugh.

"What'd you do?" she asked as she poured some of the alcohol onto a cotton ball. "Piss off some poor woman's husband?"

"First of all," he said in a strangled voice after she placed the cold, wet cotton on the first scratch. "I don't get involved with married women. Second of all, if I had, I'd have a black eye. Not scratches on my back."

"Pardon me." Slowly, so as not to sting him too much, she swiped the alcohol-soaked ball down the scratch, disinfecting it as best she could. She didn't know why she asked him how he got these. She knew. Some nameless woman couldn't contain herself in the throes of passion and dug her nails into his back. She'd heard of women who were back scratchers, but *this* was ridiculous.

"Start talking, Lace."

"Well, I was born in a little town just south of Yellowstone—"

"Nice try, Chatty Cathy. But you made me a deal, remember?"

Of course she remembered. Being this close to his naked skin and smelling his woodsy shampoo had clouded her logical thinking. She discarded the first swab and poured some alcohol on a second one.

He flinched when she placed it on the next scratch. "Holy hell, woman. Did you pour acid on that thing?"

A satisfied smile tilted one corner of her mouth. That's what he got for being so irresistible. "Sorry. Maybe next time you'll go out with a woman who doesn't have cat claws."

"Ha-ha, Twiggy."

She paused with the cotton ball halfway down his back. "Call me that one more time and I really *will* pour acid on you."

He cleared his throat. "We're getting off subject here. Tell me what's going on."

She bit her bottom lip while lightly dabbing the cotton to his marred skin, unsure of what to tell him. One more time she decided to play dumb. "It's really not that big of a deal."

"Okay, Tw—"

"All right!" she bit out with a glare at his backside, then blew out an exasperated sigh. "It's just that Ray left me with a few more things that I could do without. Well, technically it's not really Ray's fault." Ray had done the best he could with Lacy. He'd clothed her, made sure she went to school, and fed her three meals a day. Grandfathers weren't supposed to do those things. They were supposed to spoil you with extra stuff like cookies before breakfast and backyard campouts. Bless his heart; he'd had no clue how to raise a teenage girl. He taught her things like how to use a lawnmower and change the oil in a car.

"What does that mean?"

She tossed aside her current cotton ball and soaked another one. "Ray had a friend of his handling his will, if you could even call it a will. I don't know exactly what the guy did, or how he managed to get away with it, but he hadn't been entirely truthful when he disclosed Ray's assets."

Okay, so it was a bigger deal than that. Lacy really didn't want to tell him this. Why did she have to go and make that stupid deal? So she could clean his sex-induced scratches? So not worth it.

"What exactly does that mean?"

"That's the problem. I can't tell you exactly." She pulled in another breath. "The IRS is auditing me because there were hidden assets not included in the final accounting. I didn't fully understand, so I saw a tax attorney this morning. He said what the guy did was borderline fraud. Apparently the IRS has been investigating it since Ray's death and now wants to collect on these unpaid taxes." The whole thing came out in a rush, like the words had been waiting for the opportune time to force themselves out. "At the time of Ray's death, it seemed like everything was in order. And I didn't have any reason not to trust the guy."

Chase turned to face her. "How much money are you talking about?"

She lifted her shoulders in a pathetic shrug and tossed the last cotton ball onto the desk. "Somewhere in the vicinity of twenty thousand dollars," she mumbled to the ground beneath her scuffed black shoes.

"Twenty *grand*? Jesus, Lacy. When did you find this out?"

"I got a letter today in the mail."

"And this is why you need some time off?"

Time off wasn't going to fix her problem; she knew that. But, jeez, she'd never given thought to things like this. Ray had only been dead for about a year, and he'd always taken care of it. At least, she thought. She'd never even seen a bill, until the one she got this morning. Ray had been the only person in her life worthy of her love and he'd always meant the world to her. How could he have left her in this position? Or maybe he hadn't known his friend was a borderline crook?

Her eyes grew hot as moisture built in the corners. She would *not* cry in front of Chase. Dammit, she was stronger than that.

"I just need time to think and go through Ray's paperwork." Her voice came out thick from her frustration and helplessness.

"What you need is money."

No shit. Money was the one thing she didn't have.

"Gee, is that all?"

"Do you need some?"

From him? No flipping way.

She shook her head. "I'll figure something out. Maybe I'll sell the Lincoln." Upon Ray's death from lung cancer a year ago, Lacy had become guardian to an aging and outdated ranch house and a 1975 Lincoln Continental with rusty gold paint. Ray probably thought he was being generous by leaving her his most prized possessions. Lacy wasn't so sure. Half the time the Lincoln didn't start, forcing her to walk to work, which was not energizing despite what some people might think.

Chase snorted and slipped his arms into his shirt. "You won't get a thousand dollars for that piece of junk."

"Maybe I can make monthly payments to them," she

wondered aloud, more to herself than Chase. Why did she have to include him in this?

When she'd thrown out the cotton balls and faced Chase again, he'd put his shirt on and buttoned it up. Probably for the best. The last thing she needed to do was drool over him.

"I've been taking care of myself for a long time. I'll figure this out," she said again.

He stared at her with two thick brows pulled low over light blue eyes. "It's okay to ask for help if you need it. You can't do *everything* by yourself."

Desperate to change the subject, Lacy searched her brain for something to say, anything. Then she remembered he'd been watching something. She nodded her head toward the TV. "What're you watching?"

He glanced at the frozen screen of the television. "Nothing exciting."

O-kay. "In other words, you can't tell me because I'm an employee?"

His response was a smile and a nod.

"And here I thought we were sharing things."

"Sorry to disappoint you, Miss Taylor."

Well, he could just keep his secrets, then. If there was trouble at the restaurant, she'd find out eventually. Half the other waitresses were notorious blabbermouths.

She glanced at her cheap drugstore watch. "My break's over." When he didn't respond to that, she added, "So, you'll take care of the schedule?"

Once more, his bone-melting eyes raked over her ho-hum white-shirt-and-black-pants uniform. "I'll see what I can do."

Instead of uttering a *thank you*, she just smiled, not

trusting her voice to come out even. She walked to the door and opened it.

"Lacy."

Halfway through the doorway, she paused. "Yeah?"

"You can clean my scratches anytime."

Oh, for Pete's sake. The man was incorrigible!

With a shake of her head and a smile, Lacy left the office.

"Find anything yet?"

At the sound of his father's voice, Chase realized Lacy hadn't shut his door. The patriarch of the McDermott family stood in his office doorway wearing his customary Dockers and black button-up shirt.

What was the old man still doing here?

"Nothing out of the usual." The search for a thief had slipped his mind amid all his inappropriate thoughts.

Martin remained in the doorway. "Well, keep at it. There has to be something in those tapes." He turned to leave, but Chase stopped him.

"Dad, wait." He wasn't sure he should even say this. "What if it's not theft? What if Henry's just mistaken?"

His father's thick gray brows wrinkled together. "Henry's never been mistaken before." He paused. "Just humor me. If nothing comes up, then we'll consider the case closed."

Chase only nodded, knowing there was nothing he could do but appease his father. Something made him think this was a lost cause. None of his employees would steal from him. Would they?

THREE

LACY HAD NO IDEA how much useless garbage Ray had hoarded over the course of his life. Scraps of fabric and boxes of pinecones had been all she'd unearthed in the spare bedroom closet. This was exactly why she'd been putting this off. Somehow she knew she'd find nothing useful, like a DustBuster. Or, hey, money would have been good. No, Ray had to collect items like stamps from 1942.

It had been sometime after discovering her seventh jar of brown buttons that she'd decided the whole process was futile. Cleaning out Ray's effects had been continually put on the back burner since his death. Lacy didn't do sentiment. She didn't *ooh* and *aah* over babies or cry at sad movies. If that made her a cynic, so be it. The world could thank her parents for that one.

The idea of sorting through closets full of Lord only knew what just didn't make her want to jump up and down for joy. There were so many other productive things she could do with her time. Like, finding a place to live when the county took her house.

The cheerful paper she'd received in the mail remained in

the drawer where she'd stuffed it three days ago. She'd put it in there thinking, *Out of sight, out of mind*. Her plan hadn't worked. Her mind refused to think about anything else.

What the hell was she going to do? No way could she come up with twenty thousand dollars in thirty days. Unless maybe she started prostituting herself. Wouldn't dear old daddy be proud of her then?

She'd been in shitty situations before, but this definitely took the prize. Selling the car wouldn't do any good. Chase had been right; she wouldn't get more than a grand for the stupid vehicle.

After abandoning her quest to clear out Ray's stuff, Lacy headed to the only part of the house she truly loved being in: her "art studio." As a child, drawing had really been nothing more than a hobby. She'd put pen to paper and sketch the first object her eyes landed on. At the time, her hobby had merely been a way to take her mind off her father being arrested again. Or whether the woman who'd given birth to her ever regretted walking out on them. When she drew, all she saw was the paper in front of her and the object she drew.

In college, she'd hoped to be an art major and eventually make millions selling her drawings in ritzy studios. Yeah, that never happened. Her grades slipped, and she'd lost her scholarship. Unable to afford paying for college on her own, she'd been forced to drop out. Ray didn't seem to mind. As long as she was happy, or so he'd always told her. That was one of the traits she loved most about the old man. He never judged her.

She'd spent a few years working whatever jobs she could find. Eventually Ray's illness had brought her home.

Being back in Trouble was not what she'd pictured for her future.

The "studio" she'd put together after moving back was actually just an empty room. She'd managed to fill it with a few pieces of furniture and inspirational items like Ray's old rotary phone and an antique water pump. Her supplies, including pencils, charcoal, watercolors, and paints, sat on Ray's ancient and splintered desk. She'd chosen this room because it had the best light. In the early mornings, the sun streamed in full blast, setting the perfect mood to sketch whatever came to mind. She'd yet to sell anything, though—something she needed to remedy. As soon as she found a studio where an amateur could hang their work, she'd have her in.

She'd just sat down on the couch, pad in her lap, when a knock came from the front door. Considering the last someone who'd visited had come bearing unpleasant news, Lacy was a tad reluctant to open it.

She still held out hope the Publisher's Clearing House people would find her. So she got off the couch and went to the door. When she opened it, maybe she'd see a man holding a giant fake check with a camera crew behind him. No luck. It was only Chase. Her heart jumped all over her chest.

"If you have fresh scratches, you've come to the wrong place."

Chase, his eyes hidden behind a pair of sunglasses, graced her with an openmouthed smile. "You're a riot, Miss Twiggy."

She started to slam the door in his face when he slapped his palm against it, preventing her from completing her task. "What do you want, Chase?"

He held up a white envelope. "I came here to give you a present, and this is how you treat me?"

"Depends on what you mean by *present*."

One of his sexy, I-know-I'm-God's-gift-to-women laughs rolled over her when he shoved his way past her. "So suspicious."

"Do come in," she said after he already stood in the entryway. The presence of him in the house zapped all the serenity she'd been basking in a moment ago.

He pulled off his sunglasses and hooked them in the pocket of his white T-shirt. How could a plain cotton shirt threaten to make her babble like a two-year-old?

"It's such a beautiful day out. Why are you spending your day off indoors?"

She eyed the envelope in his hands. "I was actually just getting ready to leave."

One corner of his mouth twitched. "Liar."

How does he know? Maybe he pays more attention to me than I thought. Her only response was a closed-lipped smile.

He thrust the envelope at her. "Here." The sexy hint of a grin disappeared, leaving his ruggedly handsome face impassive.

Lacy didn't accept it. Chase hadn't made a habit of giving her presents, except nicknames. She wasn't any more excited to accept the envelope than she had his cutesy monikers.

"It's not a rattlesnake, Lace," he said with a roll of his eyes. "Just take it."

Only mild curiosity compelled her to take the envelope from his big, tanned hands. Feeling Chase's eyes on her, Lacy slid the flap open and pulled out a check. A check made out to her for twenty thousand dollars.

Holy hell. She'd always prided herself on being a quick thinker. This time her brain failed to offer her any kind of intelligent response. Her heart did a little jig up to her throat. She had to pull a deep breath into her lungs to keep from hyperventilating. The little check fluttered as her hand shook from disbelief and shock. Unable to look at Chase, she managed to shove the check back into the envelope. "No way." She held it out to him, but he didn't take it.

Independence had always been her first defense in her screwy world. From an early age, she'd learned to take care of herself. Accepting help from a man who'd gone from being her nemesis to the object of her fantasies put her into an uncomfortable position. While his generous offer would solve her problems, it took away something she'd always worked so hard to keep. Not even when forced would she allow Chase to be that person. He already had a power over her she hadn't been willing to admit.

"What're your other options?" Through her foggy brain, his voice came from far away, even though he stood entirely too close.

The scratched wood floor, as well as her bare feet, remained the focus of her attention. "I don't know, but I told you I'll figure it out." She shoved the envelope harder, crumpling it against his chest, which felt like tempered steel. "Please, just take this."

"Why? Afraid you'll owe me something?"

Chase probably meant his words to be a joke, but they hit way too close to home. She didn't want to owe him, or anyone, anything.

His warm hand wrapped around hers, the one holding his gift, and pulled it away from his chest. The other hand tipped her chin up. "Lacy, this is not open for debate. You need it and I want you to have it." His intense blue gaze stared into hers. "Just take the check and say 'Thank you, Chase.'"

Her hand remained in his firm grip, and she couldn't force her eyes away from his. "I don't want this," she whispered.

The same disarming half-smile returned. "I know."

"Where did you even get this much money?"

His broad shoulders lifted in a shrug. "I've invested well." They stared at each other for a few seconds; then he placed one palm behind his ear as if listening for something. "I'm waiting..."

She smiled despite herself. Chase had a magical ability to coax a grin out of her. "Thank you."

"You're welcome. Now, breathe a sigh of relief and do what you need to do with it." He rocked forward on the balls of his feet. "So, what're you working on right now anyway?"

Lacy folded the check in half and stuck it in her back pocket. "I was sorting through Ray's stuff, but that got old really fast."

"And now?"

Why was he so curious about her schedule? Lacy didn't tell many people about her love for drawing, and Chase was definitely one of those people who didn't know. Telling him would bring him too much into her private life. Best to keep him at arm's length.

She attempted nonchalance by shrugging. "Right now, nothing."

Chase, so big he practically consumed all the space around her, nodded. He looked at her in that way of his, like he saw down into her soul. How did he do that? How could one man make her unsure if she either wanted him or hated him?

"I gotta run," he said abruptly as he stepped around her and slid his sunglasses back on.

He'd made it halfway out the door when she stopped him. "Wait a minute." For Pete's sake, the man had just given her twenty thousand dollars of his own money. Shouldn't she at least offer him something? Out of nervous habit, Lacy licked her lips. "Would you like some coffee or maybe a soda?"

Coffee or soda? Is that the best you can do?

Thankfully his piercing blue eyes were hidden by his dark sunglasses. Somehow she'd made him smile, a slow I'm-going-to-give-you-the-best-orgasm-of-your-life smile. Lacy almost whimpered.

"Be careful, Miss Taylor. You might actually start to like me."

The door shut with a soft click behind him, but Lacy could have sworn she heard him laugh.

Dennis had yet to show his face in Lacy's neck of the woods. He was probably skulking in the shadows somewhere, waiting for the opporfune time to hit her up for money. Even if she *did* have money to spare, she'd rather burn it than see it in Dennis's hands.

She picked up the last of the dirty plates from the empty table, only to knock one of the glasses onto the plush carpet. Some of the leftover liquid splashed on her beat-up boots. *Wonderful.* Thinking about Dennis made her spill iced tea on her only pair of work shoes.

Why her father continued to annoy her thoughts, she'd yet to figure out. He certainly wasn't worth the pains that flared up in her chest. Years of having him appear when she least expected had her on edge. He knew she still lived in Ray's house. Would anything stop him from showing up on her doorstep? Or forcing his way in? Dennis had never been physical with her, even when drunk.

Thankfully she still had the detective's card in case he came sniffing around.

She barely made it to the kitchen with the armful of dishes she gathered from the table, but she managed to dump them into the bin to be washed without dropping any. Usually the busboy did all the clearing. Tonight was an especially busy night, so to speed things along, Lacy did the clearing for him.

"Andrew," she called to the lanky sixteen-year-old boy. "Tables six and seven need to be cleared."

The boy, who already had a bin-full of dirty dishes he'd dumped in the sink, grabbed the rag out of his waistband and ran it in the water.

"I think the entire town of Trouble is dining out tonight," grumbled Sarah, a recent high school graduate, as she waited for some entrées.

Henry, who double-checked every dish before it exited the kitchen, busily wiped the edges of the white plates for any stray sauce. Once satisfied the plates shone to perfection, he placed them in front of Sarah.

She looked at the three plates and pulled her thin, dark brows together. "I'm missing a Wellington, Chef."

Henry straightened and turned. "Larry, how much longer on that Wellington?"

The noise of the kitchen made it hard for anyone to have a normal conversation, and Henry had to shout to be heard. Add the heat that made Lacy's hair stick to her neck, and the kitchen was a pretty miserable place to be.

Larry, who frantically shifted pots around on the nine-burner stove, glanced at the head chef. "I need two minutes on that Wellington, Chef."

Henry jabbed a finger at Larry. "Make it one."

"Yes, Chef."

No one dared talk back to Henry. Everyone knew how deceiving his calm demeanor could be. When he gave an order, his cooks were expected to listen.

Henry turned around and inspected more dishes. "They're going to have to wait one more minute." One of the rules of McDermott's was all the patrons got their dishes at the same time.

A heavy sigh radiated from Sarah. Lacy had just about turned around to the kitchen door when Sarah said, "Have you seen Chase tonight?"

Lacy glanced at the younger girl. She was cute, in a preppy, cheerleader sort of way. Her shiny dark hair, pulled in a high ponytail, always swung side to side when she walked. "No, why?"

She shook her head. "Boy, is he in a bad mood. About an hour ago, I asked him if we had any more Pinot Grigio. He practically bit my head off."

It wasn't like Chase to snap at his waitresses. "What did he say?"

Sarah turned and glanced at Larry's progress, impatient for her beef Wellington. "One of my diners ordered a bottle of it. But when I went to get it from the wine cooler, there wasn't any left. So I asked Chase if he knew what had happened to it. He just shook his head and said I needed to tell them to order something else. He's had this thunderous look on his face ever since."

Lacy wasn't sure what to say to that. Maybe Chase hadn't realized they had just run out of the Pinot. Stuff like that rarely happened, though. She'd only caught glimpses of him tonight, and she hadn't been looking at his face. Fortunately for her, none of her diners had wanted any Pinot Grigio. Lacy and Chase normally didn't engage in deep conversations during work anyway. Most of the time it was snarky remarks from him and a retort from her. They had a complex relationship Lacy had yet to figure out.

"Anyway," Sarah continued as the beef Wellington was finally placed in front of Henry to inspect. "For some reason Mr. M is hanging around. I think that's partly why Chase is on edge. Just a word of caution, though." Sarah placed the dishes on her tray. "If you want a stress-free evening, steer clear of Chase." She turned on her heel and sashayed out of the kitchen, her ponytail swinging.

Heck, Lacy didn't need a nineteen-year-old cheer-leader to tell her that. Unfortunately, she couldn't manage to stay away from him.

She headed out to the dining room to check on her diners and noticed her two cleared tables now had people at them. The two-topper had an elderly couple who'd placed their menus down and sipped from their water glasses. Lacy took that as a sign they wanted to order. After taking care of both tables, she fed the orders into the machine, surreptitiously peering about for Chase. He wasn't on the floor, and after Sarah's warning, Lacy's suspicions were piqued. During business hours, he was almost always on the floor.

The dining room buzzed with the clinking of glasses and murmur of soft voices. McDermott's was always full, keeping Lacy on her toes and making the evening fly by. She enjoyed what she did, even if the pay wasn't that great. With a glance around, she noticed a man at table three drumming his fingers on the white table-cloth. The people had yet to receive the Veal Osso Buco Ravioli appetizer they'd ordered. Not wanting an irate diner on her hands, Lacy went to the kitchen to harass the cooks.

"Henry, I need the veal ravioli for table three. They're getting antsy."

The head chef didn't even glance up from inspecting the dishes. "It's coming, it's coming." He turned his head and shouted to be heard over the noise of the kitchen. "Suzanne, I need a time for that Osso Buco app."

"Uh, Chef." Suzanne, the cook assigned to the appetizer station, approached Henry with a nervous wringing of her hands. She had always been a twitchy cook. "I was just in the fridge to get the spinach to sauté it and I noticed there isn't any."

Henry jerked around to face Suzanne, who stood like a woman waiting for her execution. "How the hell can we be out of spinach?" He glanced at his sports watch. "It's only seven-fifteen."

Suzanne sputtered and looked around. "I...I don't know. The dish is ready. I just need the spinach."

"Ah, shit!" Henry, in a rare show of outrage, slammed a dish on the counter, breaking it in three sections.

Lacy backed up a step, more to avoid shards of glass than Henry's temper.

"Just plate the damn dish and bring it here," he barked, and Suzanne rushed away to her station. Henry turned his irate glare on Lacy. "You'll just have to apologize and tell them there's no spinach. How the hell are we out of spinach?" he asked again.

Poor Henry. Lacy didn't have an answer for him. It wasn't her job to check the supplies. As general manager, Chase was in charge of that. She only had to deliver the food that was ordered. Was Chase slacking on his duties? Was that why his father hung around? No, that couldn't be the reason. Chase might have been a lot of things, but a slacker he was not. No one at the restaurant worked harder than Chase. McDermott's didn't often run out of food in the middle of a dinner service, but it wasn't completely unheard of. Maybe they were just having a bad run tonight.

Even though she told herself that, something nagged at the back of her mind. Could they have a dishonest employee on their hands? She did a quick inventory of all the staff, yet couldn't come up with anyone who would steal from the restaurant. But appearances could be deceiving. Just because someone didn't seem dishonest didn't mean they weren't.

She grabbed the ravioli, sans spinach, and carried the plate to her impatient diners. Should she confront Chase about a possible theft? Would it be out of line for her to do so? Even though she'd never had a problem speaking her mind, something told Lacy to keep her mouth shut about this. Chase probably wouldn't appreciate her sticking her nose in his job. With an apology about the spinach and an "enjoy your appetizer," Lacy placed the dish in the middle of the table. Relatively sure her diners were satisfied for the time being, she decided to take a quick break to eat.

Grabbing her brown-bag dinner from her shoebox-size locker, she headed outside to the back of the building. The cool, quiet night in the outdoors beat out the stuffy, small break room. Whenever possible, Lacy ate her meal outside to get a reprieve from all the noise and heat. The time to herself gave her a moment to think about her next drawing and how to go about showing her work in a gallery. Art had always been in the back of her mind from the time she'd been about ten. As a child, she'd take her mind off her father's whereabouts by daydreaming about working in a fancy studio and selling her own paintings.

Why did she have to go and lose her scholarship? She

could have used the degree to get a job in Los Angeles or someplace more promising than this. By the second semester of her sophomore year, all the studying and work hours had been more than she could handle. Her grade point average had slipped below a 3.5, and the university had taken her scholarship away. Ray certainly hadn't had any money to support her college education and her father had slipped into whatever hole he frequented. When she'd called Ray to tell him, he'd said something along the lines of getting herself a full-time job so she could afford to stay in her little apartment. That's what she'd done. She'd applied at several art studios, hoping to get her foot in the door. Unfortunately for her, none had been interested in a kid with no art experience and no college degree. So she'd taken a job as a receptionist at a local law firm. That job had only lasted about a year before she moved on to a customer service representative for a credit card company. Needless to say, Lacy had a track record of hopping from one job to the next. Two years at McDermott's was, so far, her longest stay with an employer.

It wasn't like she had an inability to commit. Really, she didn't. After a while, she just started to feel restless with her current occupation. Like there was something better waiting for her somewhere else. She supposed that was her old man's "the grass is always greener" motto coming out in her. *Thanks a lot, Dennis.*

Lacy stuffed the last bit of her sandwich back into the bag as a white station wagon pulled into the parking lot. The headlights almost blinded her when the car stopped at the opposite corner of the building. She was too far away to identify the driver, who was a silhouette in the darkness. Not that she thought much about it anyway. People pulled in and out of the parking lot all the time. She had just reached into her lunch bag for the apple she'd packed when one of the waitresses came out of the back door and walked to the station wagon. A bag, filled with something, swung heavily from one of the girl's hands. Lacy recognized the short hair and realized it was Jessie. The high school student almost never worked on a weeknight, so Lacy had no idea what she was doing there. The driver of the car rolled down the window as Jessie approached. She said something to the other person, then handed the plastic bag through the window. It was virtually impossible for Lacy to tell the contents of the bag, but whatever Jessie had in there was big. Lacy tried not to stare. She bit into her apple and fixed her gaze on the ground in front of her. Why was she so suspicious? Just because a few items had gone missing didn't mean the waitress was sneaking food to her cohort in a white station wagon. Could be a dinner. Could be clothes. She could be returning something she'd borrowed. Not everyone was a dishonest thief like her father. Out of the corner of her eye, she saw Jessie lean through the open window and kiss the driver. Lacy didn't know Jessie that well, so she didn't say anything to the girl when Jessie went back inside the restaurant.

The car flipped a U-turn in the parking lot, making a high-pitched squealing sound as it left. Lacy discarded half the apple in her lunch bag. Jessie seemed like a nice, honest person, certainly not someone capable of stealing. But the girl hardly ever worked on a weeknight, and there just happened to be food missing from the fridge. Should Lacy voice her concerns to Chase? No. There was no need to get Jessie in trouble for something that could be completely innocent. Besides, Chase was busy enough without listening to Lacy's cooked-up suspicions.

She stood and tossed the brown paper bag into a garbage can. When she walked back into the kitchen, she spotted Chase on the other side of the room talking to Henry. Henry spoke, gesturing with his hands, and Chase had his arms crossed over his chest, giving Henry his complete attention. He looked especially good in a white dress shirt and tan slacks. He nodded at something Henry said while glancing around the kitchen. His gaze connected with hers and that familiar heat warmed her from the pit of her stomach to the top of her head. He didn't smile at her, but this wasn't unusual. He often didn't smile at her at work. Instead, his blue eyes briefly lowered to her mouth before he nodded again at Henry. Chase said something to the chef before walking out of the kitchen.

She noticed a stiffness to his shoulders and the hard set to his mouth. He obviously had something on his mind. Lacy was no Sherlock Holmes, but she had a feeling whatever made the muscles beneath his shirt so coiled was related to the shortage of supplies. Her mind returned to Jessie and the station wagon. On the surface, the scene seemed innocent. However, something told her to keep a closer eye on the waitress until she had solid evidence to bring to Chase.

Absolutely nothing.

Nothing suspicious, head scratching, or even remotely nail biting on the numerous hours of footage. The only weird thing he saw was Phil talking to himself in the fridge. But Phil was kind of a strange guy anyway, so Chase didn't give the scene a second thought. None of the waitresses or chefs had displayed any behavior that indicated dishonest activity. And he couldn't think of anyone who would steal from the restaurant. More and more, Chase leaned toward Henry making a mistake with the inventory count, although the man rarely did so. There was always the possibility of human error. For now, he'd tell his father nothing came up and to dismiss the incident as an unfortunate error.

With a sigh, he withdrew the disc from the DVD player and set it on top of the others he'd already watched. The monotonous task of viewing hours of footage had been the equivalent of watching paint dry. Chase was glad to be done with his father's little project. He only hoped now the old man would let the whole thief thing go.

The only satisfaction he found was in catching glimpses of Lacy. Her fuzzy black-and-white image flitted from room to room, her slim hips gently swaying.

Even though she couldn't stand him, Lacy was a good waitress. Her big, bright smile and soft laugh made the waitstaff like her and made her customers feel comfortable. Chase hadn't expected her to last this long at McDermott's. He knew Lacy lacked staying power. So far, she'd hung on for two years, showing up for every shift and occasionally covering for other waitresses on her nights off. That's what he called dedication.

Lacy wasn't what he'd consider a raving beauty; her looks were very average. Although, her hair was always shiny and soft-looking. She was a little on the pale side, but her skin did have a creamy glow. And she wasn't as tall as he liked his women, but she did look like she'd fit perfectly with her head on his shoulder.

Why did he constantly think about her? It wasn't like he was lacking in the sex department; Chase could get a date anytime he wanted. No, something about Lacy intrigued him. Her sassy mouth and unwillingness to succumb to his charm drew him to her unlike any other woman. Lacy had always fascinated him, but only recently had he thought about her in a sexual manner. Before she'd left town, he'd never noticed the sway of her slim hips or her full mouth. Or how her green eyes lit up when she fought with him, like she enjoyed the challenge of provoking him. And her perfume, a vanilla-orange scent, lingered like a fog whenever she walked past him and made him want to yank that hair tie out.

Chase wondered if any other man had told her these things. Lacy was the type of person who didn't respond to flattery. Her cynical mind wouldn't allow that.

He walked into his adjoining bathroom and splashed some cold water on his face. Boy, would he love to be the guy to flatter a smile onto those sexy lips. Which would probably be followed by a punch to the shoulder. Lacy was damn cute when pissed.

"Knock, knock."

His shoulders slumped in relief when he realized the voice belonged to his older brother, Noah, and not their father. Chase patted his face dry with a paper towel and walked back into his office.

"Why aren't you at home with your wife and baby?" Chase tossed the damp towel into the garbage and looked at his big brother. Noah and Avery had been married for about two years. Six months ago, Avery had given birth to a little girl named Lily. She had her mother's dark hair and her father's gray eyes and was just about the sweetest thing Chase had ever seen. One of his greatest joys in life was spoiling the little fifteen-pound bundle of cuteness.

Noah glanced at the stack of discs on Chase's desk. "I had a late meeting and thought I'd stop by." He jerked his head toward Chase's project. "What're you doing, watching home movies?"

Funny. "No, uh..." It was probably safe to tell Noah

about their father's paranoia. "There have been some things missing. Dad thinks someone's stealing. He wanted me to watch footage so I can catch the thief red-handed."

Noah must have caught the undertone of sarcasm in Chase's voice. Both of his thick, dark brows lifted. "No kidding." He ran a hand along his scruffy chin. "What kind of stuff is missing?"

Chase lifted his shoulders in a weary shrug. "Food."

One corner of Noah's mouth lifted. "Why do I get the feeling you don't agree with Dad?"

"It's not that I don't agree with him. I just think he's jumping to conclusions. Henry's the one who realized the steaks were missing. I think he made a mistake."

Noah nodded and slid his hands into his pockets. "What makes you think Henry made a mistake?"

Chase perched on the corner of his desk. "There's nothing suspicious in any of the footage," he said, gesturing to the stack next to him.

"But you did it to appease Dad," Noah concluded with a knowing nod.

"Exactly."

Noah chuckled. "I gotta go so I can kiss my daughter good night before she goes to bed." He turned to leave but stopped. "Oh, hey, Avery's throwing a welcome-home party for Courtney next month. Clear your schedule, because you're expected to be there."

A smile crept up his mouth at the mention of his sister. "I wouldn't miss celebrating Courtney's college graduation, considering how long it took her. Besides, Avery throws one hell of a party."

Noah, who always had an ear-to-ear grin at the mention of his wife, nodded. "Don't I know it? Good luck with all that, by the way."

Chase glanced his work. "I'm not going to need luck because there's nothing going on."

His brother didn't speak for a moment. He bobbed his head up and down. "Good luck anyway."

Yeah, Noah knew Chase would need luck explaining that he thought their father was wrong.

FOUR

"WHERE DO YOU WANT THIS ONE?"

Lacy glanced up from the pile of Ray's shirts she'd been folding to see Brody holding a big moving box. The wall of Ray's room was lined with boxes filled with his stuff.

"Put it in the garage with the others."

Brody hefted the box higher in his arms and carried it outside. It had taken her entirely too long to clean out Ray's room. Since his death, Lacy had been residing in her old room from high school, leaving Ray's exactly the same. The only thing she'd managed to do was change the sheets on the bed, run the vacuum a few times, and sort through his belongings. Despite that, the room had developed an unlived-in musty smell, combined with the mothballs Ray kept among his clothes. She didn't dare go into the bathroom because that's where he'd spent the majority of his time, coughing up blood and throwing up from the chemo treatments, although she had disinfected the area not long after he died. But the door had remained closed since then. She couldn't bring herself to use it with a clear picture in her mind of him leaning over the toilet.

"What're you going to do with all that stuff anyway?" Brody came into the room, wiping sweat off his brow with his forearm. With no air-conditioning, the temperature inside the house hovered somewhere in the eighties. He'd discarded his shirt about an hour ago and sweat glistened on his back. No fair how men could just take their shirts off when the temperature rose too high.

She lifted her shoulders in a helpless shrug. "I don't know. Ray didn't have any other family, so I guess I'll have to donate it all." She gave him a sidelong glance. "Unless you want some of it."

Brody eyed the shirt Lacy held up with something akin to disgust. "Uh, no thanks."

"Oh, come on. Some of it isn't that bad. What's wrong with this one?" The shirt she picked up smelled like cedar and mothballs. The color was roughly the same shade as mud and could have been made out of the same material as heavy drapery.

"That looks like something someone on the Oregon Trail would have worn."

A laugh popped out of her as she set the shirt down and folded it. "Yeah, Ray didn't have the best taste in clothes, did he?" She placed the folded shirt in the box next to her. "So, where's Little T today?" Brody's nine-year-old son, Tyler, was one of Lacy's best buddies. She'd affectionately dubbed him *Little T* when she first met him two years ago.

Brody dropped to the edge of the bed and took a swig from his water bottle. "Kelly picked him up from school."

She placed another folded shirt in the box. "But you're supposed to have him on the weekends."

"She's going to see her parents in Michigan on my weekend and asked if she could take him." He rolled his eyes after she threw him a suspicious glance. "I'm not going to tell my son he can't see his grandparents."

"I didn't say anything."

"You don't like Kelly very much, do you?"

She placed the last shirt in the box and glanced at him. "I never said I didn't like her."

"But?"

Lacy's shoulders slumped on a sigh. *How to explain this to a man…?* "It has nothing to do with me liking her. I just don't think she treated you very well during your divorce."

He lifted a dark brow. "I wasn't completely innocent, you know. It took both of us to break up our marriage."

She tucked some hair behind her ear. "I'm not saying you weren't. I'm just saying she was pretty bitter."

"I was a lousy husband, Lace. She had every right to be bitter."

Lacy shoved the full box to the wall with the others. There were still three drawers full of clothes she'd yet to unpack. The bottom one was filled with jeans. Lacy opened the rickety bureau and pulled out stacks of denim. "You're pretty defensive of her," she said with her attention focused on a worn, holey pair of jeans.

Brody was silent for a few seconds. "She's Tyler's mother."

She shook out the next pair of jeans and glanced at Brody out of the corner of her eye. Brody had always been good-looking. His father's gray eyes blinked at her and his midnight-black hair was in need of a cut. "Is that all she is?" she asked in a quiet voice.

He stared at her for a moment. While Brody was pretty darn attractive, she'd always been grateful for not having a thing for him. That would have made their friendship too weird.

"Where're you going with this, Lace?"

She shook her head. "Nowhere. I just think you talk pretty affectionately about a woman you're not married to anymore." She placed a hand on his knee. "I don't want you to be hurt again."

He narrowed his eyes at her. "You wouldn't be jealous, would you?" The small tug of his lips kept Lacy from taking him seriously.

She folded another pair of jeans and set them aside. "You're impossible."

He raised the water bottle to his lips. "Yeah, that would be odd considering you want to get into my brother's pants."

Just as he was about to take a drink, Lacy smacked his elbow and water dribbled down his bare chest and into his lap. Brody jumped from the bed as he swiped water from his chin with the back of his hand. "That was real mature, Twiggy."

She feigned nonchalance and lifted her shoulders. "That's what you get for saying something so stupid."

He picked his black T-shirt up from the floor and wiped his chest dry. "Stupid. But true."

She stared at him until he glanced at her. "Are you going to tell me you don't have a thing for Chase?"

"Yes, that's exactly what I'm saying." It was getting harder and harder for her to deny it. Damn Brody for reading her so easily.

A rude noise popped out of him. "Okay."

"You don't believe me?"

He tossed the shirt onto the floor. "No."

How to make him believe her . . . She pulled in a deep breath and focused on the next pair of jeans. Why the hell did Ray have so many pairs of jeans? "You've seen how we are together—we're always arguing."

"Foreplay."

Her temper flared for one moment and without thinking, she chucked the clothing at Brody. The denim hit his chest, then landed on the floor. He made no attempt to pick it up. Ray always said she had a temper bigger than she could handle. She inhaled deeply to calm herself down.

"No feelings, huh?"

"I hate you sometimes," she said with a smile creeping along her mouth. Brody always knew how to make her smile.

"No, you don't. I'm the only person who doesn't call you Twiggy."

She gave him a pointed look. "You did a second ago."

"You'd just dumped water down my chest," he replied while picking up another box.

"I should have asked R.J. to help me with this," she mumbled.

Brody walked to the bedroom door. "R.J. knows you have the hots for my brother too."

An unladylike groan forced its way past her lips. She dropped her head to her hands. *Damn, insufferable men.* She took another deep breath and calmly placed all the folded jeans into an empty box. Why did she let Brody get her so riled up? Because he was right? Pretty stupid reason. And here she thought she'd been going a good job of hiding her lustful feelings for Chase. Turned out his whole damn family knew. Perfect.

As she pushed the full box to the wall, someone rang her doorbell. Lacy groaned again, hoping it wasn't Mrs. Pratt with another update on the neighborhood watch. Couldn't the woman just send out a newsletter or something?

On her way to the closet, she saw Brody walk into the room. "Will you get that? If it's Mrs. Pratt, tell her I died."

Brody's soft chuckle floated over to her as he walked out of the room. Ray's closet looked like it could have belonged to a teenage boy. Clothes piled everywhere. Lacy could only take two steps into the small space. Shoeboxes were stacked on a shelf and went all the way up to the ceiling. No telling what useful things Ray stashed in those. Probably stuff like leaves and gum wrappers. She'd just grabbed a pile of sweaters from the floor when she felt a presence behind her. Knowing it was Brody, Lacy asked without turning around, "Who's at the door?"

"A girl named Megan."

She turned, almost dropping the sweater off the top of the pile. "I don't know a girl named Megan."

Brody stared at her before answering. "She says she's your sister."

In her hand, she held a check for ten million dollars made out to Lacy Taylor.

At the moment all Lacy could do was stare at the slip of paper with her name on it and an obscene amount of money printed in the box. She supposed later on she'd be in the right frame of mind to have an appropriate reaction. Right now all she could muster was disbelief. And shock. And that didn't even include the nineteen-year-old blond girl sitting at the kitchen table, claiming to be her half sister. Megan, as she'd introduced herself, had driven all the way from Southern California as per their mother's instructions. That was as far into the story as Megan had gotten before handing over the money. Lacy wasn't sure why Megan stopped in the middle to show her this check or what it had to do with her mother. Lynette Taylor had been dead broke when she left Trouble. All she'd had was a beat-up Datsun and a duffel bag full of ratty clothes. Where in the world had she gotten this kind of money?

Megan, who had one of those stylish, sleek bobs, sat at the table and played with the label on the bottle of water Brody had given her. Brody, being the super-nice guy he was, said he wanted to give them privacy and went home. But not before giving Megan a narrow-eyed look. Lacy assured him everything was okay and shoved him out the door.

"Would you mind starting over? Because I'm having a hard time believing Lynette had this kind of money."

Megan chewed her lower lip, which was free of lipstick. She pulled in a deep breath and twirled the water bottle around in circles. "When Mom came to Southern California twenty-four years ago, she met my father." Megan looked at Lacy with eyes the same green as her mother's. *Their* mother. "My father was a pretty big Hollywood producer—"

"Was?" Lacy interrupted.

"Um…" Megan tucked a strand of hair behind one petite, earring-studded ear. "He died of a heart attack a few years ago."

"I'm sorry," was all Lacy could think to say. Heck, she knew how painful it was to lose a parent.

Megan nodded and lifted her chin. "When he died, he wanted to make sure Mom and I were taken care of. He… he left her everything."

In other words, a shitload of money. Had to be if he'd been a Hollywood producer. That would explain the big fat check. But why did Lynette feel the need to give this to Lacy now after walking out on her? Why couldn't she have just been a mother? That was more valuable than any amount of money. Lacy tried to ignore the squeezing pain in her chest that occurred whenever she thought about her mother.

"So we stayed in our Malibu house until..."

Megan's words trailed off, her gaze directed at the water bottle. That bottle must have been pretty darn fascinating; Megan had spent almost the entire time staring at the thing. Was it too hard for her to look at Lacy, knowing she'd gotten the shit end of the deal while Megan had grown up with two loving parents in a trillion-square-foot house?

"Until what?" she prompted Megan gently.

Megan pulled a deep breath, shifting the expensive-looking brown silk dress against her breasts. "Until Mom died in a car accident."

Lacy heard the whispered words come out of the teen's mouth, but they didn't make sense. *Dead? How could Lynette be dead?* Lacy had always lived in a world where Lynette existed somewhere out there, perhaps thinking of the daughter she'd left and maybe considering a way to make it up to her. That pipe dream had hovered in the back of her mind for the better part of twenty years. In the forefront, however, anger and resentment clouded any affectionate feelings a daughter should feel for her mother. But dead? Now there would be nothing. No closure, no satisfaction of writing her mother a heated letter. An overwhelming sense of incompleteness consumed her, as if something had been taken from her all over again.

Lacy cleared her throat, trying to swallow the lump that made its way from the pit of her stomach.

"How...how long has she been gone?" The words came out more hoarsely than she'd anticipated.

A tear slowly ran down Megan's flawless cheek. She pulled a tissue out of her white clutch purse and carefully blotted the moisture away so as not to ruin her perfect makeup.

"About seven months," Megan replied on another strained whisper. "Afterward, when I was dealing with her will, her lawyer told me about two letters she'd written sometime before she died." She placed her little purse on the table and pulled out two white envelopes. "One is addressed to me and the other"—with one baby-pink manicured fingernail, Megan slid the envelope across the table—"is for you."

Scrawled in small, loopy handwriting was her name in black ink. Lacy didn't take the envelope right away. She stared at her name, trying to picture her mother dragging a ballpoint pen across the paper. So many things tumbled through her mind; Lacy couldn't make sense of anything. Confusion and hurt squeezed her heart until the organ almost beat out of her chest. Lynette was the most elusive, difficult person to understand. Why would she abandon her only child, move to California, birth another child, then give this obscene amount of money to the daughter she gave up? None of this made sense.

"You don't have to read it right away." Megan's voice had become a little bit stronger. "I almost wish I hadn't read mine."

Lacy pulled her brows together as she gazed at her half sister. "Why?"

The younger girl rolled her lips. "I didn't know about you until after she died. I was completely shocked when I read this," she said, holding up her envelope. "I couldn't believe she had another child that she'd given up." Megan turned her green eyes to Lacy. "The mother I knew would never have done anything like that. She just wasn't that kind of person."

"Maybe she wasn't that kind of mother to you, but she was to me."

Honey-colored brows pulled worry lines in Megan's forehead. "How old are you?"

Thrown off-balance by the question, Lacy could only stare for a moment. "Twenty-eight."

"Jeez, you're almost ten years older than me." Megan ran a hand through her highlighted tresses. "Why do you think she did it? Why did she leave you?"

That was the six-million-dollar question Lacy would never know the answer to. "I've spent almost my entire life asking myself that question." She moved her focus to the check Megan had handed her earlier. Lacy picked it up for Megan to see. "Why did you give me this?"

"That's a little bit harder to explain. I had to read my letter three times before it made sense." Megan toyed with the corner of the envelope. "Twenty million dollars was part of the inheritance my dad left for Mom when he died. In my letter, she left very clear instructions that I was to find you and give you half. She wanted you to have it."

So she could ease her guilt for leaving? Did she even feel guilty? What the hell was Lacy supposed to think about this? Yes, this money would solve all her financial problems. How could she take such a gift from someone who didn't give a rip about her? She wanted to tear it up and shove it down the disposal.

Megan must have read her mind. "I understand if you don't want to take it. I'm just trying to fulfill her wishes."

Poor girl. None of this was her fault. She didn't ask to be the one child her mother wanted. Here she was, still grieving and learning the mother she loved more than anyone left behind a child that was Megan's sister. "I'm sorry if I seem standoffish with you." Lacy pushed down her need to resent her half sister. "I don't understand any of this," she announced, shaking her head. "Why would she abandon me and then want me to have this money?"

Megan lifted her petite shoulders in a helpless shrug. "I wish I knew. She doesn't explain any of it in the letter she left for me or in her will. Maybe it's something she wanted only you to know." Her last word came out on a slight hitch. She took a sip from her water. Her chin trembled while she drank and her eyes squeezed tightly shut. Lacy felt sorry for her. It was clear the girl had been having a difficult time dealing with everything. She'd lost both her parents in a short amount of time and learned she had a half sister. Lacy could sympathize.

Neither of them said anything for a moment. Heck, Lacy couldn't talk even if she had something to say. She didn't trust her voice to come out strongly enough to say something intelligible. In the matter of an hour, her world had been flipped upside down. Nothing made sense, her chest felt tight, and unwanted tears threatened to blur her vision.

"I've decided to stay in the area for a few more days. I could really use a break from Southern California, or maybe reality altogether. It's so quaint here. People aren't in a rush and they smile at you." She pulled out a little silver pen and a slip of paper from her purse. "Here's my cell phone number in case you need"—she shrugged as she stood—"I don't know, to talk about anything. Or, if there's anything you want to know about Mom."

Lacy stood and walked Megan to the door. The girl was tall for a nineteen-year-old. Lacy was five-seven and Megan looked like she had to be at least five-ten. She smelled good too. The scent of expensive perfume, like maybe Elizabeth Arden, made a trail from the table to the front door. Lacy took the piece of paper with a cell phone number when Megan handed it to her. "Thanks for listening. I'm really sorry about...everything. I'd be happy to tell you anything you want to know about Mom."

Still not trusting her voice, Lacy nodded and offered what she hoped was a reassuring smile. Megan slid a giant pair of dark sunglasses over her eyes and walked outside. Lacy shut the door behind Megan without waiting for her to drive away. For some reason, she didn't want to see what kind of expensive luxury car her half sister drove.

The gorgeous female sitting next to him blinked her big, beautiful eyes. Dark, spiky lashes lined her eyelids and her cute, pouty mouth smiled when he brought the spoon to her mouth. She loved to be fed, and Chase loved nothing more than to indulge her. Her downy-soft hair felt like feathers beneath his fingertips when he ran his hand through her curls. He could touch her all night long, and she loved to be played with. She had the softest, sweetest giggle Chase had ever heard. He'd spent the better part of his night off making her laugh and holding her. She was one of the few females on the planet he looked forward to spending time with.

She accepted the spoon when he put it in her mouth. Her lips moved as she worked the food around, then swallowed. A satisfied smile tugged the corners of his lips when she swallowed all of the green beans. The last time he fed her green beans, she spit them all out and some of the green gunk had ended up on his cheek.

A high-pitched squeal bellowed out of her and she slapped her hands on the tray of her high chair. Yes, she really did love being fed. And Chase loved feeding her, when she didn't blow out his eardrums.

"You've got a set of lungs on you, sweetie." He dipped the tiny spoon in the jar of baby food and shoveled more greens into her mouth. "At least you're not spitting it out this time." Her answer was another scream. Little Lily was starting to become acquainted with her lungs. He'd never paid attention to how loud babies could get when they were excited.

Every once in a while, when he looked at his niece, he thought of his college girlfriend. Chase couldn't picture himself with a kid right now. He liked his single life just the way it was. Sometimes, looking at Lily, he couldn't help but wonder how different his life would be right now if the girl he'd been dating at the time had made a different decision. He knew her decision had been for the best. No way could he have handled that kind of responsibility as a college student. But her deception had hurt. The fact that he'd had to find out from a friend of hers . . .

Eleven years was more than enough time to put the whole thing behind him. And he had. He'd walked away from the situation losing his ability to commit to a long-term relationship. Now he simply stuck to the occasional date and one-night stands. That was all he needed.

Lily sucked down the rest of her dinner with minimal spit-up and lots of grins. He cleaned her up, all the while talking to her and tickling her little chin. His niece was extremely ticklish.

As soon as her hands and knees hit the floor, she took off, crawling as fast as her pudgy legs could carry her. She was quite the mover. Chase watched with amusement as she tried to pull herself up to the coffee table but didn't succeed. Her grin turned to a whine when she lost her balance and tumbled to the floor.

"I can't help you there, kiddo." He picked her up and

settled her on his hip. The child weighed about as much
as a bag of feathers. Her miniature, sticky hands reached
out and tried to grab his face. Noah had said Lily had this
thing for grabbing faces. One time she'd grabbed Noah's
face so hard she'd actually left a welt on his cheek. "No
way am I going to let you scar my face." He pulled her
hand away right before it reached his cheek. "Let's see
what Mommy packed for you."

A few stuffed animals and toys with all kinds of lights
and buttons sat by the door where Avery had left them,
stuffed in a bag. Chase took out a contraption that had a
steering wheel and a gearshift. He shook his head. Kids'
toys were elaborate these days. What happened to being
content with a few wooden blocks and Lincoln Logs?
He set the baby down and put the toy in front of her. She
kicked her legs and let out another ear-piercing shriek.
The toy lit up and sang to life when she fumbled around
with the wheel and banged on the buttons. Her dexter-
ity was practically nonexistent. Her fingers tried desperately to hit each button but she missed almost every time.
Didn't matter, though. Wherever she touched the thing,
it sang some silly ABC song. That seemed to please her.

Chase cleaned up the baby mess of jars and snacks and
had just started to munch on cold pizza when his doorbell rang. The clock above his stove said 6:15, way too
early for Noah and Avery to pick up their daughter. He
set the pizza down and scooped up Lily before he opened
the door.

Golden hair illuminated by the soft glow of the porch
light fell far beyond Lacy's shoulders. The strands looked
like they were in need of a good combing and her freckles
stood out on her makeup-free face. Slight bags sat under
her grass-green eyes as if she hadn't gotten enough sleep

the night before or she'd been crying. As much as he tried, Chase had a hard time picturing Lacy crying.

Against his wishes, his certain parts responded to the sight of her in a plain T-shirt and denim shorts. The familiar stirring below his belt had him taking a deep breath and shifting his legs. The only time he ever saw her in anything other than denim was at work. He had a feeling if his father didn't have a dress code, she'd show up in ripped jeans.

"Feeling lonely tonight?"

Lily squirmed on his hip. Chase adjusted her while waiting for Lacy to say something.

She blinked her round bedroom eyes and shifted her attention to the baby on his hip. Lacy's full, unpainted mouth curved upward when Lily let out a string of baby blabber. "Hello, little sweetie." One of Lacy's slender fingers tickled the bottom of Lily's bare, chubby foot. Lily swung her leg back and forth and shoved her whole fist in her mouth, drool pouring down her hand.

Chase stood back and decided to let Lacy enter. Her hypnotic, orangey-vanilla scent swirled around his head when she walked past him. He couldn't keep his body from responding to her even if he tried. The muscle beneath his fly twitched and threatened to embarrass him with a little tenting action.

"You're babysitting tonight?" She walked ahead of him through his foyer, giving him a view of her excellent, toned ass.

"Uh"—he cleared his throat and tore his attention away from the backs of her creamy thighs—"Noah and Avery haven't had a night out in a few months, so I offered to watch the munchkin." Now he wished he was alone.

Lacy eyed the baby paraphernalia. "If they ever need a hand, I'd love to watch her."

Chase set Lily down and she crawled over to her toy. "She's quite the handful. And noisy." To prove his point, Lily let out another baby-sized shriek when one of her toys vibrated.

Lacy squatted next to the six-month-old. "I think she's sweet. And totally gorgeous."

"She's a looker, isn't she?" Chase sprawled himself out on the leather couch and stretched his legs in front of him.

"She looks like your mother."

His mother? He gave his niece some scrutiny, taking in her brown curls, gray eyes and heart-shaped lips. Most people saw Avery and few saw Noah. Personally, Chase thought the girl was an equal mixture of both her parents.

Chase shook his head. "She doesn't look anything like my mother."

Lacy regarded the picture of Julianne McDermott on his wall and shifted her gaze back to Lily. "She looks a lot more like your mom than you realize. They have the same hair and same eyes."

"She has Noah's eyes."

Lacy tilted her head to one side, her waterfall of blond hair falling over one shoulder. "The color maybe but not the shape. That she got from your mother."

Chase narrowed his eyes at his guest and tried to ignore how long and smooth her bare legs were. "You didn't come here to talk about my niece's genetics."

A nervous giggle curved her mouth upward. "You always were observant."

As cute as they were, nervous giggles hardly ever left Lacy's lips, nor did she ever just show up at his house. Something was up.

"What were you doing? Sitting around thinking, 'I'll stop by to see my old friend Chase'?"

"You got any red wine?" she asked, completely out of the blue, ignoring his question.

"What am I, a woman?" He grinned when she rolled her eyes in a teenage fashion. "There's some Sam Adams in the fridge."

She pushed herself to her feet. "That's good enough."

His eyes stayed to her backside when she walked through the archway leading to the kitchen. The fridge door opened, then closed. A nanosecond later, she returned with a dark, cold bottle of beer. He should have asked her to bring one for him. Only the power of alcohol could tame the sexually charged atoms swirling through his body. How sick was it of him to be fending off a hard-on with his six-month-old niece five feet away? Pretty sick, indeed.

"Take it easy, Lace," he warned her after she'd chugged for a good fifteen seconds. "Everything okay?"

She lowered the bottle and licked a bead of liquid from her lower lip. Lily crawled into Lacy's lap, begging to be held. After setting the bottle on the coffee table, Lacy picked the baby up and turned her green, saucer-sized eyes to his. "My mother's dead."

FIVE

THERE WERE ALWAYS THOSE PEOPLE in life who walked around with the proverbial black cloud over their heads. No matter how sunny or warm the weather, that black cloud lingered, promising nothing but gloomy, rainy days. Lacy, bless her beautiful heart, was one of those unfortunate people. The woman just couldn't catch a damn break.

For the past hour, while downing two full beers, she'd told the story of the half sister she'd never known existed and the death of her mother. She spoke with a composure that Chase was sure she held on to by a very thin thread. The way her brows pulled together or her teeth continually stabbed into her lower lip showed him she was a hair away from cracking. That was little Twiggy. She had a tougher exterior than most men. How many times in the past few days had he wondered how soft she'd be underneath her suit of armor? More than the entire time he'd known her.

During her revelation, he'd said little, letting her talk as much as she wanted. And, man, could the lady talk. Under normal circumstances, Lacy wasn't a chatterer.

Her smart-ass retorts had always been precise and to the point.

Then she dropped the bombshell.

"Ten *million* dollars?" *Holy shit.* Chase had no idea what he'd do with that much money. "Where in the world did your mother get that kind of money?"

"Weren't you listening? She married a wealthy producer." She lifted her shoulders beneath her teeny-tiny shirt. "I guess she got struck with a guilty conscience."

He let his gaze stray down to her breasts for one forbidden moment. They weren't very big, just perfectly round and perky. "What're you going to do with all that money?"

She pulled at the frayed end of her shorts. "I don't know if I'm going to take it."

Was she serious? "Lacy, you'd be crazy not to take it. It's a shitload of money."

She threw him a droll look from the recliner she'd settled herself in. "Thank you for that insight." Then she said on a tired sigh, "How can I accept money from a woman who turned her back on me? I feel like I'm making a deal with the devil or something."

Chase kept an eye on Lily as she crawled to the sliding glass door and looked outside. "It's really not that complicated. Taking the money doesn't make you a bad person. Just smart."

"Smart?" she repeated with a shake of her head. "I don't feel very smart."

"That's because you're emotionally attached. Just take the check and deposit it." He ran his gaze over her again. She sat cross-legged in his brown leather recliner, her bare feet tucked under her legs. She looked like a scared, confused little kid. "You'll be financially secure for the rest of your life."

"That thought has occurred to me." She tucked a strand of silky blond hair behind one petite ear. "I almost gave it back to her."

"I'm glad you didn't. You deserve this. Go treat yourself to a spending spree."

Her hands twisted around each other in her lap. Then she took a deep breath and refocused her attention on him. "How's your back?"

Her question coaxed a smile out of him. "Healing, thanks to you." This morning after stepping out of the shower, he'd caught a glimpse of the scratches. The three angry red marks had dulled to a dark pink. The burning sensation had finally subsided, and now they just itched like a damn mosquito bite. Maybe Lacy would scratch them for him. The scandalous thought had only entered his head when Lacy's mouth turned up in a sly grin. "What?"

She rolled her lips. "I was just thinking I hope the woman was worth the memory because those scratches are probably going to scar."

Damn, little Twiggy was a lot more observant than he gave her credit for. Why had he tried to pass them off as something else when any idiot with half a brain would know they came from a human nail? He decided to go out on a limb and provoke her. "There are ways for you to erase her memory."

The beer bottle, the last little bit of liquid sloshing on the bottom, paused just before reaching her mouth. Her green eyes, full of the sparkle he loved to put there, narrowed at him. "Are you hinting what I think you're hinting?"

He stacked his bare feet on the coffee table. "You're a smart girl, Lace."

The muscles in her slender neck moved subtly when she downed the last of the beer. Out of the corner of his eye, he saw Lily crawl to her diaper bag. Chase kept his gaze locked on Lacy as she lowered the bottle and set it on the end table next to the recliner. The corny cliché "cutting the sexual tension with a knife" was the only thing that came to mind as the two of them assessed each other from across the living room. Over the past few years, Chase had become so used to Lacy's glares that anything else was like trying to understand a foreign language. Her eyes left his face and touched his chest before lowering to his nether regions. In about point-zero-five seconds, said regions sprang to life and pulsed against his zipper. He almost shifted to hide the result of his reaction but stayed where he was. Better to let her see what she did to him, if only to coax a reaction out of *her*. Coaxing reactions out of Lacy had fast become one of his favorite pastimes.

"What would you say if I agreed?" Her soft bedroom voice dropped an octave as if she didn't want Lily to hear.

The baby, completely oblivious to their conversation, babbled over a book she'd pulled out of her diaper bag.

"I'd say," he answered slowly, "that you're treading in dangerous water."

A mischievous glint lit up her gaze. "You're the one who brought it up."

That he did. And what in the holy hell had he been thinking making a comment like that? Any other woman would have laughed it off. Leave it to Lacy to call his bluff. It was actually kind of amusing. Debating a hypothetical affair with her was the most fun he'd had all day.

The intense, sexually charged moment lasted a few more rapid heartbeats before being interrupted by a knock on the front door. Chase had enough time to stand from his chair before his brother and Avery walked in. The married couple looked satisfied and refreshed from their kid-free evening out.

As usual, Avery's hair was styled in its perfect, not-a-hair-out-of-place fashion. The sophisticated updo suited the crisp, stick-straight blue dress that fell just above her knees. One would never know of her background from talking to her. She was one of the most grounded, big-hearted people Chase ever had the pleasure of knowing. And she made his brother grin like the Cheshire cat. That in itself was reason enough to love her. But it didn't hurt that Avery always looked like she belonged in a limousine headed to a star-studded party in Beverly Hills rather than Trouble, Wyoming. Everything about her polished appearance screamed, "I come from money."

Lily squealed when she saw her parents and crawled as fast as her pudgy arms and legs could carry her. Her two-toothed, slobbery grin stretched from one miniature ear to the other as Avery scooped Lily up and tossed her in the air.

"Mama missed you, sweetheart," Avery cooed, and placed loud smooches on her daughter's chipmunk cheeks.

"She give you any trouble?" Noah asked as he stuffed toys back into the diaper bag.

"She's never any trouble. I would ask what you two did, but the wrinkled shirt is a dead giveaway," Chase muttered so Avery wouldn't hear. Noah's only rebuttal was another stupid grin.

"Hey there, Lacy," his brother called out to Chase's visitor, who'd remained in the background. "You're, uh, not working tonight?" Noah's question was accompanied by a suspicious glance thrown in Chase's direction. Chase ignored his brother's look that said, *What in the heck is she doing here?*

Instead of answering Noah's question, she said, "Your daughter is the most beautiful thing I've ever laid eyes on." Clever, little evasive Lacy wasn't fooling Chase. Her once-relaxed limbs were now folded across her too-thin frame. A typical defensive posture if Chase ever saw one. The ever-present, mile-high protective wall was firmly in place, keeping any priers safely out. His brother included. The move brought Chase's too-curious side out.

If Noah picked up on the underlying currents, he didn't let on. "Isn't she, though?" He tickled his daughter's wet chin. "Lucky for her she looks like her mother."

Avery rolled her chocolate-brown eyes. "You always say that, but we both know better. Lacy, you have to come to Courtney's welcome-home party next month. I'll send you an invitation."

"I'd love to come. I haven't seen Courtney in years—that is, if the boss will give me the night off."

Chase directed his attention to Lacy. None of the tension that made her body practically vibrate only moments before showed on her angelic face. One of her blond brows arched above her eye. The little witch was testing him. Well, he could dish out as good as she could give. He folded his arms across his chest. "That all depends on your performance."

The gleam in her eyes turned into a glare as they narrowed. *Yeah, right back at you, sweetheart.*

Someone cleared their throat. Chase turned at the sound and found Noah and Avery staring at him with Lily once again shoving her whole fist in her mouth. A pregnant pause filled his living room as no one said anything.

"So...thanks for watching Lily," Avery offered in a pretty poor attempt to fill the void.

Noah had the gall to actually smirk, reading more into the situation than there was. Setting Noah straight would have to be his first order of business. Tomorrow. For now, he'd have to deal with Lacy and whatever she had on her mind.

Noah rocked back on his heels and gestured with his thumb toward the door. "I guess we'll go now."

"Uh, yeah. Okay." *Jeez, dumbass. Real articulate.*

He walked his brother and sister-in-law to the door. Avery stepped through first with Lily in her arms, the little girl staring back at Chase with her round, thickly lashed eyes. Noah stopped before continuing down the walkway. "What's that all about?"

Chase was already shaking his head before Noah had all the words out. "Not now. I don't even know myself."

With a pointed look and another devilish smile, Noah said, "Good luck." He turned on his heel, whistling some stupid, cheerful tune as he walked away and climbed into his SUV.

Even though he couldn't see her, Chase felt her gaze linger on his backside. The attention felt like a woman's soft fingers floating over his hot skin, making his dick twitch in response. Just when did Lacy start having this effect on him? The fact that he didn't have an answer was as unnerving as what she did to him.

He turned, knowing he'd find her watching him and sure enough, she was. Her fathomless green eyes searched his for several heat-filled seconds. He stood by the door, waiting for her to make a move. She remained coiled up in his chair, her legs crossed in front of her, and her arms folded in her lap. Her long hair cascaded over her shoulder like a golden waterfall. Despite her serene expression, Chase sensed something else just beneath the surface. What exactly that was, Chase hadn't figured out. Could have been sexual tension with the way she'd been eyeing him all night, like he was a prime steak and she wanted to slather A1 Steak Sauce all over him.

Chase had seen probably a dozen layers to Lacy's personality. Lacy had always been very choosy with whom she let get close much less who she exposed all her inner workings to. Brody had been one of the few people who'd seen the candid Lacy. Chase wasn't sure how his brother had always been able to peel back the onion layers to the sweetness within. And Chase was... well, he wasn't sure what he'd been to Lacy. The idea should have annoyed him. Instead, it intrigued him. He always did love a challenge.

Lacy abruptly stood, smoothing her paper-thin shirt over her sorry excuse for denim shorts. Chase forced his eyes to remain on her face instead of allowing his gaze to fall on her creamy thighs. She didn't speak as she took the empty beer bottles to the kitchen and disposed of them in the garbage. The silence in the room grew into its own entity that both of them refused to acknowledge. Both were too stubborn to break it first.

Finally he couldn't stand the growing static in his ears. "Headed home?" he asked when she came back into the room.

"I suppose." She slid the tips of her fingers into her shorts pockets. "Thanks for the beer."

"Anytime."

Well, they'd managed to exchange half a dozen words before they went back to staring again. That was certainly progress.

"Why'd you come here, Lace?"

The delicate muscles in her throat moved as she swallowed. "I don't know. Would you believe I was just in the neighborhood?"

He couldn't help the upturn of his mouth. "No."

"I guess I'm busted, then."

"That you are." He made no attempt to hide his assessment of her. He let his eyes wander from her face down to her tiny, feminine feet. Besides being practically see-through, her shirt looked like it was held together by a few fragile threads. The frayed shorts had no doubt been cut from a pair of equally pathetic jeans, and they'd been cut too short. They made her legs appear a mile and a half long, more than enough length to wrap around his hips while he slipped into her with agonizing slowness…

She needed to leave. Now.

"I need to get home." As if she'd read his X-rated thoughts, she yanked her purse from where she'd dropped it on the floor and pulled it onto her shoulder with jerky movements.

Sweet, innocent Lacy Taylor had no idea of the power she held over a man. A man like him. Unknowing women like her were the most dangerous kind.

"I guess I'll see you at work tomorrow night."

Chase didn't move from his spot by the door as Lacy stopped in front of him. Her bare, soft arm brushed along his harder one as she reached for the doorknob. A shock of awareness shot from his fingertips down to his groin, making every hair on his body stick straight up as if her body contact had electrocuted him. She must have felt the sensation too. Her eyes lifted to his and lingered, two seconds too many. Chase took advantage of the opportunity and snaked one arm around her slim waist. He expected to be able to feel every one of her ribs. Instead he found the subtle curves and a softness found only on a woman. The feeling surprised him, as did most things concerning Lacy Taylor.

He didn't attack her with his mouth like he wanted to. Her body slowly came against his, pressing in all the right places, from her small breasts to her trim thighs. Her gaze lowered to his mouth and her tongue darted out and licked across her lower lip. For the second or third time that night, his dick thickened and this time, it nudged her belly. He knew she felt the evidence of his arousal when her eyes widened at the contact. Her breath went from slow and even to rapid and huffy, fanning across his neck.

Surprising him yet again, Lacy slid one arm around his neck and threaded her fingers through his hair. She nudged his head lower, then stood on her tiptoes so her mouth could reach his. Her warm, pliant lips brushed along his, skimming instead of kissing. Her breath mingled with his when her lips parted just the tiniest bit. Chase took that as an invitation and slipped his tongue inside before she changed her mind. Lacy didn't seem to mind the intrusion. Her tongue was equally enthusiastic as it swirled around his in an erotic dance that had his arm tightening around her waist. Both of them opened their mouths wider, inviting each other to do as each wanted.

Chase turned his head to change the angle of the kiss. Something landed on the floor with a thud, and he realized she'd dropped her purse so she could slide her other arm around his neck. He backed her to the door and pressed her against it so he could feel every inch of her body along his. She grunted as her back hit the wood. The kiss grew more intense, their tongues moving in and out of each other's mouths.

Chase couldn't remember the last time he'd really kissed a woman without thinking about how long it would be until they got naked. The next step had never been far from his mind. With Lacy, he'd be satisfied to kiss her against his front door for the rest of the night. He thrust one hand into her hair and tilted her head back to deepen the kiss. The strands of her hair sifted around his fingers and felt just as soft and downy as he'd expected. Her vanilla-orange scent traveled up to his nose and filled his head with visions of her running naked through an orange grove. He pictured the sun high, sending rays over her smooth skin. The image made his dick strain painfully against his fly. Lacy's response was a gasp that he swallowed into his mouth. She wanted him.

She tore her mouth away from his. "Chase, I want you," she said as if she'd read the very words that had just entered his foggy mind.

Oh, he knew she wanted him. Her heart beat a rapid, hard punch against his chest. Her pupils widened, filling the green to a deep onyx. Orgasms were easy to fake. But no woman could fake a reaction like this.

"Are you sure?"

She skimmed one of her hands down to his chest and rested it above his heart, which beat just as swiftly as hers. "Yes." The whispered words came out in a rush.

That was all the confirmation he needed.

In one hasty move, he whisked her away from the door and lifted her up against his pelvis. She immediately wrapped her legs around him and resumed their kissing. Her tongue invaded his mouth again, threatening to make him lose his concentration to put one foot in front of the other. The stairs were going to be a challenge if she didn't stop rubbing her little tits against his chest. Then again, the sensation of her pebbled nipples rubbing against his chest would be well worth tripping and falling. Somehow, he managed to take the stairs two at a time, if only to get her on the bed that much faster. Once in his room, he kicked the door closed with more force than necessary. Lacy slid down his hips, languidly stretching her body along his. Damn, the woman knew how to tease.

For one tension-filled moment she stared at him and then slipped her nimble little fingers beneath the hem of his shirt. The second her fingertips made contact with his skin, his stomach coiled and contracted and he hissed in a breath through gritted teeth. The little tease had the nerve to smile as though she knew exactly how much torture she inflicted. Inch by painfully slow inch, she lifted his shirt until she'd pulled it over his head and threw it to the floor. Her eyes ate up every speck of his naked flesh and the tips of her fingers left a trail of fire on his skin as she floated them from one side of his chest to the other.

He ought to be awarded the freaking Medal of Honor for how long he managed to stand still. What he wanted to do was toss her onto the bed and drive himself inside her for a few hard, fast pumps until all the breath left her body.

A quick wet feeling replaced her fingers. Chase's already heavy eyelids slid shut at the feeling of her small, warm tongue on his nipples. She circled them slowly with a featherlight caress, traveling from one nipple to the next. The attention almost had him shooting off in his pants and ending their good time before they got to the great stuff.

"Enough of this one-sided action," he rasped, and grabbed her by the shoulders.

"But I'm enjoying myself," she protested as he shoved

her back on the bed. She landed with a gasp, her hair falling into her face.

"Not as much as you're about to." He stalked her on the bed, crawling over her like a predator about to take its prey.

Anticipation animated her feminine features. A small smile turned up the corners of her mouth and her teeth dug into her lower lip. As he glanced down at her body, he realized she was still clothed. Well, he'd have to remedy that.

With aching slowness, he lifted her shirt, following the hem with his mouth and dropping kisses along her belly. Her hoarse moan filled the quiet static of his room. She arched off the bed, offering herself to him. As soon as he had her shirt off, he slid one arm behind her back and undid the clasp of her bra in the one-handed way he'd taught himself as a teenager. Once he had her breasts free, he closed his mouth around one, lavishing the same attention upon her nipples she'd showed his. He allowed no mercy, swirling his tongue in endless, rapid circles until her nipples were as hard as diamonds. One of her hands cradled the back of his head, encouraging him on. The other hand circled his waist and slid beneath the waistband of his jeans. She dug her hand as far as she could reach, and Chase realized she was hinting at him to take his pants off. He didn't oblige her, instead focusing on her breasts. They were so delicious, he was happy to let his tongue linger for as long as he liked.

After a few more torturous moments, he lifted his mouth and worked on removing her shorts. She was so thin, the denim slid easily off her hips. She kicked them and her underwear free and soon she lay completely naked before him.

He supposed now would be a good time to savor the sight of a buck-naked Lacy Taylor, willing and ready for him. But all he could think about was getting inside her. He leaned over her, letting the crisp hairs of his chest brush across her nipples as he reached into the nightstand next to her pillow for a condom. She sucked in a quick breath. He barely had his jeans over his hips when she snatched the condom from him and deftly rolled it down his rigid length. The brush of her fingers sent an electrical shock from his dick all the way down to his toes.

The second she had him suited up, he kneed her thighs apart and flexed his buttocks, sliding just the very tip of himself between her wet folds. Instantly, warm, slick heat surrounded him and milked his length as he inched the rest of the way into her tightness, which gripped his penis like a squeezing, wet fist. It took every ounce of his self-control to hold himself still, instead of ramming her like a jackhammer. He wanted to make this last longer than the three seconds it would take for him to come.

He focused his attention on her face to gauge her reaction. So far, she hadn't made a sound except for the occasional moan. Where he expected to see tightly closed eyes or maybe an expression of pain, there was an openness about her that was so uncharacteristic of Lacy. Long, dark lashes swept in almost slow motion over dilated pupils. Her lips, wet from his kisses, parted with her heavy, labored breathing. She licked her lower lip, prompting him to take her mouth with his again. He swept his tongue inside, still not moving his hips in order to build the anticipation. Her arms went around his neck and she floated her hands over his back.

She lifted her hips in a grinding motion against his, a movement so unexpected it rendered a groan from deep within his chest. The sound went into her mouth and he felt her smile against him. He returned the favor by circling his hips in one direction and then the other. Lacy tore her mouth away from his and let out a cry of pleasure. Her fingers, once stroking over his back, now dug into his flesh, no doubt creating little crescent-shaped indents with her nails.

When he finally decided they'd both done enough waiting, he gently pulled himself almost all the way out, then plummeted back into her body. Another anguished scream from Lacy mingled with his heavy breathing. She lifted her legs higher, wrapping them around his hips. He repeated the pulling out motion again, this time with more force and speed until he had a steady rhythm going. His room was soon filled with the sound of the headboard thudding up against the wall mixed with their moans and sighs.

As the speed of his hips increased, he leveled himself up and hooked one of his elbows behind her knee, lifting her leg high and deepening his penetration. Sharp teeth bit into his shoulder, propelling him to slam into her harder and faster. Lacy let go of his shoulder and sobbed her release. The inner muscles of her silky walls contracted around him, massaging his dick. The feeling of her orgasm around him felt so fucking good that his own orgasm blindsided him like a hit to the back of the head. Hot, milky semen shot out of him and into the condom. Every muscle in his body coiled like steel beneath his sweaty skin. He buried his face in Lacy's sweet-smelling neck while his hips jerked and bucked through the rest of his orgasm. The whole time she held him tightly and kissed his neck. Her hands had moved down to his ass so she could pull him in as deep as possible.

After he'd emptied every last ounce of bodily fluids into the tip of the condom, Chase lay on top of an equally exhausted Lacy, trying to steady his breathing. The two of them didn't move for a few precious seconds, both of them too drained to even speak.

Finally, Lacy broke the silence. "I think you killed me," she rasped.

"*I* killed *you*?" he muttered into her hair. "I can't move."

She let out a pathetic, sleepy chuckle and glided her soft hands across his back. Blessed sleep was about to take him and Chase carefully disengaged himself from Lacy's body and rolled over. He pulled in a steadying breath and looked at the shadows of the trees stretched across the ceiling. He was sure the repercussions of this would hit him later. But for now Chase decided to bask in the satisfying afterglow of a healthy round of sex. He peeled the sticky condom off and lazily tossed it onto the floor. Whatever. He'd pick it up tomorrow.

"That was"—Lacy exhaled and rolled over to face him—"the best orgasm I've ever had."

He slanted a look at her out of the corner of his eye. "You don't have to flatter me that much."

"I'm serious. I've never had sex that good."

Women had told him that before and he'd always chalked it up to cheesy flattery. The slumberous look on Lacy's face and relaxed body put a genuine meaning behind her words. He didn't want to think that highly of himself, but he had to admit that had been one of the most intense rounds of sex he'd ever had.

Just as Lacy lowered her head to his shoulder, a thought occurred to him. "What if we made this a regular thing?"

"When you say 'this,' do you mean me crashing your babysitting party and stealing one of your beers?"

The comment earned her a smile. "It was two. And I think you know what I'm talking about."

This time she snorted. "Be serious, Chase."

He ought to be the one saying those words. Instead, he pressed on. "I am serious. We're pretty good together, don't you think?"

"I already told you how good it was."

He sensed a "but" coming. "So . . . ?"

She was so still for a minute that he actually thought she'd stopped breathing. "I don't think it's a very good idea for us to get involved."

"Reason being?"

She pulled one of the hairs on his chest. "Well, for one thing, you're my boss."

"A minor detail that can be overlooked."

Her breath tickled his skin when she giggled.

"Any other excuses?"

"Yeah, your father has that no-dating-employees rule."

"Another minor detail."

"I wouldn't really call that a 'minor detail.' Plus there's the fact that he despises me."

"Where'd you get an idea like that?"

She lifted herself onto an elbow and gazed down at him. "Your father has never liked me, Chase."

He tucked her hair behind her ear. "That's not true." Actually it *was* true. Martin had never really been fond of Lacy. Because of her father's actions, he'd always felt her a bad influence on Brody. The only reason Lacy had been hired was because Martin didn't involve himself with hiring staff. That was Chase's job. His father hadn't jumped for joy when he saw Lacy taking orders one day. But she'd proved herself a good waitress, so Martin kept his thoughts to himself. Lacy had also been right about his father's no-dating rule. He strictly forbade the staff to date each other and refused to hire boyfriends or girlfriends. He always said it encouraged irresponsible behavior that ultimately led to a hostile work environment. Chase never shared those sentiments, but he supposed his father was smart to be cautious.

Lacy idly drew circles on his chest with her blunt nail. "I don't know."

Her walls were firmly back in place. "Why are you so unsure?" He wrapped a hand around her thigh and pulled it up higher so it rested across his hips.

She nibbled her lower lip and kept her attention on his chest. The gears in her head were working overtime to come up with some excuse. Lacy always chewed on those sweet lips when she tried to process her thoughts fast enough to come up with a response.

Finally, he tipped her chin up so she met his gaze. "I'm not asking you to marry me, Lacy. I'm not even asking for a commitment. I'm just suggesting that we—"

"Be sex buddies?"

"For lack of a better term, yeah."

"And how would that work? Whenever you get horny you'll just call me and say, 'Hey, Lace, come over here and let's bang'?"

He narrowed his eyes at her. "Give me a break, Lace. I'm not that crude."

Her impassive look turned suspicious.

"Okay, I can be sometimes." He ran a fingertip over her shoulder, smiling in satisfaction at the intake of her breath. "But it wouldn't be like that." When she failed to respond, he went on. "If it makes you feel better, you can have complete control over our arrangement."

She shifted her thigh over him, brushing his penis. "Meaning?"

"Meaning I won't push you to do anything you don't want to. You can decide when and where we get together and even if you want to end things." She would no doubt want to end things with him sooner or later. He knew she had problems trusting people, especially men. He didn't fault her that, given everything she'd been through. When she still didn't respond to his offer, he pushed her onto her back and settled between her thighs. She stared up at him with a small smile pulling at her mouth. He lowered his head and eased her lips apart with his tongue. She let him inside, as he knew she would, and he glided his tongue along hers.

"I can tell you need a reminder of the best orgasm you've ever had—which I gave you," he said when he lifted his mouth from hers.

She rolled her eyes in a dramatic fashion. "I'm going to regret saying those words, aren't I?"

"That's up to you." Looking at her nude body and remembering the feel of her around him made him grow hard again. He retrieved another condom out of the nightstand drawer and tore the packet open. He was about to roll it down when Lacy yanked it out of his hands.

"I'll take care of that, thank you." She pushed him onto his back. "I think I did a pretty good job last time."

He grinned like a man who'd just won the lottery and folded his arms behind his head. Like the artist she was, Lacy slithered down his body and reminded him just how good she was.

"No one can know about this," Lacy announced as she shimmied into her shorts sometime before sunrise.

Chase, who'd been uncharacteristically quiet since she'd slid out of bed, lay with his head propped on one muscled arm, watching her every move. His scrutiny unnerved her, as did his silence. Chase *always* had something to say, so why should now be any different? He'd asked her to stay for breakfast, which she politely declined. She was on lunch shift today and wanted a shower before going in to work.

After snapping her shorts, she spared him another glance. He was as still as a Greek statue. "Chase, I'm not kidding."

"I heard you."

She swiped her shirt off the floor and pulled it over her head. "No one in your family or at the restaurant can know. Especially your father."

"I won't say anything if you don't want me to."

"Thank you."

The predawn sky had a murky, grayish tint to it but wasn't enough to cut through the inky blackness of Chase's room. The only light was coming through the thin slats of the wooden blinds and that was pathetic at best. She couldn't see his face very well, only his big form on the bed. The sheet draped over his waist, leaving the rest of him exposed. The sight of his bare chest, which she'd explored, touched, and kissed for the past several hours, made her want to slide back into bed next to him. If she didn't leave now, she'd be too tempted to play hooky.

"You're going to walk out without a kiss good-bye or even a thank you?"

"I just said thank you."

He slowly shook his head. "Uh-uh. That was for something else."

She couldn't help the topsy-turvy feeling in her stomach. The man really was impossible. "You really do have an ego, don't you?"

"I haven't had any complaints so far."

"I don't doubt it."

"So, are you going to kiss me or what?"

"You'll have to come and get it."

"But I'm naked."

"A fact of which I'm well aware."

It was too dark to tell, but Lacy got the distinct impression that Chase was grinning. In no hurry to fulfill her request, he slid out of bed and sauntered, completely unabashed by his own nudity, to where she stood. Unable to help herself, her eyes dropped to his . . . area. And what an impressive area it was. His penis hung heavily between his powerful thighs. It grew thicker and longer with each step he took closer to her. By the time he reached her, the shaft stuck straight out at a ninety-degree angle and poked her abdomen.

"Trying to convince yourself to stay, Miss Taylor?"

The jerk had caught her ogling him.

She tried desperately to stop the smile curving her lips upward. "Not even for money."

"I bet I could convince you." He tilted her face with the tip of his index finger. His mouth felt like pure magic and sin all wrapped up in one knee-weakening kiss. His warm palm cupped her cool cheek as his tongue glided inside her mouth one more delicious time.

"Think about that while you're working." He turned her around and smacked her denim-clad rear. The tingling sensation on her bottom left her wondering if she'd made a deal with the devil.

SIX

THE SECOND SHE WALKED IN THE DOOR from her lunch shift, Lacy kicked off her shoes and headed straight for her drawing room. Without bothering to remove her sweaty, stinky work clothes, she grabbed a sketch pad and pencil. On the way to work, she'd spotted a tree in some-one's yard that had the most beautiful pink flowers. Every square inch of the tree's branches was dotted with baby-pink blooms, and a thick blanket of the flowers covered the ground. She'd never noticed the tree before, but on this particular morning, the angelic beauty of it instantly caught her eye. She'd been struck with a fierce urgency to capture its softness with her pencil. On the way home, she slowed her car to a crawl to get one last good look. It was the sort of tree under which families had picnics or lov-ers held each other during an afternoon nap. Such events had never taken place in her life and few people had been worth spending that sort of time with.

Regardless of that depressing realization, the fully bloomed tree had been first and foremost in her mind all afternoon. She plopped herself cross-legged on the floor and dragged the pencil across paper. For the next thirty minutes, she focused only on the charcoal lines as they started to turn into the image she had in her mind. The tree stood by itself with no other occupants crowding its space. The majesty of it was far too great to share the spotlight with things like dogs or small children. She also accentuated its size, drawing it taller and fuller than the original version. All the flowers were in full bloom, none dead, or wilted, or lying on the ground for people to trample on. No, this tree deserved much better than that. Lacy was determined to do the magnificent plant justice, to give it a perfect existence in an imperfect world. She owed something with such exquisite splendor the absolute best.

Different versions of the tree took up six separate pieces of paper. If not for the cramp in her hand, she'd have kept on going. Satisfied she'd exhausted the tree from her mind, Lacy set the pad aside and studied her work.

This afternoon of drawing had reminded her of why she'd started in the first place.

Solitude.

Escape.

Perspective.

She refocused her attention on the pink-blossomed tree.

Compared to her other sketches, the lone tree was simple, and borderline lonely. Something about this particular drawing struck a chord within her that none of her other drawings had, not even the ones of small children. She could imagine her sketch situated inside an aged, antique frame, perched on someone's mantel or, better yet, on the walls of city hall. Of course, that would require her actually selling it. Last year the town of Trouble had its annual fair where local merchants, quilt makers, and others of different trades sold their goods to people from the area. Brody had tried talking her into reserving a space for her own booth, but she'd been too much of a coward. She didn't want to stand there like a hopeful fool while people passed her by for things like kettle corn and organic baby clothes. She knew, deep down, she had a better shot of selling her drawings at the local fair than she did at any art gallery. Most galleries didn't want to waste their time on an artist who didn't have a résumé.

This year's fair was about four months away, and she could really use the extra income—that is, if she even sold anything. Now would probably be the best time to reserve a slot since last week's newspaper had run ads advertising open booths. Wishful thinking had made her cut the ad out and stick it under a magnet on her fridge. Then the unpleasant news of her father's whereabouts and the unexpected visit from a half sister forced her pipe dream to the back of her crowded mind. After all, there was only so much room in her brain for exhausting possibilities. This was all, of course, not including the possibilities from last night.

Chase wanted to have an affair with her. She'd left his house without giving him a concrete answer, but she had the distinct feeling he'd made the decision for them. That was sort of his personality. While the lovemaking had been electrifyingly phenomenal and had left her mind foggy all day, an affair with Chase was the last thing she needed. With her father's annoying presence looming around her and a ten-million-dollar check practically screaming to be cashed, sex with her boss would definitely muddy the waters. Chase was one person Lacy needed to focus on keeping a platonic relationship.

In fact, that line never should have been crossed to

begin with. Ignoring the ethical side of things, a relationship with him could never go anywhere. He'd made a career out of bedding women and Lacy had problems trusting men. An affair between the two of them had *dismal failure* written all over it. Contrary to what her past said, Lacy did not like getting involved with men who were destined to break her heart.

But how marvelously delicious the sex had been. Before last night she'd never known it was possible for her body to go numb from one orgasm. And Chase, the selfless man that he was, had given her several. By the time she'd left his house, she hadn't known which way was up.

Lacy left her drawing room and headed to the kitchen for a bottle of water. Boris snored from his spot on the worn rug and didn't so much as twitch an ear at her presence.

Last night, Lacy had meant to go see Brody. Then she remembered he'd mentioned something about going on a date. Chase's house was on the way to Brody's, and for some reason, the sight of his chrome and black Harley in the driveway had made her stop. Without giving herself time to change her mind, she'd knocked on his door and everything had sort of evolved from there. She hadn't *planned* on sleeping with him. In fact, the thought had never even entered her mind until he opened the door, holding his chubby niece. The entire time she'd sat in his living room, she'd tried thinking up ways how she could get out the door without throwing herself at him. She hadn't even gotten the door open, much as she suspected would happen. All the dramatics of late had forced her to do something desperate. That, and the fact that she hadn't had sex in way too long. The end of her rope had come into view and Lacy had needed something to take her mind off recent events. Chase had been the perfect solution.

Never would she have suspected him to suggest they get involved.

Lacy took a sip of the cold water, hoping it would extinguish the hot images from last night. It didn't.

Boris stirred and pushed himself up onto long, lanky legs. He ambled over to her as fast as his old, worn-out body could take him. Poor dog. Lacy had no idea how much longer the dog would live. His cold nose nudged her thigh and she glanced down to find his enormous brown eyes gazing up at her.

"I'm going to take that as a hint that you're hungry."

Boris's response was a more forceful nudge. Lacy pulled out leftovers from the other night. Ray had never bothered with things like buying dog food. He'd always slopped whatever leftovers were in the fridge into Boris's bowl. Boris had always seemed content to scarf down things like mashed potatoes with gravy and red beans and rice. He wasn't picky.

Lacy scooped cold turkey into the dog's dish and Boris didn't waste any time sloppily eating it. Half the food ended up on the floor, but she knew the dog would eventually get around to eating it all. Boris could sometimes take a few hours to eat one bowl of food.

She left the dog to his meal and walked to her bedroom. After the long day she'd had, a shower sounded like absolute heaven. Just as she started to peel off her shirt, the top dresser drawer caught her eye. A few days ago she'd placed the letter in there. The letter written by her mother. Her *dead* mother. Her mother's passing still hadn't sunk in. Lacy thought that by now she'd start to feel something. Loss. Grief. Denial. But she felt nothing.

After all, her mother's death didn't really affect her life. The woman left a long time ago and her dying was of no real relevance to her abandoned daughter. Except for the money she'd left her. Lacy still hadn't come up with a solution to that. Should she burn the check like her initial reaction told her to? Or should she take it, pay off her debts, and give Chase his money back?

Megan had said the letter explained everything; Lacy still didn't have the guts to read it.

Her shirt fell to the floor as she walked to the dresser and opened the drawer. The envelope lay upside down, the way she'd tossed it in there. She eyed it before slamming the drawer shut with enough force to rattle the lamp sitting on top.

"No," she said with a shake of her head. "I don't owe her anything."

She peeled off her black pants and started the shower. The water shot out of the showerhead and splattered on the dingy, cracked white tiles of the back tub wall. She eyed the water running down the drain and tried not to picture her mother sitting down to write a letter to her abandoned daughter. How long ago had she written it? What had been going through the woman's mind? Had she cried? Had she felt anything at all?

With a groan of frustration, Lacy left the shower running and returned to the dresser drawer. The envelope lay in the exact same position it had one minute ago.

"Did you really expect it to move by itself?"

This time she picked it up and turned it over to see the front. Her name was scrawled in tiny, lowercase letters with a little line underneath. She turned it back over and ran her finger along the seam. Back and forth her finger went like a hypnotist swinging one of those old pocket watches. With a weary sigh, she placed the envelope on top of the dresser instead of inside the drawer. She wasn't sure why, but for some reason the top of the dresser just seemed like a better place. Maybe seeing it every time she walked in and out of her room would motivate her to read it. For now, she just didn't have the strength. It wasn't like the letter was going anywhere, anyway.

Twenty minutes later, after a too-long shower, Lacy walked out of her room refreshed in a pair of cotton shorts and a tank top. She'd just walked into the kitchen to start dinner for herself when someone knocked on the door. Maybe Chase had come to continue their supposed affair.

On the other side of her door stood Mrs. Pratt, the head of the neighborhood watch. Lacy managed to stuff down her groan when she saw the elderly, four-foot-nothing woman. Mrs. Pratt wasn't a bad person; she was just incredibly nosy. Lacy didn't appreciate people prying into her life.

"Hi, hon. Mind if I come in?"

Sure, she was just thinking to herself how she wanted to spend her evening with the neighborhood gossip.

To Lacy's knowledge, Mrs. Pratt had never smoked. Yet she had the voice of a woman who'd smoked unfiltered cigarettes since birth. Every time Lacy was around the old woman, she wanted to tell her to clear her throat.

To avoid being rude, Lacy stepped back. "Sure, Mrs. Pratt. Come on in."

The woman's distinct odor, like mothballs and cedar, washed over Lacy in a nauseating wave. She shut the door and watched Mrs. Pratt show herself into the living room.

Stiff, cornflower-blue pants encased Mrs. Pratt's legs

along with a long-sleeved, sunflower-yellow shirt. Her snow-white hair was pulled back in a loose, sloppy bun with one of those 1920s beaded combs as an accent. The comb was actually quite pretty but on Mrs. Pratt it looked out of place, like she wanted to look classy. A lot of words came to mind to describe her neighbor but *classy* wasn't one of them.

Either the old woman was color-blind or she just didn't give a damn what people thought of her. Given her personality, Lacy would guess the latter.

"How've you been doing lately? I noticed your car making a funny noise the other day as you left for work. Sounds like your timing belt." Mrs. Pratt shuffled around the room in her ugly orthopedic, brown leather shoes. Her sharp blue eyes darted around the room as though she was looking for something to fix—or gossip about.

Lacy had noticed the squealing noise, too, but had no idea what was causing it, not to mention she didn't have the money for a major auto repair. Unless she cashed that damned check. Why was it every time she turned around, life gave her a reason to take her mother's guilt money when it was the last thing she wanted to do?

"Did you hear Annette had her triplets the other day? She named them April, May, and June. Isn't that the tackiest thing you've ever heard?"

Lacy *did* consider it sort of cruel to give your kids such cheesy names, but the tacky thing was Mrs. Pratt gossiping about it. "Yes, that is pretty tacky." Agreeing was easier than arguing, especially with Mrs. Pratt.

Lacy searched her brain for the fastest way to get the woman out of her house. "What brings you by today, Mrs. Pratt?"

She turned to face Lacy, her mouth pulled into a

disapproving frown. Lacy noticed her pink lipstick had bled beyond the lines of her lips into the wrinkles gathered around her puckered, disapproving frown. "You got any iced tea?"

"Ah, sure." Momentarily thrown off by her request, Lacy went into the kitchen for her last bottle of Snapple and poured it into a glass. Actually, she'd been planning on saving her peach iced tea for dinner, but whatever. If it would expedite this visit, then so be it.

Mrs. Pratt wrapped her bony, arthritis-warped fingers around the glass. "I was hoping for something homemade but I guess this will do."

We all can't be Martha Stewart.

The glass trembled slightly in Mrs. Pratt's unsteady grip as she took a shallow sip. Lacy didn't bother asking the woman to use a coaster as she set the glass down on the coffee table.

"I'll admit Snapple does know how to make good tea. Though it's nowhere near as good as the sun tea my mother used to make. Have you ever made sun tea?"

While growing up, Lacy was lucky she'd learned how to use the microwave. "No, I've never tried. You'll have to teach me sometime." Even though the last thing Lacy wanted was lessons on how to make sun tea from Mrs. Pratt, she didn't want to be rude, either.

Mrs. Pratt settled her hunched-over frame into Ray's brown corduroy recliner. Lacy expected her to ask for the remote so she could watch reruns of *My Three Sons* and make herself at home.

"Pardon me if I sit down for a minute. My legs don't hold me up so well."

Great, now she felt bad for wanting to usher the woman out. As far as she knew, Mrs. Pratt didn't have any family.

Her husband had passed away about twenty years ago and the couple never had any children of their own. Mrs. Pratt had lived alone in her ancient, outdated house for as long as Lacy had known her. She still drove a light-blue Cadillac the size of a small luxury liner. And every Saturday, she got out in her yard, with her sombrero-sized straw hat and pulled the weeds in her beloved rosebushes. For eighty-something years old, the woman was surprisingly efficient. Lacy often gave Mrs. Pratt a hard time because of her affinity to worm her way into other people's lives, but loneliness probably played a big part in that. She knew the feeling. She suddenly hoped she wasn't such a nosy, busybody biddy when she was in her eighties. And alone. Oh…shit.

Lacy took a seat on the couch. "How's your day been, Mrs. Pratt?"

She waved a weathered hand in the air. "Oh, the usual. Couldn't get myself out of the bathtub this morning; then I couldn't remember where I'd put my arthritis medication. Do yourself a favor, Lacy—don't ever get old. It all starts going downhill after fifty."

The comment made Lacy smile. Mrs. Pratt could be annoying, but she was as spry as she was nosy.

Lacy knew she'd regret saying these next words but she did anyway. "If there's anything you ever need from me, I'm just right down the street."

Mrs. Pratt's faded blue eyes lightened. "That's sweet of you, hon. But the ladies at my church do everything for me that I need." She spared her enormous, digital wristwatch a glance.

"I should get to the reason I'm here so I can get to the pharmacy before they close." She jerked a craggy thumb over her shoulder. "You know the Hutchisons at the end of the street? Don and Jenny, with five kids?"

They'd moved to the neighborhood a few years ago, so Lacy didn't know them that well. But she did see their oldest riding his bike up and down the street almost every afternoon.

"Anyway," she continued before Lacy could confirm. "Jenny was at the park with her three youngest and she said she saw some guy with blond hair and one of those long, handlebar mustaches lurking around the playground. She said he wasn't doing anything bad, but he was sort of creepy. Have you seen anybody like that around here?"

Lacy slowed her breathing and waited for Mrs. Pratt to finish speaking. Dennis had blond hair, and five years was more than enough time to grow facial hair. Most people in town knew her situation and what a worthless bastard Dennis was. But Jenny Hutchison was so new to the town she wouldn't know Dennis Taylor if she looked him in the face. Mrs. Pratt would undoubtedly know him. She'd lived in Trouble her entire life and had been good friends with Ray.

She wasn't sure how to respond to the information. It wasn't Dennis's style to lurk in a place that wasn't going to be beneficial to him in some way. If her father really was back in Trouble, then the blond man Jenny saw could very well have been him. If she made her suspicions known to Mrs. Pratt, it would likely send the woman into a panicked frenzy, and the FBI would probably be here within the next twenty-four hours.

She forced herself not to fidget her fingers, which was a nasty habit of hers when nerves took over. "No, I haven't seen anybody like that around here," she said, which technically wasn't a lie. Lacy really hadn't seen Dennis.

"I figured as much. He was probably some man Jenny

hadn't seen before. I've just been going house to house and letting people know to keep an eye out and report any strange things to me. If you happen to see this guy, will you let me know?"

Well, that depends.

Lacy gave her a reassuring smile. "Of course I will."

Mrs. Pratt placed her hands on the armrests of the chair and pushed without any success. The recliner rolled back and forth at her failed attempt to stand. Lacy felt sorry for the woman and offered a solid hand of help. Mrs. Pratt's breath went in and out with a rapid, wheezing sound.

"Thanks, hon," she said on a breathless note. "That chair's harder to get out of than it looks."

"Ray always had trouble with it too," Lacy replied, if only to make the woman feel better. Mrs. Pratt's bony-fingered hand held on to Lacy's arm as she led the old woman to the door. Once there, Lacy held it open for her. "I'll let you know if I happen to see this blond-haired guy." The words of reassurance made her feel like a hypocrite. Lacy had no intention of telling Mrs. Pratt anything that concerned Dennis Taylor. That was her burden to bear and no one else's.

The soles of Mrs. Pratt's leather shoes scuffed down the cement walkway and took her over to the next house. Lacy closed the door, trying to tell herself what she'd just heard didn't mean anything; it was nothing more than a coincidence. There were lots of blond men in town and some of them probably had mustaches. Just because a guy with the same hair color as her father's happened to be at her neighborhood park didn't mean Dennis really was here. Or even looking for her, for that matter.

So why did that cold feeling snake its way down her back as it did whenever he was near? Something didn't feel right. But then again, things seldom felt right in her life. Forcing deep, even breaths, Lacy walked down the hallway to her drawing room. On the floor sat the sketch of the pink-blossomed tree. She picked it up and studied the charcoal lines on the paper. This wasn't the best work she'd ever done, but it was definitely her favorite.

She tossed the paper back onto the floor, feeling antsy and nervous. Damn him. Dennis wasn't even in her life and he was still ruining her serenity. All she had to do was consider the possibility of him being in the area and her nerves went into overdrive. How did he have this hold over her? Lacy had been taking care of herself for a long time; she'd never needed him.

Unsure of what to do with herself, she power walked back to the kitchen and pulled some cookie-dough ice cream out of the freezer. After heaping several spoonfuls into her mouth, Lacy failed to feel better. Instead she felt fat as well as on edge. She returned the ice cream to the shelf and walked to her room.

The sight of her unmade bed reminded her of the previous night with Chase. Going to his house now was out of the question. Not only was he at work but also jumping back into bed with him was likely to confuse her even more. She needed to keep her distance from him for a little while.

After pacing for the better part of ten minutes, Lacy exchanged her shorts for a pair of Capris and slid on her best-looking sandals. They had the fewest amount of scuff marks on them.

Her purse lay tilted on its side from where it landed after she walked in the door. She scooped it up and walked into the garage where she got behind the wheel of

Ray's rust bucket. After she sent up a prayer of desperation, the car finally started.

Without any real destination in mind, Lacy drove through the town of Trouble and ended up at McDermott's.

SEVEN

SLAMMING DISHES AND VOICES from the busy kitchen indicated the dinner service at McDermott's was well under way. Servers came and went to the dining room, balancing dishes with expert ease. Lacy spotted Becky-Lynn just as she swept through the kitchen doors. She placed a hand on the girl's shoulder. "Is Chase on the floor?"

The blonde tossed Lacy a distracted glance. "I think he's up in his office." She left the explanation at that and power walked to the dining room. Becky-Lynn was one of those people who didn't talk unless you initiated the conversation. Even then the girl usually left her answers at three to four words. Lacy didn't know that much about her except she'd graduated from a local city college and had yet to move on to something else. Despite that, there was something about the young girl that hit Lacy close to home. They may not know each other that well, but Lacy had always felt a connection with Becky-Lynn. She saw something of herself in the girl, the same lack of direction in school and the same wariness of others.

"Hey, Lacy. What're you doing back here?" Diane, a

forty-something mother of four, said as she fed orders into the computer. The frazzled mother would give you her last dollar if you needed it. She'd been forced to return to work after her husband suffered some sort of work-related injury and was restricted to bed rest. Her rosy cheeks and permanent grin gave her a sort of Mrs. Claus demeanor. Premature streaks of gray accented her dark hair, which was cut into one of those short, spiky styles. Lacy always thought the cut didn't really suit Diane's personality. It looked more like something that belonged on a seventeen-year-old boy.

"I forgot to pick up my paycheck earlier." Lacy stepped out of the way of another server who walked swiftly to the kitchen. "It's a madhouse tonight."

Diane inhaled deeply. "Tell me about it. I stayed to pick up an extra shift but now I'm wishing I'd gone home. I think I'd rather face my four rowdy boys than this mess." She finished typing in her order and turned to face Lacy.

Diane had been picking up a lot of extra shifts lately. In fact, the woman worked almost every single night. The amount of time she put into the restaurant left Lacy to wonder how Diane had time to take care of her ailing husband and kids. Was her family that desperate for money that she had to work seven days a week? Was workman's compensation not enough for them?

"Haven't you worked almost every single night this week?" Lacy asked, not able to keep her curiosity at bay.

Diane glanced at Lacy. "I haven't had a night off in two weeks. I need the extra money."

The poor woman. Lacy's heart went out to her. "Doesn't workmen's comp help out?"

Diane snorted. "It's barely enough to cover groceries.

I had to tell my second oldest son that he couldn't go to band camp this summer."

Lacy placed a hand on the other woman's arm. "I'm so sorry, Diane. I wish there was something I could do."

"I appreciate that," she answered with a close-lipped smile. "But it won't last forever. We'll get back on our feet soon."

If I ever get the nerve to cash that check, I could use some of the money for good. Like helping out Diane and her family.

Lacy glanced around the restaurant and decided to change the subject. "How's the service going so far?" At the very last second, she held back a comment on the recent shortage of supplies. Lacy didn't want to be the one starting rumors about thefts, or whatever the heck was going on, if the whole thing turned about to be innocent. She certainly didn't want to think Diane, of all people, could be responsible. So far all she had was the incident in the parking lot. Hardly solid evidence.

Diane nodded and her long, dangly earrings swung back and forth. "Other than being crazy, it's good. The tips tonight have been great." She picked up her black order book. "I've got to go check on some dishes. I think Chase is in his office."

She walked away before Lacy had a chance to say anything else. It wasn't like Chase to be holed up in his office on such a busy night.

The noise of the dining room faded away when she walked through the door that led upstairs. The blinding industrial light was always a shock after the dim interior of the candlelight downstairs. Why Mr. M chose such unflattering, hideous lighting was a mystery to her. Must be a man thing.

The door to Chase's office was closed when Lacy approached. She knocked softly three times but didn't hear a response. After waiting a good minute, she pushed down the silver handle and opened the door. Inside the room, Chase stood at one end of his desk with his arms crossed over his thick chest. Opposite him was his father, looking considerably more at ease with his hand in his jeans pockets. *Wow, jeans. Mr. M must be feeling especially lighthearted today.*

Mr. M had always scared the shit out of her as a child. His snow-white hair was so thick it looked almost unnatural for a man his age. The sheer size of Chase's father never ceased to intimidate Lacy. The man had his son by probably a couple inches and towered over Lacy by what seemed like three feet. He was the kind of man who created a hush over a room when he walked in. His legs were miles long and roughly the size of tree trunks. But when he smiled, the whole intimidation factor melted away from him. Unfortunately, he didn't direct his smile at her too often.

When he spotted her, his thick white eyebrows shot up his wrinkled brow. "Good evening, Ms. Taylor." Oh, and he always felt the need to address her as "Ms. Taylor" like she was some formal acquaintance he'd just met. Never mind the fact that his son was one of her best friends.

She lingered by the door, fearful of him squashing her like a bug if she took one step farther into the room. "I didn't mean to interrupt anything. I can come back."

Chase, who'd inherited his father's dominating personality, remained motionless and speechless. Lacy wasn't sure he'd so much as blinked.

She kept her gaze trained on his father.

"No, that won't be necessary. We're finished here."

An awkward silence, the kind that followed when someone made an inappropriate comment, nearly suffocated Lacy. Clearing his throat, Mr. M turned on his heel and Lacy moved out of his way as he left the office. Her nosy side reared its ugly head, tempting her to say, *What the heck was that about?*

Instead she settled for, "Is everything okay?"

The muscles in Chase's jaw flexed and his lips flattened into a hard line, creating a don't-mess-with-me look.

"Just business stuff," he replied out of barely moving lips.

She took that as her cue to change the subject. "I need to get my paycheck."

His penetrating blue gaze raked over her, as if seeing the naked flesh beneath her clothing. Instant, hot memories of last night flashed before her eyes, like a broken movie reel spinning the same scene over and over again. Scenes of heavy breathing, a rocking mattress, and bare, intertwined limbs had her sucking in a steadying breath. Chase was a man who knew how to satisfy a woman in bed and leave her wanting more. He was like an addictive drug she'd experimented with and now had to have another taste. And if not careful, she could become an addict.

"Sure," he said in a more normal voice, bringing her thoughts back to the subject at hand.

His long, confident stride took him to a locked cabinet against the wall.

Pure self-indulgence made her check him out the same way he had her. His hard ass filled his slate-gray slacks to bone-melting perfection. Powerful, muscle-bound thighs strained beneath the expensive fabric of his pants. A narrow waist flared out to mile-wide shoulders that she'd run her hands and had hooked her legs over. What a dirty mind she'd developed.

He turned in time to catch her gawking. There was definitely no bouncing back from that. He gripped her check in one large, blunt-fingered hand, the same hand that had touched every touchable inch of her body. Okay, time to leave before she stripped and offered herself up like a sacrificial lamb.

"Here you go." He held it out to her.

For a moment, she only stared before she realized he expected her to come and get it. Boy, he really knew how to play the game.

Fine. She could be within touching distance and maintain her composure. She closed the short distance between them and slid the check from his hand. He didn't let her get away so easily. His long fingers ran along the backs of hers and each and every little hair on her arm stood on end in the wake of his touch. The man didn't play fair.

"You busy later?"

She ran her free hand through her long hair and contemplated his question. "Later as in tonight?" *Tonight as in, when it gets dark and people do naughty things?*

"Yeah, tonight." His eyes danced with dangerous mischief.

Rather than admit pathetically that she was indeed free, she sidestepped his question with one of her own. "Why?"

He pinched her chin with his thumb and index finger. "Keep your light on for me."

Apparently he'd made the decision about his proposed affair for her, which Lacy didn't much appreciate. She was perfectly capable of making her own decisions, thank you very much.

She crossed her arms in an attempt to stand her ground. "I never said I didn't have plans. For all you know I could have a date."

"You don't have a date."

Hot irritation burned her cheeks to roughly the same temperature as a volcano. How dare he insinuate she didn't have a date? How did he know she didn't have a horde of men lined up around her door? Did he think she was that pathetic?

She lifted her chin and narrowed her eyes at him. "I beg your pardon? You don't know that."

It was his turn to narrow his eyes. "Do you?"

She didn't answer at first, hoping to let him suffer in silence. Then with a teeny-tiny bit of defeat, she admitted, "Well, no—"

"Wait up for me, then," he said, then turned his back and walked to his desk, effectively ending their discussion.

Of all the pigheaded...

"Excuse me—" she started, when a voice from the doorway stopped her.

"Chase, there's an issue in the kitchen," Marie, the hostess, announced in a rushed voice.

He expelled a weary breath. "This seems to be the night of issues."

Marie's announcement slammed shut the proverbial door on their conversation. Lacy took the opportunity to slip out of the office before Chase turned thunderous. She left the restaurant with her check in hand and mixed feelings in her heart, especially sexual anticipation. All the way home she wondered if Chase was serious about seeing her later or if he'd bluffed just to keep her on her toes.

• • •

The night ended on a decidedly sour note, turning his shitty mood even shittier. One catastrophe had turned into another, starting with one of his waitresses flaking on him and ending with the register drawer fifty dollars short. He'd remedied that with the teeth-gritting solution of pulling some cash out of his own wallet. His father didn't need to know. By that time the old man had gone home where he belonged. And it wasn't like fifty bucks would put Chase in the poorhouse. But the drawer *never* came up short. Chase simply didn't allow things like that on his watch. He ran a tight ship here and hardly anything ever went wrong. Until recently. Between missing food and now missing money, it grew harder and harder to chalk it all up to human error. There were just too many coincidences.

How was all this happening under his nose? The only employee who was ever here without him was Henry. The last thing Chase wanted to think was that his head chef was stealing from them. But so far what little evidence he did have pointed in the chef's general direction. But how in the world would he have taken cash from the drawer? Henry never left the kitchen and if he did, someone would have definitely noticed him. So where did that leave Chase? With a few strange occurrences and thirty potential suspects. Not exactly a recipe for a nail-biting mystery. Maybe he ought to go over the surveillance again to make doubly sure he hadn't missed anything.

He leaned back in his desk chair and scrubbed a tired hand down his face. The whiskers from his all-day beard growth scraped along his palm.

The mantel-style clock on his desk showed it was a few minutes past ten-thirty. Everyone in the restaurant had gone home, leaving him alone to contemplate the business's problems. The nightly deposit envelope with the day's take, including his fifty dollars, sat on his desk.

With nothing left to do, Chase gathered the envelope and his helmet, locked the place up, and mounted his bike. The Harley growled to life and vibrated with a comforting strength between his legs. There was something about having the ability to harness the power of a motorcycle that sent adrenaline through his veins like a pleasure-inducing drug. With every sleek turn of the handlebars, he felt as if he possessed some sort of superhuman power. He rumbled down the quiet streets of Trouble, not really in any hurry to reach his destination. But Trouble, being the small town it was, meant the bank came into view in practically no time. He tossed the bag with the deposit slip into the slot and tucked the envelope into the bike's small compartment.

For a moment, he sat atop his motorcycle in the parking lot of the bank, contemplating where to go. Of course, he hadn't forgotten about his earlier conversation with Lacy. *Leave the light on for me.* Why did he have to go and say such a stupid-ass line? His stupidity had been worth it after seeing her cheeks turn a tomato red. Lacy was so easily riled. She liked her independence and wasn't going to let someone like him order her around. She'd wait up for him if she damn well wanted to, not because he asked her to. *Oh, but she wanted to.* Last night had been too phenomenal for her not to. He'd watched her super-fine backside sway out of his house this morning knowing she'd be back for more.

With a smile of anticipation, he made a left turn out of the bank parking lot and headed toward the older part of town. A right turn down a side street took him to an older neighborhood where Lacy lived. Most of the houses in this part of town were sadly dilapidated because the owners were older than dirt and couldn't have any pride of ownership on their limited fixed income. There were very few yards with neat, green grass. Several houses had shutters that hung off on one side and others had paint peeling from the shingles. Chase knew the only reason Lacy stayed here was because she couldn't afford to move.

Actually, she could afford to move if she used some common sense and took the money her mother gave her.

He eased his bike into the driveway and turned off the engine before anyone complained about the ruckus. Out of all the houses in the neighborhood, Lacy's was the least sorry-looking. The grass was green and neatly trimmed. Bright, happy flowers sat in the planting bed at the base of the one and only tree. However, the milk chocolate–brown paint was faded and peeling from twenty years of wear and tear. And the streetlight on the sidewalk flickered like a bad strobe light.

He hooked his helmet over the end of the handlebar and walked up the cracked, uneven walkway to the front door. She'd left the light on just as he'd asked. The faint, buttery glow of the living room lamp shone through the curtains covering the front window. The door opened just as he poised his fist to knock.

"I wasn't waiting up for you," Lacy said.

Yeah, right, liar. She stayed up for me. The thought brought a satisfied smile to his mouth.

A few wispy tendrils of hair had escaped from her sloppy bun and hung straight down around her face. She blinked at him out of huge green eyes as though surprised to see him, despite his earlier announcement. Her fair, even skin had a freshly scrubbed glow. And she'd traded her work attire for gray cotton shorts and a baby pink T-shirt with a picture of a Care Bear on it. Bare feet completed her look.

The whole ensemble made his dick jerk awake.

"What were you doing, then?"

She twisted her hands in front of her. "I was just going to bed."

He peered around her into the living room. "With a bottle of red wine?"

She glanced over her shoulder, showing him the back of her slender neck. "It's empty." A few more strands of hair came loose when she whipped her head back around, eyes wide. "I mean it was almost empty when I opened it." She continued when he lifted a brow. "Obviously I didn't go through an entire bottle of wine in one night."

Miss Twiggy was flustered. The thought was a nice boost to his ego.

After eons of staring at him, she stepped aside to let him enter. He walked by too close, purposely brushing her arm with his. Her uneven breath didn't go unnoticed on his part.

"Everything okay at the restaurant tonight?" she asked after closing the door.

Playing dumb seemed like the best course of action. "What do you mean?"

She gestured lamely in front of her. "It just seemed like you and your father were . . . having a moment."

Lacy had always been perceptive. Because she was an employee, he couldn't tell her anything. "It was just business stuff."

She nodded. "Why don't I believe you?"

"Maybe it's your suspicious nature."

The comment earned him a soft giggle. "I have some more wine if you want it."

He snorted. "I told you I don't drink wine. If you have beer, I'll take some of that."

"Sorry to disappoint."

He lifted a shoulder. "Guess we'll have to settle for staying sober. Which is a shame because it would be fun to get you drunk."

Her fingers played with the end of her shirt. "I haven't gotten drunk since college."

"I'd say you're overdue."

One corner of her mouth turned up. "Maybe some other time." She waltzed past him, bare feet shuffling along the scarred wood floors. "Want to sit down? You look like you need to unwind."

He had an entirely different way of unwinding that didn't involve sitting on a couch. Good things came to those who waited. He could be patient.

Lacy folded her thin frame into the corner of the couch and picked up her half-empty glass of wine. The rim slid between her delectable lips when she took a slow, shallow sip. She drank like a woman who was on borrowed time and wanted to savor every last drop of what she had left. He'd never seen anyone drink with such longing, with her eyes closed and slow swallows that worked the muscles of her delicate neck. It was almost like watching a piece of artwork come to life, like one of those pearly white statues of a Greek goddess lounging in nothing more than a toga. Put her in a toga and Lacy would outshine any goddess.

A dewdrop-size bead of moisture lingered on her lower lip before she smeared it away with her thumb. The gears in her head, which never took a day's rest, looked to be in overdrive.

"Got something on your mind?" Chase toed off his boots and crossed his ankles.

"My mother." A halfhearted smile created faint lines in her cheeks. "I haven't spared the woman a thought in I don't know how long. Now all of a sudden I can't think about anything else."

"I'm going to go out on a limb here and say you haven't done anything with that check."

She tossed back the last few sips of her wine and placed the glass on the end table. After a moment of silence her only answer was, "No."

Jeez, the woman brought new definition to *stubborn*. A check worth enough money to feed a small country was now in her possession and she couldn't see past decades-old feelings. Okay, so she'd been hurt as a child and despised the woman who'd given her life. Knowing what it was like to lose a parent, Chase understood the emptiness that replaced parental love. However, he couldn't fathom how someone who should love you unconditionally turned heel without so much as a backward glance. Lacy one-upped him on that one. The battle of guilt and conscience that raged inside her was something only she fully grasped. Maybe it was his ability not to lead with his emotions that made the choice so blaringly obvious. But he didn't want to seem like an insensitive ass.

He tried to impose his opinion as gently as possible. "That money could solve a lot of your problems, Lace."

"Nobody knows that more than me," she replied matter-of-factly.

And the problem is? "Maybe," he started slowly, "your mother wanted to right a very big wrong."

A snort, followed by a bitter, humorless laugh escaped

her. "My mother didn't have a chivalrous bone in her body."

All right, then. "I hate to play devil's advocate here, but do her reasons really matter?"

She turned her head to look at him and he saw the battle going on in her eyes. "It matters to me."

He held his hands up in defense. "Okay." Clearly a touchy subject, so he tried a different route. Risking bodily harm, he placed a comforting hand on her small shoulder and dragged the tip of his index finger over the curve. "You should read the letter."

"What I should do and what I can do are two different things. I'm not ready yet." One of her velvety legs lifted and slid over the other one, effectively pulling her short shorts practically up to her butt crack. His eyes instantly zeroed in on the sight, bringing back memories of them spread wide around his hips. "I had an interesting conversation with Brody tonight," she blurted out, destroying the image in his head. "Apparently Kelly's getting married."

"No kidding? To that guy she's been seeing?"

"Yeah, the one Brody refers to as a jackass."

Chase chuckled and rested his left foot across his right knee. "Why does Brody call him that?"

Lacy lifted one shoulder in a halfhearted shrug. "I think he's jealous."

"Jealous of the guy who's marrying his ex-wife?" he asked with a trace of doubt. "I don't think so. Brody's not the jealous type."

She tucked a few loose strands of hair behind one ear and didn't deny his statement. "I think he still has feelings for her."

This time he shook his head, knowing she was wrong. "No way. He was never in love with Kelly."

She threw him a droll look. "They were married for seven years, Chase. He had *some* feelings for her."

Her logic made sense, whether he wanted to admit it or not. He stretched his arm along the back of the couch. "What did he say to you?"

"He didn't have to say anything. His demeanor was a dead giveaway." Her gaze briefly dropped to his lap. "He's having a hard time."

Even though he loved his brother, Chase's concern for him was shoved to the back burner in light of Lacy's appraisal. The way her fingers fidgeted and tapped an erratic rhythm against her bare thigh told Chase she was turned on. So did the way her chest lifted in deep breaths, pushing her breasts against the thin cotton of her old shirt, revealing her hardened nipples. The question was, did she plan on acting on it or on calling it a night and politely showing him to the door?

"It's late and I have to work tomorrow," she said as if the realization had just hit her. She unfolded her slender frame from the couch and picked up the wineglass from the table. She walked toward the kitchen, rewarding Chase with a prime view of her spectacular ass. The confident, feminine sway of her hips spoke of a woman who knew how to use her curves. Although Lacy wasn't a particularly curvy woman, the gentle back-and-forth motion accentuated what she did have. How did women learn how to walk like that? Was it something they taught each other in high school? *How to attract a man's attention in five seconds or less?* However the technique came to them, women as a whole knew exactly what they did to a man's libido when they sashayed like that. Women weren't stupid creatures; a little swivel of the hips and they could set every man's tongue wagging like a panting dog's. Lacy was no different. She was fully aware of how he reacted to her.

Her green eyes connected with his when she peeked over her shoulder at him. "Are you coming?"

Hell, yeah was about to force itself out of his mouth. Self-control had him tamping down his crude side for Lacy's sake. Never say he couldn't be a gentleman when he wanted to be.

Instead he remained on the couch, letting his eyes meander down her lithe body. "Are you sure?"

"Isn't that why you came over here?"

When he stood, his six-foot-three frame towered over her, with the top of her head reaching his collarbone. He stepped close enough to invade her personal space but didn't touch. The edge of her cotton shirt kissed the front part of his slacks. Despite the whisper of contact, minimal and hardly enough to start fireworks, his dick leaped to life and pushed with all its strength against the inside of his boxers. Never one to miss anything, Lacy let her curious eyes drop to the action behind his pants. Chase knew she wanted him. But Lacy never wore her emotions on her sleeve. She masked them quite well when she lifted her eyes to his.

"Do you want me to stay?" Although he had all the confidence in the world, the words came out with an uncertain, uneven tone. With a mere lift of her long, black lashes, Lacy turned him into a quivering idiot.

Her soft breasts nudged his chest when she inhaled deeply. His hands twitched at his sides, eager to feel her nipples grow to little raspberries.

"Yes," escaped on a whisper as if she'd read his thoughts. Lacy returned the wineglass to the end table, grabbed his large hand in her smaller one, and led him to her bedroom.

• • •

Sometime later, after even the moon had disappeared, leaving the sky an ominous coal-black, Lacy kicked the covers off her perspiration-dewy body. The lack of air-conditioning had grown from a minor inconvenience to a downright annoyance. In the aftermath of hers and Chase's vigorous lovemaking, her bedroom had turned into a humid, muggy sauna. The sheets felt like thick damp washcloths against her already-damp skin. Kicking them off served no other purpose than to transfer them to the end of the bed. The air around her still brushed over her skin like hot, putrid breath. She wished she could at least have a fan in her room, but her one and only oscillating fan finally had bit the dust after about a thousand years of use.

Chase had thrown his covers off with a grumpy, "It's too damn hot in here," immediately after rolling off her. His ability to fall asleep in about three seconds struck a chord of envy in her. And he took up an enormous amount of the bed, which wasn't that big to begin with. With a six-foot-three and two-hundred-whatever-pound man taking up two-thirds of the bed and pumping out buckets of body heat really cramped her sleeping style. Lacy was one of those sleepers who liked to spread out in the middle of the bed. She'd carved a nice little indentation for herself right in between her two pillows. But the man who'd so generously given her two orgasms was currently in her favorite spot. The only reason she forgave his invasion of space was because she basked in a rather satisfying postcoital bliss. Besides, he outweighed her by a hundred pounds; she had absolutely no hopes of scooting him even one inch.

At least the man was unbearably gorgeous, lying on

his stomach with both his arms folded underneath her pillow, his fine body gleaming with sweat, hers to enjoy. Wide shoulders tapered down to a narrow waist, which then curved into those two round, very hard ass cheeks. His long, muscular legs stretched to the end of the bed where his feet hung off the edge. Lacy smiled at the sight he made, a man too big and too masculine for her girly full-sized bed.

Unable to sleep for the humid air clinging to her, Lacy slid out of bed and searched for her clothes. They were nowhere to be seen, but Chase's blue shirt lay in a heap, still where she'd hurriedly thrown it. Not wanting to put that much effort into finding her own clothes, she swiped his shirt off the floor and shrugged into it. Having the cotton material caress her skin should have made her even hotter. On the contrary, the scent of him lingering on the fabric surrounded her in a delicious cloud of manliness that was all Chase. She buttoned the shirt while padding barefoot down the hallway to the living room. Her stomach growled, but Lacy had always read the worst time to eat was the middle of the night. She ignored her demanding hunger and instead curled up on the couch and turned on the television.

A frustrated sigh flowed out of her at the lack of good programming at... what did the clock say? Lacy squinted at the mantel clock. Good Lord, it was three-thirty in the morning? She tossed the remote onto the cushions next to her and settled for watching a rerun of the evening news. An apartment fire in a neighboring town and the night's lottery numbers hardly made for edge-of-your-seat viewing. The middle-aged woman, with every shade of blond highlighted into her badly teased mane, droned on in an annoyingly cheerful tone about events in the greater

Cheyenne area. Lacy picked up the remote, hoping some new programs had cropped up since her last attempt to scan the channels, when the anchorwoman moved on to her next story.

"In local news, the citizens of Trouble should start double-checking the locks on their front doors. Late last night, a woman called authorities when she discovered a man trying to enter her home through a bedroom window. She told the police she beat the man back with a broom, then called nine-one-one. The man, apparently spooked, took off running before the police arrived on the scene. Here's what the woman had to say about the incident."

The scene then cut to an older woman with a plump face telling the story about how she defended her home against a would-be intruder. The woman, whose identity was only revealed as "the victim," told her story with an unnatural calm, as though she encountered that sort of thing every day. Even as she listened to the woman retell her story for the six o'clock news, Lacy's "Dennis radar" went from dormant to hyperactive in about three seconds. The interview was cut off when the anchorwoman returned to the screen and announced they had a sketch from the victim's detailed description of the perpetrator.

By the time the sketch flashed on the screen, she knew without a doubt the man the police needed to search for was Dennis Taylor. Forensic artists really did have an amazing ability to capture a person's essence without ever having laid eyes on them. This artist had done an impeccable job of setting Dennis's nose at just the right angle so that it looked like a miniature pelican's beak. The eyes were the same shape, a little bit on the large side and farther apart than they should be, but they possessed the same dark, not-quite-sane look they always had in real life. His hair, which looked like it was only days away from falling out, was too thin and wiry and hung almost to his shoulders like a bad imitation of Russell Crowe's style. All in all, there really wasn't anything attractive about Dennis Taylor. He was the sort of man women avoided eye contact with in a bar, with his I'm-a-loose-cannon-stay-away-from-me air. Luckily for Lacy, she'd taken after her mother. The only thing she inherited from Dennis was his blond hair.

For the entire ten seconds the sketch remained on the screen, she forced herself to look at the black-and-white illustrated eyes. Even in a drawing, his stare had the same effect as it did in real life. It was as if he were sneering, *I know you're out there, sweet daughter, so you'd better prepare yourself.* No matter how strong she pretended to be, Lacy couldn't stop her heart rate from escalating to marathon status or the hairs on her arms from shooting to attention like an electrical charge had just coursed through her. Dennis always created this reaction whether he was in her life or not. The impending doom of storm clouds always hovered over her indefinitely until he crawled back into whatever hole he'd come from. She reverted to her old nervous habit of wringing her hands until she finally shoved them under her bare legs.

The anchorwoman repeated the age-old mantra of asking anyone to call such-and-such number if they had any information of the assailant's whereabouts. Paralyzing nerves kept her rooted to the couch until the number, jumbled and nonsensical to Lacy in her panic, disappeared from the screen. She had no hope of remembering them in her scrambled mind. Instead, her thoughts centered on Dennis and the possibility of him appearing at her door. She'd never actually asked herself what she'd do if he did show his ugly face; for the past five years, he'd always been someone else's problem and she'd been happy to let them deal with him. Gracing her with his unpleasant presence was starting to become a real possibility, and Lacy didn't have the slightest clue how to deal with that. In the past, she'd always given him whatever spare cash she had, for no other reason than to rid herself of him. Now she didn't have any spare cash. Okay, maybe she did. There was the matter of a ten-million-dollar check; however, Lacy would rather see that burned to ashes than in the hands of the worthless man who'd fathered her.

The news took a brief commercial break, snapping Lacy back to reality. She used the opportunity to rid herself of her overactive nerves and stood. One advertisement rolled on after another but Lacy paid no attention to such things like how to make millions over the Internet or free financing for the first year on a brand-new car. She stepped over Boris's unconscious form as she walked in circles around the living room, trying to come up with a plan.

She'd missed the telephone number the news gave out, but she did have the business cards for the two detectives who'd come to see her. They'd said to call them anytime, but would they remember that when their phone rang in the middle of the night? Was there anything they could do at three in the morning anyway? Then again, what would they say when she told them she saw the report hours before calling them? Would that make them suspicious? Discredit her character?

She released a long, frustrated breath at the lack of answers her brain generated. The flickering light of the television skittered across the walls, creating uneven, chaotic patterns. Boris yipped in his sleep and his front paws twitched. The refrigerator hummed a low, comforting sound that would normally lull her to sleep. All the sounds of home that should have calmed her overworked nerves sounded like they came from someplace far and unreachable. Dennis's face appearing on the screen had invaded her privacy and the safe little bubble she'd created for herself, yet another reason for her to resent him. As if she didn't have enough reason as it was.

She continued on her trip around the living room, stepping over Boris, then walking past the kitchen. After ten minutes of mindless pacing, Lacy felt as unsettled as she had before. She made her umpteenth trip around the coffee table and came to an abrupt stop when a tall figure standing at the end of the hallway made her heart punch its way through her rib cage.

Chase leaned against the wall wearing nothing but his black boxer-briefs and a shadowed, unreadable expression. "Trying to burn off more calories?" His deep, rumbling voice chased away the paranoia that had consumed her for the past ten minutes.

Instead of answering his question, she countered with, "How long have you been standing there?"

The low volume of the television filled the living room for a moment before Chase answered. "Long enough to know something's on your mind."

"I couldn't sleep."

"So you thought you'd wear yourself out by walking in circles around the living room?"

The man paid way more attention to her than she was comfortable with. Dennis was a part of her life that wasn't easy for her to open up about, especially to Chase. He'd always loathed Dennis, as he rightfully should. The possibility of Dennis being in town wasn't something Chase would take lightly. No, she needed to deal with this on her own until Dennis was either in jail or in another part of the country.

"I was just feeling restless," she finally answered.

Chase didn't move so much as an eyelash. At least she didn't think he did. The room was so blessedly dark, save what little light the television generated, that his face was in complete shadow. A shame, considering how disgustingly handsome he was.

"You mean our earlier activities didn't wear you out?"

A warm, tingly feeling started in her cheeks and snaked its way down to the depths of her belly. His words caressed her skin as though he'd actually touched her with those masterful hands of his. Even though she couldn't see his eyes, she felt their touch on every part of her, from her hair all the way down her bare legs. The man was seducing her from across the room. Without a word, he held out his hand.

She clicked the television off and accepted his invitation. Once back in bed, she curled herself around his hard, warm body and let his hands, drifting up and down her back, melt her into a dreamless sleep.

EIGHT

DAWN BROKE ENTIRELY TOO EARLY and brought with it annoyingly cheerful sunshine. Lacy wasn't ready to face the day yet, so she rolled over with a groan that sounded almost inhuman and slipped back to sleep. A short while later she woke up to the sun's merciless rays pouring into her room with more force than before. She admitted defeat and swung her sleep-sluggish legs over the edge of the bed. The events of a few hours ago made her feel exhausted, both physically and emotionally. Her eyes felt gritty and her brain mushy, and her thighs burned and quivered from her and Chase's strenuous activities. Last night he'd introduced her to positions she'd never even heard of and twisted her body in ways she didn't think possible. Lacy didn't want to think about where he'd learned some of that stuff and how he'd gotten so good at it. Or how he knew to tell her to rotate her hips in just the right direction in order to heighten her orgasm. But she liked to think he'd read about it somewhere rather than having practiced it on other women. She hadn't survived this long on her own by being naïve. Chase had had a reputation of bedding one woman after another for as long as she'd known him. So long as he wasn't screwing other women while they were…whatever it was they were.

She remained on the edge of the bed and glanced at him over her shoulder. He lay on his side and faced the window, giving her a view of his back. She took a closer look at the tattoo on the back of his right shoulder. He'd had the barbwire-looking thing that circled his left bicep since he was about eighteen. Lacy vaguely remembered Brody telling her how upset Martin had been about his son permanently marking his body. All four of the boys had gotten tattoos when they turned eighteen. Lacy never understood why they felt the need to mark themselves, as though they needed visible proof they were becoming men. The one on his back was a lot smaller than the one circling his bicep. The black-and-white design was small and intricate with some sort of weave pattern. Upon closer scrutiny, she saw the tattoo wasn't some nonsensical twisting weave pattern but actually a cross. She leaned across the bed to study the crisscrossing lines and ran her index finger over hard muscle where the tattoo was located. Before she could touch him further, as she ached to do, Chase stirred and rolled over onto his back to face her.

"Sorry. I didn't mean to wake you up."

He pressed the backs of his hands into his eyes and stretched. "That's all right. I need to get up anyway."

She admired his strong muscles as they flexed and moved when he stretched. "When did you get that tattoo on your back?"

"College."

"I didn't realize you had more than one."

His blue eyes dropped to her bare breasts. "I have

three, actually." He unfolded his hand from behind his head and shoved the sheet past his hips. There, at the very bottom and intimate part of his abdomen, were the words *Twelve Inch Wonder.*

Good grief, the man thought highly of himself. Lacy sat back and rolled her eyes. "Twelve inches?" He was big, but not *that* big.

One side of his delectable mouth turned up. "It was my nickname in college."

"And who gave you this nickname?"

"A friend of mine."

She crossed her arms over her bare breasts. "A girlfriend?" Why in the world did she ask that?

His eyebrows twitched and something dark flashed in his bottomless blue eyes. "Wouldn't you like to know?"

Wasn't that why she'd asked? Lacy knew next to nothing about Chase's dating history. Granted, it was none of her business, but the curiosity was killing her. He'd always been very tight-lipped about it, like he had some deep, dark secret he didn't want anyone to know. To anyone else in his life, Chase was usually an open book. But this one subject was kept under lock and key.

He pulled the sheet back up and ran his calloused palm over her thigh. A shiver rippled through her naked body when his hand abandoned her leg and sought out her breast.

"What time do you have to be at work?"

Her eyelids became heavy and drifted closed when he skimmed his thumb over her nipple. "Five."

He pushed himself up and lowered her to her back, all the while dropping kisses on her neck. "I don't have to be there until eleven. How about a quickie?"

How romantic. "My thighs hurt." Despite her protest,

she lifted her legs around him and ran her hands over his back.

"I'll be gentle."

Heat gathered in her abdomen and spread south when she felt him probing her entrance. His warm tongue left a wake of moisture on her neck and his hands floated down her sides.

"Chase..."

"Hmm? Do you want me to stop?"

Yes. "No." *Oh man, his hands.* His hands were everywhere, touching every part of her. Lacy squirmed beneath him and ran her legs along his. He hadn't entered her immediately. Instead, he'd started this little teasing game where he rubbed the tip of himself along her slippery entrance. Lacy was just about to surrender to another round of mind-altering sex when her doorbell chimed. At first, the soft ringing was barely enough to penetrate her foggy mind. Chase's mouth made a deliciously wet path from her throat to her belly, thwarting her attempts to disentangle herself from him. Since her body was already in sexual la-la land, Lacy closed her eyes and willed her mind to follow. However, the bell rang a third time, letting her know that whoever stood on the other side was determined she get up and answer it.

In a pathetic and halfhearted attempt, Lacy shoved on Chase's steel-like, mile-wide shoulders. "Chase, someone's at my door."

"Who cares? They'll eventually get the point and come back later." He skimmed his magician's hands up her inner thighs, prompting a gasp from her.

No, they needed to stop. They'd already done it countless times since last night. One of them needed to rein in their libido and rejoin the human world.

Putting more effort behind her movements, Lacy wiggled her legs out from under him and gave his shoulders a determined shove. He sat back with an "Are you crazy?" expression on his sinfully handsome face. She ignored his look and scrambled off the bed.

"You're insane." The remark was softened by his slightly upturned mouth.

She kept her back to him while pulling on yesterday's clothes with jerky movements. Where Chase was concerned, she practically had no sanity and if she looked at him, she'd be out of her mind again. Out of the corner of her eye, she caught the disbelieving shake of his head, yet another thing she chose to ignore as she padded barefoot to her front door.

A breezy, overcast day greeted her when she swung open the door, as did the retreating backside of her half sister. The heavily leafed tree in the front yard swayed back and forth as if beckoning anyone walking by to come and "sit a spell," as Ray had always said. A particularly strong gust whipped the short strands of Megan's chin-length hair, which she tried to hold back with one hand, across her youthfully beautiful face. Her white linen skirt, which was probably worth more than Lacy's car, swirled around Megan's shapely knees.

"Oh, you're home." She turned and looked at Lacy. Her voice was as breathy as the air that blew around them. "I was just leaving."

"Yeah, sorry." What was she supposed to say now? *I was just about to have sex when you rang the bell*? Instead, she stepped back from the door and decided not to offer an explanation. "Do you want to come in?"

A childish sort of delight lit up the younger woman's innocent green eyes. "I'm sorry to just show up like this,"

Megan said as she stepped through the doorway. She turned to face Lacy. "Last night I went for a drive, and it hit me that you're really the only family I have left. I just thought it would be a shame for us not to get to know each other."

Something inside Lacy melted at Megan's words. Lacy knew what it was like not to have a living soul left to make that familial connection with. Even though Lacy couldn't erase the tiny bit of resentment she felt toward Megan, the girl had been just as affected by their mother's actions. It wouldn't be right for Lacy to take her hurt and betrayal out on her half sister.

Before Lacy could comment on Megan's announcement, the girl's eyes widened at something behind Lacy. She turned and found Chase standing at the end of the hallway. Megan's eyes grew to the size of grapefruits at the sight of the imposing man with a bad case of bedhead and twenty-four-hour stubble.

"Uh, I can come back."

As far as awkward moments went, this was one of those and it was guaranteed to be locked in her memory until they put her in the ground. She searched her muddled brain for some sort of intelligent response, anything other than, *Um, yeah, this is my boss, who spent the night and I'm not really sure what our relationship is.* This also would have been a good time for one of them to clear their throat or crack an inappropriate joke. Chase, saint that he was, broke the silence first.

"You must be Megan." He walked toward them and offered his hand in greeting.

Megan stared at Chase's outstretched hand as though she'd never gone through a hand-shaking ritual before. Then she placed her manicured palm in his and offered a shy, close-lipped smile.

Lacy tried to repress the hundred-degree temperature that crept into her cheeks. Heaven only knew what Megan must be assuming. Two nights ago, Lacy had gone through this song and dance about not telling a soul about her and Chase's affair and yet here Megan was. Granted, she lived like five states away, but discretion was always the safest route and one Lacy intended to stick to.

Chase released Megan's hand and turned to Lacy. "I've got to run. I'll just grab my shirt and show myself out."

Way to be discreet, bucko.

Megan, a soft, rose-colored blush high on her cheekbones, glanced at Lacy. "I really didn't mean to intrude on anything."

Lacy waved a hand in the air before Megan could finish her sentence. "There's no intrusion, believe me. He knows his way out." She forced a smile in an attempt to downplay the situation.

Megan's delicate brows twitched in dismay. "Okay. Well, I was actually out in search of some coffee and thought maybe you'd like to join me. We could use the time to talk."

To be honest, Lacy was surprised the other girl hadn't run screaming back to California after twenty-four hours in Trouble, Wyoming. People who were raised with chauffeurs and seven-figure trust funds didn't often find themselves basking in the stench of manure.

So, what was Miss Hollywood still doing here?

On the other hand, Lacy didn't often have a prayer of starting her day until she had sufficient caffeine flowing through her veins.

She found herself nodding at the teenager. "If you can give me ten minutes, I'll put on something more respectable."

Before Lacy could retreat to her bedroom, where Chase still lurked, Megan's eyes widened for the second time since walking through the door.

The *click-clicking* of toenails on the floor, followed by a cold wet nose on Lacy's hand, revealed Boris's presence. The old dog had been snoozing all morning and had no doubt decided he needed his meal.

Lacy scratched Boris's ears in an attempt to show Megan the beast was tamer than he looked. "Oh, this is Boris. He's harmless."

"Wh-what is he?" Megan took a step back when Boris aimed his nose at her delicate skirt.

"He's an English mastiff. Don't worry, he won't hurt you," Lacy reassured her when Megan still edged backward. "He's about a hundred years old and can't hear or see worth a damn. But his sense of smell is still keen, so it's probably your perfume that piqued his interest. Just give him a little nudge and he'll leave you alone."

A thick, mile-long thread of drool stretched down from Boris's droopy jowls and threatened to ruin Megan's leopard-print, peep-toe stilettos. The girl moved her foot back just in time and touched the very tips of her fingers on Boris's wet nose. The dog's pink tongue lolled out and didn't even come close to reaching Megan's hand.

Boris, having been satisfied with a little pat-pat, ambled his arthritic bones to the kitchen. Lacy grinned after him. Boris possessed the charisma of a housefly.

"Just give me a minute to feed him and change my clothes."

Chase was just pulling his shirt over his head when Lacy entered the bedroom. *What a shame, covering up all that hard muscle.*

"Are you okay?" he asked as he came toward her.

Lacy discarded her clothes and pulled some fresh ones out of her dresser. "Yeah. Why wouldn't I be?" Playing tough never worked with Chase, but she tried anyway.

"She's a piece of your mother. I know that's a difficult subject for you."

How did he understand her so well? Had he always known these things about her? She tugged on a pair of denim shorts, then faced him. "I'll be fine. We're just going to get some coffee."

He touched a strand of her hair. "Are you sure? Do you want me to come?"

Oddly enough, she did. She wanted him to have coffee with her. Then she wanted to share dinner with him and crawl into bed next to him so she could feel his warm skin against hers. Despite those desires, this was something she needed to do on her own.

"I promise I'll be okay. Thanks anyway." *Last night was really great. Let's do it again. Every night.* The words were on the very tip of her tongue when Chase leaned down and brushed a soft kiss over her lips. Sweet electrical currents shot down to her toes.

"I'll see you later," he said after ending the brief kiss. He sauntered out of her bedroom and toward the front door.

Lacy squashed down her urge to run after him as she yanked a shirt over her head.

Thirty minutes later, she blew on her nonfat, no whip, white-chocolate mocha while Megan took a sip of her green tea chai latte. The coffee shop's attempt at creating an attractive outdoor patio had failed miserably, mostly because they hadn't provided any umbrellas to shield customers from the sun. Plus the café didn't deem it necessary to scrape away the oodles of bird droppings littering the tabletops and chairs. Lacy guessed most people didn't want the essence of bird doo-doo with their morning, midday, or evening coffee. The two of them opted to sit indoors where the only redeeming qualities were a functional air conditioner and a television running the day's news. Suffice it to say, Trouble's only coffee shop was certainly no Starbucks where customers could enjoy the low hum of music and sit at tables that didn't wobble on uneven footing. But it was a step up from filling your own cup at the corner gas station.

Megan scooped a dollop of whipped cream with her straw. "Thanks for agreeing to come out with me."

Lacy grinned after placing her cup on the table. "I appreciate you asking me. Actually I'd thought you'd have gone back to California by now."

The girl pursed her baby-pink lips. "I'm just kind of going day by day right now. Plus, I got tired of being in that enormous house by myself. It started to feel like I was being swallowed up." Megan glanced at their surroundings. "It's different here. Not as chaotic as Los Angeles."

That was an understatement. "You have no plans as of now?"

"I don't know. I'm not sure what I want to do with the house. And I'm not in any hurry to get back there until I make that decision. I'm leaning more toward selling it."

Lacy imagined a ten-thousand-square-foot house with a bowling alley and movie theater in the Hollywood Hills and couldn't fathom anyone not wanting to live in a place like that. Megan undoubtedly had her reasons for not wanting the house anymore, and who was Lacy to judge?

"So what do you do here, Lacy?"

"I wait tables at McDermott's. It's a steak house," she

added when Megan looked confused. "It's not glamorous work, but it's pretty good money."

Megan's brow crinkled. "Haven't you cashed the check I gave you? You wouldn't have to wait tables anymore if you did." She set her paper cup down and slapped a hand over her mouth. "I'm sorry. I didn't mean..." Short blond hair dusted the tops of Megan's shoulders when she shook her head. "I didn't mean that the way it sounded."

Lacy found herself smiling. "It's okay. Waitressing was something that was supposed to be temporary because of my circumstances at the time. But it just kind of stuck with me over the past two years. I find myself complaining about it, but I enjoy what I do. As for the check..." Lacy twirled her coffee around. "I'm not ready yet."

"What did you do with it?"

"It's sitting on my dresser."

The other girl took a sip of her latte. "Didn't the letter explain anything?"

Lacy hesitated before answering. "I haven't opened it yet."

Megan lifted her gaze to Lacy's. Something similar to nostalgia washed over Lacy when looking into green eyes so very much like her mother's.

"I'm sorry," Megan said. "I'm being incredibly nosy."

Oh, hell. Guilt heated Lacy's face and washed up to her hairline. "Don't worry about it. I don't blame you for being curious. *I'm* curious." She inhaled deeply. "I'll get around to it sometime. Just not now."

Lacy watched as a young woman accompanied by two little girls walked through the door of the coffee shop. One girl hovered by her mother's side while the other girl ran to the display counter and begged for a muffin.

"I've been spending the past few months trying to understand why she did it," Megan said.

Lacy tore her gaze away from the six- or seven-year-old girl with yellow overalls and disheveled black hair. Megan's words took a second to register in Lacy's brain. "You mean why she left me?" The harsh tone in her voice had been unintended. As Megan had told her before, she'd been shocked to learn she had a half sister. Those circumstances had been well beyond Megan's control and she didn't deserve the brunt of Lacy's anger and resentment.

"Yes," Megan answered before Lacy had a chance to apologize for her callous tone. "I know I said this before, but the mother I knew would never have done anything like that." She picked up her paper cup, then set it back down. "I went through a period of anger after my father died, but it's probably nothing compared to how you felt."

Well, she didn't want to rub it in Megan's face or anything, but, yeah, Lacy doubted that too. She swallowed some more hot mocha and decided to change the subject. "Do you go to school back home?"

Megan nodded. "I just finished my first year at UC San Diego as an undergraduate. I plan on getting a degree in psychology. Then when I'm done, I have to get my masters in clinical psychology."

"Wow. What do you plan on doing with that?"

Megan wrinkled her nose. "I was planning on being a forensic psychologist. But I never realized how incredibly *boring* it all is. Not to mention a ton of work. Not that I thought I could sail through it in a few years." She shook her head, sending her caramel tresses across her jaw. "There're about half a dozen degrees to earn and I have to work side by side with a chartered forensic psychologist in the field. And there's an exam I have to pass so I can get certified."

Lacy smiled. "No offense, but what in the world made you want to go into that line of work?"

A lighthearted laugh bubbled out of Megan's full mouth. "I don't know. Watching too many crime shows, I guess. My dad said he never understood why I would want to do something so morbid and depressing. He wanted me to major in fine arts at Chapman University because that's where he went." She tucked a short strand of hair behind her ear. "Fine arts and theater and all that other stuff never interested me. I don't have a creative bone in my body. I'm more of an analytical sort." She took a deep breath. "Not at all like either one of my parents."

Lacy sucked down some more coffee. "How long will all this take you?" No way could she imagine spending that much time studying in school.

"If I'm lucky, I'll have a stable job by the time I'm thirty. At the rate I'm going, I'll finish my undergrad by the time I'm twenty-three. I was going to go for my doctorate but those can take up to seven years." She sipped her chai latte. "Anyway, I think I'm going to transfer to Pepperdine to get my masters. If I have the stamina, I'll try to do my fieldwork and study at the same time."

Never in a million years would Lacy have imagined that someone who drove a Lexus convertible and wore four-inch heels would have an affinity for science. The two went together about as well as chocolate and lima beans. Then again, Lacy knew firsthand how flawed it was to judge a person by their looks. According to half the town, when she was a teenager, she was just as much a criminal and drunk as her father. Thus far, Lacy had tried not to judge Megan, however unsuccessful she'd been.

She shook away the thoughts and swirled her drink around. "So what exactly does a forensic psychologist do?"

"It's kind of hard to explain. Basically, they get inside the mind of a criminal and try to understand why they do the things they do. A lot of their practice happens in a courtroom and their evaluation of a criminal's sanity is for purposes of testimony. They need to have a great understanding of legal language and the judicial system." Megan's short fingernail drew circles on the faded tabletop. "A lot of it is pretty boring and sometimes I second-guess my career choice."

"It's never too late to change your mind."

"Yeah, I figured since I've only got one year of my undergrad done, I could change my mind and not have to start over. But in most cases, the beginning classes of any major are unexciting. I think I'll give myself one more year; then I might switch to forensic science. Though I don't think I'd have the stomach to examine a dead body." Megan's thin frame shuddered and she ran her hands up and down her bare arms.

Public toilets held more appeal to Lacy than cutting open and cutting apart human bodies. She'd barely managed to stomach dissecting frogs in high school.

The two of them enjoyed their drinks in companionable silence while the other woman in the coffee shop tried to corral her two daughters at a table. As Lacy swallowed, an unsettling thought occurred to her.

"Do you have any brothers or sisters?"

Megan grimaced. "I have a stepbrother from my dad's first marriage. But he's way older than me and was already out of the house by the time I came along." She pursed her lips and pulled her thin brows together. "Paul, who lives in San Diego, and my dad had a strained relationship because of my dad's divorce from Paul's mother." One thin shoulder lifted in a negligent shrug. "We're not very close. No brothers or sisters for you?"

She shook her head. "No, it's just me."

Megan tilted her head to one side. "What about your dad?"

Delving into Dennis's criminal background and lack of paternal skills was entirely too deep a discussion for morning coffee with a person who was practically a stranger. "I was mostly raised by my grandfather." Not a total lie and about as much as Lacy wanted to share at the moment. "He died about two years ago and I decided to move into his house. He was pretty much the only family I had."

Megan nodded. "I never knew any of my grandparents. My dad's father died years before I was born and his mother lived on the East Coast and died when I was three. And Mom, well...she never mentioned her parents."

"I never knew them either. I asked Ray about them once before and he said..."

"Said what?" Megan prompted after the words died off Lacy's tongue.

They're as worthless as your mother, was what he'd said. But Megan, who obviously had a much different perspective of their mother than Lacy, would only be hurt and confused by such a statement.

"He didn't have a whole lot to say about them. If they remained in the area all these years, then they never bothered to get to know me."

Pretty sad and pathetic but true. Lacy could draw her entire family tree on a Post-it note.

Megan tipped her head back and downed the rest of

her drink. Lacy realized an hour had passed since the two of them had sat down at the table; it was as if only a few moments had gone by. Even though her half sister had gotten the better end of the parental deal, she was easy to talk to. The resentment Lacy had felt upon first meeting the girl had disappeared, and its departure left room for things like companionship and the warm, fuzzy feelings that came with making a new friend. Although, Lacy wasn't sure she was quite at the friendship stage with Megan. Old habits made it difficult for her to open up and allow people to see her vulnerable side. Ray was one of the few people who'd seen Lacy's weaknesses and faults, yet loved her despite them. The same trust issues she'd always had prevented her from letting anybody else get close enough to see that side of her. That was probably one of the reasons why she didn't have very many close friends, save Brody.

Could Megan turn into one of those people? Their relationship was still in the infant stage, making it hard for Lacy to judge either way. So far, she liked what she saw in the younger girl, so there were definite possibilities of veering into the acquaintance category. After that, only time would tell.

"Before I forget, I have something for you," Megan announced. She set her cup down on the table and grabbed her purse off the back of the chair. She dug around for a moment, then retrieved a small white box. "I thought about giving this to you the other day, but I didn't want to bombard you all at once."

Lacy sat while Megan slid the box across the table. "A few months ago, while I was going through Mom's things, I found this. She had it wrapped in some tissue with a pink ribbon tied around it. At first I wasn't sure what to do with it, but now I'm sure I want you to have it."

Lacy's heart thumped up into her throat and threatened to choke her. She took the box and ran her tongue along her suddenly dry lips. Megan had good intentions; Lacy knew that. The girl only wanted Lacy to know the mother she had known. Her fingers trembled when they removed the lid to the box and placed it on the table.

Inside, nestled on a pad of soft cotton, was a delicate gold locket. The chain was whisper thin, and etched in fine lines on top of the heart-shaped locket was a single, tiny rose. Lacy took the necklace out of the box with sweaty fingers and managed to open the heart. A faded, ancient baby photo of herself stared up at Lacy. She ran her thumb over the picture and tried to imagine the jewelry fastened around her mother's neck. Had she ever worn this? Had she kept it as a reminder of the daughter she walked away from? So many unanswered questions still tortured her.

Hot tears burned her eyes and threatened to spill over onto her cheeks.

"I'm sorry," Megan blurted out. "I didn't mean to upset you. I just thought maybe you'd like to know that she never forgot you."

"It's okay," Lacy whispered. "Thank you."

"That's pretty damning evidence, don't you think?"

Chase didn't respond to his assistant manager's question, mostly because she was jumping to conclusions. The fact that his father had been breathing down his neck for the past two weeks was the only reason Anita was reading between the lines of the less-than-impressive surveillance video.

He picked up the remote and reversed the footage. The employee backtracked his movements, jerkily taking three potatoes out of a paper sack and placing them on the shelf. He then walked backward and out of the food storage area.

"I think it's pretty safe to say this is the reason we've been short lately."

Anita was the sort of person who stood in the middle of a crowded room, waved her hands around, and screamed, "Look at me!" until every eye focused on her. But her sharp eye and refusal to take shit from anyone made her a good right-hand man—or woman, in this case.

"I mean, look at him." She waved a hand at the screen and sent the silver bracelets on her wrists jingling. "He does it in plain sight. And there's no evidence showing he tries to return them."

Anita made a valid point. At no time during the remainder of the employee's shift did the disc show the potatoes being returned to their rightful spot. On the other hand, there was no evidence showing the employee leaving the restaurant with them. The tape only showed them leaving the pantry.

Chase turned to Anita. "How do we know he wasn't taking them out for Henry to prepare?" Forgive him for playing devil's advocate, but Chase couldn't bring himself to fire an employee based on three seconds of surveillance.

Anita's dark brown, heavily made up eyes lifted toward the ceiling. "How many times do you see the waitstaff going into the food storage area to retrieve supplies for Henry? That's the sous-chef's job."

Again, another point and one Chase already knew. But something about this didn't add up. The tingling sensation on the back of his neck told him there was more to this than the DVD showed.

"What about the money? There's no footage of him taking money from the cash drawer."

Anita rubbed her thumbnail along her sun-spotted cheek. "You're right about that. However, that was one incident and it happened several weeks ago. I'm leaning more toward human error."

"I counted that drawer three times. That was no human error."

"So you're telling me that someone took money from the drawer and managed to dodge all our cameras? Not likely."

He crossed his arms over his chest. "What are the chances of having two thieves on our hands? Whoever took money also has been depleting supplies. And what's puzzling about this"—he jerked his thumb at the frozen television screen—"is that no one reported a shortage of potatoes that night."

Anita's too-thin brows pulled together over her eyes. "I think it's worth at least a conversation. Your father's demanding answers, and right now we don't have many to give him."

No shit. Martin had been spending more and more time at McDermott's, as though his mere presence would scare off the thief. Chase had gone so far as to scrutinize the schedule and try to find patterns in the thefts. Just when he thought he had someone pegged, something would go missing on a night that person had off, forcing Chase to dismiss them as a suspect.

The incidents had no rhyme or reason. He'd even been forced to scrutinize Lacy, much as he hadn't wanted to. As one of his head waitresses, she worked almost every time something was reported. To his relief, when she appeared on the footage, she'd never been doing anything she wasn't supposed to. He'd dismissed her along with almost everybody else. He already knew he hadn't been the one taking things, nor his father. That left him with Henry, the sous-chefs, and even Anita. He was pretty sure Anita wouldn't steal from them. In fact, he was pretty sure none of the chefs would steal either, which left him where he was when this whole thing started: at square one.

The only common thread was the person who reported the crimes.

Henry.

In Henry's defense, the head chef was at the restaurant all the time and did all the checking and double-checking of the supplies. Naturally when the numbers didn't add up, Henry would be the one to discover it first. For some reason, that fact wasn't enough for Chase to disregard him. So far, the DVDs had revealed no suspicious behavior on Henry's part, leaving Chase with nothing.

"Want me to bring him in?" Anita asked.

Chase stared at the television screen a moment longer before shaking his head. "No. I'll keep a close eye on him, though. In the meantime, don't tell any of the employees what's going on. I'd rather whoever's doing this get sloppy and eventually show themselves."

Henry's name floated around his head but didn't leave his lips. Those suspicions were his alone and Chase didn't want to alert anyone that he thought McDermott's head chef was stealing from them.

NINE

"I STILL THINK YOU SHOULD SIGN UP for the art festival."

"You do, huh?" Lacy tucked her cell phone between her shoulder and ear as she shoved her purse in her work locker.

Brody continued with his sales pitch. "I absolutely do. I know a guy who's on the organization committee and he says there are still a few booths available. I could have him hold one for you."

Her locker shut with a clang. "I don't know, Brody. The art festival is the last thing on my mind right now. I don't even think I have anything worth showing."

"I don't believe that. You've always underestimated your talent."

In *his* opinion. Lacy had seen some of the artwork that had been in the festival before. They were works of art from local artists who had already established themselves in statewide galleries. Even in her wildest pipe dream, she was nowhere near that good. During a moment of pure wishful thinking she had imagined selling a few pieces and catching the eye of a gallery owner who'd take a liking to her, but who was she kidding? Her black-and-white trees and local mountain ranges wouldn't so much as spark a glimmer of interest.

Bless Brody's heart. He was a true friend who'd say her drawings would make M. C. Escher jealous, even though they both knew he was full of baloney.

"Okay, here's the deal," he continued as she turned to the mirror in the break room to make sure her white shirt looked crisp and fresh. "Steve, the guy I know on the committee, says he'd be willing to look at some of your pieces and let you know whether they're good enough to show."

"And what if he says they're not?" One of her biggest fears had always been having her drawings rejected.

"Trust me, he won't. I wouldn't have even brought it up to him if I didn't have complete faith in you." He was silent a moment, then said quietly, "You need to believe in yourself more, Lace. You have a talent."

That's what Ray used to always say. But he was her grandfather, and grandfathers were supposed to say things like that.

She remained silent, then stepped into the bathroom when Becky-Lynn entered the break room.

"I need to think about it." *And decide what I have that's worth showing*.

Brody's resigned sigh vibrated through her cell phone. "I have until the end of next week to let him know. If he doesn't hear back from me, he's going to give the booth to somebody else. This could be your chance. Don't let another year go by."

A grateful smile curled along her mouth. "Thanks, Brody. You're the best. Oh, hey," she said before he could hang up. "Bring Tyler by sometime, okay? I miss my buddy."

Brody waited a beat before answering. "He's still out of town with Kelly. I'll bring him by as soon as they get back."

She shifted her phone to her other ear. "How're you doing with all that, by the way?"

More silence. "I'm dealing. I'll be okay, Lace."

"I'm worried about you."

"I'm a big boy. Besides, as long as Tyler's happy, that's all that matters to me."

Lacy inhaled a breath and grinned. "You're a good dad. Tyler's lucky."

"Lacy—"

"I have to go. My shift is getting ready to start," she interrupted, not wanted to hear the sentimental "your situation was unfortunate" crap she'd heard a thousand times before. "I'll let you know about the fair."

After disconnecting the call, Lacy went back into the break room and found Becky-Lynn rooting around in her locker. The younger girl slammed the door shut, then turned her shy smile to Lacy.

"Thanks again for filling in for me the other night."

Lacy opened her locker and tucked her cell phone back into her purse. "No problem. I'm always happy to pick up an extra shift when I can." The other girl's yellowish blond hair, natural tan, and sky-blue eyes always reminded Lacy of a Swedish model's. Even in the dead of winter, Becky-Lynn possessed coloring most women went to tanning booths to achieve. Tonight, however, the girl looked different, like she'd gone too long without sun exposure and her color had faded to an unnatural pale. Bluish circles sat underneath her normally bright eyes.

"Are you okay?" Lacy asked her.

"Do you know if Chase or Mr. M is here tonight?"

Everyone knew Chase took Mondays and Tuesdays off. Becky-Lynn had been working at McDermott's long enough to know the GM wouldn't be there tonight.

"I don't think either one of them are here."

Becky-Lynn slowly blinked her long, thick black lashes.

"But Anita's here," Lacy added.

A handful of dull, unwashed-looking blond hair slipped out of Becky-Lynn's ponytail when she lowered her head. "I really should talk to Chase. I can't keep this from him anymore."

That sounded ominous. Lacy and Becky-Lynn hadn't exchanged more than a handful of sentences in the entire time they'd worked together. Lacy didn't know anything about her beyond that Becky-Lynn was a twenty-two-year-old college graduate who'd yet to pursue a career that didn't involve waiting tables.

"Okay," was all Lacy could say to the girl's cryptic statement. "I'm sure he'll be here on Wednesday."

Becky-Lynn shook her head and looked everywhere in the break room but at Lacy. "I don't work again until Friday."

"I'm sure Anita can take care of whatever's on your mind." Well, she actually wasn't sure. But heck, Becky-Lynn looked lost and tired and...something that wasn't quite right.

"She can't. I need to talk to Chase." She glanced at her black, sporty-looking watch. "I have to go clock in."

The conversation ended as abruptly as it had started, leaving Lacy with no other choice but to follow Becky-Lynn into the dining room. After clocking in and grabbing an order pad from the computer station, Lacy surveyed her section and took note of who sat where and who didn't have food in front of them. Along the left wall in one of the booths sat a woman with dark curly hair, all by herself, reading a menu. The woman's name eluded Lacy but she recognized the diner as a local.

She approached the woman, whose silver earrings hung halfway down to her shoulders.

"Good evening. I'm Lacy and I'll be your server," she said, giving the woman her most practiced smile. "Have you been given tonight's specials?"

"I'm waiting for Chase," the black-haired woman answered without taking her attention off the menu.

Lacy held the smile on her face like a shield. It wasn't any of her business what and who Chase did. But that didn't make it easy to accept. "Chase doesn't work on Mondays."

"Oh, he'll be here. He asked me to come." The woman's gaze ran over the thick, leather-bound menu. One of her white-tipped manicured fingernails tapped an even rhythm along the edge of the linen-finish, twenty-four-pound paper. In the dim, romantic lighting, an emerald the size of a tennis ball winked from its place on the woman's thin ring finger. Whoever she was, she certainly wasn't here to enjoy a steak dinner by herself.

Something very closely resembling jealousy, even though Lacy didn't want to admit it, ran thick and hot through her midsection. This woman's polished, sex-kitten appearance was the polar opposite to Lacy's I-barely-managed-to-run-a-brush-through-my-hair persona.

She finally shifted dark, chocolate-brown eyes up to Lacy. "Can you tell him I'm here?"

Even though Chase never mentioned anything about having an exclusive dating relationship, Lacy had come to assume while they were...doing their thing, he wouldn't be running around with women who wore so much mascara they looked like they had tarantula legs growing out of their eyes.

Okay, that wasn't such a nice thing to think. Just because this person was under the impression that Chase would make a special trip to the restaurant on his day off didn't mean he was banging her.

Lacy's blunt fingernails dug into the cover of her ordering book. "I already told you, he's not here. He won't be back until Wednesday."

Tarantula Woman placed her menu down on the white tablecloth. "He told me to come by. So I'm sure he's here. Besides," she continued, and held up a brown paper sack, "I have something for him."

The look on the woman's face was along the lines of *Oh you dear, sweet thing, you have no idea what you're talking about.* One thing that got beneath her skin more than anything else was pity. Pity was for losers who couldn't take care of themselves.

Lacy reminded herself Tarantula Woman was still a customer and could stiff her on the tip if Lacy showed so much as a hint of irritation. She forced another smile onto her face and tried not to picture scenarios in which Chase would be acquainted with this...person.

She yanked her ballpoint pen out from behind her ear. "Can I get you something to drink while you're waiting?"

The woman offered a close-lipped smile. "I'll have a bottle of Cabernet."

Lacy froze with her pen above the ordering pad. "You want the entire bottle?"

"Yes." The words *you moron* were implied.

Lacy didn't mention the fact that their Beringer Private

Reserve ran at about one hundred dollars. If this woman wanted to blow a hundred bucks on a bottle of wine to drink all by herself, that wasn't any of Lacy's business.

Forming as pleasant a smile as she could muster, Lacy turned from the table and went to feed her order for a single bottle of wine into the computer.

As she darted from one table to the next, taking orders and serving food as fast as she could, Lacy's gaze invariably landed on the lone female diner in the booth. Had Chase really asked the woman to meet him here? Did he plan to dine with her? The curly-haired lady certainly seemed to think so. And where would she have gotten an idea like that, unless Chase had planted it there? In all the years she'd known and sparred with him, she'd never taken him for a two-timer. In fact, she had no knowledge of him doing such a thing. But that didn't mean he didn't have it in him. He was, after all, a man. All men had their weaknesses. Maybe Chase's was curly-haired women with gaudy emerald rings.

On the other hand, they'd never labeled their relationship as anything official or exclusive. It just sort of happened and they hadn't taken the time to hash out the nitty-gritty details.

Lacy's uncertainty stemmed from her lack of knowing Chase's history. Or, more importantly, the women in his past. The other morning, after seeing his tattoo, she'd attempted to get some sort of insight out of him. She'd hoped he'd take her open-ended question as an invitation to be up front with her. His evasive answer had been cute and all, but Lacy had been left unsatisfied. What was it, specifically, that he didn't want to talk about?

As Lacy waited at the pass for Henry to plate the dishes, she thought back to Saturday night. Chase had shown up at her door sometime before midnight with finger-combed hair and a disarming smile. After drinking in his deliciousness for several moments, she'd grabbed his hand, led him to her room, and they hadn't surfaced until morning. She'd woken up to a featherlight kiss on her bare shoulder and the sound of him walking out the front door. The following twelve hours had been spent remembering little things like the heavy feel of his weight on the mattress next to her or how his eyes crinkled at the corners when she regaled him with stories of her college years. He'd asked her what her apartment looked like and how late she slept in on Sundays. Then he distracted her from her answers by running the tip of his finger down her spine and over the curve of her buttocks. When she asked him about college, he'd clammed up tighter than a virgin, with nothing more than a few vague answers such as, "It was an uneventful four years," and "I don't know, I was a typical college student." Lacy seriously doubted that. Not many men had their penis size tattooed on their abdomen, even if it was a slight embellishment. After failing to elaborate on what Lacy suspected was more, Chase had distracted her yet again by rolling her onto her stomach and dropping kisses down her backside.

A tactical battle strategy if she ever saw one. There was a singular event, or perhaps several, that he didn't want her to know about. Maybe no one knew it. What could have happened to him that he didn't want her to know about? Kicked out of school? No, that wasn't it. She remembered Brody talking about Chase's graduation. Arrested for a DUI or something along those lines? The arrested part was entirely possible, considering he had several minor arrests in high school. That particular scenario, Lacy couldn't rule out. But what was the big deal with that? Chase had never been embarrassed about his brushes with the law before, so why now? Maybe it was something really scandalous like possession of drugs or a sex tape, which seemed to be the running fad lately among the rich and famous. For whatever reason, Lacy had a feeling this thing correlated with his dating past. The unknown was starting to get to her, like an itch she couldn't satisfy.

Not that it was any of Lacy's business. It's not like they were a married couple and were obligated to share their deepest, darkest secrets with each other. What they shared was nothing more than compatible sex. Well, more than compatible. Downright combustible. But still, hardly a reason for him to tell her something he wasn't comfortable with.

Henry plated a cowboy rib eye and a stuffed chicken breast for Lacy to deliver. After Phil added garlic mashed potatoes and sautéed asparagus, Lacy picked up the two plates and hustled them out to the dining room.

Certainly she didn't *need* to know Chase's big secret, if there even was one. She probably was reading between the lines of their conversation, although instinct told her he hadn't been a hundred percent honest with her.

The two diners receiving the rib eye and stuffed chicken shoved their glasses out of the way and grinned like people being handed a pot of gold. Lacy wished them a good meal and stopped by the table next to them to clear salad plates. Thirty minutes had passed since she'd first spotted the curly-haired sexpot waiting for her rendezvous with Chase. Just as Lacy had known would happen, the woman was still alone. Only now, a noticeable rose-colored blush filled her high cheekbones. Her elegant fingers, once tapping a smooth rhythm, now spun the long-stem wineglass in circles. *Hmm, the sign of a pissed-off, stood-up woman?*

After dropping the salad plates in the sink, Lacy pushed her way into the dining room once more.

"Would you like to look at the menu again and make a selection?" Lacy asked the agitated lone diner.

She turned her tight-lipped grimace to Lacy. "What I'd like is for you to tell Chase I'm here so I don't have to wait for him anymore."

Did the woman not understand basic English? Maybe Lacy ought to run her up to Chase's office so she could see it was locked up tighter than a fortress.

"Honestly, what is he doing?" The woman craned her head around Lacy's frame. "I haven't seen him once. Shouldn't he be on the floor?" She waved a hand in the air, allowing the lights to twinkle off her emerald ring. "I don't know, supervising or something?"

Lacy pulled a patience-inducing breath into her lungs. "Like I said before, Mondays and Tuesdays are his days off. He won't be here until Wednesday. Our mushroom risotto is one of the best items on the menu. Would you like me to have them fire one up for you?" *Because if you don't order something, I'm going to have to kick you out, which I really don't want to do, considering your attitude so far.*

"Fine, bring the risotto." She lifted her wineglass and sucked down an unnaturally large gulp. "Do me a favor and have Chase deliver it. But don't worry, I'll still give you a tip."

Good Lord, the woman put new meaning to the term *dense.*

The subject of Chase's absence wasn't something Lacy wanted to debate with her any longer. Lacy scribbled *mush risotto* on her ordering pad and stabbed the entry into the computer.

Ten minutes later, Lacy placed the app in front of the year's worst diner. Muttering, "Enjoy your appetizer," Lacy spun on her heel like her ass was on fire and walked to another one of her tables.

"I was beginning to think you had a camper over there," Diane muttered in Lacy's ear when the two of them stood at the pass.

"I might still. She's waiting for Chase."

Diane snorted and placed a plate on her tray. Henry dutifully inspected the other four while Diane waited.

"She's going to be waiting awhile."

Lacy grinned. "I tried to tell her but she's hell-bent on sticking around. I managed to talk her into ordering an app so I wouldn't have to kick her out."

"That's always an ugly scene," Diane agreed.

Lacy glanced at her watch and continued to wait for her entrées. "How's Tom doing?"

Diane bobbed her head from side to side and ran stubby fingers through her spiky hair. "He's coping. The pain pills knock him out, so he spends most of his time sleeping. The doctors say he needs to spend at least another six weeks off his leg; then he has to go to physical therapy before he can return to work."

Lacy felt sorry for Diane. She placed a hand on the other woman's round shoulder. "Hang in there. It'll get better."

Henry finally placed the last four dishes on Diane's tray. "I just keep praying." Deep laugh lines bracketed Diane's heart-shaped mouth when she smiled. Lacy had to give the woman credit; she never lost face.

Lacy placed four dishes on her tray, then carried them

out to the dining room. After setting them in front of the diners, she checked on two more tables and took drink orders for three others. Chase's so-called date remained by herself. The bowl that held her mushroom risotto sat empty and discarded in the middle of the table. A sleek black cell phone was pressed up against the woman's ear but her lips weren't moving. After a second, she pulled the phone away from her ear and tossed it into her purse with a disgusted snort. Lacy didn't want to, but she approached the table to take the empty dish, only because she was obligated as the woman's server.

"Are you ready to order an entrée?" *Please say no and take your evening somewhere else.*

"I just want the check," she muttered while digging through her purse.

Thank the good Lord.

Lacy processed the check faster than she'd ever done in her two years of waiting tables. Within a minute, she had it printed up and delivered to Miss High-and-Mighty, who'd already pulled cash out of her wallet. She tossed a hundred-dollar bill and a fifty onto the table.

"And you can give this to Chase while you're at it." The brown paper bag landed on the tabletop. "He asks me to drop them off, then doesn't even show up."

Lacy's gaze remained fixed on the paper sack while Tarantula Woman huffed out the door.

"Diane, will you keep an eye on my section for a minute?" Lacy asked after she'd snagged the bag.

Diane barely had time to get out a "Sure thing" before Lacy let herself into the break room.

What kind of person did this? Lacy wasn't the nosy sort who rifled through other people's stuff. Normally. But she supposed since Chase had been *inside* her, several

times, that gave at least a reason to be curious, if not a
right to know just what that woman wanted with her lover.
Okay, maybe not full-on rights. Still, she was damn curious, and, really, who would know if she unrolled the top
of the bag and took a little look-see?

Ten seconds later, Lacy wished she had just left the bag
closed and tossed it into her locker.

Inside the bag sat Chase's black boxers, neatly folded.

A line of sweat trickled down the indentation of his spine;
the cotton waistband of his shorts absorbed it until that,
too, was wet. The circa-1950s oscillating fan, which sat
on his workbench, did nothing more than stir the musty
air of the garage, giving him no reprieve from the humid-
ity. The stuffiness didn't slow him down. Instead, Chase
continued to lift the chest press away from his torso until
the muscles in his arms quivered from the strain and a
bead of sweat materialized at his temples. With practiced
care, he lowered the chest press back down, then pressed
it up again. Just for shits and giggles, he'd decided to add
an extra ten pounds to his normal two-fifty. After the first
few reps, he'd developed a steady rhythm that had lasted
for the past half hour.

That morning he'd been greeted by a cheerful phone
call from his father, saying the cash drawer had come
up ten dollars short last night. Chase hadn't been at the
restaurant, so he had no explanation for the shortage. For
some reason Martin seemed to think Chase could give
some reasonable account for the missing money. But he
couldn't. The only people who had access to the cash
drawers were the restaurant key holders: Anita, Martin,
Henry, and himself. Short of jerry-rigging the drawer, no
other employee had access to it.

The case of money coming up short was more baffling than the missing food. *Anyone* could get their hands on the food and other various supplies. While Henry seemed like the logical culprit, as much as Chase didn't want to admit it, that didn't explain the cash. Henry was never anywhere near the cash drawer.

In any event, Chase didn't have an answer for his father. The old man was growing impatient and wanted Chase to start interviewing employees. Suffice it to say, he and his father differed in opinion. Martin was ready to pounce on any employee who so much as raised a hair of suspicion. So far the collective evidence was weak at best. With the exception of one of the waiters taking potatoes off a bin, they had nothing. Chase wasn't in the habit of accusing innocent people. As for interviewing employees, he told his father he'd compile a list of staff who had worked on days things were taken.

He had a feeling his old man wouldn't be satisfied until one of his waitstaff was escorted from the premises in handcuffs. After everything, Chase hoped it wouldn't come to that.

In addition, there were a few people on staff Martin wasn't crazy about, including Lacy. He'd never said so directly, but most likely he kept Lacy in the forefront of his mind as a suspect, purely because of her father. Martin had always loathed Dennis Taylor and Lacy had never fared much better. But Martin didn't know Lacy like Chase did. She possessed lightness and a determination that Dennis lacked. The only thing Dennis was determined to do was sit in jail.

To appease his father, he'd interview Lacy and prove to his old man she was not the dishonest thief her father was.

Chase lowered the chest press to its stand and sat up.

Sweat glistened on every surface of his body. His heart beat a satisfying pounding rhythm through his veins. The last time a workout had this much effect on him was Saturday night in Lacy's bed. He'd rolled off her with his heart beating just as fast and the same beads of sweat popping up on his skin. They'd spent three nights together this past week. Three hot, erotic, mattress-rocking nights filled with tangled limbs and life-altering orgasms. Chase didn't often make a habit of returning to the same woman's bed multiple times. Unless, of course, the sex happened to be outstanding, as was the case for maybe three or four women he'd known over the years. After the newness wore off, he'd move on to the next conquest. But there was something about Lacy that kept drawing him to her. He kept expecting the novelty of being with her to wear off. Seeing her smile light up her eyes and hearing her whisper his name was like a tight fist around his heart every time. His defenses around her grew weaker by the day.

A torn, permanently stained white towel hung haphazardly on the edge of his workbench. Chase swiped it up and ran the coarse fibers over his face and chest. He stepped inside the house, tossed the towel into the laundry basket, and headed to the kitchen.

So far, he had no explanation for returning to Lacy's bed time and again. Other than the fact that she was hot as hell and had stamina strong enough to match his own. Maybe it was because she'd yet to show him the real her. She was a woman with secrets. What would it take to coax some of them out? Sex would only go so far. There had to be a way to get her to show that deeper side.

He grabbed a bottle of water from the fridge, downed a refreshing sip, then started up the stairs to take a shower.

Just as he entered his bedroom, a harsh pounding came from his front door. Ignoring it seemed like a great idea, so he kept walking toward the bathroom. But the pounding got louder and more insistent. He bounded down the steps and yanked the front door open, not at all pleased to have a visitor.

Bright afternoon sunshine sifted through the trees of his front yard and reflected off the candlelight-colored strands of Lacy's hair. He drank in the sight of her standing on his front porch. Long, smooth legs emerged from a pair of white cotton shorts, and high, round breasts strained beneath a fire-engine red, spaghetti-strap tank top. The only thing that stopped him from pressing her against his sweaty chest and dragging her fine ass to his bed was the look in her eyes. Thunderclouds swirled behind the green depths of her eyes. Her full, beautiful, unpainted mouth was pressed in a flat line. Chase knew a pissed-off woman when he saw one.

"What's going on, Lace?" he asked, instead of inviting her in.

"I have a present for you." She lifted her toned arm to reveal a brown paper sack dangling from her hand. "One of the notches in your bedpost brought this for you." Her mouth lifted in a smile that didn't reach her eyes. "She wasn't too happy about you standing her up."

What the hell? More cryptic words had never been spoken. The tone in her voice told Chase she hadn't come bearing a freshly baked batch of brownies. And who the heck was she talking about?

"Um...okay," he replied. "You want to come in and show me what you have?"

"I'd rather not." She shoved the bag against his chest with enough force to throw him off balance. He rocked back on his heels and managed to hold on to it before it landed at his feet. Without waiting to see if he'd received her gift, Lacy spun on her petite heels and marched back down the concrete walkway with all the fury of a woman scorned.

But what the hell was she scorned about?

He unrolled the wrinkled paper sack and peeked inside to see his boxers folded up in a neat little square at the bottom of the bag.

Where in the world had she gotten these, and why was she so peeved about them?

"Lacy!" he called after her right before she opened her car door and sat in the driver's seat. The bag fell from his fingertips as he sprinted to the driveway just before she could shut the car door. He grabbed the door seconds before it closed. "You gotta give me some answers."

She stood from the driver's seat and pushed him away from the car. "I don't have to give you anything. I should have known better than to get involved with you."

He grabbed her arm before she slid back into the car. "Where'd you get those?"

"It doesn't matter where I got them." She twisted her arm out of his grasp and tried to get into the vehicle. "Let go!" she spat when he wrapped his hand around her other arm. Her attempt to pull herself away from him was futile. He outweighed her by a good eighty pounds.

"Dammit, stop," he said through gritted teeth after she kicked him in the shin. "Lacy, stop," he said with more force this time when she stepped on his bare foot. She wasn't very big, but the girl was determined. The only way he was able to subdue her assault was to pin her arms behind her back and press her against the car with his body. Her round breasts heaved up and down against his chest. Chase forced his thoughts away from the thin cotton of her tank top rubbing against his bare skin. Now would not be a good time to sport a boner.

"Now, start at the beginning and tell me what the hell is going on."

Her breath came out through her nose in short, uneven puffs. Shallow lines bracketed her angry mouth. "You don't have to manhandle me."

"I do when you're trying to beat the shit out of me." He couldn't help the tilt of his mouth.

"You deserve it," she said through clenched teeth. Two spots of red colored her high cheekbones.

"For what?"

Her pointy chin trembled. "For two-timing me."

Huh? "Lacy…"

"Forget it." She struggled against him again, twisting her shoulders this way and that. "Will you let me go? You're going to cause a scene with your neighbors."

"Then calm down." He loosened his grip on her hands. "Take a deep breath and tell me what's got you so upset."

To his surprise, she pulled in a breath that pushed her breasts harder against his chest. "I already told you. That bag is proof you can't keep your pants zipped."

Astonishment lifted his brows. "You think I've been running around behind your back?" *Was she insane?* When she didn't respond, he said, "Lacy, I haven't slept with anyone else since you and I got together."

Her beautiful green eyes narrowed and her nostrils flared.

"You don't believe me?" he asked her.

"How can I? You're going to tell me your underwear climbed their way out of your drawer, walked down the street, and found their way into that woman's house all by their itty-bitty selves?"

"What woman?" he asked her again.

"I don't know! Some woman with dark curly hair. What the hell does it matter?"

This time he let her wriggle her way out of his arms. Taking a deep breath, he stepped back from her and ran a hand through his hair. An explanation was on the tip of his tongue, but Chase held back. Lacy was in one of her moods and in no frame of mind to listen to what he had to say. He could say something like, "I can explain those," or "It's not what you think" or some other stupid thing that would make him sound even guiltier. Even though he wasn't guilty of anything to begin with.

Sonja had some serious brass balls to stroll into the restaurant, hand his freakin' underwear to Lacy, and ask her to return them. She could have burned them for all he cared. She was one demented woman if she thought their night together would lead to some sort of courtship. He'd made it clear from the beginning he had no intention of entering a relationship with her. And while he was fully aware he never should have slept with her to begin with, it was a mistake he couldn't undo. The only thing he regretted was Lacy getting hurt in the process. No doubt she'd deny being hurt, because Lacy portrayed herself as being too strong to let a man hurt her. Chase was no dummy. The strain in her voice and trembling chin told a different story.

"Lacy," he started anyway, even though he knew his efforts were useless. "I swear I haven't been with anyone else since the first night we slept together. I'm not that kind of guy."

She crossed her arms in front of her. "Then how did she get a hold of your underwear?"

Okay, this is where it got tricky. He'd have to tell her something she wouldn't want to hear in order to explain them away. "I left them at her house."

Her chin lifted, then lowered in a slow nod. "Right. See you later, Chase." She grabbed the door handle of the car with an unsteady hand.

"Lacy." Dammit, it couldn't end like this. She had to believe him. He placed his hands on her slim shoulders and turned her to face him. "I would never do anything like that to you. Yes, I did sleep with her but that was before we got together." A single tear leaked out of her eye and rolled down her cheek. He swiped it away with his thumb. "You believe me, right?"

Her gaze dropped down to his mouth, then lifted up to his eyes. She was so beautiful his heart ached. "I have to go to work. It would probably be better if we didn't see each other anymore."

TEN

One month later

SOME PEOPLE THOUGHT LACY WAS JADED. Perhaps ... *annoyed* was a better word.

Although she tried to portray the essence of someone who had a *Little House on the Prairie* upbringing, sometimes she failed miserably. To her credit, she never let her shortcomings show at work. Always the consummate bundle of joy, she had a smile plastered on her face and a bounce in her step. She figured the happier she was, the happier her customers, hence better tips. Big tips were forever welcome.

To add to her list of things to be happy about, the state of Wyoming could no longer take her house away. In her haste to beat the deadline that had been imposed on her, she'd grabbed the check Chase had given her, drove to the clerk's office in Casper, and paid them the sum of twenty thousand dollars. Normally, Lacy wasn't a procrastinator. On the contrary, putting duties off until the last minute was something she avoided.

So why did she use Chase's money after what happened

between them? Well…she didn't really have a logical answer to that, especially when the check her mother had left her sat in her dresser drawer. Lacy *still* couldn't bring herself to use it. She'd chosen the lesser of two evils. It was either hang on to her pride for dear life or keep her house. Lacy chose to keep her house.

Even though she hadn't heard anything about him, there was always the chance of her father showing up. There hadn't been any more reports on the news or moms seeing creepy men at the park. For some reason no news made the hair on the back of her neck stand up more than if there had been sightings. It was sort of like seeing a spider and not killing it before the thing disappeared in the bowels of the house. Lord only knew where it would show itself next.

Lacy tied the final knot in her running shoes, then stepped outside. The afternoon was unusually cool, giving her a reprieve during her afternoon jog. Last week she'd been reminded how out of shape she was while lifting boxes out of the garage and into the bed of Brody's pickup truck. By her third box, she'd reached the point of hyperventilating. Brody had patted her on the back and said she needed to take a trip to the gym. Like she could afford a gym membership. Because she'd given it up, Lacy had lost her ability to jog without becoming winded within forty-five seconds.

Whatever. It was all about the effort, right? Power walking was better than sitting on the couch like a bum.

She jogged for another thirty seconds before slowing to a walk. A strong gust of wind picked up, cooling her skin where perspiration had formed.

She missed Megan. Two weeks ago they'd had lunch together, as they'd made a habit of doing, when Megan announced she could no longer put off returning to Southern California. Things there awaited her, like deciding what to do with the house and getting ready to return to school. Prior to leaving, Megan had called Lacy and said she'd come back at the end of summer before school started. As much as Lacy would miss their acquaintance, she understood.

She power walked past Mrs. Pratt's house, then picked up her pace to a light jog again. The old woman was in her flowerbed, a sun hat the size of a satellite dish covering her thin gray hair. She lifted a frail hand in Lacy's direction. Lacy grinned, waved back, and kept going down the street.

The one unfortunate thing about running, besides the sweat, was the amount of time it gave her to think. As much as she forced her thoughts to stick to her surroundings, her mind always wandered...to things like Chase. The other day at work Lacy had noticed a few of the female diners in the waiting area eyeing the GM as he walked through the dining room. In the kitchen she'd told him, "You have a fan club waiting for you." To which he tugged on her ponytail and said, "You sound jealous, Miss Twiggy." However much she'd been hurt by the way things ended between them, she still considered Chase a friend. And she had been hurt. After calming down, Lacy had realized Chase had been truthful with her. He hadn't been with another woman. After two weeks of being intimate with him, Lacy felt things for Chase that were definitely more than friendly. She hadn't gotten to the point where she'd been able to put a label on those feelings. Chances were they'd start to veer into the "deeply caring" category, if not all-out love. The last thing she needed was to fall in love with someone like Chase. Better to have ended things when they did.

All in all, she had no regrets. Being with Chase had been a fun and unique, if not adventurous, experience. He made her laugh, made her feel beautiful, and gave her orgasms unlike anything she'd ever felt. No, she absolutely didn't regret any of it.

After turning around, Lacy slowed to a power walk again and headed back to her house. Sweat formed between her breasts and coated her backside by the time she walked through the front door. At hearing the door open, Boris pushed himself onto shaky legs and waddled his way to her.

"Are you finally ready to eat?" Lacy asked him after scratching his ear. She pulled last night's chicken out of the fridge, shredded it up with a knife, and dumped the food in his bowl. He touched his nose to the meat, gave a gruff sniff, then lopped his tongue out. Only about half the meat actually made it into his mouth. The dog didn't seem to care. She left him to his meal and peeled her sweaty clothes off as she headed to the bathroom.

Half an hour later, Lacy was sweat-free and smelled like gardenias. She took the time to blow-dry her hair, something she rarely did, and slathered on vanilla-scented lotion. She'd walked into the bedroom to pick up her dirty clothes when a cool breeze flowed through the doorway and brushed along her freshly scrubbed skin. The only way that sort of airflow could get into the house was through an open window. Lacy knew without a doubt she hadn't opened any of the windows. And Boris didn't make a habit of standing up on his arthritic hind legs and opening the windows for his sheer pleasure.

Had she not shut the front door all the way? Yes, the thing was old and sat off balance on its hinges, but she'd never had a problem with it failing to latch. She tossed her clothes in the hamper and walked out of the bedroom. Another refreshing breeze blew across her face just before she rounded the corner. The front door stood halfway open, partially revealing her front yard, in need of some TLC. Maybe she hadn't shut the door with enough force, although she could have sworn hearing the latch click. What other explanation could there be? Doors didn't open by themselves.

She placed one bare foot in front of the other and pushed the old door closed until the latch clicked. Just to be extra cautious, she gave the handle a tug to make sure it was actually in place.

"Next time you might want to throw the dead bolt."

Before the sentence was even finished, she immediately recognized the speaker. Lacy spun around and couldn't stop the gasp from leaving her lips. There, in Ray's torn, faded corduroy recliner sat the elusive, yet borderline psychotic, Dennis Taylor. His long, spindly legs, clad in a pair of pathetic paint-stained jeans, stretched out in front of him. His thin, bony hand ran circles over Boris's head; the traitorous dog had perched his head on Dennis's lap.

With her back pressed hard against the door, her breath came in short, shallow gasps. In the past few weeks, she'd lived in the dream world where Dennis had moved to the other side of the galaxy. As unlikely as that seemed, Lacy just *knew* her luck couldn't be so good. Dennis, the low-life bottom-feeder, *always* resurfaced.

Lacy closed her eyes briefly and forced herself to calm down.

Okay, Dennis has never been violent before. All he wants is money to get his next fix or drink himself silly.

"You've put on weight. Don't take that as an insult, though. You were too thin last time I saw you." His voice sounded like it belonged to someone who'd had a cigarette in his mouth since birth. The past five years hadn't been kind to him. If it was even possible, his voice had gotten rougher. His discolored white shirt had holes along the hem at the neckline and practically hung off one sharp shoulder. The skin on his forearms looked like rawhide with hair, and lean, sinewy muscles made him look more lanky than strong.

"Your dog doesn't look good. It looks like he's got cataracts." He directed his attention to Boris, who shoved his head farther up Dennis's lap.

"He's old," was all she could reply. Why, oh why didn't she dead bolt the front door? "Why are you here?"

"I was in the area and wanted to see you." He didn't take his attention off Boris's snout.

Dennis almost never wanted to stop by and "see her." He always had an ulterior motive.

"I don't believe you." She pushed away from the door. "Tell me what you want, then leave."

He turned his dull brown eyes to her. Years of drinking and mild drug use had etched deep crevices in his gaunt face. Multiple bags pulled his beady eyes down. Several lines stretched across his forehead. Overall, Dennis Taylor was not a good-looking man. Not for the first time, Lacy wondered what the heck her mother had seen in him.

"If it's money you want, you can forget it," Lacy said when Dennis failed to reply to her first demand. She grabbed the doorknob with a trembling hand. "I made it clear the last time I saw you that I want nothing to do with you." She yanked the door open and the afternoon breeze blew through the living room.

Dennis didn't move from his spot. He just sat there,

running his hand over Boris's head and drilling her with his menacing gaze.

The skin on the back of her neck itched.

"Word has it you've come into some good times recently."

At first his words eluded her. *Good times?* Then she thought over the past month and a half.

The check.

All the blood that had rushed to her head upon seeing Dennis now rushed down to her belly and left her feeling light-headed and sick to her stomach. Playing dumb was her first instinct but Dennis wasn't stupid. The man might have made bad decisions, but Lacy never accused him of being dense.

She cleared her throat. "How did you know about that?"

"Your grandparents," he replied, like she should have known he kept in touch with her mother's parents—people Lacy had assumed were dead because they'd never attempted to have a relationship with her.

Dennis continued. "Your bitch of a mother had the audacity to leave all that money to you."

The shock of his words was like a kick to the midsection.

She didn't let the effect of his words show. "You think you're entitled to some of it?"

He nudged Boris's nose off his lap. "Well, I only raised you and used almost all my meager income to clothe and feed you. I think for damn sure that woman owes me something in return."

Actually, Ray had done all that. Dennis hadn't so much as pitched in a nickel for his daughter's well-being. He could have scraped together the money for a new pair of shoes or a backpack when her old one had fallen apart, but, no, he'd been too busy using his pathetic income on whiskey and meth, or whatever the hell his drug of choice had been at the time.

And he was delusional enough to think he was actually entitled to something?

"What makes you think I didn't tear it up?" She crossed her arms over her chest.

"'Cause you're not stupid."

Obviously she was if she forgot to lock her front door.

"The only thing you deserve is a one-way ticket back to jail, Dennis." She held the door open wider. "Get out."

His thin, honey-colored eyebrows twitched. "You're going to throw me out of my father's house?"

Her teeth ground together. "No, I'm throwing you out of *my* house. And you have no right to call him your father—you weren't even at his funeral." The memory of standing beside Ray's casket, knowing Dennis couldn't drag himself out of whatever hole he was in to attend his father's funeral made tears burn in her eyes.

"I'm two seconds away from calling the cops, Dennis. Leave."

A tense, pregnant pause filled the air between father and daughter. The lines in Dennis's cheeks grew deeper when the corners of his mouth turned down, a look that was a permanent fixture on the old man's face.

Without saying a word, he stood and stretched to his unimpressive height. He stabbed his fingers through his thin, strawlike hair. Lacy was surprised he didn't pull out huge chunks.

She kept her gaze fixed on the hardwood floor as Dennis's tennis shoes softly scuffed toward her. The second he stepped out into the sunshine, she threw the door closed with enough force to make the wooden door frame creak. She hoped she slammed it hard enough to send him on his scrawny ass.

Only when she was alone did she allow all the breath to leave her lungs. Dennis had a way of draining her energy.

Showing up uninvited was nothing new. He had a track record of popping in wherever she happened to be. However, this was the first time he'd set foot inside Ray's house in years. When she was eighteen, just before leaving for college, he'd stopped by right after serving time for possession of an illegal substance. Ray had seen how Dennis's appearance had upset Lacy and had asked his son not to come back. To Dennis's credit, he'd obliged his father's word, most likely because he'd spent more time in jail.

She walked into the kitchen. There, inside her junk drawer, was the business card of one of the St. Helena detectives who'd visited her in May. Without hesitation, she picked up the phone and dialed the cell number for Detective Parks.

She received his voice mail and left a message. Immediately after hanging up, she dialed Detective Whistler's cell phone. Again, she got voice mail. A frustrated groan gurgled in her throat and she jabbed the portable phone back onto its base. Should she call the Trouble Police Department? Was there anything they could even do? It's not like she had a restraining order against him and the front door had been unlocked. And as far as she knew, he hadn't done anything illegal. But she still needed to report him considering he'd already broken into one person's home. She plowed both hands through her hair.

"Boris, what should I do?" The dog lifted his head and looked at her through bleary brown eyes. He dropped his large muzzle back onto the worn area rug and went to sleep. "Thanks a lot," she muttered. She turned around and leaned her emotionally exhausted body against the cracked tile countertop. Her surroundings blurred as tears gathered beneath her eyelids.

Crying was a weakness Lacy hardly allowed herself. Tears never solved anything and only left her tired and red-eyed. But in the quiet solitude of her kitchen, she didn't bother to fight the moisture that leaked over her eyelashes and trickled down her cheeks. One by one the tears fell until she hiccupped and slumped to the floor. Using the heel of her palm, she swiped away the wetness that covered her face.

"So stupid," she muttered. "Why am I crying? He's nothing to me." An encounter with Dennis didn't usually affect her so deeply. When had she gotten so weak?

"Stop." She stood and grabbed the dishtowel that hung on the oven door. "You have a life to live that doesn't have anything to do with him." She used the towel to blot the stray tears from her face. "You're better than him." Just as the words left her mouth, her gaze settled on the whimsical, colorful invitation to Courtney's homecoming party Avery had sent her. She dropped the towel on the counter. "Ah, shit that's tonight." She blew out a deep breath, went into her bathroom, splashed some warm water on her face, and slathered on more moisturizer.

Twenty minutes later, after changing into a khaki skirt and an emerald-green blouse, Lacy drove to Noah and Avery's house.

Two dozen cars lined the street outside the McDermott home. Okay, so she was fashionably late. Like, an hour late. There were so many people, she doubted anyone would notice little old her.

She parked her boat at the very end of the street and walked. The sun had already slid behind the surrounding rolling hills, casting the sky in soft blues, blending into a deep purple. A summertime Wyoming sunset had a way of capturing the splendor of Mother Nature unlike any other place Lacy had been.

Childish laughter and booming voices grew louder as she approached the house. Brody's pickup truck sat in the driveway, behind Chase's motorcycle. Lacy had known he'd be here. Her heart sped up and danced in her throat at the thought of being near him again. The two of them were adult enough to be in each other's presence outside of work and exchange intelligent words. Then again, there were probably enough people here that maybe she could avoid any personal contact with the man.

She tapped her knuckles on the intricate stained glass window in the middle of the white front door. When no one answered, she rang the doorbell. She was about to walk around to the back gate when the door opened and the always-stunning Avery McDermott stood in the entranceway, an ear-to-ear grin lighting up her classically pretty features. In one arm, she held Lily, who sported an adorable floral-print sundress, and she held a pitcher of iced tea in the other hand. The woman was a true multitasker.

"Sorry about that," she said with a smile. "I was just running inside to grab some more tea when I heard the bell. I told Noah to put a sticky note on the door to tell people to let themselves in, but apparently it slipped his mind." She hefted Lily higher on her hip.

"Here, let me take that," Lacy said, and reached for the pitcher of tea.

"Oh, thank you. Come on in," Avery said, and closed

the door. She turned and walked through the natural wood foyer that led to a great room with a vaulted ceiling. "I'm glad you came. I was beginning to think you weren't going to show."

"To be honest, I forgot." Not the most honorable excuse, but at least it wasn't a lie.

"You haven't missed much anyway." Avery walked into the kitchen and pulled a platter out of a cupboard. "Courtney didn't get here until about thirty minutes ago." She pinned Lacy with a wry grin. "Only Courtney would be late to her own party."

"Yeah, that's our Court." Courtney Devlin had always marched to her own beat. That's why Lacy loved her.

Lily squealed, then wriggled her round little bottom on Avery's hip, a clear sign the seven-month-old wanted away from Mommy. "Oh no, you don't, Princess. I know what you want." Avery tightened her grip on the baby and opened another cabinet.

Lacy set the pitcher down on the jet-black granite counter. "Can I help you?"

Something on the other side of the kitchen beeped. Avery rolled her eyes. "Yeah, you can take the tea outside and set it down on one of the tables. Then you can grab this little terror and put her in her playpen."

Lord only knew how mothers juggled so many things at once. The only explanation was that those motherly types had to have been born with a chip in their brains that allowed them to hold a baby and cook a meal at the same time. Lacy definitely didn't have that chip.

"Here, let me have her." Lacy walked around the island with the built-in cooktop and took the baby from Avery.

"Beware, she's a kicker," Avery said, then tickled her daughter's bare foot. "I really appreciate it."

Lacy rubbed her nose along Lily's satiny-soft cheek. "Are you kidding? I'll use any excuse to hold her. She's such a doll." Lily reached one chubby, hot hand toward Lacy and almost managed to grab a chunk of her hair.

"Oh, she likes to pull hair too. I'm surprised I don't have a bald spot." Avery hustled to the oven, her knee-length, swirly printed dress floating around her.

Lacy hung on to the baby with one arm, grabbed the pitcher with the other, and walked out the double French doors. There, on the other side of the patio, stood the man who'd seen every intimate part of her body and kissed them too. His mouth tilted up in a toe-curling grin when he spotted her.

Chase couldn't keep his attention off Lacy. Instead of her usual ponytail, her hair fell like a blond waterfall over her shoulders, sparking memories of it brushing along his chest or spread out on his pillow. The muscle beneath the fly of his pants stirred at the memory of the two of them late one night in his kitchen. He'd let her through the front door and offered her something to drink. After closing the fridge, he'd turned to find her staring at his ass with her teeth sinking into that beautiful lower lip. Instead of making the long trek up to his room, he'd set the bottle of water down and lifted her onto the counter. No objections flew from her mouth when he'd stripped them both of their bottoms and slid into her right next to the coffeemaker.

When he approached the porch swing that she sat on, her eyes lit on his and the corners of her mouth turned up in a smile.

"Can I sit, or are you still mad at me?"

"Only if you rock us. My leg's getting tired."

He sat next to her and pushed the swing back with his foot. "I'll take that as a peace offering."

She slid her green gaze to his. "I never said I wasn't still mad at you."

"You make a career out of being mad at me."

She curled one leg under the other and her bare toe poked his thigh. "You make it so easy."

He stretched one arm along the back of the swing. "I aim to please you, Miss Taylor."

"What, no Miss Twiggy?" she asked with a small smile.

He leaned close until his lips were next to her ear. "I've seen you naked enough times to know you're anything but twiggy."

Her hand shot out and shoved him back. "Do you have to do that?"

"Would you rather I say it loud enough so everyone can hear? I'm trying to conform to your 'no one can know about this' rule."

She lifted one shoulder in a shrug. "There is no more 'this,' so say whatever you want." When he merely stared at her, she said, "I meant it when I said it would be better if we stayed just friends."

"You consider us friends?" His gaze dropped to her breasts, which were covered in some shiny green material.

Again, she shrugged. "Why not? There's no reason why we can't be friends. What?" she demanded when he blinked at her.

He ran a hand along his chin. "I've never slept with a friend."

She crossed her arms beneath those spectacular breasts. "Curly-haired underwear woman wasn't a friend?"

Chase glanced to the other side of the patio when

Avery stood from the table and lifted Lily out of Tyler's arms. "No."

Thankfully, Lacy didn't pursue that particular subject. No way did he want to have that argument again. Avery disappeared inside the house with the baby.

Lacy nudged his elbow with hers. "You're falling behind on the job."

"Sorry." He pushed at the ground with his foot and rocked them higher.

"Did Becky-Lynn have a conversation with you recently?"

He tore his attention from the partygoers and settled it on the woman next to him. "At the restaurant?"

"Yeah. Not too long ago she was acting kind of weird and said she needed to talk to you."

"How long ago?" Was Becky-Lynn party to whatever was going on at work? He hadn't found any evidence so far.

"I don't know. About a month ago. I told her to talk to Anita but she said she could only talk to you."

Becky-Lynn was a young, quiet girl and one of the more solid waitresses he had. He'd never had any issues with her being late or not showing up, and she earned good tips. "She hasn't said anything to me."

"There's something going on at the restaurant, isn't there?"

His gaze settled on hers again. "What do you mean?" How could she have guessed that? Had she seen something that she needed to tell him?

"I'm not sure. Things just seem different there lately, more chaotic and disorganized." She turned sideways in the swing so she faced him. "*You* seem different at work too."

Did all women have that freaky intuition where they just knew stuff? How could she have picked up on that?

He nudged her chin with his knuckle. "Paying a little too much attention to me?"

She swatted his hand away. "Oh, and you would like that, wouldn't you?"

"I'm not complaining."

"So, Becky-Lynn never talked to you?" she asked to get them back to the subject.

"What exactly did she say?"

Lacy picked at the hem of her skirt. "The day she talked to me, she asked if you were working. I said you weren't and maybe Anita could help her with whatever was bothering her. She said no, that she had to talk to you."

Chase lifted his index finger and ran it through a few strands of her sleek hair. What did she put on her head to make her hair so damn irresistible? "She hasn't said anything to me." His finger made a journey from her hair to the outer edge of her ear. Her gaze dropped down to his mouth.

"You have a one-track mind." Her voice had gone from normal to raspy in the amount of time it took his finger to make little circles around her ear.

One side of his mouth tilted up in satisfaction. "You like my one-track mind."

"Maybe at one time," she said, and pushed his hand away. "But we're not there anymore, remember?"

How could he forget? She made it a point to let him know they were no longer together. Fine, he could settle for being friends. At some point, she had crossed that friendly acquaintance line and had become something else. When that happened he wasn't sure, nor was he willing to dissect it. All he knew was that theirs was a complex relationship. Chase wasn't sure he'd ever understand Lacy.

"I guess Becky-Lynn changed her mind, then," she said.

"My father thinks someone at the restaurant is stealing," he blurted out without thinking. Technically, he wasn't supposed to share this information with her. On the other hand, Chase was one hundred percent sure he could trust Lacy with it. Unable to stop himself again, he lifted his hand and tucked some hair behind her ear.

She swatted his hand away. "I can't concentrate when you touch me. Say that again?"

He dropped his hand. "Forget it. I really shouldn't be talking to you about this."

"No, you can't do that." She nudged his thigh with her foot. "You brought it up, so now you have to tell me. Why does your dad think someone is stealing?"

Lacy gave new meaning to the word *tenacious* and would never back off now that he'd mentioned the whole stupid thief thing.

"Let's go for a walk. I don't want to talk about this here." He stood from the swing, which sent Lacy swinging back under the absence of his weight. "Come on." With a tug of his hand, he pulled her up.

ELEVEN

L ACY SLID HER SANDALS ON and followed Chase out the side gate.

Once on the sidewalk, they fell into a companionable silence and walked side by side.

"Does the shortage of supplies have anything to do with this?" she asked after they'd walked for about a minute without talking.

He didn't bother asking how she knew. Lacy had already proved to be more observant than anyone gave her credit for.

"My dad seems to think so."

She glanced at him. "You say that like you don't agree with him."

A boy on a multicolored ten-speed flew down the street in the opposite direction. "I'm not sure what to think yet. So far, I have no solid evidence against anyone. Except maybe Henry."

Her attention jerked to his when he said that. "Henry? No way would he steal from you. He's the head chef."

"True," he agreed. "But every time something goes missing, he's the first to notice."

"Wouldn't he anyway? He's always doing inventory counts."

"I know." They walked around a car that hadn't been pulled into the driveway far enough and blocked the sidewalk. "But right now, I have no actual evidence and a whole bunch of things that don't add up. In all the years I've been running this place, nothing has ever gone missing before. It doesn't make sense."

"Maybe Henry is miscounting or overlooking some things. There's always the possibility of human error."

"That's what I told my father." Unfortunately, his father didn't agree with that. And then there was the matter of the missing money.

"Your father doesn't think Henry is stealing, does he? I honestly don't think Henry would do anything like that. I mean, he's been working there longer than you. Why would he start stealing now?"

Chase was silent a moment and studied the cement beneath their moving feet. "That was my logic too."

"Was?"

He lifted a shoulder. "Now I just don't know. Henry being the thief would account for the food but not the money. That part doesn't add up."

Her gaze locked with his. "Money's come up short too?"

"A few times. And it's only been small amounts, which leads me to believe that maybe the drawer isn't being counted properly."

Lacy tucked her hands in the front pocket of her skirt. "So you either have a dishonest employee on your hands or a very sloppy one." They fell silent again. A man and a woman with three small kids and a golden retriever walked by on the other side of the street. The man lifted his hand in greeting, which Chase and Lacy returned. "What're you going to do if you can't find any real evidence?"

"I don't know. I'm going to have to start double-checking all of Henry's numbers and keeping a closer eye on the staff." This solution most likely wouldn't appease his father, but Chase was running out of options. The only thing he hadn't done was interview the employees. Luckily for him things had been pretty quiet in the past few weeks. Business was steady, and nothing had come up missing or short. Maybe their would-be thief had decided to back off.

They turned around at the end of the street and started back toward Noah's house.

"Do you think whatever Becky-Lynn has to say has anything to do with this?" Lacy asked after neither of them said anything.

"I think she's as likely to steal from the restaurant as I am." He glanced at the evening sky. "Maybe she's got some personal problems."

"I'll keep my eye open for you while I'm on the floor."

He glanced at her. The street lamp cast an orangey glow on her hair. "I'd appreciate that."

Her delectable mouth turned up in a smile. "We're friends, remember?"

"I can't think of too many friends I've seen naked."

"Ditto."

Against his better judgment, he skimmed the back of his index finger down her soft cheek. "Are you sure you don't want—"

"Yes."

His thumb traveled across her lower lip. "Maybe you don't remember how good it was."

She pushed his hand away. "Oh, I remember."

"Because I specifically remember you saying it was the best sex you'd ever had."

A frustrated groan flowed out of her. "I *knew* I was going to regret saying that."

"Your buttons are too easy to push," he said with a grin.

"Only when you're around."

"I think you love having me around, Miss Twiggy."

She stopped in her tracks and gestured toward Noah's house. "Weren't you just saying before—"

He slid his arm around her and forced her to keep moving. "That time I said it for fun."

She glanced at him out of the corner of her eye. "It's hardly fun."

"It is for me."

"You and my entire family will be happy to know I have a date tonight."

Lacy glanced up from her sketch to look at Brody sitting beside her on the park bench. Anita had given Lacy three days off in a row, an unusual event. Not that Lacy was complaining; it was nice to have a little time to herself. She'd decided to take Brody's advice and signed up for the art festival. Yesterday and today she'd used as time to perfect her drawings and come up with new ones. Ever the perfectionist, Lacy had yet to deem anything worthy of public showing. "You shouldn't live your life for the rest of us, Brody."

His gray gaze followed Tyler as the boy climbed across the monkey bars on the playground in front of them. "Tell that to my family."

Her pencil flew across the paper to complete the lines

of the domed clock cupola of the Trouble town hall. The bench they sat on was the only one that lent a full view of the historical building. Trouble had precisely two historical buildings: town hall and the Masonic center. It had been a dream of hers to draw the Trouble town hall for years. After getting approval from Brody's friend Steven, Lacy decided to go balls out and sketch the 1915 building.

"They only want you to be happy," Lacy replied after tearing her attention away from her drawing.

"Yeah, I have the world's most worrisome family."

Brody might complain about his family, but he loved them. What wasn't to love? He had two parents who actually put effort into their kids' happiness and a whole slew of other people who had his best interests at heart.

"Consider yourself lucky," she reminded him.

He patted the top of her head as if she were a dog. "Yeah, I know. You have people, too, Lace."

"Such as you?" She flipped over a page in her sketch pad and started her drawing over. Something about the scale of the building didn't look quite right.

"You know it."

"So, who's the girl?"

Tyler jumped down from the top of the monkey bars and ran to the small rock-climbing wall.

"She was the student teacher in Tyler's class."

On the third version of the town hall, Lacy started from the cupola and worked her way down. "Student? How old is she?"

"Twenty-five. That's only a four-year difference."

She lifted her shoulders and hid a grin. "I didn't say anything. What's her name?"

"Elizabeth. I bumped into her when I picked Tyler up

from summer school yesterday. I'd always thought she was kind of cute."

Lacy turned her head to look at him. "Do yourself a favor and don't tell her she's cute to her face." She returned her attention to the work in her lap. "That's the kiss of death."

"What're you talking about?" He took his gaze off his son. "Isn't that a compliment?"

Men really didn't understand women, did they? "Women generally don't appreciate men using the same adjective to describe them as they would a puppy. Choose a different word like *gorgeous* or *beautiful*."

"Women are so sensitive," he muttered. He nudged her shoulder with his hand. "You and my brother looked mighty comfortable with each other the other night."

If Brody only knew. "We were talking about the restaurant." Okay, only a half-truth. Not even for money would Lacy mention the other things she and Chase had talked about. Brody most likely wouldn't understand. He had a dominantly protective streak when it came to her. He probably thought Chase would use her, then dump her. Sometimes Lacy thought Brody overestimated her.

"What about it?"

Lacy tried to capture the post–Civil War character of the old building. "Your father thinks he has a thief among his staff."

"Does he really?" he asked, his attention focused on Tyler racing around the playground. "Based on what?"

"Based on a meager shortage of supplies."

Brody rested one foot across his knee. "Dad's always been kind of paranoid about the businesses. I'm sure it's just an unlucky streak."

"Only time will tell," she muttered absently while

dragging the pencil across paper. This version was better but the cupola still didn't look right. Something about the way she had the dome shaped didn't match the actual thing. Perhaps she was sharpening the cornices too much. She lifted her pencil to measure the slope of the angles and proportions.

"Lace, that's great. You should display that at the festival," Brody said after glancing down at her paper.

Lacy shook her head. "I don't know. It doesn't look right." She flipped back several pages to the first sketch. "See with this one, I made the building too wide. And this one"—she turned two pages over—"I made it look too modern."

"And what's wrong with the one you're doing now?"

To any onlooker, the latest drawing of the old building looked spot-on. Lacy had always been her own worst critic. There were a few nitpicky details that jumped off the page at her like blinking neon lights. "I can't pinpoint any one thing. It's several things that make the whole sketch look ... off."

"You're too hard on yourself." He ran his thumb down one of the pencil lines. "Blow it up to a portrait size and you could sell this sucker. Are you going to include this in the festival?"

"That was the plan."

Tyler climbed down from the rock wall and ran to the water fountain. "I keep forgetting to ask you when Kelly's wedding is." She tucked the sketch pad and pencil into her bag with the rest of the supplies.

"It's early September."

"Are you going?"

A muscle twitched in his stubble-covered jaw. "I don't know. If I do go, it'll be for Tyler's sake."

She placed a hand on the hard muscle of his shoulder. "Despite what everyone else says, I know you're not in love with her."

He turned his head and pinned her with gray eyes like his father's. One side of his mouth turned up, revealing a dimple. "Thanks."

"Would you have married Kelly if she hadn't ended up pregnant?"

A light breeze blew some dark hair back from his forehead. "Hard to say. We'd only been together for a month when she got pregnant. We went from fooling around to getting married in less than a year." His shoulders lifted beneath his soft blue T-shirt. "I was trying to do the right thing."

"A fact that I'm sure she'll always love you for."

"I doubt that."

"Brody," she said, and then waited until he looked at her. "You married her and provided for your son. Stop painting yourself as the bad guy. How come you two didn't have any more kids?"

"We just never got around to it. Kelly went on birth control right after Tyler was born. She mentioned it once, but Tyler was only two, and I hadn't finished school yet and wasn't ready to have another one. After I graduated and went to work for my dad, I told her I was ready. But she told me she wasn't sure she could handle two kids at home by herself." He ran a hand along his square jaw. "The subject never came up again after that."

"And you were extra careful after having one 'oops,'" she guessed.

He shook his head. "Not my ideal way to have kids, no."

She brushed a lock of hair back from his forehead. "Kelly was lucky to have you."

He lifted an arm around her. "You're a good friend."

"Just trying to return the favor," she said with a small smile.

The enthusiastic gallop that had propelled Tyler a short while ago had reduced to a fast walk. Sweat made the ends of his blond hair stick to his skin. The boy came to a stop in front of them. Tyler had inherited his mother's sun-streaked hair and his father's facial features and gray eyes. Height was another thing Brody had passed down to his son. Tyler towered over most other nine-year-olds and was actually almost as tall as Lacy. He was a soft-spoken, sweet kid who had his mother's manners and his father's disposition.

"What do you say, Champ, are you tuckered out yet?" Brody asked as he ruffled the top of his son's head.

"Dad," Tyler replied with an "Aww shucks" tone and ducked out from under Brody's hand.

Brody glanced down at his thick black watch. "You ready to have some dinner? I have to drop you off to your mom in about an hour."

The boy scuffed his tennis shoe in the dirt. "Can't I go in the morning? We're supposed to go to Aunt Lisa's house. It's boring there. And it smells like cat poop."

A laugh popped out of Lacy at the honesty of little kids.

"No can do, son. You have to go tonight. That's the deal." At Tyler's dramatic sulk, Brody added, "I'll tell you what. We'll get some ice cream on the way there. Sound good?"

Tyler's gray eyes lit up with delight. "Can we go to Dairy Queen and get a Blizzard?"

A dimple peeked in Brody's cheek when he grinned at his son. "I was just thinking Dairy Queen sounded perfect. You want to come have some food with us?" he asked Lacy.

She shook her head and grabbed her art bag. "You guys go ahead. I'm going to go for a walk before I go home. See ya, Little T."

Tyler laughed when she poked him in the ribs.

They parted ways, Brody and son climbing into Brody's truck and Lacy walking through the park toward home. The park wasn't exactly down the street from her house, but she'd opted to walk for the exercise. Plus, it'd been such a beautiful day and now an even more beautiful evening. The sky was crystal-clear with a faint breeze ruffling the overgrown trees. Lacy hooked her bag over her shoulder and left the park behind.

She'd just reached the end of Main Street when a vehicle pulled up beside her.

"Well, look at this. You need a ride and I just happen to be driving by." The deep voice that haunted her lonely nights came from the open truck window.

Lacy didn't slow her pace. "I don't need a ride." She tossed Chase a glance. "But thanks anyway."

"Don't tell me you're walking for the sheer pleasure of it." Dark sunglasses rested on top of his head.

"Actually, I am." She came to a stop. "And what are you doing out here? Shouldn't you be at the restaurant?"

His mouth curled in a mischievous grin. "I'm playing hooky."

Lacy's heart rate kicked up to supernatural speeds. Recent memories of him flashing that same smile just before drowning her in pleasure flooded her mind.

"You live and breathe your work," she argued. "What are you really doing?"

"I wasn't supposed to work today, but I came in for a few hours anyway. I'm on my way home now."

She took a step closer to his truck. "I knew it."

He threw the truck into park and rested one hand on top of the steering wheel. "Where are you going? I'll give you a ride."

"I'm just going home."

"Home?" he asked with raised brows. "You're walking all the way home from town?"

"It's not that far," she said with a shrug. She didn't trust herself to be that close to him.

He quirked a brow at her. "It's five miles."

"So?"

His mouth crept into another smile. "So, let me give you a ride."

Lacy took a step closer. *Do not get in his truck. You'll just get sucked back into bed with him again.*

But it was oh so tempting. She allowed her gaze to eat up his masculinity, then took another step closer to his vehicle.

"Afraid to be alone with me?" he teased.

Yes. "No."

He leaned across the seat and opened the passenger door. "Then hop in."

TWELVE

LACY TRIED TO KEEP HER EYES in front of her and not on the man sitting so casually in the driver's seat. She shouldn't have gotten in the truck with him. Now he'd walk her to the door and she'd be tempted to press her lips to his. Or do much more than that.

Her eyes kept straying to his long legs, so beautifully wrapped in a pair of gray slacks. Then she reminded herself of the way things ended between them. The thought was like a cold bucket of water over her head.

"So, tell me something," he said, breaking the silence between them. "Why are you out walking through town to begin with?"

"I had the day off and wanted to spend the day outside."

"Okay."

She tossed him a glance. "Why do I get the feeling you're questioning my ability to be physically active?"

He came to a stop at a red light and turned his attention to her. His gaze swept down her body. "I'm not questioning anything. Your stamina could put me to shame."

"Chase..."

He held up a hand. "Sorry, I couldn't help it. You left

that wide open." He reached across the front seat and pinched her chin. "Besides I love ruffling your feathers."

She swatted his hand away and he chuckled, a deep rumble that slid over her skin like a lover's caress. *Bad idea getting in this truck.*

"Lighten up, Lace. You're not still mad at me, are you?" The light turned green and Chase continued toward her house.

"Why would I be mad at you?" If anything, she was mad at herself for reacting to him as if she were a teenager.

"Did you forget about shoving my underwear at me?"

Hell no, she hadn't forgotten. But what ate away at her was the way she'd handled the situation. There were a dozen different ways she could have responded. How about calmly asking him for the truth, instead of jumping to conclusions?

"Yeah, about that. I overreacted."

He snorted. "You think?"

"Will you shut up and let me apologize?"

His answer was a devious tilt of his mouth.

She exhaled. "I'm sorry for the way I reacted." She risked a glance at him. His eyes scanned the road ahead of them. "I know you're not the type of guy to run around behind a woman's back. I should have known that, but it was a shock having your underwear handed to me at work."

He turned onto her street. The muscles in his jaw hardened. "Sonja shouldn't have done that. I guess it was her tacky way of getting me back to her house. She's tried it before, but the woman can't take a hint."

Maybe you should have stayed out of her bed to begin with.

No. Chase's past with women was none of her business.

"Anyway, I'm sorry. I should have given you a chance to explain."

His eyes softened when he looked at her. "I appreciate that." He reached out to trail his finger along her jawline. "You know I would never do anything like that to you, right?"

She smiled and tried to suppress the goose bumps that threatened to show themselves. "I know. I've been so emotional lately, and I don't know why."

He pulled into her driveway and cut the engine. "Are you going to protest me walking you to your door?"

"Would it do any good?"

He flashed her a quick grin. "Not a bit."

They climbed out of his truck and then Chase followed her to the front door. "Thanks for the ride." She slanted him a look. "Even though I could have walked."

He leaned against the door frame. "I know, but I'll use any excuse to be near you."

She stopped just before sliding her key into the lock. "Chase, I can't go there again with you. We're friends. We work well together and I don't want to ruin that." *He's giving you an opportunity to drag his gorgeous hide back to bed and you're turning it down?*

"You couldn't ruin it, Lace."

Oh yes, I could.

His arm snaked around her waist and pulled her flush against him. She went willingly, just because she wanted to feel him one more time. Was it so bad to allow herself this one last indulgence?

He plucked her keys and bag out of her hand and dropped them to the concrete beneath their feet. Lacy only had eyes for the man pressed closely to her as he very slowly slid out the tie holding her hair back. Chase tunneled his hands into her hair as it fell free around her shoulders. He threaded his fingers through the strands until they reached the end. Their mouths hovered just centimeters from each other's, Chase's warm breath tickling her face.

"Invite me in," he said in a hoarse whisper.

Her eyelids drifted closed. His mouth was so close. All she had to do was lean forward ever so slightly, and she'd be able to feel the lips that she'd been dreaming of since they'd been apart.

"Chase, I can't," she managed to say. A heated flush rushed through her entire body and lights danced behind her closed eyelids.

"But you want to."

Why wouldn't he kiss her already? Why was he torturing her by not allowing his lips to take hers? Barely being able to feel the heat and softness of his lips was maddening.

"I know you want me, Lacy." He held her face between his warm palms. His mouth still refused to settle on hers. "Just one more time together."

She almost gave in. The feel of his much bigger, much harder body against hers had her coming close to uttering the words he wanted to hear. Memories of them together, him on top of her, tortured her to the point of insanity.

Common sense had her stepping back, out of his embrace. "I meant it when I said I can't. And we both know it wouldn't be just one more time." One time had never been enough for Chase. During their few weeks together, he'd barely given her enough time to remember her own name before taking her again.

He brushed his thumb along her cheek. "Okay."

She picked the keys up from the ground, inserted them

in the lock again, and turned. The dead bolt didn't unlatch with the key. After Dennis's unwanted appearance, Lacy had been diligent about locking her doors. Before leaving earlier, she'd thrown the dead bolt and now the dead bolt wasn't in place.

"What's wrong?" Chase asked when she froze in the act of opening the door.

The hairs on the back of Lacy's neck stood. "I locked the door when I left and now it's not locked."

"Are you sure?"

She licked her suddenly dry lips. "Positive."

Chase placed an arm in front of her and moved her back from the door. "Stay here."

The old wood creaked when he swung it open. Lacy held her breath as he stepped over the threshold and into the house. The interior was inky dark. Why hadn't she thought to leave a light on? Would Dennis be so bold as to enter her home a second time?

The seconds ticked by agonizingly slowly as Lacy held her breath and waited. Little beads of sweat formed in between her breasts and on her back. If someone was in her house, then Chase was potentially putting himself in danger. Or, more accurately, *she'd* put him in danger by bringing him here. Her teeth stabbed into her lower lip while she waited for him to come back and tell her the coast was clear.

He didn't. Instead, a series of thumps and curse words came from inside the house. Something loud crashed to the ground, like several pieces of wood had splintered into a thousand pieces. The commotion had Lacy jumping back and squealing. Had someone really broken into her house and had Chase stumbled across them? What if he was hurt? Stabbed? Strangled? Oh, Lord, she'd never forgive herself if something happened to him.

Ignoring his command to wait outside, Lacy went into the house and followed the sounds of a struggle. Just for extra protection, she grabbed a frying pan from the kitchen and gripped it in her sweaty palms. Glass shattered, and more curses came from her bedroom. Her heart thudded up into her throat, but she forced one foot in front of the other until she came to her bedroom door.

The sight before her almost made her drop the frying pan. The old rocking chair that had once sat in the corner of the room was now reduced to toothpicks. Every single drawer in her nightstand, as well as her dresser, was open, their contents tossed about the room. Half the knick-knacks from her dresser top were broken and scattered everywhere.

However, those material things didn't matter to her. What had the breath whooshing out of her were the two men on the floor. Chase had Dennis pinned on his stomach, his knee buried in the middle of Dennis's back, the older man's head turned to one side at an awkward angle. Chase had trapped Dennis's hand behind his back, locked in his tight grip.

Dennis tried to wiggle out from underneath Chase, but he was unable to escape.

A thin stream of blood ran down one side of Chase's face. Lacy dropped the frying pan, and it clattered to the floor as she rushed to his side.

"I told you to wait outside," he barked.

"I heard a horrible sound. I thought you were hurt."

Dennis tried to raise his head off the floor. "I know that check is here somewhere. You owe me!" He wiggled, but it was no use. "Just give me a little. I promise I'll leave you alone."

"Shut up," Chase said through gritted teeth. Dennis

groaned when Chase dug his knee harder into her father's back. The fierce look on Chase's face softened slightly. "As long as you're in here, you might as well call the police. I don't know how much longer I can sit in this position."

Lacy sprinted back to the front porch where Chase had dropped her purse. She dug her cell phone out with shaky hands and punched 911. She rattled out the information for the dispatcher in as even a tone as she could manage. Lacy walked back into the bedroom with the cell phone pressed to her ear, while the dispatcher tried to calm her down. Dennis had given up his futile attempts at getting free.

In moments, sirens screamed in the distance. Lacy ended the call and stood outside to wait for the police.

"Thank you so much for coming," she said in a border-line shaky voice to the two officers who had arrived and approached her.

"Are you all right, ma'am? Can you tell us what happened?" the younger officer asked her.

She led them through the door while explaining how she'd realized her door had been unlocked and how Chase had captured her father. They followed her down the hallway and the three of them came to a stop outside her bedroom door. Lacy stood aside while the officers relieved Chase and slapped handcuffs on Dennis's wrists. One officer spoke to Chase in hushed tones while the other one read Dennis his Miranda rights. Lacy couldn't bring herself to look at the man who'd fathered her. She shouldn't be surprised he'd tried to rob her. He'd done this same thing to other people in the past whenever he needed money for a fix. But this was the first time he'd done something like this to her.

What if she'd been home? What if she hadn't allowed Chase to walk her to the door? Lacy had never been afraid of her father before. She was now.

She stood back while the officer escorted Dennis out of the bedroom.

"You should probably have that cut looked at, sir," the younger officer said to Chase.

Chase's eyes lit on hers and then roamed down her body. "I'm fine."

The other man turned his kind eyes to her. "Would you like to press charges?"

Lacy walked farther into the room and stopped next to Chase. He grabbed her hand and gave it a comforting squeeze. "Yes," she replied.

The officer nodded once. "All right. We'll have to get the suspect processed and we'll be in touch in a couple of days. In the meantime, I'll need to get both your statements."

For the next thirty minutes, she and Chase retold their story. She described to the officer how she found her front door unlocked. Then Chase explained how he found Dennis rifling through Lacy's drawers, tossing her clothes all over the bedroom. Lacy immediately suspected drugs when Chase mentioned the wild look in Dennis's eyes. She should have known the man couldn't stay off the stuff for long.

Lacy swayed on her feet as the Trouble PD took her father away and the commotion died down. Chase came to her rescue again when he wound his arm around her shoulders.

"Are you okay?" he asked, pulling her close to him.

"Me?" she asked him in disbelief. "You're the one who's hurt." She touched the thin line of blood on his face, which had dried.

"It's nothing. Just a scratch."

To keep from completely breaking down, Lacy pulled away from him and went to her bathroom. She grabbed the washcloth from the sink and ran it in warm water. "It's not nothing," she said after forcing him to sit on the bed. "How did this happen?"

Chase didn't even flinch when she touched the cloth to his wound. "He pulled a fast one on me and threw something hard at my head. It was dark and I didn't see it coming until it clocked me in the forehead."

Lacy furiously blinked back tears at the idea of Chase being hurt. He'd all but stormed into the house on his white horse in an effort to protect her. And she hadn't even asked him to. He was lucky Dennis hadn't had a real weapon with him.

"It's obvious he came here looking for that check," he said as Lacy blotted away the dried blood. "How did he know about it?"

Lacy had never wanted to drag outsiders into her problems with Dennis, least of all friends.

"He said my mother's parents told him about the money." She turned the washcloth over to a clean side.

"He said?" Chase asked sharply. "You mean this is your *second* run-in with him? I thought he was in jail."

"I'm not sure how long he's been out. I stopped keeping track of him a long time ago."

"So what happened?" He pulled out of her reach and looked at her. "He was here, wasn't he?"

Lacy nodded and Chase stood from the bed, a myriad of expletives flying from his mouth. "Jesus, Lacy. Why didn't you call the police?" he demanded.

She lifted her shoulders in a helpless shrug. "I don't know. I guess I didn't want to deal with the headache. I just wanted him gone. Plus, he technically didn't do anything wrong. I'd left the door unlocked."

His face turned thunderous. "Didn't do anything wrong? That's trespassing."

Her gaze followed him as he stalked from one side of the bedroom to the other. "I realize now I should have called the police. This incident tonight wouldn't have happened." She turned the washcloth over in her hands. "I'm sorry you got dragged into this."

"Sorry?" he repeated as he gripped her shoulders. "Have you thought about what would have happened if I hadn't been here?"

Drugs always made Dennis volatile and unpredictable. If she had stumbled across him, what would he have done? Would he have been physically violent with her like he had with Chase? A shudder ran through her at the thought.

"I can see you're giving it some thought now. I just wish you would have told me about the first time he came here."

"And what would you have done? Stood guard at my door every night? It's not your job to protect me."

The thunderous look on his face softened. He let go of one of her shoulders and brushed his hand over her hair. "It may not be my job, but I want to help you. You can't do everything alone."

Why not? I've been living like that a long time.

In fact, she'd been taking care of herself for so long that the idea of someone coming to her rescue had never occurred to her. Chase wanted to be that man, but could she let him? She wasn't used to depending on people.

He dropped his hands from her. "I can see you're tired."

"Wait." She grabbed his hand just as he turned away. "Don't go yet."

He lifted a brow in question.

She didn't have the strength to jump back into bed with him and walk away. She wouldn't go unscathed. But the thought of sleeping here alone, knowing her father had invaded her privacy, made her skin crawl. Every time she closed her eyes, Chase's depiction of tonight's events flashed across her mind. Knowing her father had been digging through her personal belongings made her stomach churn in knots.

"I just—" She cleared her throat. "I don't want to be alone."

His thumb glided over the back of her hand. "Do you want me to sleep on the couch?"

She shook her head.

"In here? Are you sure?"

"Yes."

Within seconds, he had her stripped down to her underwear and placed under the covers. There was nothing sexual about it. She knew he didn't plan on jumping her bones for an all-night sexual marathon. This was his way of showing he wanted to take care of her. Lacy was too tired to protest. Her eyes followed his movements around the room as he picked up her discarded things.

"You don't have to do that," she said in a sleepy voice.

"I know." He picked up a handful of her underwear and placed them back in the drawer. "Just relax."

Her eyes drifted shut. The sound of his footsteps around the room as he tidied things was an odd sort of comfort. Just knowing he was close by allowed her tension-filled body to relax by slow degrees. She forced thoughts of Dennis and his unpredictable behavior out of her mind. This being-taken-care-of thing wasn't so bad.

Several minutes later, the mattress dipped under Chase's weight as he slid under the covers. His body heat surrounded her in a cocoon of masculinity and strength. He brought her to him, and she went willingly, only too eager to feel his bare flesh against hers. She sighed in contentment as his arms went around her and she drifted to sleep.

THIRTEEN

LACY HAD ABSOLUTELY NOTHING TO SHOW at the art festival. A week since she'd drawn the Trouble town hall, she'd accumulated probably a dozen different versions of the same building. None of them had sparked any sort of "wow" factor that some of her others had, like the one of the tree she'd done a while back. Now *that* was wow. She kept the original for herself, simply because she couldn't stand to part with it, and had had a sixteen-by-twenty copy made, matted, and framed. All of which had cost her a pretty penny. She figured if she priced this baby right, she could make a small profit. And hopefully catch the eye of a gallery owner who'd love to buy a hundred copies of her work and sell them.

Still wishful thinking, but the festival was a step in the right direction.

Her studio floor was littered with every drawing she'd ever done, scattered as she attempted to find something else to accompany the tree. A small pile of three possibilities sat on the couch.

One, she'd done of the Arizona desert just outside of Sedona. As majestic as a sunset over the desert was, something about it was a little bland. Maybe she'd break open her box of colored pencils and add a little pizzazz to the sky.

The second was of an eagle perched on top of a tree. Most times when Lacy went looking for inspiration, she'd take her camera with her to capture the moment. One afternoon, while driving, she spotted the eagle soaring through the air before landing on the highest branch of a nearby tree. Something about the way the bird's cat-like eyes scanned every square inch around him had been so mesmerizing that Lacy had pulled over, grabbed her camera, and shot half a dozen pictures. Later that day, she uploaded the photos to her computer and sketched the bird from the images on the screen.

The third drawing was of the historic governor's mansion in Cheyenne. Her original reason for the sketch had been a sentimental one. When she'd been about six or seven, she, her father, and Ray had driven into Cheyenne and on a whim had taken a tour of the historical building. While the tour had bored her to tears, the trip was one of the few happy memories she had of her father. At that point in her life, Dennis had been clean for about two years and had provided for her the way a father should have. Not long after that, he'd fallen onto hard times again and she'd gone to stay with Ray for a few months.

"There has to be something else I can use," she muttered as she sifted through random drawings. Maybe she needed to do some new ones. Most she had here either weren't good enough or were unfinished.

With a sigh, she stood from her crouched position and gathered the three sketches she'd placed on the couch. She'd just set them on the drawing table when her doorbell rang.

A quick peek through her peephole showed Chase on the other side. A pair of dark sunglasses hid his eyes and his big, well-toned body was covered in a black T-shirt and a pair of khaki cargo pants. Why did her heart have to skip three beats every time she saw him? And why couldn't she breathe normally around him like she did with other men?

"I can hear you moving around on the other side of the door, Lace. Open up." Even through a thick piece of wood, his deep voice turned her inner muscles into Jell-O.

His deliciously full mouth turned up in a slow, heart-melting grin when she opened the door.

"How did you hear me?"

He tapped the threshold with one large boot. "Your floorboards creak."

Ah, another thing that was wrong with the house.

She crossed her arms under her breasts and willed her heartbeat to slow down. "What're you doing here?"

"I want to take you for a ride." His grin widened when she lifted her brows. "On my bike. Although I'm willing to do the other thing you're thinking."

"Not a chance," she said with a shake of her head.

Both his thick, wide shoulders shrugged. "Can't blame a guy for trying."

Her eyes dropped down to his powerful thighs and suppressed the memory of them in between her own. She cleared her throat so her voice had a prayer of coming out evenly. "I'm not a big fan of motorcycles, Chase."

"But you like mine." He tugged on a strand of her hair. "I've seen you eyeing me on it before."

Did he have to be so in tune to her every move? His weird sixth sense made it difficult to be discreet about how much she still wanted him.

"All right, you want the truth?" He whipped off his sunglasses and pierced her with eyes the same color as the sky. "I still feel bad about the way things ended between us."

"And you want to make it up to me by sticking me on that thing?"

He tossed a backward glance over his shoulder. "That's not the only thing I have planned. Come on," he said when she still didn't agree. "Live a little. What else do you have to do?"

Well, when he puts it that way…

She dropped her arms and turned from the door. "Give me one minute." This was going to get her into trouble. Her willpower was weak at best where Chase was concerned.

Her flip-flops lay discarded on the bedroom floor where she'd kicked them off the night before. She slipped them on, then on a whim grabbed her art bag and walked to the front door. There had to be something among the Wyoming scenery beautiful enough to make it on her sketch pad. She snagged her purse off the kitchen counter and locked the front door behind her.

Chase leaned against his bike like the irresistible badass he was. He held out a monstrous black helmet when she approached.

"Do you have any idea what that's going to do to my hair?"

"Do you have any idea what smacking your head on the pavement will do to your brain?" One side of his mouth kicked up and he plopped the helmet on her head. "Nothing could make your hair look bad." His big fingers brushed along her chin and jawbone when he fastened the strap of the helmet, sending little lightning bolts to her midsection. "Here," he said, and took her art bag and purse off her shoulder. A duffel bag–sized compartment sat on the end of the bike, and Chase deposited her belongings into it.

"You have to get on the bike, Lace," he said after he threw one long leg over the motorcycle and she only stood there.

"Right," she said more to herself. The bike was taller than she'd anticipated and her toes barely touched the ground when she mounted. Chase's body heat felt way too good, not to mention how divinely hard his back muscles would be, so she opted for leaning back and grabbing the seat behind her. Spontaneously combusting on a motorcycle in the middle of the open road was not on her "to do" list.

"That's not going to work," he said over his shoulder. "You need to hold on to me."

No way could she handle being plastered to all that muscle. "I think I'll be okay like this."

"No, seriously." When she didn't move so much as a toe, he turned in the seat so he could see her. "You're not afraid to touch me, are you?"

"Of course not," she said with a weak smile. *Yeah, that was real convincing.*

A heavy sigh radiated from his big body. "Give me your hand." When she placed her palm in his much bigger one, he yanked it forward until her arm was wrapped around him. He settled it on his abdomen, then held out his right hand. "Other hand." His fingers wrapped around her wrist and gently tugged until her hand rested on top of her other one. "Don't let go. But feel free to let those drift lower."

"You're pushing it," she growled next to his ear.

His back vibrated against her chest when he laughed. Man, he had a sexy laugh. The low, rough timbre had a way of skipping along her nerves until her bones all but melted. Lacy always tried to shield herself, but he managed to sneak past her defenses.

The motorcycle rumbled to life and sent her loins vibrating to match the rest of her body. Chase maneuvered them out of the driveway, then sped down the street. Within ten minutes, Trouble faded into the distance and all that surrounded them was the vast openness of the Wyoming foothills. Lacy kept her arms tight around the man in front of her, more from fear of falling to her bloody death than savoring the feel of him. Of course, the fact that he was so gosh dang masculine made clinging to him much more enjoyable.

He handled the bike with the ease and grace of someone who'd been born on top of one. The machine fit beneath his lean, steely muscles like he'd had it custom made just for him. So he'd caught her watching him ride his bike a time or two. She hadn't denied it because he was right, and they both knew it. Watching him roar down the streets of Trouble had been a temptation too great for her to pass up. She'd indulged in her fantasy. So sue her.

Thirty minutes or maybe an hour passed before Chase took a side road off the main highway. Thick, white clouds drifted across the crystalline sky as though they had a particular destination in mind. Aspens and other species of trees Lacy couldn't name bent from side to side in the pleasant breeze. Summertime was really the best time of year in Wyoming. Although the temperatures tended to skyrocket, the wind didn't blow so badly.

As they flew by the scenery, Lacy pressed herself as close to Chase as she could get. Her arms tightened around his torso. Her inner thighs gripped his bigger, harder ones and her breasts smashed into the sculpted muscles of his back. This was the closest she'd been to him since the last time they'd spent the night together. Not that she'd thought about those nights with the dreamy intensity of a teenager. Because she hadn't. Nor had she remembered how simply divine he felt on top of her or how his skin burned hers up. Or how he could perfectly synchronize his kisses with his pumping hips so that she couldn't form a clear thought.

No, she hadn't daydreamed about *any* of that. Not even a little.

Sometime later, Chase turned down another road, then came to a stop at a manned gate with a sign in the front that said FLAMING GORGE NATIONAL RECREATION AREA. He dug his wallet out of his back pocket and paid the uniformed ranger the necessary fee to enter the park. Once the arm of the gate lifted, the two of them set forth again.

Their surroundings opened up to brilliant red cliffs that reminded Lacy of the Grand Canyon. Although the Flaming Gorge Recreation Area was well known throughout the state, Lacy had never been there. Chase seemed to know where he was going. Another significant chunk of time went by with the two of them speeding past more and more cliffs until they came to a body of water.

"This is the Green River," Chase said after he shut the bike off and dismounted. "I come here sometimes to fish."

"You fish?" she asked as he helped her off the bike. Chase the restaurant manager. Chase the badass who rode a motorcycle. Chase the expert at giving orgasms. But Chase the fisherman? Never would she have guessed.

"When I can get away." He took the helmet from her

and hooked it over the handlebars of the bike. "Which isn't very often. Here." He opened the back compartment and pulled out her art bag. "What's in there?"

"Stuff I like to travel with sometimes."

Chase didn't know about her sketching, much less seen any of her pictures. If she planned on showing her stuff to the general public, then surely she could show them to a man who'd seen her naked more than anyone else. Plus, she could really use this time to capture something worthwhile to go with the others.

He eyed the bag with interest and speculation and pulled more stuff out of the bike's compartment: a blue plaid blanket and a grocery bag full of to-go containers.

She lifted her chin toward his things. "What's all that?"

"Well, I can't cook worth a damn, so I brought some of Trouble Café's home cooking."

"So this is like a picnic?"

His seductive mouth turned up in a grin. "I suppose."

She narrowed her eyes and followed him to the shoreline of the river. "You're not by any chance trying to court me, are you?"

"Why, do you want to be courted?" he asked as he walked ahead of her. Her eyes remained glued to his world-class ass.

"No," she replied when they stopped walking.

He set the bag of food down, then spread the blanket. "That's not how you felt a few weeks ago."

The blanket was huge and had patches of holes where the earth beneath poked through like little fingers. She kicked her shoes off and sat down. The blanket may have been old, but the fibers felt like feathers beneath her legs.

"That's not what we were doing. We were—"

"Fucking?" he supplied as he sat down next to her.

A sigh flowed out of her. "That's not how I'd put it, but yes. Either way there was no courting involved."

His blue gaze jumped to hers as he opened the bag of food. "So the moral of the story is you don't want to be courted?"

She took one Styrofoam container out of the plastic bag and set it on the blanket in between them. "I would appreciate that, yes."

"I live to serve you, Miss Taylor."

He unloaded three more containers from the bag and spread them out on the blanket, along with two sets of plastic utensils. He then placed two bottles of water next to their food.

"What did you get?" Whatever it was smelled fried and pretty damn good.

"Fried chicken wings, mashed potatoes, dinner rolls, and apple turnovers." He grinned at her. "All the basic food groups."

"I know I'm too skinny, but jeez."

His bone-melting gaze dropped to her thighs. "You're not too skinny. Dig in. I promise you won't be disappointed."

"No plates?"

He handed her a plastic fork and gestured to the open containers. "These are our plates."

Worked for her. The food smelled too good to debate whether or not they had dishes to eat on. The aroma drifting to her nose prompted a low rumbling in her tummy.

The chicken was crispy and tasted like Cajun seasoning. The mashed potatoes were creamy with a few lumps, and the bread practically melted on her tongue. Lacy's childhood lacked a lot of things and home-cooked meals were one of them. The extent of Ray's culinary skills didn't usually go beyond a microwave or prepackaged oven meals. Never in her life had she tasted anything like this, as though the person who prepared it put their heart and soul into the food. Each of the dishes complemented each other in a way that made them taste that much better.

"Oh my gosh, I think you killed me," she said after she'd inhaled half the box of potatoes.

One side of Chase's mouth kicked up when he reached for another chicken wing. "Don't tell me you've never eaten at the Trouble Café."

She shook her head and tore off a piece of bread.

"You've lived here how long and you've never been there?"

"My salary doesn't exactly afford luxuries like that."

"Hmm. Your boss should give you a raise."

She dug her fork into the potatoes. "Maybe you could put in a good word for me."

He opened the bag of turnovers. "Yeah, we are pretty tight. Are you ready for one of these?"

Her eyes narrowed. "You really *are* trying to kill me, aren't you?"

"There are better ways to go than this, believe me." Just to get his meaning across, his eyes lowered to her shirtfront as though he saw the flesh beneath. Her heart did a little triple beat beneath her rib cage. If he meant in bed with him, then he was damn right.

"Just have a small bite." He tore off a corner piece with his thumb and forefinger and held the treat out to her. A dollop of apple filling oozed out like molasses and fell to the blanket.

Before she had a chance to say, "No stinkin' way," Chase put the turnover to her lips and forced them open.

Caught under the hypnotizing spell of his very blue eyes, Lacy opened her mouth just wide enough to let his fingers inside. His index finger touched the tip of her tongue before letting go of the food. Just because he was a teasing little sneak, he let his index finger linger so that her lips closed around it.

"That was sneaky," she said after regaining her voice.

He inhaled half the turnover in one bite. "But fun."

She unscrewed the cap to her water bottle and took a sip. "If I eat another bite, I'll explode."

"Good stuff, huh?" They'd killed off the chicken wings, so Chase closed the lid to the container and stuffed it back in the bag.

"I can't believe I've been missing that all this time. Their cooking ought to be illegal."

A chuckle rumbled from his thick chest. "It reminds me of my mother's cooking."

Only half the potatoes remained, so Lacy shut the Styrofoam lid and helped Chase clean the rest of their mess. "Do you remember anything about her?" Maybe his memories of his mother were a lot clearer than her memories of her mother.

He tossed the last napkin into the plastic bag. "I was only seven when she died, so my memories of her are pretty fuzzy. I remember her cooking, though. She used to make biscuits that absolutely melted in your mouth."

Lacy had never tasted anything like that until today. "I'm sorry I never got to meet her. She sounds like an amazing woman."

Chase leaned down on one elbow and stretched his long legs out. "She had to be, to tame three boys."

She crossed her legs under her. "You were the wildest one, weren't you?"

"What gave you that idea?"

"Oh, I don't know," she said, then lifted his shirtsleeve to reveal the tattoo beneath.

He glanced down at his bicep. "Oh, that. You know, Noah and Brody have the same one in the exact same spot."

She nodded and let her hand linger on his arm. "And they each have one that says *Twelve-Inch Wonder* too?"

He lifted a muscled shoulder. "I can't help it if I'm bigger than them. Besides"—his gaze ran down to her toes—"you have enough firsthand experience to know the tattoo is pretty accurate."

"You know, despite what some women tell you, size doesn't always matter."

The gorgeous man had the gall to laugh. "They only say that when the man they're with is too small."

Right, and he'd never had that complaint because he was the "Twelve-Inch Wonder," a name most likely given to him by a woman. Lacy had a sneaking suspicion men didn't go around naming other men's penises. She shook her head and decided to change the subject. Discussing body parts associated with sex was not the wisest idea.

"How did it go at the police station yesterday?" he asked after they'd both been silent for a moment.

"As well as can be expected." She'd officially filed burglary charges against her father the day before. This wasn't the first incident where she'd filed charges against Dennis. But something about yesterday left her feeling almost sick to her stomach. Maybe all these years of being more responsible and mature than her father were finally starting to wear on her.

"You did the right thing," Chase reassured her. "So what happens next?"

"They'll have a formal hearing, then the judge will decide whether the case will go to trial."

"If it does go to trial, will you have to testify?"

"I don't know. I just want to forget about the whole thing."

A cool breeze sifted through the leaves in the trees around them. Lacy let her eyes drift shut and her body float down to the blanket. She settled her relaxed bones next to Chase and savored the rare moment of having absolutely *nothing* to do.

"Are you sure you want to be in this position?" The man next to her spoke in low, bedroom-voice tones.

One of her eyelids cracked open. Her former lover leaned closer than he should have with his elbow resting against her shoulder. Half a day's worth of light-brown stubble covered his square jaw and made him look even more disreputable. Within the past few seconds, his face had gotten closer. How had he done that without her noticing?

He traced her bottom lip with his index finger. "You make it so easy, Lace."

Huh? Make what easy? His words didn't make sense. His blue eyes darkened and dropped down her mouth where his finger ran back and forth. A wave of goose bumps followed his finger down her neck and over one collarbone. Her eyes drifted shut again and her breath turned from even to shallow and erratic when his finger traced along the neckline of her shirt. How did he do that? Where did he learn these moves and how to turn a woman to a bowl of cottage cheese by touching her? Good grief, if he didn't stop, she'd forget her friend rule and pull his mouth down to hers.

"If I'm not mistaken, I'd say you're turned on," he whispered next to her ear.

She placed a hand on one of his shoulders. "A good enough reason for you to stop."

His lips found her neck and she tilted her head to one side. "Actually that's a good reason to continue."

She gave his shoulder a shove. "Did you bring me here to seduce me?"

"We both know I don't need to bring you way out here to do that." His kisses grew more insistent, following the path his finger had taken moments before. Lacy sighed when his mouth found hers. His warm tongue danced along the seam of her lips, then slipped inside when she granted him entrance. Tingles worked their way down her body when his tongue swirled around hers. He inserted one thigh between her legs and shifted himself more fully over her body. He was so big, his body covered her much smaller one as if they'd been designed to go together. Oh, how she'd missed this and the feel of him on top of her. She missed how he made her feel beautiful and desirable, how one curl of his lips made her forget everything else in her life.

One of his hands slid into her hair and gently gripped the side of her head. His fingers massaged her skull lovingly. She arched into him, savoring the feel of all that masculinity. Without breaking contact, he shifted the angle of the kiss and plunged his tongue even deeper into her mouth.

All sense of time and reality drifted away from her as she wrapped her arms around Chase's shoulders. The man was a master at making her forget her own name. All he had to do was crook his finger and she turned to mush.

His tongue continued to slide along hers in a delicious, erotic dance; her heart cracked in two.

He finally lifted his head and skimmed his thumb along her swollen lips.

"We really shouldn't do this," she managed to say.

His mouth twitched in a small smile. "I'd say we already did."

She pulled in a cleansing breath to clear her head. "I mean anymore."

"You don't sound too sure," he said after disengaging himself from her.

"I'm not. That's why we shouldn't."

His hand sifted through her hair again. "You tie me up in knots."

"It's not on purpose. In the meantime I should be getting home."

"All right."

They reluctantly pulled themselves off the comfort of the ratty blanket and cleaned their picnic mess. Chase disposed of the garbage while Lacy folded the blanket and stuffed it back in the motorcycle. Once mounted, with Chase gripping the handlebars and Lacy wrapped around him like a glove, he pulled the motorcycle out of their spot and started their journey home.

All the way there, Lacy allowed herself to enjoy the feel of him against her front. He was so irresistible that it was all she could do to keep from begging him to stop the bike and continue his seduction. Instead, she dropped her head to his back and rested her cheek there for the remainder of the ride.

By the time he pulled into her driveway, twilight had set on their tiny town. She dismounted from the bike and replaced her belongings with the helmet in the back compartment. He didn't kiss her or touch her, probably because he knew she wouldn't want him to. She really did, but for the sake of her sanity it would be better if there was no touching at all.

"Have dinner with me," he demanded just before she wished him good night.

"Chase..."

He held his hands up in surrender. "No seducing, I promise. I won't even touch you unless you touch me first."

"Just dinner?" Why did she get the feeling they were stepping into the dating category?

"Nothing else."

She pursed her lips and hitched the art bag higher on her shoulder. "You have to take me someplace I've never been before. Someplace nice."

He grinned and her insides melted like butter over a hot muffin. "I think I can manage that."

She turned to walk to the door, then spun around at the last second to catch him watching her. "Thanks for the afternoon out."

His response was another grin; then he kicked the motorcycle on and backed out of the driveway.

What in the world had she just agreed to? Her friendship rule wasn't going to stay in effect if she kept letting him take her out. Even if he had promised not to touch her, Lacy couldn't promise herself she wouldn't be the least bit turned on. Her body might be safe from him but her heart was another story.

"You are a glutton for punishment," she chastised herself as she opened the front door and went inside.

Boris didn't even twitch from his usual spot. The reason she knew he was alive was because he snorted, then let out a low whine. Ray's old dog was so predictable. She walked past the living room and almost made it by the kitchen when something beeped.

Her sandal-covered feet stopped in their tracks. Had

she set a timer and forgot what it was for? The house didn't have an alarm, nor did she have an answering machine.

Her cell phone. For some reason she hadn't stuck it back in her purse from the last time she'd used it. Instead, the device sat on the kitchen counter where she'd absent-mindedly placed it.

She picked it up and touched her thumb to the touchpad. *One new voice message* blinked on the screen.

Her eyebrows pinched together as she listened to the voice mail.

"Miss Taylor, this is Officer Williams with the Trouble PD. I just wanted to let you know we're processing the charges against your father. I also encourage you to give me a call, should you remember anything else of importance. I'm available anytime."

He rattled off his phone number; then the message ended with the automated voice telling her to press seven to delete. Lacy pushed the END button and dropped her phone. With a loud *clack*, it hit the cracked tile countertop where it had rested a moment ago.

She'd been through this process before with Dennis. Something inside her churned like an unsettling thunderstorm ready to break. Little white stars danced before her eyes. Her once-warm skin turned clammy cold until a thin layer of perspiration built up in between her breasts and upper lip. Just as she took a step down the hall, the floor tilted and her stomach somersaulted. She sprinted the rest of the way to her room, kicked open the bathroom door, and tossed all that home-cooked food into the toilet.

Damn Dennis. Damn him straight to hell for affecting

her like this. She ought to be throwing a celebration party for the bastard's return to jail. Instead, she was leaning over the toilet, hair hanging in her face, and throwing up the last of her delicious lunch. Right down to the tiny bite of apple turnover.

What the hell was wrong with her?

FOURTEEN

CHASE PULLED INTO LACY'S DRIVEWAY at six-fifteen and cut the engine to his truck. The temperature today had soared near one hundred. The sun was not even close to setting and the heat made the material of his navy blue polo stick to his skin as he walked up the concrete path and rang the doorbell. The *click-clicking* of heels sounded through the old wooden door a second before it swung open. This time when his shirt stuck to his skin it had nothing to do with the unusual heat. His gaze drifted up a pair of smooth, bare legs, hips hugged by some weird stretchy material, and breasts barely supported by a scooped neckline. He had to peel his tongue off the roof of his mouth when he got a load of floss-thin spaghetti straps that barely held the dress up over her body. For some insane reason, the deep, emerald-green color made her blond hair shine even more than it already did.

After moving back to Trouble, Chase had conceded that Lacy had grown into a stunningly beautiful woman, but *damn*. If he'd never seen her naked, he never would have known she had the sort of body to make men fall to their knees.

She flipped her long, silky hair behind one shoulder. "I'm probably overdoing it with the dress, but I thought, what the hell? I splurged on it a few years ago and haven't had anywhere to wear it."

"No, it's uh…" He cleared his throat and let his eyes drop down to her spectacular breasts. "I mean, yeah… yeah," was all he could get out. *Real genius. Way to make her feel good.*

Her painted pink lips turned up in a satisfied grin. "Thank you."

Her *fuck-me* heels stepped out onto the landing; then Lacy shut the door behind her. "So where are we going?"

"A place in Cheyenne I went to once, a few years ago." When he glanced at her, he meant to look at her eyes but for some unfathomable, insane reason his gaze automatically went to her boobs. "I think you'll like it."

She stopped a few feet from his truck. "If you're going to spend the whole night staring at my breasts, then we're going to have problems."

He tossed his truck keys from hand to hand. "You can't wear a dress like that and expect me not to look. Take it as a compliment, Lace."

One of her thin eyebrows lifted as though she didn't like his explanation but was willing to accept it anyway. Because she didn't expect him to, he followed her around to the passenger side and opened the door for her. It also gave him an excuse to touch her when she needed help climbing into the vehicle. Underhanded and sneaky, yes, but he couldn't help himself.

"What kind of place is this?" she asked once they were on the road.

He draped one hand over the steering wheel and used the other to aim the air-conditioning vent toward his face.

Little beads of sweat had formed at his temples when Lacy sat on the seat, then lifted one leg to cross it over the other. Instant images formed in his mind of those legs wrapped around his hips as he jackhammered into her tight little body.

Okay, this is going to be a long night if you keep thinking things like that. She made it clear she has no intention of going to bed with you again.

"Chinese food. But it's not just ordinary Chinese. It's weird like, Asian fusion or something."

"You're taking me to a place that has weird food?"

He chuckled and made a left onto the main highway. "No, the food is excellent. When I ate there before, I just thought Asian fusion sounded strange."

Her eyes roamed over his face. "Did you go there with a woman?"

What would she do if he said yes? He almost did just to get a reaction out of her. "Actually, no. We went there for Carol's birthday." He took his eyes off the road for a second. "Does that make you feel better?"

She was silent for so long, her green eyes blazing into his, Chase didn't think she was going to answer. "Yes," she said, then turned to look out the window.

The twenty-minute drive into Cheyenne was spent talking about things like Boris's arthritis and Chase possibly adding a game room to his upstairs. Lacy was easy to talk to. She didn't keep her answers to simple yes and no. Everything she said was like a little story. And she asked a ton of questions. Things like, "Why do you think they still put directions on the back of shampoo bottles?" and "Instead of building a game room, why don't you build a workout room so you don't have to use a garage?"

Shit, he didn't have answers to things like that. And the garage wasn't that bad to work out in. A little stuffy, but not awful. In his opinion, a suitable place to put a pool table was much more important.

When he told her that, she just shook her head and said, "I don't understand men."

He pulled off the freeway and drove into downtown Cheyenne where the restaurant was located. Cheyenne wasn't a beautiful place, but it had all the essentials of a major city, including good food.

Lacy didn't wait for him to open the car door for her, like the independent woman she was. She beat him to the punch and fell into step beside him. His instinct told him to reach out and grab her hand or put an arm around her shoulder. When he'd asked her to dinner, he swore there would be no touching or anything of that nature. As much as he wanted to pin her sweet little ass to the side of the building and take her in a very public way, he wouldn't. Chase prided himself on being a man of his word, and Lacy for damn sure deserved someone like that.

Once inside, he gave the hostess his name, and he and Lacy followed the young girl to a table in the back.

"Okay, I don't know anything about Asian fusion," Lacy announced after they'd been handed their menus and left alone.

"They have good curry. And Carol had the sushi and she said it was really good."

She wrinkled her nose as her eyes ran over the menu. "I don't think I can handle anything spicy. I've never had tempura but for some reason it sounds like heaven."

He scanned his menu. "Tempura, huh? I don't know, I'm thinking of getting Schezuan beef."

They placed their food orders, along with a bottle of

red wine, with the waiter. When they were alone, Lacy took a sip from her water glass.

"So how're things at the restaurant?" she asked him after lowering the glass from her lips.

His eyes dropped to her full mouth when a bead of moisture clung to her lower lip. "You mean have I uncovered any thieves?"

"Yeah. The last time I worked, things seemed pretty normal."

"On the surface, sure. But my father's been breathing down my neck to figure out what's going on."

She flipped some hair behind one shoulder, revealing her collarbone. "And you still think nothing's going on?"

"So far. I showed Dad the surveillance to prove to him we have no solid evidence but he's still not convinced. And I've already had a talk with Henry to double-check all his numbers so there aren't any more discrepancies. Since then there haven't been."

"Maybe Henry was just being careless." She picked up her wineglass when the waiter set their drinks on the table. "I seriously don't think he'd steal from you."

Chase stretched his arm along the back of the booth. "I don't either, but for a while he was all I had to go on. He's the only one, besides me and Anita, who has access to the restaurant after hours."

She tilted her head to one side. "But why would he risk his job like that?"

"If someone gets desperate enough, they'll resort to anything."

"And Becky-Lynn never talked to you?"

He lifted both shoulders. "Nope."

"Why don't you approach her? She sounded like something was really weighing on her mind."

One of his brows lifted. "Obviously not, since she's yet to bring it up. And I have no reason to suspect her for anything."

"You have no reason to suspect Henry," she countered.

"More than I do Becky-Lynn," he answered. She watched him with those bottomless green eyes over the rim of her wineglass. "What was in that bag you had with you the other day?"

Her brows pulled together. "When?"

"At the lake. You pulled out a bag of stuff but then never opened it."

Her gaze dropped down to the black tablecloth. The swell of her breasts pushed against the hemline of the dress when she inhaled. "Those were my art supplies."

"What sort of art supplies?" he asked after shifting his eyes to hers.

The tip of her fingernail drew patterns on the table. "A sketch pad and pencils."

An adorable yet sexy blush colored her sharp cheekbones. She bit her bottom lip before lifting her glass and taking a swallow. If he didn't know better, he'd say Miss Taylor was embarrassed about something. Lacy had too strong a backbone to let anything get to her. How could some paper and pencils make her blush like a little girl?

She lifted one delicate, bare shoulder. "I do some drawing in my spare time."

"How much?"

A defeated sigh escaped between those beautiful lips. "It's sort of a passion of mine. I started in high school."

Lacy had a passion for drawing? He never had any idea she'd taken up sketching as a pastime. Why wouldn't she mention anything?

"I didn't see you draw anything at the lake." Had she not wanted him to see?

The same rose color filled her cheeks again. "You sort of distracted me."

"You didn't seem to mind."

She put down her wine. "Regardless. Anyway, I guess I changed my mind about drawing that day. It was kind of nice not having anything to do."

Their food was delivered on contemporary, square plates. Lacy picked up the black cloth napkin and folded it across her lap. A set of plastic-wrapped chopsticks sat beside their flatware in case they wanted to be authentic. Lacy bypassed those and stabbed her fork into some tempura chicken. Her delectable lips closed over the chicken, then slid to the end of the fork as she pulled it out of her mouth. Long, black eyelashes swept down over her eyes as though she'd eaten a piece of gold.

"Aren't you going to eat?" Lacy asked.

He blinked himself out of his trance and shook his head. "What kind of stuff do you draw?" he asked after stirring his beef in with the white rice that came with his dish.

"Mostly landscapes and architecture. Sometimes I'll do animals. I tried doing people, but that's not my strong point."

"So, what happened?"

She paused with the fork in front of her mouth. "What do you mean?"

"I get the feeling this is what you planned on doing with your life. But something stopped you. What was it?"

Her gaze ran across his shoulders before she inserted the fork in her mouth. When she swallowed, she said, "It started in college. I got so overwhelmed with my studies and working and other things that my grades slipped and I lost my scholarship. I couldn't afford to pay for school out of pocket and neither could Ray, so I had to drop out." She stopped when he blinked at her. "You don't look surprised by that information."

He shrugged. "Brody told me you had to leave school."

"Big mouth," she muttered. "Anyway, I had to get a full-time job to keep paying for my apartment and my sketching sort of got put on the back burner." She scooped some rice onto her fork. "I even tried getting a job in an art gallery so I'd have my in, but nobody wanted a college dropout with no experience."

"So you gave it up completely?" That didn't sound like the Lacy he knew.

A chunk of silky hair slid over her shoulder when she shook her head. "No, I still draw every once in a while. And it's still my dream to sell my drawings in a studio. But after Ray got sick, I put all my energy into him and I've been stuck in this rut ever since."

He picked up his wineglass. "Have you tried any of the galleries here in Cheyenne?" There had to be someone out there willing to give her a chance. Even though he'd never seen her work, Chase had a feeling Lacy was good at what she did.

"A few." She pushed a few pieces of chicken around, then finally stabbed her fork into one. "I always get a polite 'thanks but no thanks.' On a positive note, your meddling brother has convinced me to reserve a booth at the art festival in October."

"Brody?" he asked, surprise lacing his voice.

Of course, dumb-ass. What other McDermott would she be talking about?

She nodded and swallowed her food. "Every year he

tries to get me to participate, and I don't know, I guess I've been too scared."

"What made you change your mind?"

"If I'm going to be serious about having a career in art, then I have to start getting myself out there."

He set his fork down and leaned back in the booth. "Why do you doubt yourself? I'm sure you're better than you give yourself credit for."

The corners of her mouth turned up. "That's what Brody always says. Maybe this year will be my break." She shoved her plate away and leaned back. "I can't eat anymore."

"You want some dessert?" he asked after finishing off his own food.

"No way," she replied with a shake of her head. "I'm so full I could puke."

Chase grinned at her honesty. No woman he'd ever been out with had talked about puking. They'd always been too busy showing off their assets or coming off as sophisticated and glamorous. Lacy didn't have a vain bone in her body. There was no extra agenda to end up in bed. She was content to have a nice dinner out with a friend.

Their waiter was efficient and exchanged plates for their check. Chase shook his finger at Lacy when she reached in her purse to pull out money.

"Let me at least give you money to cover the wine," she tried to protest.

He'd already handed the waiter his credit card. "What kind of guy would I be if I ask you to dinner then make you pay?"

"You're not making me do anything. I want to pay."

"If it's that big a deal to you, you can get the next one," he said a short time later when they were in his truck.

Lacy leaned her head back against the headrest and closed her eyes. "There's going to be a next one?"

He kept his eyes on the road. "Didn't you enjoy yourself?"

"Very much. The food was great."

"Then why wouldn't we do this again?"

She didn't say anything for about a minute, so Chase thought she'd fallen asleep. "It feels too much like dating."

"And you don't want to date?" Why did the woman always keep everyone at arm's length? "Why can't we just be two friends who have a casual dinner every once in a while?"

She lifted her head off the seat and pinned him with her emerald eyes. "Because you know it'll be more than that."

They passed a sign announcing the Trouble town limits. Chase took a turn off the highway and headed back to town. "What're you so afraid of, Lace?"

Her finger skimmed along the leather stitching of the armrest. "I'm not afraid, just cautious."

"Not everybody has plans to abandon you," he said quietly.

His statement only earned him silence, which was how they spent the rest of the ride back to her house. Lacy was a talker but only about things she was comfortable with. Bring up family dynamics or fears of being alone and she threw the old familiar wall right back into place. That was okay. The complexities of Lacy Taylor were something well worth the amount of patience it took to know her.

The porch light by her front door gave off a weak yellow illumination. The fixture looked like it was a hundred years old and sat crookedly on the wood shingles.

Lacy climbed out of the truck before Chase had a

chance to pull the door handle. Did she plan to beat him
to the front door and let herself inside before he could
even say good-bye?

To his surprise, she didn't. After unlocking her front
door, she turned to face him.

"Dinner was really nice. Thank you," she said with a
tight smile.

Yep, those walls were firmly back in place. "You're
welcome." The porch light made her blond hair look like
a halo around her head. Her skin had a creamy glow to it
and Chase wanted to run the back of his hand down her
cheek. Then he remembered his promise not to touch her
and jammed his hands in his pants pockets.

"Will I see you tomorrow at work?" he asked when she
didn't move or say anything.

"I don't have to work again until Thursday." Her tongue
darted out and touched her lower lip. His dick swelled to
twice its normal size when her attention focused on his
mouth.

"Don't look at me like that," he said in a near-growl.

She tilted her head to one side. "How would you like
me to look at you?"

He took a step closer to her. "Like you don't want to get
into my pants."

"You're extraordinarily sure of yourself," she mur-
mured, but didn't back up when he got close enough for
her breasts to brush his chest.

He broke his promise not to touch her and placed
his index finger under her chin. "No, you're just very easy
to read." Then he dropped his hand and turned to walk
away.

The front door opened and closed behind him. Little
Miss Twiggy was flustered. The knowledge that he could

at least crack that unbreakable wall of hers had him smiling the whole way home.

She'd been caught red-handed. The evidence was as damning as it was surprising. At first Chase thought he must have been seeing things. Then Anita had rewound the tape so they both could gape at the footage.

Becky-Lynn had been one of McDermott's most dependable and reliable waitresses. True, the girl was always a little quiet and on the shy side. Since he'd known her, she'd never displayed any suspicious activity or given him reason to look twice at her. With the exception of her calling in sick recently, there'd been nothing strange about her behavior.

"I'll go get her," Anita said in a solemn voice before leaving the office.

He felt exactly as she sounded. This was the ugly side of the job and one Chase hated. No pleasure could be taken from firing someone. And unless Becky-Lynn had a really good, reasonable explanation for what he and Anita just watched, her ass was grass.

Upon first viewing, the footage looked almost exactly the same as the one with the other waiter taking potatoes and stuffing them in a bag. However, when Chase questioned the boy about it, he'd had an excuse for what he'd done. Apparently it had been a busy night and Phil asked the waiter to grab some potatoes from a bin. Not something Chase would have considered, as under normal circumstances the sous-chefs didn't use the waitstaff to run errands. The story hadn't been so outrageous that Chase wasn't inclined to believe the kid. When Phil corroborated the story, Chase and Anita dismissed the incident as nothing.

The door to his office opened and Anita stepped inside, followed by Becky-Lynn. The college graduate was a cute girl. Her short, dirty-blond hair always hung down and brushed her shoulders. Her makeup was usually understated, which enhanced her youthful look. But the girl who stood before him now looked like Becky-Lynn's worn-out sister. Her hair, pulled back in a messy ponytail, closely resembled the color of dishwater. Pale skin, accented by a smattering of freckles across her nose, stretched tightly across her face and puffed beneath her eyes. It was a wonder her appearance hadn't scared off half her customers.

"Anita said you wanted to see me," Becky-Lynn said when she came to a stop in front of his desk.

"Yeah," he said, and pulled one of the chairs away from his desk. "Have a seat." When she lowered herself at a snail's pace to the chair, Chase picked up the remote to the television. "There's something I need you to watch."

The screen flickered to life and once again showed Becky-Lynn entering the kitchen. Chase and Anita stood back while Becky-Lynn watched herself take a dinner roll off a tray that had just come out of the oven and stuff the whole thing in her mouth. Next, she removed two more and shoved them in the pocket of her pants, all while no one around her noticed. In a matter of ten seconds, she'd managed to basically steal three rolls, then stroll out of the kitchen without anyone being the wiser.

When Chase stopped the DVD, what was left of the color in Becky-Lynn's face had completely drained. Her tired-looking eyes were round and unblinking.

"I..."

"Didn't expect us to catch you?" Chase supplied when her thin, soft voice trailed off.

Her throat muscles worked in rapid succession and she lifted her blue eyes to his. "I was going to tell you. I've just been trying to work up the courage because I feel really guilty. But I swear it won't happen anymore."

Yeah, a likely story and one guilty people always told when they didn't want to get into trouble.

"Do you have a reasonable explanation for this, Becky-Lynn?" Anita asked.

Becky-Lynn turned in the chair to focus her attention on the assistant manager. "I have an explanation but I don't know if you'll think it's reasonable."

Chase crossed his arms over his chest. "Why don't you start from the beginning?"

FIFTEEN

T HURSDAYS WERE USUALLY PRETTY BUSY at McDermott's, but tonight at least half the tables sat empty. At ten minutes after seven, Lacy figured it was pretty safe to say they wouldn't be getting a whole lot of other diners. Not that she minded. Normally Lacy thrived on the hustle and bustle that dominated the dining room. But the lack of customers made her pounding head and unusual fatigue easier to bear.

After tossing back two painkillers about an hour ago, her headache lessened to minimal pressure in her skull. As for being tired...she didn't have an explanation for that. She'd slept a good ten hours the night before and now felt dead on her feet.

"Are you okay?" Diane asked as the two of them waited at the pass for their dishes. "You don't look so hot."

Lacy ran a hand across her perspiration-coated brow. "Yeah, I just have a mild headache."

"I have some Tylenol in my bag," Diane offered as she drummed her fingers on the stainless-steel counter.

"I took something already. Maybe it hasn't been long enough to take effect."

A flushed-face Henry hustled to the pass and set down two dishes. "You two gabbing like a couple of mother hens and hovering over me isn't going to make the dishes go faster. Why don't you go make yourselves useful by checking on your diners?"

Diane's heart-shaped mouth dropped open at Henry's orneriness. The head chef was in a bad mood tonight. Lacy had been informed by Becky-Lynn that the inventory count of zucchini hadn't added up. Henry had stormed from one end of the restaurant to the other with a thunderous look on his normally calm face.

"I bought five pounds of it at the market this morning," he'd said as if trying to work out the logic for everyone to hear. "Now there are only four and a quarter pounds. How does a whole three-quarters of a pound of zucchini just *disappear*?"

Becky-Lynn said Henry's face had been as red as a fire truck; then he'd disappeared up to Chase's office and hadn't come down for an hour. Phil had tried to reason with Henry and suggested the guy at the market had made a mistake. Henry only shook his head and produced a receipt, proving he had indeed purchased five pounds of zucchini.

The organization of the bins and walk-in refrigerator could make a general proud. Simply misplacing or losing sight of the zucchini among all the other stuff wasn't possible. Ever since the zucchini caper, Henry had been snappy, impatient, and all-around unpleasant to work with. The sous-chefs had barely said anything other than the necessary words to their head chef.

Diane took her dishes without a word from Henry and did an about-face to the dining room.

Suzanne placed a steak dish in front of Henry, which

he inspected by sticking his finger in the middle. A heavy sigh exploded from him when he jabbed the pan back at Suzanne. "The order was for medium-rare. That's rare. Do it again."

The assistant chef knew better than to argue. Muttering, "Yes, Chef," she marched back to her station and replaced the steak in the oven.

Henry wiped away the beads of sweat along his rust-colored hairline, using a towel he kept slung on his apron. Outbursts from Henry were few and far between. The staff had learned to deal with them when they came and stay out of the chef's way. Lacy was pretty thick-skinned and knew Henry's verbal attacks were more out of frustration and weren't personal.

Without so much as a glance at her, Henry practically tossed the plates on Lacy's tray.

After delivering her dishes, Lacy retreated to the break room to eat her dinner. She'd just tossed her instant meal in the microwave and settled down with a magazine one of the other employees had left at the table when Becky-Lynn walked into the room.

Several chunks of lackluster hair had slipped free of her sloppy ponytail. Deep, crisp wrinkles patterned her white work shirt, which wasn't tucked into her black slacks. Becky-Lynn's eyes were bloodshot and dull.

Lacy set the magazine down when Becky-Lynn sniffed and stopped in front of her locker.

"Are you okay?" Lacy asked when the other girl sniffled a few times.

"I have to leave," Becky-Lynn said in a thick, low voice. "Chase just fired me."

The metal chair scraped across the floor when Lacy stood. "He what?"

With a shaky hand, Becky-Lynn pulled her purse out of her locker. "I don't blame him. What I did was wrong. But I thought maybe he'd just reprimand me and send me home for the night. Now I don't know how I'll pay for prenatal care."

"What're you talking about?" Lacy asked after she placed two hands on Becky-Lynn's defeated shoulders. "You're pregnant?"

The younger girl turned her tear-filled eyes to Lacy. "I have to go."

"Wait a minute." Lacy tried to stop Becky-Lynn before she walked out of the room. "What did you do?"

The muscles in her throat moved up and down. "I'm not supposed to say. It was nice working with you, Lacy." She pulled out of Lacy's grasp and left the break room.

"What the hell?" Lacy asked the empty room. Surely Becky-Lynn wasn't the thief Chase sought out? The girl wouldn't do anything like that. And she was pregnant? Was Chase aware that he'd just put a young, pregnant girl out on her ass?

Her microwaved chicken enchiladas sat forgotten as Lacy left the room and headed upstairs to Chase's office. This was *so* not proper waitress protocol, questioning one's boss. But Becky-Lynn was a solid server and surely deserved another chance. She ignored her common sense and opened the door to Chase's office without knocking.

Inside, the man in question sat behind his desk with Anita standing on the other side. They both turned their heads to look at their uninvited guest. Fully aware that Anita stood right there, Lacy said, "You fired Becky-Lynn?"

Chase held his hand up. "Not now, Lacy."

Once again she ignored common sense and stopped in front of his desk. "No way do you think Becky-Lynn is the one who's been stealing?"

"You know about that?" Anita asked, then tossed an accusatory glance in Chase's direction.

Lacy kept her eyes on Chase. "You're making a mistake by firing her."

Thick, dark brows pulled low over thunderous blue eyes when Chase stood from his chair. "I said not now. Anita and I have this handled."

Lacy jabbed her hands on her hips. "Really? Because it doesn't seem like it."

Okay, wrong thing to say. The muscles in Chase's square jaw ticked as though he ground his teeth to enamel dust. With slow, deliberate steps, he rounded his desk and stopped in front of her. "Go back to work," he ordered through gritted teeth.

Her chin shot up in the air. "Not until you promise to give Becky-Lynn another chance."

Before she could so much as squeak a protest, Chase placed his two big hands on her shoulders, turned her around, and marched her to the door. Then he lowered his mouth to her ear and whispered, "You're going to pay for this later." A not-so-gentle shove placed her on the other side of his door a second before it slammed shut behind her.

Yeah, she probably should have thought that through before speaking her mind. Poor, poor Becky-Lynn had looked so lost and defeated that something inside Lacy had turned ugly. The girl deserved to have someone stand up for her. This had to have been a misunderstanding. Lacy couldn't help but think that Chase jumped to conclusions and fired Becky-Lynn to get his father off his back. The girl didn't deserve to be anyone's scapegoat.

A deep growl vibrated low in her belly. Her chicken enchiladas didn't seem so appealing considering she'd thrown up her last two chicken dishes. Was it possible to develop a food allergy to chicken halfway through one's life? Lacy had never heard of such a thing. Maybe the chicken she'd eaten at the restaurant with Chase a few nights ago hadn't been cooked all the way and that's why she'd gotten sick that night. She supposed it was possible. Like an automaton, she marched back down the stairs, went through the kitchen, and entered the break room again.

Inhaling her dinner gave her a chance to clear her confused head. Although she stood by her judgment that Becky-Lynn was most likely innocent, Lacy conceded she shouldn't have confronted Chase like that. Especially in front of Anita. It'd been unprofessional and rude. Once again she'd fallen victim to her habit of acting without thinking first. Now Chase was mad at her and swore she'd pay for it later. Whatever the heck that meant.

"Gross," she muttered, and tossed half her uneaten instant dinner in the trash. The enchiladas had been rubbery and drenched in grease, a combination that had her stomach turning over on itself. TV dinners were far from five-star meals but *jeez-louise*. "I don't think I can handle any more upchucking," she said to herself before walking back to the dining room and finishing her shift. Luckily for her stomach and her headache, which had never fully diminished, the rest of the night passed relatively quickly. For the next two and a half hours, Lacy took orders, delivered dishes, and pocketed generous tips.

Not long before she clocked out, Chase reappeared from his office but neither of them said a word to each other. Fortunately for her, Anita was still there to review

Lacy's orders for the night and log her tips. The hard set of his mouth and lines of tension above his eyes told Lacy that Chase was in no mood to converse with people. With the exception of Henry and Anita, Chase got away with keeping to himself until closing. Not that she minded. Lacy wasn't exactly in the mood to exchange words with him either.

After walking into her house through the garage door, she paused long enough to drop her purse on the kitchen counter. During the drive home, her headache had returned with a vengeance, along with a dull ache in her lower back. The only thing Lacy could figure for the backache was that her old tennis shoes had finally bitten the dust. Maybe she ought to pick up a new pair that had better shock absorbency.

She dragged her tired bones down the hallway to her bedroom and snagged a bottle of pain reliever out of the bathroom. Even though she'd already conceded wrongdoing in Chase's office, Lacy still felt like she owed him an apology. The look on Anita's face had been enough to let Lacy know she had been out of line. Chase had taken a chance on telling her something he shouldn't have. Not only had she made herself look like an idiot, but she'd also made Chase look like a blabbermouth. The last thing Lacy wanted was to breach the trust between Chase and his assistant manager.

On the other hand, Lacy couldn't help but feel like Becky-Lynn had been wrongfully fired. True, Lacy didn't know the circumstances of the girl's situation. Over the past few years, she'd seen plenty of other members of the staff given second chances after messing up. In Lacy's opinion, everyone deserved a second chance. Unless what Becky-Lynn had done was beyond unforgivable.

Could the girl be the thief Chase and his father sought? A nagging feeling in the pit of her stomach told Lacy that Becky-Lynn wasn't that person. Of course, that feeling could also be from the inedible dinner she'd had. Something about those enchiladas hadn't set right with her.

After tossing back the two pain pills, Lacy sank on the edge of the bed and toed off her sneakers. Definitely time for some new shoes. Her little piggies were an unattractive shade of red and her lower back throbbed like someone had kicked her with a steel-toed boot. On the upside of her pain, she'd earned almost two hundred dollars in tips. Yes, sirree, that was a good night indeed. First thing tomorrow, she'd go out and get herself a good-quality pair of walking shoes.

Boris hadn't been fed all day, so Lacy changed out of her work clothes and went back to the kitchen. The dog currently indulged himself in his favorite pastime: snoring like a B-52 bomber. Most people wouldn't be able to sleep with all that racket; Lacy had learned to ignore it years ago. Boris didn't so much as twitch a toe when she dumped leftover beef stew in his bowl. Whatever. He'd get around to eating it eventually.

With no more chores for the night, Lacy padded barefoot to her bathroom and brushed her teeth. Following that, she gave her face a good scrubbing with cleaner and smeared on some moisturizer. The red numbers on the bedside clock glowed 11:30 when she slid herself beneath the cool, clean sheets. *Ahh, nothing beats a big, soft bed after a long day.* Her heavy eyelids had just dropped closed when a furious pounding on the front door had them flying open. Her heart just about punched a fist-sized hole through her rib cage and she shot to a sitting

position. She held her breath for a few seconds as she listened to the house. Nothing, not even the dog or the sound
or her faulty air-conditioning. She sighed and slid back
under the covers when it happened again.

Bam, bam, bam.

This time she jumped out of bed and stood motionless as though her late-night visitor would come barrel-
ing through the door at any moment. To assure herself no
ax-wielding murderer waited outside for her, Lacy walked
to the front door and peered through the peephole.

When she saw her visitor, every bone in her body
melted and she leaned her forehead against the door.
When the wood shook under Chase's thudding fist again,
she squealed and jumped back.

Of all the nerve…

"What the hell is wrong with you?" she demanded
when she yanked open the door.

The thunderous look in Chase's narrowed blue eyes
said he wasn't a man to be messed with right now. But
jeez, he'd just given her a mild heart attack by his
not-so-subtle late-night call. She supposed since she was
the one who'd been rudely jerked out of bed, she deserved
some sort of explanation.

The angry yet gorgeous man on her doorstep pushed
his way past her and yanked the door out of her hand. He
slammed the thing shut with a loud crack.

"What are you doing?" she demanded again when he
towered over her.

He took one step closer and pointed his index finger
in her face. "Don't ever question my authority in front of
another employee again."

She swatted his hand away. "Get your finger out of
my face. I'm sorry for barging into your office, but I

stand by what I said. I don't think you should have fired Becky-Lynn."

"Apology *not* accepted."

She jammed her hand on her hips. "You came all the way down here and forced me out of bed to tell me you don't accept my apology?"

He stepped even closer to her so their torsos brushed together. "You don't know anything about the situation. You were way out of line."

"I said sorry for that. But"—she held up a finger when he opened his mouth to reprimand her again—"I know enough to know you're jumping the gun for no other reason than to get your father off your back."

The muscles in the corner of his jaw clenched as his gaze drilled into hers. "I never should have said anything to you. You're too damn headstrong to keep your opinion to yourself."

Her chin lifted in defiance. "No one put a gun to your head and made you tell me anything. At least I'm being honest."

He jerked back from her. "And I'm not?" he asked loudly enough for Boris to raise his head off the floor.

"How seriously are you taking this thief thing?" she countered.

"I fired Becky-Lynn, didn't I?"

"Based on what?"

"Oh, I don't know." He placed a finger on his chin as though thinking. "Based on the video that caught her red-handed *and* the fact that she admitted to it."

Huh? Had Lacy totally misread the situation? Or was there something else going on she didn't know about? Perhaps Chase was too pissed off at her right now to let her in on anything else.

"I see that shut you up," he said when she didn't reply to his announcement. "Still think I should give her a second chance?"

"Well, I don't know, Chase. Don't you think everyone deserves a second chance? Where would we be as a society without second chances?"

His blue gaze ran over her. "That doesn't sound like the hard-ass Lacy I know. Did you give *me* another chance?"

She held up a finger. "First of all, I'm not that much of a hard-ass." At least not intentionally. "And second of all, what you did was pretty bad."

He threw his hands up in the air. "I didn't *do* anything. You want to know what I think? You needed a reason to bail and took the first opportunity you got."

"I beg your pardon? Don't you dare turn that around on me. I'm not the one who had my underwear floating all over town."

"This has nothing to do with my underwear and you know it," he said as he closed the distance between them again. "You got restless and scared."

The fact that he was partially right was completely beside the point. The fact that he'd figured it out...that's what astounded her. That, and the fact that he stood close enough so his body heat wrapped her in a warm blanket of delicious masculinity. She wanted to be mad at him. In fact, she was. Furious. Being dragged out of bed at this late hour and yelled at by someone who looked good enough to lick was not something she appreciated. The combination made her feel all discombobulated and out of sorts. The only thing Lacy felt comfortable with was being in control. And she most absolutely, without a doubt was not in control of her uneven pulse. Thanks to the man standing in front of her.

Chase continued even though she stood there and hadn't countered his accusation. "You had a good thing going and got freaked out that it would blow up in your face."

"Well, you could say it did."

He poked at her again. "Because *you* allowed it to."

Again, she pushed his finger away. "I didn't allow anything. It just happened, because shit always happens to me. That's why it's better for me to be alone."

"Because you're afraid," he said.

Her teeth ground together. "That's the second time you've said that and it didn't go down well the first time."

"Then just admit it, Lacy."

She stood on her toes, hoping she had a prayer of being eye level with him. "I am not afraid," she bit out through her clenched teeth. "If anyone is scared, it's you."

"What the hell do I have to be scared of?"

"You're afraid to talk to me."

One of his dark brows lifted. "*I'm* afraid to talk to *you*?"

"Why is it whenever I ask you about college, you evade the subject?"

He took a step back from her. "Why are you so interested in my college years?"

It was her turn to get in his face and jam a finger at him. "I told you things that I'm not proud of, things nobody else knows. Do you think I like admitting I had to drop out of school and take dead-end jobs I hated? Those are things that aren't easy for me to talk about. But when I asked you about college, you gave me nothing."

"That's because nothing happened."

"I don't believe you."

His eyes darkened even more.

"You're hiding something and for some reason you're afraid to tell me. Am I the only person you've kept this from?"

His lips barely moved when he spoke. "It's nobody else's business."

"So there is something," she concluded.

He threw his hands up in the air. "You seem to be so sure there is."

"I *know* there is. You willingly gave me information about the restaurant you shouldn't have and yet you can't talk about a few years at school? It's the one subject you clam up about." She stepped closer to him and poked him in the chest. "You're the one who's afraid, Chase, and until you tell me—"

Her words were cut off by his mouth crushing down on hers. One of his hands slid underneath her hair and wrapped around her neck. Her hand, which had been up against his chest, was pinned between them when Chase wound his other arm around her waist and yanked her flush against him. Because Lacy had no willpower where Chase McDermott was concerned, her mouth immediately opened underneath his to allow his eager tongue inside. The man flat-out knew how to kiss. His tongue did a skillful little dance around hers, then darted in and out before he tilted his head to change the angle. Lacy managed to wrench her arm from between them and then dipped the tips of her fingers beneath the waistband of his slacks. His butt cheeks were hard and smooth beneath her hand. Chase reciprocated the move and molded both his large hands over the cotton material covering her bottom. He always had a way of touching her that felt like absolute pure heaven. Every time his hands came so much as a foot from her skin, her heart gave a predictable triple beat, like Pavlov's dog salivating at the sound of a bell.

Within the next nanosecond, he'd spun them around and had her perched on the edge of the entryway table. The table wasn't very big and barely managed to hold her. She had to scoot to the very edge and hold on to Chase's shoulders. The sneaky bastard had probably done that on purpose. Once he had her comfortably situated, his mouth left hers and traveled down her neck. She willingly tilted her head to one side so he had the most access possible. His hot tongue left a deliciously wet trail from her ear to her collarbone. How did he know just the right spots to spark lights dancing behind her eyelids? After their first time together, he'd already memorized all her erogenous zones and how to work them *just* right. And apparently she had a lot of them. More than she ever thought possible. The man ought to be awarded a master's degree in the art of pleasuring women.

She attempted to return the favor by grabbing two fistfuls of his shirt and pulling the hem out of his pants. Once she had the shirt free, she ran her hands underneath, up to his chest. He really did have the most amazingly fantastic pecs, sculpted and smooth but with a soft, thin layer of hair that tickled her fingertips. Her favorite thing had been to lay her cheek over the hair and savor the feel of it against her skin. She circled her index fingers around his nipples and smiled when the points puckered.

Chase tore his mouth off her neck and stepped out of her reach. "You infuriate me," he said on a growl, then yanked her shirt over her head.

He infuriated *her*? Lacy couldn't make sense of her thoughts when he touched her.

Once her shirt hit the floor, his masterful hands

grabbed the ends of her shorts, slid them down her legs, and tossed them aside with an impatient flick of his wrist. No way did she want to be the only one clothed; plus, she really loved a naked Chase. Without bothering with the buttons, Lacy shoved the shirt up his chest and ripped it over his head. Then, with shaky hands, she undid his slacks and pushed them down his legs. His penis, magnificently long and thick, pointed directly at her. Unable to wait a second longer, she wrapped one hand around him and squeezed. *That* got his attention. A deep, chesty groan vibrated up through his throat and his eyelids dropped closed. Just to torture him a bit more, she glided her hand over the silky skin of his shaft. The memory of this powerful organ inside her sent the same shivers through her that went through Chase. Just as she got a good rhythm going, Chase shoved her hand away and grabbed her hips with his hands.

A startled gasp left her lips when he pulled her almost off the table and entered her with one long, deep stroke.

"Chase, the bed—"

"Too far," he said when he withdrew and slammed himself back in.

Her panting turned into a cry when his pelvis bumped up against hers, creating a breathtaking friction against her sweet spot. The rickety table wobbled beneath the force of Chase's powerful hips. Lacy felt incredibly vulnerable hanging halfway off the table; the only thing holding her up was where the two of them joined. To remedy that, she braced one hand behind her and wound the other around his neck. After a few slow but enthusiastic pumps, Chase's pace grew faster and more vigorous. Lacy lifted her hips in perfect synchronization to his, then dropped her head back to let out a low cry when the base of his shaft hit *just* the right spot. He took advantage of her exposed neck and placed openmouthed kisses just below her ear. Warm, swift breath fanned across her skin when he rammed against her with enough force for her elbow to buckle. The unexpected loss of support startled her, making her slide the rest of the way off the table. Lacy had no idea how he did it, but somehow Chase managed to react quickly enough to keep her from falling on her bare ass.

With the skill of an acrobat, he held her up while managing to stay inside her. She sucked in a shallow breath, when his arm pulled her hips closer to his. The strange move he pulled to keep them joined was almost like having an out-of-body experience; he actually moved deeper into her. Her head dropped to his shoulder and she moaned against his skin. The next thing she felt was wood against her back when Chase lowered the two of them to the floor. He shoved her legs farther apart with his knees and she took the invitation to lock her ankles around his lower back. Once they had a comfortable position established, his hips resumed their pumping. After about four hard, deep pumps, Lacy's inner muscles started contracting as her orgasm broadsided her with the force of a category-five hurricane. Her fingernails scored into the steely muscles of his shoulders and her eyes drifted shut. The feel of his iron thickness dragging against her sensitive, clenching flesh had her letting out a high-pitched cry. The pleasure of it all was almost too much for her to take. For a second, Lacy thought she might have actually blacked out.

Immediately following her orgasm, every muscle in Chase's body coiled tight like a snake; then he groaned low and deep against her throat.

SIXTEEN

"D O YOU REALLY THINK I MADE A MISTAKE firing Becky-Lynn?"

Three days after their confrontation in the front hall of her house, they were still discussing this. "Yes." Lacy didn't look up from the drawing in her lap. Her pencil curved over the paper with a deliberate slowness as she tried to re-create a photo of a full-grown bull moose she'd taken at Yellowstone years ago. So far she'd gone through two versions of the photo before scrapping the drawings. Problem? Chase kept distracting her.

"Tell me why," the man sitting at the foot of the bed demanded.

A weary sigh flowed out of her. She dropped her pencil to the paper and lifted her attention to him. "Because she's a kid who made a mistake and I think she deserves a second chance. Don't you?"

He pulled the last piece of pizza out of the box and shoved it into his mouth. The man could put down food like a dang horse. "Thievery isn't tolerated at McDermott's," he answered after swallowing. "Do you have any idea what my father would say if he found out I didn't fire the person who'd been stealing from us?"

"I really don't think Becky-Lynn is that person. She ate a dinner roll for crying out loud."

"And then proceeded to shove three more in her pants pockets."

Okay so that part was a little more difficult to explain. Surely the girl had a good explanation for that?

"What did she say when you confronted her?"

Chase shoved the last bite of pizza in his mouth. "Are you going to eat these?" He gestured to the two pizza crusts on her discarded paper plate. Lacy shook her head. "Becky-Lynn is pregnant."

She slowly lifted her eyes to his just as he crammed half the crust in his mouth. "I know."

Chase licked his fingers and grabbed the last crust. "You know?" When she didn't respond, he shook his head. "Apparently she was feeling extra nauseated and needed something to eat to prevent her from throwing up all over the dining room. According to her it was a one-time thing."

"I still have a hard time believing it. She's what, twenty-one?"

"Twenty-two."

She shook her head. "Exactly why you should give her another chance."

One of Chase's thick brows flew up his forehead. "What kind of example would I be setting if I brought her back after she stole from us?"

"No one would have to know." She set aside her drawing and stacked her feet in Chase's lap. "Becky-Lynn was one of your best waitresses. I know she made a bad judgment call, but I really think you should give her one more chance. If she messes up again, then fire her. For heaven's sake, Chase, the girl is pregnant. Don't add unemployed to her list of troubles."

"Her pregnancy isn't my problem," he said as he wrapped a hand around her ankle and pulled her foot to the center of his lap. Her heel rested on the manly part of him, which was covered by a pair of soft gray boxers. Neither of them had bothered with much clothing since forcing themselves out of bed long enough to order a pizza. Chase had hastily pulled on his underwear for no other reason than to keep the delivery boy from reporting him for indecent exposure. The closest thing to his bed had been the tank top Chase had thrown on the floor. After digging her underwear from the depths of the sheets, she pulled the top on in time for the pizza box to be dropped on the center of the bed. For the past half hour, the two of them munched on pizza and shot the breeze about varying topics. She'd refused to listen to her stomach and had unwisely shoved two pieces of pizza in her mouth. Her insides had been turning over on themselves ever since.

"Okay, I know you're not that insensitive," she said, returning to the subject at hand. Hey, he asked for her honest opinion. Lacy had never been one to sugarcoat her feelings.

"Maybe I am," he said with a wicked tilt of his mouth.

She settled deeper in the sheets and leaned her head against the backboard. "You're a closet sensitive, Chase." When his blue eyes narrowed, she giggled. "You pretend to be tough, but on the inside you're all mush. Ow," she complained when he pinched her baby toe. "You can deny all you want but I see right through you."

"See, I don't think you're thinking clearly."

The grin remained on her face when he skimmed his thumb along the arch of her foot. "I can't imagine why."

"Do you want me to stop?"

"Depends on where you plan on going with this." The man had never-ending stamina. Lacy had barely been able to keep up when he'd roused her from a light slumber and turned her over on her stomach. Sleep was something she valued above anything else. When Chase's hands floated to her hips and lifted them, Lacy had only been able to sigh in contentment. The groan he let loose in her ear had traveled through her nerve endings down to where their bodies joined. Lacy had never experienced anything like that. Being taken from behind while Chase buried his face in her neck had made for an intensely erotic orgasm, one that had left her unable to handle any more for at least a few hours. He'd taken pity on her by letting her grab another hour of sleep before ordering the late-night pizza. While she thought food would calm her stomach down, all that grease had left her feeling...odd.

The man seated at the foot of her bed had sensed her stomach issues and grabbed a bottle of Tums from his bathroom. They'd helped enough to the point where she'd been able to settle back in bed comfortably.

"I think you've had enough for one night," he concluded when her eyelids grew droopy.

"I think I probably agree with you."

Several hours later, the room was draped with the inky blackness of a moonless night. Lacy had drifted in and out of sleep for Lord only knew how long. Chase shifted and turned over just as many times as her, leaving the sheets a tangled mess around their legs. After settling in a semicomfortable position on her side, Lacy blinked into the darkness and willed sleep to take her tired body. Just as her eyelids swept down over her eyes, Chase shifted again and folded one arm behind his head. A soft sigh filled the quiet space of his room.

"What's wrong?" she asked when she realized he joined her in non-slumber land.

"Just thinking."

She rolled onto her back next to him and stared at the ceiling. "Don't stress over the Becky-Lynn situation. You were right about setting an example to the employees."

"I wasn't thinking about Becky-Lynn."

She turned her head on the pillow and glanced at his handsome profile. "What's got you so restless, then?"

He was silent for a moment before answering. "Something I've been keeping to myself for a long time."

Though this was what Lacy desired most from Chase, a little honesty, the tone of his voice had the hairs on the back of her neck standing up. Things that were intentionally buried were never good topics of conversation. Certain unsettling events in a person's life were usually left undiscussed for a reason. Lacy ought to know. She had a very good one named Dennis Taylor.

Not even a hair on Chase's body moved. His gaze bore into the ceiling as though looking directly at whatever plagued his mind. A sudden heaviness had settled over them, making the skin on the back of her neck itch.

"What is it?" she finally asked.

"My college girlfriend."

A thick, tense pause filled the air around them. His college girlfriend? Was he serious? Didn't he know that mentioning a woman, especially an old flame, while in bed with another one was enough to have his naked ass kicked out the door? The man certainly had balls; she'd give him that. But why now? Why, after how many years after the fact, would he be thinking about some girl he dated in school?

"I'm not reminiscing about good times, if that's what you're thinking," he reassured her after he took his attention off the ceiling and placed it on her.

"Of course not." She tried not sounding flippant but failed.

He rolled onto his side and slid some hair over her shoulder. "We dated for a little over a year and were thinking about getting an apartment together off campus."

An unwanted burning sensation developed in her chest. Lacy tried to tell herself it was more heartburn but even she wasn't that delusional. "Don't need to hear all the details."

"Jealousy is very becoming on you, Miss Taylor." He flicked her nose.

She swatted his hand away. "Go on with your story."

"Are you sure?" The uncertainty in his voice sent her heart all aflutter. No way in heck could she fall in love with him. Her sanity couldn't afford that sort of head-over-heels tumble.

"Will it help you sleep?" she asked after forcing her voice to come out normal.

One corner of his delectable mouth tilted up. "Only one thing will help me sleep."

She resisted the urge to roll her eyes. "I'm out of commission for a while after that last time."

"Wore you out, did I?"

"Most undoubtedly," she said with a slight grin. "And I'm sure, by the way. So keep going."

His bare chest puffed when he inhaled a deep breath. "She had an abortion without telling me."

For the first time in . . . well, Lacy wasn't even sure how

long she'd last been at a loss for words. Her speechless-
ness made it difficult for her to determine which issue
to address first: the fact that Chase had never told a soul
about this, yet decided to clue her in, or how in the world
his girlfriend could do something so deceitful and hurtful.

She exhaled and pillowed her arm beneath her head.
"How did you eventually find out?"

"I found out a week later through a mutual friend.
Needless to say, I ended the relationship."

Chase's expression was unreadable due to the lack of
light, but his hushed voice held a twinge of regret. "Why
would she tell you about the pregnancy if she was planning on aborting it? That seems a little unnecessary, not
to mention cruel."

His soft chuckle lacked humor. "The cruel part
probably never entered her mind. As for telling me, well,
she said the abortion was a spur-of-the-moment decision
when she realized having a baby was the last thing either
one of us needed. I told her she didn't have the right to
make that decision for me—then I stormed out of her
dorm room."

His thick shoulder was tense beneath her hand. "I'm
glad you said that to her. Most guys would have been
relieved or not even cared."

"I can't say I wasn't relieved but I was furious as hell
that she did that behind my back. Looking back now"—
he lifted the shoulder beneath her hand—"it was probably
the right decision."

Did Chase not want kids? Did he not see himself as a
father one day? "What makes you say that?"

Silence was her answer for a moment. "Before that
happened, I hadn't exactly been a model student. I was
going nowhere fast. But after..." His eyes closed for

a brief second. "I was hit with a large dose of reality. I stopped the all-night partying and got my ass in gear."

No matter how much Lacy thought she knew about Chase, he'd whip something else out and blindside her with all sorts of surprises. In fact, the lack of predictability in him was one of the things she loved most about him.

Love?

Oh, hell.

She cleared the lump out of her throat. "Why did you never tell anyone?"

Like before, he waited before answering. The knuckle of his index finger ran over her collarbone, then dipped down between her breasts. The caress was whisper-light but powerful enough to send waves of shivers along her skin.

"I didn't want to give them a reason to be disappointed in me," he finally answered.

Well, what do you know? Chase really *was* all mush. His I-don't-give-a-damn attitude toward everyone in his life was nothing more than a smoke screen. Despite what she thought about him, he had just as many deep scars as she. While most of the town knew about hers, Chase kept his under lock and key.

Without a word, he rolled from the bed and stalked across the bedroom, completely unabashed of his own magnificent nudity. "I shouldn't have told you any of that," he muttered before disappearing into his bathroom.

As she lay in bewildered silence, the shower in the bathroom turned on. Jeez, the man went from hot to cold in less time it took Boris to fall asleep. And Boris fell asleep *really* fast.

So, Chase had told her something he hadn't even told his own family. Why? Maybe he'd been feeling especially chatty and needed to get that burden off his chest. Or, the more desirable option, he felt she was special enough to share something he couldn't tell anybody else. Yeah, in a perfect world. More than likely she was nothing more than a good lay to him. No, she refused to think of herself that way. He had to feel something more than that.

Dammit, her heart went out to him. He'd gone through a difficult situation at a young age. Someone he may or may not have been in love with betrayed him on the deepest level possible. And he'd dealt with all that alone. Lacy, more than anyone, knew what it was like to feel utterly alone. No one to spill your troubles to or understand how those troubles kept you awake at night. How had he handled the outcome? He'd focused on what needed to be done and made something of himself. He'd finished college and now ran a successful restaurant.

Without asking him to, he'd confided in her. What had she done? She'd laid there and let him pull away from her. And now he was in his shower. Alone.

Just like he'd been before.

Determination had her tossing the covers aside and walking to the bathroom. A cloud of steam greeted her when she opened the door. With a stealthy silence, she tiptoed across the floor, grabbed a handful of the shower curtain, and peeled it back far enough to step in. Chase had his back to her with all the cords of muscle pulled tight and bunched together. His hands were braced on the wall above him and his head hung down between his shoulders. Her heart practically cracked open at the defeated sight of him.

He lowered his hands from the wall and, as though sensing her presence, turned his head and looked at her over his shoulder. Something close to sadness darkened his blue eyes.

Lacy placed a hand on his shoulder. "I'm sorry," she whispered.

Water ran down over both of them and plastered their hair to their skin. Steam swirled around their two wet, naked bodies. The muscles in his jaw clenched when Chase reached a hand out and then snaked his arm around her waist.

She went to him as though she had no choice in the matter, because really she didn't. All he had to do was glance at her and she practically melted. Her breasts smashed against his wet chest. His powerful thighs, dusted with soft hair, brushed against her softer, feminine ones. She wound her arms around his neck as he buried his face against his shoulder. They remained that way for a long time, holding each other in a silence only two people comfortable enough with each other could do. As the water ran cold, Lacy no longer could deny that she was totally and completely head over heels in love with him.

"I'll come visit you on one condition."

Lacy held her cell phone to her ear with one hand and used her free hand to turn the steering wheel. Megan had called her about five minutes ago just as Lacy had walked out of the framing store with a sack full of frames and matting for her drawings. The two of them had chatted about their summers while Lacy drove through town and headed back home.

"Okay, what's your condition?" Lacy asked as she turned down her heavily tree-lined street. Mrs. Pratt had her head buried in her bright pink azaleas and two little boys rode their bikes down the street, enjoying their last two weeks of summer before school started.

"You have to read Mom's letter."

Dang it, Lacy just *knew* Megan was going to say something like that. The letter had sat forgotten on her dresser for almost three months now. At one point she'd almost tossed the letter without even opening it. No sense in irritating old wounds, right? Her mother had left for greener pastures, in essence shaping the person Lacy had become, and there wasn't a damn thing she could do to change that. Lacy didn't give a flying rip about her mother's so-called sentiments or explanations. They were twenty-five years too late.

"I know you don't want to," Megan continued as though reading Lacy's cynical thoughts. "But I think you need to. And don't take this the wrong way but you're a little bit on the jaded side. I know you care, even though you say you don't."

Lacy hit the button on the garage door opener when she pulled into the driveway. "It's not that I don't care. I just"—she sighed and dropped her head back to the headrest—"I'm still not ready."

"Are you ever going to be ready? It's like a Band-Aid. You've got to just get it over with. Look"—Megan's voice dropped to a softer tone—"what Mom did to you was pretty unforgivable. And, trust me, it's taken me a long time to accept that she actually did that. I just think you'll regret not reading it. I won't come see you if you don't."

"You drive a hard bargain," Lacy complained after pulling the car into the garage.

"Tough love, my dear sister. It's for your own good."

Shouldn't Lacy get to decide what was for her own

good? She wasn't used to people caring about her like this.

"Just promise me you'll try. School starts in three weeks."

Lacy turned the car off and tossed the keys in her purse. "I promise I'll try," she found herself saying. Megan had been just as much a victim as she and at least deserved Lacy's good word.

"Thanks. I'm late for my spinning class, so I've got to go. Call me next week and let me know."

Lacy disconnected the call, grabbed her bags, and walked into the house. Maybe she really did need some tough love. After all, her stubbornness at times served as her own worst enemy. Sometimes it really did take a relentless force for her to see the error of her ways. And she missed Megan. Lacy saw a lot of herself in the girl. They both had the same shade of honey-blond hair, both had their mother's green eyes. And both of them had been hurt by the woman who'd birthed them.

However, Lacy wasn't so stubborn that she'd refused to see her own sister because she couldn't bring herself to read a stupid letter. It wasn't like the letter needed to mean anything to her. They were only words written by a person who meant nothing to her. Now Lacy's reasons for ignoring the letter seemed childish and immature.

"Hey, buddy," Lacy greeted Boris when the dog came ambling through the kitchen. He must have been eating his leftovers and heard her open the garage door. Her ancient, semicrippled, partially blind friend was always there for her. She gave the dog an absentminded scratch behind the ears before carrying her purchases down the hallway.

Over the past week, Lacy had gotten her butt in gear

and finally selected her top pieces to display at the festival. All in all, she was pretty satisfied with her wide variety of drawings. Since the frames and matting were so expensive, she'd opted to frame about half of them, set a higher price tag for those, and sell the others "as is." The whole project of blowing up the drawings to a large portrait size and buying the framing had set her back a pretty penny. So much so that she'd decided to put off getting her hair cut for another few weeks.

She placed the bag of frames and mats on the couch in the drawing room and carried her other bag of purchases into the bedroom. On the way home from the framing store, she'd made an impromptu visit to the drugstore to pick up a few things she'd been running low on. She tossed a tube of mascara in the makeup drawer, placed a small bottle of vitamins in her medicine cabinet, and pulled a package of cotton balls out of the grocery bag. Just as she set the cotton balls inside the cabinet underneath the sink, her eyes landed on a light blue box of tampons.

An unopened box of tampons.

With a slight frown, she took the box out of the cabinet and set it on the counter. When had she bought these? It had been so long ago, she couldn't even remember. The tip of her index finger ran along the seam of the carton as she thought back. During her previous menstrual cycle, she'd used the last tampon she had. Because she hadn't wanted to be unprepared, she'd purchased another box the next day. How long ago had that been? Her stomach turned over and a fine sheen of perspiration coated her forehead.

Not being able to remember her last period was not a good sign. No way was this happening to her. Her heart slowly sped up to an unnaturally rapid beat. Lacy hadn't made a habit of keeping track of her periods with a calendar, but she walked to the pantry anyway and took the calendar down. With unsteady, sweaty fingers, she flipped the pages back several months, hoping to trigger her memory of her last cycle. It didn't help. She flipped the pages back to August. Only one week remained until September. She knew for a fact she hadn't had her period yet this month and was almost positive she hadn't gotten it in July. What about June? She turned back to May. She and Chase had spent two weeks together in May and had been broken up by June. Then they'd gotten back together in July. Now they were almost in September. Had she bled in June? Dammit, she couldn't remember!

The timing was too suspicious for her to write it off as an irregular cycle. Sometimes her cycles were off, but not that off. She simply couldn't ignore the fact that she hadn't had her period in at least two months, possibly three. How had she not noticed until now?

Fear and anxiety like she'd never known before made her hyperventilate. She turned from the counter and paced to the living room.

Okay, don't freak out. You need to think.

First of all, Chase always wore condoms. At least she was pretty sure he did. Was it possible there had been at least one time when both of them had forgotten? Immediately popping into her head were a few occasions back in May that had been especially hot and frenzied. One had been in this very living room where she currently paced a hole in the already threadbare carpet. They'd just finished sharing a bottle of wine when Chase had lowered her to the couch. If her memory served her correctly, he'd pulled a condom out of his pants pocket seconds before slipping into her. So, that couldn't be it. The second memory was from his kitchen. The whole thing had happened so fast, Lacy hadn't had time to catch her breath before he'd entered her. He'd given her one look, then lifted her onto the countertop. For the life of her, Lacy couldn't remember him rolling on a condom. Could that be it? Could that one moment of lust-filled, passionate insanity resulted in an unexpected pregnancy?

How could they have been so careless and stupid?

Telling herself not to freak out didn't work. Tears of helplessness gathered beneath her eyelids. Her trembling, clammy fingers swiped away the first of the moisture just as it slipped over her cheeks. Crying had become a nasty habit of hers over the past few months. When had she become such an emotional person?

Okay, maybe she was jumping to conclusions. Maybe Chase had used a condom and she simply couldn't remember. The only way to know for sure was to take a pregnancy test.

She made a mad dash for the drugstore and grabbed the first pregnancy kit her eyes landed on. Back in her bathroom, three pink plus signs confirmed her suspicion.

SEVENTEEN

T HANK YOU SO MUCH FOR GIVING ME another chance."
A single tear rolled over Becky-Lynn's puffy lower
eyelid. A week and a half had passed since the girl had
left work with her tail between her legs. True, what she'd
done was wrong and Chase had a feeling being fired
was a big enough lesson learned. However, when the
cash drawer had shown up twenty-five dollars short last
night, he realized his hunt for the thief was far from over.
Besides, Lacy was right. Becky-Lynn was one of his best
waitresses. The last week of August was always a difficult time to find extra help since all the college students
in town had returned to school. Chase figured since he
hadn't clued his father in on what happened with Becky-
Lynn, no harm had been done.

"Here." He handed her a tissue off his desk. "I don't
think your customers will be inclined to tip an emotional
waitress."

Her hitch-filled sniffle reminded him of a small child.
"Thank you," she whispered. "I promise I won't let this
affect my job. And I think I'm over my morning sickness,
so this shouldn't be a problem anymore."

He uncrossed his arms and straightened from the corner of his desk. "Even if it is, tell me and I'll do whatever I can to help you." He tipped her chin up to meet his gaze. "All right?"

She closed her red, puffy eyes and nodded. "Thank you."

"You'd better go clock in."

The girl walked out his office door, her long ponytail swinging and her shoulders held back.

Anita walked in a moment later. "You did the right thing," she announced after closing the door behind her.

"I think so too." Becky-Lynn had left a small pile of wadded-up tissues on his desk. Chase grabbed them and tossed them in the garbage can. "She just needed to be scared straight."

Anita nodded and pursed her thin, lined lips. "I agree. She's a good kid. Now that we have that situation settled, we need to go over what happened yesterday." His assistant manager pulled a folded piece of paper out of the back pocket of her crisp, black slacks. "I looked at yesterday's schedule and wrote down everyone who worked."

Just what he did not want to do. The only two upsides to this were the absence of his father and the fact that Lacy had had the day off yesterday. Not that he ever believed she had anything to do with the thefts. But her absence made him breathe a little easier. And the only bad thing to admitting fault to the Becky-Lynn situation was also admitting he still had a stealing problem on his hands.

"Okay, let's have it," he said as he lowered himself to the leather chair behind his desk.

Anita sat down and crossed one skinny leg over the other. "Well, the obvious ones are you, me, Henry, and Phil. The rest of the kitchen staff yesterday was Suzanne, Bryn, and Eric. The waitstaff, including lunch, was

Robert, Chelsea, Diane, Lenny, Matthew, and Christina. Then we have the hostess, Claire, and the dishwasher-slash-busboys Andrew, Nate, and Darryl, all of whom were in the general area of the cash drawer." Anita folded the paper back up. "Except for Claire, who remained in the front of the house all night."

"So we're able to eliminate one whole person." Chase pinched the bridge of his nose in order to dull the onset of a headache.

"Actually," Anita chimed in, "I think we can safely eliminate anyone who wasn't here yesterday. Including Becky-Lynn."

The woman did have a point. See, this was why Anita was so damn good. The two of them had always made a dynamite team.

Chase dug the heels of his hands into his weary eyes. He hadn't even stepped foot on the floor yet and he was already waist-deep in shit. The first hour he'd poured over yesterday's numbers thinking maybe, just maybe, he'd made a mistake when counting the drawer. Then he'd dealt with Becky-Lynn and her never-ending tears of gratitude. To top all that off, his father was supposed to make an appearance during dinner service tonight to take care of some paperwork. Keeping the Becky-Lynn incident from his old man had been easy enough. But Chase couldn't morally keep this mess from his father. Martin would have to know the restaurant was still having problems. And Chase would get no less than this shit hitting the fan when the time came.

USS *Martin* left quite a wake.

"I've got to get my story together before my dad comes in. All right," he said as he leaned his elbows on the desktop. "Who's coming in today who was here yesterday?"

Anita tugged on her pearl earring. "Aside from Henry

and Phil…Suzanne's got the day off, so Bryn and Eric will be here. Chelsea and Matthew are working lunch and Diane and Lenny will be here for dinner service. Claire is coming in tonight, too, and I think Darryl will be here as well."

Chase picked up the silver personalized pen his father had given him for his birthday last year and tapped it on the desk. "Here's what we're going to do. Tell each of them, including Bryn, Eric, and Phil, that I need to speak to them when their shifts end. But not together. I want to talk to each of them separately, so they'll have to wait outside my office."

"All right. But Chase…" Anita pursed her lips, a habit of hers when anxiety took over. "I really think you should talk to Henry too. I know you don't want to think he's the one behind this, but he's the only one who has a key to the cash." She lifted her narrow shoulders. "He's the most logical suspect."

Didn't he know it? Henry certainly made for an easy target but the fact wasn't any easier to swallow. Henry had been a loyal employee of McDermott's since Chase was in high school. And, as Lacy had pointed out, why would Henry start stealing now after all this time?

"Maybe you should let your father deal with him," Anita concluded when Chase didn't respond to her statements.

Chase shook his head. "No. I don't want my father thinking I can't handle this." Lord, Martin McDermott thinking his son was incompetent at his job was the last thing he needed. Chase had worked his ass to the bone for the past eight years trying to prove he could single-handedly run this restaurant successfully. And he'd done a damn good job, if he did say so himself.

His watch read 9:15. "Is Henry still in his office?"

When Anita shook her head, a strand of black hair slipped in front of her ear. "He's in the kitchen, prepping."

"Do me a favor and tell him I need to talk to him."

Anita slipped from his office without a word.

Anxiety had his muscles humming and vibrating like tight coils. To alleviate the tension from his overworked body, Chase bounded from the chair and stalked from one side of his office to the other. One thing that Henry had in his favor, and would most likely be his key defense, was the amount of time the chef spent in the kitchen. Rarely was Henry on the floor, as he didn't have any need to be. In fact, Chase couldn't remember the last time he'd spotted Henry someplace other than the kitchen or his office. So how would he have time to sneak out of the kitchen and take money out of the cash drawer without someone noticing? The waitstaff spent much more time around the cash drawer than anyone else. Any number of the people who'd worked yesterday would have had a much better opportunity to slip twenty-five bucks into their pocket. They often had to make change for those diners who paid cash for their meals.

Like Anita said, Chase needed to speak with Henry if only to eliminate him as a suspect.

Chase plowed a hand through his hair and walked back to his desk.

What if the unthinkable happened and something had snapped inside Henry, forcing the man to steal from a place that had employed him for fifteen-plus years? How could Chase bring himself to let the man go? Henry was someone his father and his stepmother, Carol, considered a family friend. He was also an absolute genius in the kitchen. His New York strip practically melted in a person's mouth.

Henry was just as much an integral part of McDermott's success as Martin McDermott. The man was practically indispensable.

"Anita said you needed to speak with me."

Chase's head whipped around at the sound of Henry's voice. The chef's crisp white uniform was already stained with various shades of orange and red.

"Have a seat, Henry."

The other man closed the door with a soft click and lowered himself to a chair facing Chase's desk. The russet-colored Fu Manchu that graced Henry's full upper lip looked like it had been recently snipped to perfection. The hair on his head was a different story. The darker brown strands curled over the top of Henry's ears like he hadn't bothered to comb his hair after showering.

"I read over the specials earlier and they sound good." *Why the hell are you stalling? Just get this over with.*

Both Henry's thick brows pulled together. "You told me that already. That's why I went ahead with prep work."

Chase ran the tip of his index finger along the edge of his desk. "You're right, I did." *Now you're not even thinking before speaking.* "Okay, here's the thing," he plunged in before having second thoughts. "Someone's been stealing from the restaurant, including the cash drawer. Every once in a while, money comes up short at the end of the night. You, Anita, and I are the only ones who have access to the drawer."

Silence stretched between the two men. "And?" Henry asked. Deep lines of tension speared across his forehead. "Are you asking if I'm the one who's been taking money?"

"I'm just trying to get to the bottom of this." Chase leaned back in his chair.

Henry's whiskey-colored eyes turned hard. Then the frown on his face broke into a grin. "I have to be honest with you, Chase. I'm pretty shocked you'd even consider me a suspect. Your father pays me way too much money for me to resort to stealing."

Wasn't that the truth? Henry's paychecks were only a fraction smaller than what Chase earned. Chase lifted his hand off the desk. "I know that. But you have to understand where I'm coming from. I wouldn't be doing my job if I didn't consider everyone."

"Have you talked to Anita? She has just as much access to the cash as I do. And when was the last time you saw me in the front of the house?" Over the course of the past minute, Henry had scooted his average frame to the edge of his seat, as though ready to pounce on Chase should any accusations be tossed about.

"Actually, I have considered Anita. The problem with that is she's been absent on days when money has gone missing." Chase lifted one shoulder. "I've had to eliminate her."

Henry's face relaxed as he leaned back in his seat. "I'm the only one who's here every day."

Chase dropped his gaze to the desk. "That's a fact I can't ignore."

The chair Henry had been sitting in tumbled to the floor when the man shot to his feet. The action took Chase so off guard that his heart just about beat a hole through his rib cage. "How about the fact that I've been a loyal employee here for longer than you? Or the fact that your father is one of my best friends?" Henry's complexion turned from a milky white to fire-engine red. A bluish purple vein bulged beneath the skin of the man's sweaty forehead. He planted tightly balled fists on the surface of Chase's desk. "I can't believe you'd accuse me of stealing."

Chase didn't like to be looked down on by anyone. He slowly pushed to his feet. "Technically, I haven't accused you of anything. I'm trying to do my job by exploring every avenue. I wanted to eliminate you as a suspect so I could breathe a little easier."

The muscles in Henry's jaw bunched beneath long sideburns.

Chase pulled in a deep breath and told himself not to react to Henry's unusual temper. "Do you think I wanted to consider you were the one stealing? That's the last thing I wanted."

Air flowed rapidly in and out of Henry's flared nostrils. Then he straightened and ran his thumb over his facial hair. "I apologize for that. You know me well enough to know I don't ever lose my cool like that."

"I know."

"I just…" The chef turned from the desk and walked to the opposite wall. "This place is like my home." He turned back to Chase. "Martin is like a brother to me. After what he went through when your mother died, and struggling to get this place off the ground—" Henry's words broke off when he shook his head. "I have way too much respect for your father to ever steal from him. For a brief second, I thought maybe you actually believed I was a thief."

Chase walked around his desk and placed a hand on Henry's tense shoulder. "I never really believed that. But I have to be fair and talk to everyone."

"I understand. And, again, I'm sorry for losing my temper like that." He clapped a hand on Chase's back. "You're a good GM, Chase."

"Thanks."

"I'd better get back to my prep work. I was behind already." He turned and walked toward the door, then paused with his hand on the knob. "You want my opinion? Take a closer look at Diane."

"You can't possibly be serious with this color." Courtney, bless her outspoken, imaginative heart, held a paint sample up and tossed it down on the coffee table. The little card landed on top of a growing pile of colors his sister had eagerly vetoed. Courtney was the most creative person he knew. He'd asked her to help him pick out some colors for the new addition to his upstairs. So far she'd hated every single one.

"And what the heck is this?" She held up a tan sample. "They ought to rename this one Baby Poop. Where did you find these? Ugly Paint Colors 'R' Us?"

Chase leaned back against the couch and stacked his hands behind his head. "They're all very popular colors, Court."

A snort popped out of her pink lips. "Yeah, if you have no imagination." She twisted on the couch to face him. "Why don't you give me a blank check and I'll surprise you."

"Not a chance."

Her hands slapped down on her bare knees. "Why not?"

"Because I'll end up with an exercise room the same shade of hot pink as this." He tugged on a strand of her short, spiky hair.

One of her thin eyebrows lifted. "Now you're saying you don't like my style?"

No one dared insult Courtney Devlin. "Hot-pink hair is one thing. Hot-pink walls are just wrong."

She tossed the paint sample on the table. "Fine, be boring." Her too-thin shoulders slumped over.

He nudged her elbow. "What's got you all pissy?"

"Nothing," she said to her knees. "It's my mother. She's driving me crazy." His sister surged off the couch. "First she complains that I'm not out on my own. Then she says I need to give them rent money. I mean, hello?" She lifted her arms in the air before letting them flop down to her sides. "How am I supposed to save up for a place of my own if they're going to charge me rent?"

"Did you say that to her?"

She tossed a droll look over her shoulder as she paced to the fireplace and back. "Of course. Then she said we could work out a deal." Court made quotation marks in the air with her fingers. "I'd only have to pay a hundred dollars a month plus buy my own groceries, which I'd have no problem with because I can't stand all that fatty red meat and soda she buys."

Courtney's eyes bounced over pictures of Chase's mother.

"I told you before you'd be welcome to stay with me. I have three other rooms."

Her nose ring twinkled when she wrinkled her nose. "I really don't want to listen to my brother's bumping and grinding at all hours of the night. But thanks anyway."

He chuckled at her honesty. "And listening to our parents bumping and grinding is better?"

"Parents don't bump and grind. That's common knowledge."

"No, that's childhood fantasy."

Her blue eyes shot daggers at him.

"What about R.J.?" he asked around a smile.

"I barely made it through my teen years without killing him. I don't want to go there again, thank you."

Chase held his hands up in defense. "Pardon me." Man, she was touchy today.

Her hands were planted on her thin hips as she floated from one side of his living room to another. "I'll figure this out on my own. I always do. In the meantime"— she twisted her wrist and dropped her gaze to her thick, lime-green watch—"I have to get to work. On my way home I'm going to pick out some paint and you're going to like it."

He stood and gathered the discarded paint samples. "The room's not even built yet."

"Regardless. It's never too early to make decisions." Her sandals flapped across the wood floor. "Um, Chase?"

"Yeah?"

Courtney stood in front of one of the windows with her attention outside. "Why is Lacy Taylor pulling into your driveway?"

Little details never slipped past his sister's notice. She was one of those people who could walk into a crowded room and notice a hairline crack on a far wall. He had no earthly clue how she did it. Maybe it was that freak-ish intuition women always bragged they possessed. Either way, he could feign nonchalance but she'd see right through it. And who cared if she did? Lacy was the one who wanted to keep their affair as secret as the real iden-tity of the *Mona Lisa*.

Instead of answering, he slid his hands in his pockets and leaned against the wall next to her.

She narrowed her eyes at him. "There's something sus-picious going on here, and I'm going to find out what."

He only grinned.

She jabbed a finger at him. "You don't fool me, Chase." She brushed by him in a flurry of huffiness and let herself out the front door. The woman was like a damn fortune-teller.

Lacy glided up the walkway in a pair of light gray cotton Capris and a plain white T-shirt. A friendly open-mouthed smile broke across her face when she approached Courtney. The two girls engaged in an extended mushy hug that most women do when they see each other. Why did women always act like it'd been a lifetime since exchanging a conversation?

Chase lounged against the open doorway and waited for Lacy to finish talking to his sister. Lacy's brilliant green eyes lit on his, then roamed down his body when she approached him. His predictable dick stirred and hardened when she drew near. Her shiny hair hung free over her shoulders. He gave in to his impulse and tunneled his hand underneath the soft curtain of strands. She melted into him when he pulled her toward him and slanted his mouth over hers.

She traced her index finger over his lower lip. "What was that for?"

"I couldn't help myself." *And because I am just so damn happy to see you.* When was the last time he'd been this pleased to see a woman? Never. What made Lacy so different?

Chase had a feeling that whatever "it" was very closely resembled love. Only one other time in his life had he allowed himself to fall in love with a woman. He'd walked away with a broken heart and a promise to never let himself fall under a woman's spell again. Lacy, with her sexy, kissable lips and soft touch had him wondering if he'd fallen yet again. The fact that he didn't know for sure had the skin on the back of his neck itching. In the past, he'd always been able to define his feelings for a woman. Now he floated around in a sea of uncertainty.

He closed the door behind Lacy, just as Courtney backed out of the driveway, and led her into the living room.

"What's all this?" She picked up one of the samples from the table and held it up in a ray of sunshine that spilled in through one of the windows.

"Paint colors for my new exercise room."

Her arm lowered and she pinned him with a look. "You've decided to take my advice about an exercise room after all?"

The smugness in her voice had his mouth turning up in a grin. "I think so. I picked those up on a whim a few days ago. Courtney was here giving me her blatantly honest opinion on them."

"Let me guess, she hates all of them."

He closed the distance between them and tucked some hair behind her ear. "Very vocally so, yes."

Her tongue darted out and ran along her lower lip when his hand curled around the back of her neck. "I didn't come here for a quickie," she said when he skimmed his lips over her jaw and nibbled her ear.

"I'm not asking for one," he whispered.

Her blunt fingernails dug into his shoulder. "You're doing a pretty good job of showing me you do."

Well, hell yeah, he was always up for a quickie. However, over the past few months, Lacy had become more than a convenient screw. The postcoital bliss spent talking about meaningless things was what he'd come to cherish the most. And Chase had never been that postcoital guy. He'd always been more of the "okay, thanks for the great time, but I need to be going" kind of guy.

Something about Lacy made him want to spend that time with her. He wanted to talk about her childhood and hear about her college years. He wanted to watch her teeth bite into her lower lip when she flew her pencil over a sketch pad. Did that mean he was in love with her?

Her hands shoved at his shoulders, which pulled him out of his thoughts and away from her lush curves.

In the span of about a minute, her shoulders had gone ramrod straight and her hands twisted in circles around each other. She paced away from him and stood in front of the wall that housed several photos of his mother. Her chin lifted and her shoulders pulled back.

"What's wrong?" he asked after she'd gone from hot to freezing cold.

Her eyes darted over one photograph after another. She remained silent for so long, Chase thought she wasn't going to answer him.

"I'm pregnant," she finally replied.

For the first time in his life, he didn't know what the hell to say.

EIGHTEEN

S AY THAT AGAIN?"
Lacy turned from the pictures and pierced him with those green eyes that always went straight to his heart. Without a word, she dug into her purse and pulled out an envelope. Her feminine little fingers trembled when she handed the envelope to him.

With this heart jackhammering up in his throat, he practically tore the envelope when he took out a fuzzy black-and-white picture. In the middle of a sea of blackness was a white, kidney-bean-shaped...thing. Was that supposed to be a baby?

"What's fifteen weeks?" he asked after trying to read all the little computer information in the corner of the photo.

"That's how far along I am." Lacy's voice sounded distant, as though he'd drifted out of his living room and viewed the two of them from far away. Was this what an out-of-body experience felt like? If so, he didn't like it one damn bit. In fact, he'd rather roll over a bed of nails than feel his heart beat like a bass drum in the bottom of his stomach.

Then Lacy's words finally fought their way through the cloud of anxiety in his brain. "Fifteen weeks? That's like…" He did the math in his head, slower than he'd be able to calculate it under normal circumstances. "You've been pregnant since May? It's September. How the hell long have you known?"

She snatched the photo back from him. "Calm down. I found out last week, but I didn't see my doctor until yesterday. I wanted to be completely sure before I told you."

He plowed sweaty hands through his hair and turned away from her. "Fuck. How the hell did this happen?" The words were meant for his ears only. After stalking halfway to the kitchen, he turned and faced Lacy. "How the hell did this happen?" The question came out more forceful than he meant it to. His uncertainty and bewilderment leaked into his tone.

Lacy's light brown eyebrows pulled together over her troubled eyes. "What do you mean, how did this happen?"

"I mean we always used protection. So I'll ask you again, how did this happen?"

Her bare lips pursed. "If I didn't know any better, Chase, I'd say you're blaming me."

He mentally counted to ten in order to rein in his temper. "I'm not blaming anyone. I'm trying to figure out why you're standing here telling me you're pregnant when I used protection."

"I bet if you think really hard, you'll be able to figure it out." She lifted a hand and gestured behind him. "Remember a little incident in your kitchen about four months ago?"

Hell, there had been several incidents in his kitchen. The one she referred to that occurred in May didn't ring any bells. Except… well… he did have a vague memory of not being able to keep his hands to himself. In a feverish move, he'd lifted her onto the countertop and dropped his pants practically all at once. But he'd slipped on a condom, hadn't he? Oh hell, maybe he hadn't. How had that not crossed his mind? Okay, he knew damn well how. He'd been so hot to get inside Lacy and feel those trim thighs around his hips that thoughts of protection hadn't even occurred to him.

This is what you get for thinking with your dick: another knocked-up girlfriend.

All right, he could handle this. He wasn't the same immature, inexperienced kid he'd been in college. When Allison told him she was pregnant, jittery nerves had taken control of his sensible thinking. Without so much as an encouraging word to her, he'd left her standing in the middle of his dorm room while he'd driven around town. Abandoning her like that probably hadn't been the best way to assure her he could handle having a baby at the ripe old age of twenty. Perhaps his departure was what propelled her to abort the child. He would not freak out on Lacy the same way he had Allison.

"I can tell by the look on your face that I've triggered your memory." Lacy's soft voice pierced his thoughts.

Jeez, he was stupid.

"I'm due in February, in case you're wondering." Her light sigh filled the silence between them. "Look, I don't want anything from you, okay? I didn't tell you to trap you into anything. I was just trying to do the right thing because you have a right to know. You don't need to feel obligated to me in any way."

He held the photo up for her to see. "This is my kid. Of course I'm obligated." Then he blurted out the next words before he could stop himself. "Marry me."

Her eyebrows shot up her forehead. "What?"

Nothing made sense. At the moment he couldn't make heads or tails of his own thoughts. He didn't know which way was up or down. He only knew he wanted to be with Lacy.

He only knew that he loved her.

"Chase, we're not getting married," she answered with a shake of her head.

"Why not?"

She tossed her hands up in the air. "Because we don't love each other," she said with exasperation.

He closed the distance between them. "How do you know I don't love you?" Damn, the woman had zero self-esteem.

Her blond hair flew around her shoulders when she whipped back toward him. "Do you?"

He set the photo down on the table next to them and wrapped his hands around her shoulders. "Maybe I do."

"*Maybe* is not an answer." Her small hands gave him a hard enough shove that he took a step back from her. "I don't want you to marry me because you feel obligated or because you *maybe* love me." She snatched the picture off the coffee table and shoved it with trembling fingers back into the envelope.

"Lacy..."

She sidestepped out of his reach. "I wanted to do my part by telling you. I didn't think it would be fair to keep you in the dark about this."

"I appreciate that but—"

She stopped in front of the door and turned to face him. "I don't want a last-minute marriage proposal tossed out because of a baby. I want someone to marry me because they can't live without me. I want someone to respect and cherish me the way I deserve."

"You can't just show up here, tell me you're pregnant, and expect me to know exactly what to say." His feet ate up the ground between them. "You've had a week to get used to the information. I've had about five minutes."

"Which is exactly my point. You're not thinking clearly." She yanked the door open and early afternoon sunshine spilled in. "Think about what you want out of this. Until then, I don't think it's a good idea for us to see each other."

Her sexy, curvy hips swayed under her thin cotton pants when she practically ran back to her car. Dammit, she wouldn't even give him a chance to explain himself. He didn't need time to think. He needed to tell her he loved her. Why hadn't he just said so instead of stumbling over his words like an incompetent moron?

And why did she always have to leave like that?

"I really appreciate your help with this," Lacy told Brody again.

"I'm glad I could help. It's taken you long enough to make a decision about this." Brody sat next to her at her kitchen table, making a list of local churches and charities. "But here's your one problem." He kept his attention on the list in front of him. "This is a large amount of money, so the bank is going to put a hold on the check for up to a month."

Lacy paused with a spoonful of chocolate mousse halfway to her mouth. "A month?"

"Banks are finicky people who tend to want to cover their bases. Chances are they'll let you have access to about a hundred dollars. But the rest of it, they'll let you have in small chunks over the course of several weeks."

She wrapped her lips around the chocolate dessert, then swallowed. "But it's my money."

Brody set the pen down and drilled her with his gray eyes. "I know that. But they don't. They need to verify the income before they'll let you take it out. You can't deposit the check and then turn right around and withdraw the entire ten million. For all they know the check could be a forgery and you just screwed them out of a large chunk of money."

Her shoulders slumped over, mousse forgotten. "So I can only have a hundred dollars?"

"For now." He turned his attention back to his list. "After the funds have been verified, they'll only let you take out a few thousand dollars every five or six days."

Her spoon scraped along the bottom of the container until she'd consumed the last of the chocolate. "It'll take me a year to withdraw the money at that rate."

"Probably."

Well, wasn't that just the greatest thing? She finally made a decision about what to do with this money and she wouldn't even be able to *do* anything with it. After her less-than-successful encounter with Chase, she'd returned home and thrown herself a little pity party. Her one guest, Boris, had faithfully stuck by her side when she'd resorted to her predictable pacing. Jittery nerves had her feeling restless, almost as though she'd hung on the precipice of an anxiety attack. In order to feel like she had some semblance of control over her life, Lacy had made an executive decision about her inheritance. She'd made a hasty phone call to Brody and asked him to help her come up with possible organizations to donate the money to. As tempting as ten million dollars was, Lacy couldn't morally keep the total sum for just herself. She'd come up with a figure that would allow her to renovate the house, buy a new car, and set money aside for the baby. The rest of the dough would be better served in the hands of the community.

There were undoubtedly a lot of people out there who could use the help, namely kids. The thought of anyone wanting for anything the way she had made her heart twist. Lacy would do everything she could to make sure others in need had the best life possible. With this money, she now had a way of doing that and wasn't about to waste one penny of it.

After coming to a satisfying decision, Lacy had shoved her conversation with Chase, along with his impromptu, completely unromantic marriage proposal to the back of her overworked mind. Sleep had taken over a short time later, allowing her to block the events of that day.

She stood from the table and disposed of her trash. "So after I deposit the check, I automatically get a hundred dollars?"

"If you want it." The rickety dining chair scraped along the wood floors when Brody stood. "You could probably set up some sort of automatic deposit with the bank and have them transfer the maximum amount of funds as soon as they become available." He set the list down on the counter for her to look at. "Here are all the local organiza- tions that could use the extra money."

Half a dozen churches, the Masons, a senior center, the youth club, and the local schools were what Brody had come up with. Lacy had a soft spot for youth centers, con- sidering she knew what it was like to crave a connection with other humans that gave a person a sense of purpose.

The youth center had been around as long as she'd lived in Trouble. Her father had never bothered to enroll Lacy in any of the activities, such as the drama program or summer camps. Being able to give something to children who didn't have that opportunity created a warm, tingly feeling around her heart.

"You did well with this."

"You could also just endorse the check over to whoever you want to have it," Brody said, ignoring her comment.

She leaned against the counter as he opened the fridge and took out a bottle of water. "But I don't want to give all the money to just one place. I want to spread it out."

He chugged several gulps, then lowered the bottle. "Then you'll have no choice but to wait until the funds become available."

Why couldn't banks be more customer-friendly? Okay, she understood the need to make sure she wasn't trying to defraud them. But only being able to withdraw a few thousand dollars at a time?

She nibbled her bottom lip. "All right. If I have to wait, then I have to wait."

He flashed her a crooked grin and ruffled the hair on the top of her head. "Good girl."

The chocolate mousse she'd inhaled hadn't made a dent in her never-ending hunger. She stepped around Brody and rooted in the fridge for something to curb her appetite. Thankfully, her days of tossing cookies seemed to be over, leaving her free to consume everything in sight without repercussions later on. Except gaining tons of weight, which she'd begrudgingly accepted.

"By the way, how was Kelly's wedding?" she asked, after grabbing a container of cottage cheese and a spoon.

"It was all right. I watched them exchange their vows, kissed her on the cheek, then left."

Her brows lifted up her forehead. "You didn't stay for the reception?"

Brody shrugged. "I stayed long enough for dinner. Then Tyler and I went to a movie."

She dug her spoon into the cottage cheese. "How does Tyler seem to be taking his mother remarrying?"

"He's good. He really likes what's-his-name."

She tried not to laugh at Brody's refusal to accept Kelly's new husband. No matter how much he denied it, he still had feelings for the woman. "You mean Collin?"

"Whatever."

"You don't sound the least bit jealous," she said after swallowing a huge mouthful and digging the spoon back in.

Brody's dark eyebrows pulled together. "Slow down, Lace. You'll get sick eating that fast."

"I think I'm going to give the bulk of the money to the youth center, then split the rest of it up among the churches and schools." She ignored Brody's comment. The last thing she needed was him becoming suspicious of her condition. After all, it was only a matter of time before her belly grew round enough for everyone to notice. Heck, some of her pants were already too tight. This morning she'd opted for cotton because her denim shorts wouldn't stretch around her thickened waist. She'd had to change out of the button-down shirt she'd put on, because the buttons wouldn't snap over her enlarged breasts. The things were so sore she'd barely been able to wash them in the shower.

On the other hand, guilt tore at her insides for not being honest with her friend. Brody was one of the few people in her life who knew all her fears, anxieties, and goals. Having an affair with his older brother that ultimately led to an unexpected pregnancy was something she couldn't share with him yet. Something told her he wouldn't take the news well.

"Are you sure you're leaving enough for yourself?" The question pulled her out of her guilt-induced thoughts.

"I think a million dollars is enough."

"You know, if it were me"—he glanced at their surroundings—"I'd sell this place and buy something new."

"But this was Ray's house."

He tilted his head. "It's not like Ray's still here."

No, but the memory of him is here and that's the only happy thing I have to hang on to.

"Lace," he said in a softer tone. "I know you don't want to let it go, but I think you'd be better off starting fresh."

But I want to raise my child here, was what she almost told him. Instead she replied with, "I don't expect you to understand, Brody. I was raised here. I'd rather fix it into something that would have made Ray proud."

He placed a hand on her shoulder. "Ray's proud of you no matter what you do."

Proud that she got herself pregnant? She doubted it.

Brody pushed away from the counter. "At the end of the day it's your decision. Just make sure you leave yourself enough to live comfortably."

"I promise I'll be okay." *At least I think I will.* She set the empty cottage cheese container aside. Had she really eaten all that? "You're such a good friend to me, Brody." Her arm went around his thick torso. "Thank you," she whispered. The familiar sting of tears gathered behind her closed eyes. Maybe all the crying bouts that had plagued her recently were a result of those pesky pregnancy hormones.

"What're you doing?" he asked, after stepping away from her. His thumb swiped a tear that trickled down her cheek. "You're not a crier."

"I don't know what's wrong with me." Technically not true. Man, she couldn't stand lying to him.

"We're all allowed to have a few vulnerable moments. Trust me, I've had my share over the past few years." He did her a favor and grabbed the empty cottage cheese container and tossed it in the garbage can next to the fridge. "You wouldn't be human if you didn't allow yourself to—"

The last of her tears got soaked up in the paper towel she'd grabbed when Brody paused and stood frozen by the side of the fridge. His gray eyes remained fixed on something pinned to the side of the appliance that faced the back door. Then it hit her and Lacy's eyes dropped closed. Last night after coming home, she'd absentmindedly stuck the sonogram picture underneath a magnet. The garbage can that Brody had meandered over to just happened to be on that particular side. Why, oh why did she not think of that? This was not how she wanted her friend to find out about this.

If you'd been honest with him from the beginning, you wouldn't be in this pickle.

Dammit, she hadn't been ready. She'd barely had enough time to get used to the idea herself before telling Chase. He, above anyone else, needed to know first. The emotional roller coaster she'd been on hadn't settled down long enough for her to start having that discussion with people. The "who's the father" questions she'd no doubt be hounded with weren't something she wanted to deal with. All she'd wanted was a little time before having to explain herself.

She stood rooted to the spot like the coward she was, while Brody took the photo off the fridge and examined it more closely.

"Something you want to tell me, Lace?" he finally asked, looking up from the sonogram.

She squared her shoulders and prayed for strength. "I was going to tell you."

"Are you really pregnant?" His gaze bore into hers.

Her heart pounded up into her throat. "Yes. I'm sorry I didn't tell you at first—"

"It's okay. You don't owe me any explanations. I'm happy for you."

She shifted her footing. "You are? You're not mad?"

He set the picture down on the counter and took a step closer. "Why would I be mad?"

"Because…" Well, now she felt like an imbecile. "Usually I tell you everything and I wasn't ready to start telling a whole bunch of people."

"It's all right," he reiterated. "The most important thing is, are you happy?"

Was she happy? She'd been so concerned with telling Chase about his impending fatherhood, trying to decide what to do with the money, and the upcoming art festival that her own happiness wasn't something she'd given a lot of thought to.

"I'm getting there," was the best she could come up with.

"I'll accept that," he said as he placed a comforting kiss on her forehead. "Not so fast." He stopped her when she turned away from him. "Who's the father?"

Shit. Okay, *this* she was not ready to talk about. Brody

could have all the pregnancy details he wanted but as to who fathered the baby . . . that subject was off-limits. Especially to the father's younger brother. "It doesn't matter."

"People always say that when it matters." He placed two gentle hands on her shoulders and turned her to face him. "This man's identity is none of my business. But whoever he is, I sincerely hope he plans on taking care of you."

Unwanted tears built up in her eyes again. "He wants to marry me."

"And do you want to be with him?" he asked as he blotted a tear away with her discarded tissue.

"Yes." Heaven help her, she did. For all his pigheadedness and stubborn ways, Lacy loved Chase. "Yes, I do want to marry him."

One corner of his mouth turned up. "Then why don't you?"

"Because I'm an idiot who has too much pride." Another tear slid past her lashes.

"I doubt that."

She pushed away from him. "No, I am. He asked me to marry him and I got mad at the way he asked. It was a stupid thing to get mad about."

"How did he ask you?"

"He just blurted it out like it was some last-minute decision. Like without me being pregnant, the thought of marrying me would have never occurred to him."

Brody stepped up behind her and turned her around again. "Let me explain something to you about men. We're not good with words. Put us in a complicated situation with a woman we have feelings for, and nine times out of ten we'll screw it up. Chances are he felt a bit overwhelmed and didn't know how else to express himself."

Her teeth bit into her lower lip. "I don't know."

"I think both of you just need some time to think. Do I need to kick his ass for making you cry?"

"It's Chase." The words came out in such a tumbling rush, Lacy hardly realized what she'd done until it was too late. The huge weight that had lifted off her shoulders made her feel like she practically hovered in the air.

Brody's dark brows slammed together. "*What's* Chase?"

She pushed away from him again and stalked into the living room. "I didn't want anybody to know at first. I thought if we kept it a secret it would, I don't know"— she lifted her shoulders and let them fall back down—"be easier."

Not even a hair on Brody's body moved. "Are you trying to tell me you slept with my brother and got pregnant?"

She bobbed her head up and down.

They stared at each other from across the room.

"I have to go," he blurted.

"Brody..." Her only answer was the slamming of the front door.

NINETEEN

CHASE RAN BLEARY EYES OVER THE NOTES he'd made of the employee interviews from the day before. With the exception of Henry's cryptic comment about taking a closer look at Diane, nothing even remotely suspicious jumped out at him. He'd kept the chef's words in mind when interviewing her. Admittedly, the perspiration that glistened on her forehead and the erratic tapping of her finger against her thigh were a little suspect. But they were hardly anything to slap handcuffs on her wrist for. The only thing she had going against her was her schedule. Aside from Henry, she was the only employee who'd been at the restaurant every time something had been taken.

On the other hand, Diane had been a loyal employee for the past three years. Why would she risk her job like that? She seemed as likely a thief as Henry. Though, her husband had been injured on the job and had been forced to take unpaid time off. He knew her family was strapped for cash due to their meager disability income. Anita had been good about giving Diane extra shifts in order to help the woman out. Was Diane the sort of person to stoop that low when desperation took over? With no hard evidence,

Chase only had speculation and mild suspicion, exactly the same thing he had several months ago when food first went missing.

The only thing he'd been able to suggest to his father yesterday was to install newer, more efficient cameras around the restaurant. Martin hadn't blinked an eye. "I'll get right on it," was what he'd said.

On an upside, Chase had been able to dismiss several employees as suspects, which pleased his father. As it stood, Diane was the only person of interest.

He shoved away from the dining table and went to change into his workout clothes. Maybe a good, pounding workout would help him figure out what to do about Lacy. He didn't need an MBA to figure out he'd completely blown it with her. The past twenty-four hours had given him time to reflect on the situation.

Did he see himself having kids? Sure, someday. But someday had always been in the distant future, not right around the corner. Nevertheless, that didn't change the fact that it had happened.

In hindsight, he'd realized he'd acted hastily in asking her to marry him. Lacy didn't want to marry anyone, least of all him. True, the two of them had had an out-of-this-world time in bed and got along great, and they were even going to be parents together. Did that mean they needed to walk down the aisle? Truthfully?

He didn't *need* to marry Lacy; he *wanted* to marry her. That much he was absolutely clear about. Lacy, on the other hand…he wasn't sure what she wanted. In fact, he wasn't sure even *she* knew what she wanted. Her unstable past had left her jaded enough to be wary of men. Chase had a feeling she'd lumped him in with all the other lowlifes who'd scarred her big heart.

After dressing in workout clothes, he went into the garage and set his treadmill on high speed. The pounding of the soles of his running shoes on the rubber surface echoed in his otherwise quiet garage.

Perhaps he needed to take a few days and let Lacy cool off. And, as Lacy wisely pointed out, he needed some time to figure things out too. He wasn't the sort of man who would default on his responsibilities. He'd take care of Lacy and his child by whatever means he could. If Lacy refused to marry him, then he'd do the next best thing by being as involved and active in the baby's life as he could.

Lacy was too good of a person to keep Chase from his own kid. She knew from firsthand experience what it was like to feel abandoned by a parent.

After a twenty-minute run, he shut off the treadmill and picked up his free weights. Thirty minutes of pumping iron did nothing to quiet his thoughts. He'd give Lacy until tomorrow. Then they'd resolve their issues.

In the meantime, he showered the sweat from his body, then went back downstairs to give his notes one last look-see. His father had requested a copy so he could make his own assessment of the situation. Chase had just made the copy from his printer/copier when someone kicked open his front door with enough force to make the wood crack back against the wall. He pounded out of the office to see who felt the need to ram through his front door like an eighteen-wheeler.

Brody's hard eyes glared at Chase. He stalked toward Chase like a predator, with his hands balled into white-knuckled fists and his eyebrows lowered like two angry, dark slashes. He was just about to ask Brody what the hell had jumped up his ass when Brody jabbed his fist out and tagged Chase right in the jaw. The whole thing happened so quickly that Chase didn't have time to react or dodge the punch. His head snapped back and the sharp, coppery taste of blood filled his mouth. Bright lights danced in front of his eyes and an instant, skull-cracking throbbing overcame his entire head.

Chase gingerly touched his mouth and came away with red on his fingers. The son of a bitch had bloodied his mouth.

"Nice shot," was all Chase could say. He worked his jaw side to side to make sure nothing was broken.

Chase saw the blue flecks in Brody's eyes when he took a step closer. "Of all the women in this town to screw, why her?"

His little brother had always had a fierce protective streak when it came to Lacy. It was like Brody didn't think Lacy could handle herself and he'd unofficially dubbed himself her bodyguard. Chase understood, even respected, Brody's big brother–like nature toward her. And if Lacy wanted to confide in her friend, that was her prerogative. But they were brothers for hell's sake.

Given the thunderous look on Brody's face, Chase decided playing dumb was not the wisest course of action. "I don't know what Lacy told you, but this is between me and her."

"You hurt Lacy, so now you have a problem with me," his brother said through gritted teeth.

Chase brushed past his brother. "That's very noble of you, but it's still none of your business."

Brody grabbed Chase's shoulder. Chase spun around and shoved Brody away. "Punch me again, and we'll have a real problem. And before you start lecturing me, I offered to marry her and she turned me down flat."

"She turned you down because you're an ass."

A snort popped out of Chase's mouth when he turned his back on his brother again. "I'm an ass because I tried to do the right thing?"

Brody followed Chase down the hall. "You know, you wouldn't even have to worry about this if you'd been thinking with your head instead of your dick."

"Is that what Dad said to you when you first brought Kelly home?"

Tense silence was his answer. Chase stopped in his tracks and turned around. The muscles in his brother's jaw grew hard like tempered steel. Thick, dark clouds practically swirled above Brody's neatly combed hair.

He jabbed a finger in Chase's direction. "The difference between you and me is that Kelly was never in love with me. But I wasn't blinded by my own love not to see the truth staring me in the face. And you're not an ass because you tried to do the right thing. You're an ass because you're letting her push you away."

With those pearls of wisdom hanging in the air between them, Brody stormed through the still-open front door.

Great. Maybe Chase ought to go piss off his neighbors so he could be on their shit list too. He scrubbed a hand over his coarse whiskers and gritted his teeth at the pain in his jaw. Such an outburst of emotion from Brody was rare. The youngest McDermott had always been as cool as a cucumber. Just what had Lacy said to him? Had she been all tears about how Chase was the big jerk who knocked her up?

She told him he hadn't been thinking clearly. While she'd been right, that didn't change the fact that he *did* want to marry her. His delivery had been a little unorthodox. How could he make her see he wanted to be with her, not out of obligation, but because he didn't want to live without her?

When Lacy returned home after her lunch shift, a white van with an air-conditioning company logo adorning the side was parked along the curb in front of her house. A short man with a receding hairline and a blue uniform slammed the back doors to the van and walked across her freshly mowed grass.

"What the heck?" she asked herself as she hopped out of her car in the driveway without bothering to pull it into the garage. Her tennis shoes crushed the short blades of grass when she followed the man to the side of the house. "Excuse me? What're you doing?"

Deep brown eyes encased in years of laugh lines stared back at her. "I beg your pardon? Are you one of the neighbors?"

"Am I—" Lacy shook her head. "No, I'm the homeowner."

The man returned to his task of whatever he was doing with her air-conditioning unit. "We're here to install the new air conditioner."

Okay, either she'd slipped into the twilight zone or someone was playing a prank on her. "I didn't order a new air conditioner." Although she needed to. The ancient one the man currently tinkered with had become obsolete.

"I've got the work order right here." He held a pink piece of paper between sausage-like fingers.

Lacy snatched it out of his hand and scanned the words down the page. Her eyes darted back up again and landed on one Chase McDermott. "Is it too late to cancel this?" As much as she understood Chase wanting to do something nice for her, Lacy had never been one to accept handouts. She certainly didn't need it. She now had more than enough money to purchase her own air conditioner.

"It's already paid for, lady. Take it up with the guy who placed the order." The man continued to show her the top of his thinning hair as he ran his hands around the unit.

She placed the pink paper down on top of the A/C unit and shuffled toward her front door. Chase had to know that she wouldn't sit back and let him do this without demanding an explanation.

Boris lifted his enormous head when she shut the front door. His droopy brown eyes gave her a once-over, then drifted closed again. Lacy tossed her purse on the kitchen counter, dug her cell phone out, and punched in Chase's number.

"Hello." His deep baritone sent a tidal wave of goose bumps from her hairline all the way down to her toenails.

She inhaled a deep breath to steady her uneven heart. "There's a man outside installing a new air conditioner. Care to explain that?"

"Think of it as a baby present."

A sigh flowed out of her. "Chase, you didn't have to do that. I can afford my own air-conditioning."

"I know I didn't have to. I wanted to. And before you start arguing with me and giving me your 'I'm used to being independent' speech, let me say one thing."

He paused and Lacy walked down the hallway to her bedroom. "All right," she said after a moment.

His voice dropped a notch when he spoke again. "First, I need to apologize for last week. I didn't handle the baby news very well."

She sank to the edge of her bed. "You handled it just fine."

"No, I didn't. I was shocked, to say the least. And you were right—I wasn't thinking clearly."

"I had just dropped a huge bombshell on you. You're allowed to be a little frazzled. And I wasn't exactly sympathetic either. I was sort of still getting used to the idea myself."

"I think it's safe to say neither of us got an A-plus for our actions. But I appreciate you being honest with me from the beginning." He paused. "That really means a lot to me."

Her fingers wrapped tighter around her phone. "I won't do to you what she did."

More silence. "I know."

Lacy dropped her gaze to the chocolate-brown shag carpet. "So, back to the subject at hand…"

His soft chuckle was like a warm caress down her back. "I would love to give you an opportunity to demand an explanation from me but the restaurant is crazy and I need to get back on the floor. I'll stop by after work and we can talk then."

He ended the call before she had a chance to reply. Well, *that* hadn't gone as planned. Then again, nothing during the past several months had gone according to any sort of plan.

She'd gained a sister, lost a mother, gotten her father thrown back into jail, had an affair with a man she liked but could barely tolerate, became a millionaire, got pregnant…what else was there? Oh, yeah. She'd tumbled head over heels in love with the same man who inspired both feelings of love and hate.

If that wasn't the picture of a life in chaos, she didn't know what was.

A knock on her front door interrupted her thoughts.

Lacy strolled out of the bedroom and opened the door to Mrs. Pratt. Lacy allowed the woman to enter so she could get some reprieve from the heat.

"Hi, hon," she said in a breathy voice. "I was just going door to door to let all the homeowners know the good news."

"What's that?" Lacy asked.

Mrs. Pratt ran a weathered hand through her thin, gray hair. "The blond man seen lurking around the neighborhood was arrested and thrown in jail. Turns out he was also wanted for some robberies too. And I saw something funny in the paper. The man they arrested looked suspiciously like your daddy."

Lacy knew precisely which article Mrs. Pratt referred to because she'd read the same one earlier that morning. Dennis had pleaded guilty to his charges, and they'd skipped a trial. Given it wasn't Dennis's first offense, the judge had slapped her father with the maximum sentence—fifteen years without parole. Turns out their neighborhood lurker had also been her father.

"Yes, that was him." Lacy had learned long ago to curb her embarrassment for having such a father.

Mrs. Pratt cupped a paper-thin, soft hand over Lacy's cheek. "Poor child. I never thought that man deserved you. Now you don't have to worry about him for a long time. Focus on taking care of that baby."

All the blood drained from Lacy's head. "What do you mean . . . ?"

The old woman made a *tsking* sound. "You think I don't know a pregnant woman when I see one? You have that look about you."

Lacy could only stand there, completely stunned, as Mrs. Pratt let herself out of the house. So much for keeping her condition a secret. The whole town would know by next week.

Later that night, as Boris settled back down on the floor and Lacy slathered on the last of her moisturizer, a soft knocking came from her front door. Her heartbeat picked up with each step she took down the hall until the organ was practically up in her throat. Would she ever be able to react normally when Chase was around? He sucked the oxygen out of her lungs and left her dizzy and disoriented. It was like being a teenager with a crush all over again.

Her porch light never got turned on, which left Chase's devilishly handsome face in shadow. His tall frame and thick, wide shoulders filled the doorway the same way thoughts of him filled her head. He stepped inside when she stood back to let him enter.

"Feels good in here," he said as cool air from her brand-new unit pumped in through the vents on the floor.

"Definitely better than before." She closed the front door and let her eyes roam down his deliciously hard derriere and powerful thighs. Wicked images of those same thighs pinning her to the mattress as he thrust her higher up the bed flew around her brain. The new air-conditioning was much welcome right now. "About what you did…"

"How about you just say 'thank you'?"

She narrowed her eyes at his backside. "It would have been nice to have some warning."

He stopped in the living room and faced her. "Then you would have said no."

Did he really know her that well? "Then at least let me—"

"I don't want you paying me back either."

She lifted her eyes to the ceiling and reined in her

instinct to argue with him about intruding on her independence.

He took a step toward her and tucked a long, free strand of hair behind her ear. "When was the last time someone gave you something?"

His thumb circled her ear and ran down the column of her throat. The contact had her eyelids fluttering and goose bumps trailing in the wake of his thumb.

"I'm not trying to encroach on your independence or using this to manipulate you. I wanted to do something nice for you."

Her mouth grew dry and she touched her bottom lip with her tongue. "There has to be something I can do to thank you."

"Say 'thank you.'"

Lacy considered herself an articulate person. Speaking her mind had always been something that came naturally to her. But when Chase was around, all those instincts flew out the window. Words tumbled over themselves in her brain and eventually found their way around her twisted tongue. Even as a teenager, Chase had had the ability to make her lose all logical thinking and it was part of the reason she'd disliked him as much as she craved him. At twenty-eight, things were no different. Except for suffering from lust, she had an especially bad case of undying love.

"Thank you," she finally managed to say. Then her eyes dropped down to his mouth. There on his bottom lip was a partially healed, crescent-shaped cut. Her index finger glided over the wound. "What happened?"

"Brody punched me."

She dropped her hand from his mouth. "He did what?"

Chase stepped away from her and walked around the

room. "Let's just say Brody and I aren't too happy with each other right now."

Lacy held up one hand and stepped over Boris. "Wait a minute. Brody punched you because of me?"

"I guess you could say that."

She tossed her hands up in the air. "You men and your stupid caveman tendencies."

"You're the one who told him. I thought you didn't want anyone knowing?"

"I didn't. But then he saw the ultrasound picture on the fridge and I couldn't lie to him." It'd been four days since she'd seen Brody and she missed him like crazy. Was he still mad at her? Would he talk to her if she called him? She sank down on Ray's battered recliner. "What does it matter now? Everyone's going to find out eventually."

"Have you told anyone else?"

She shook her head. "I didn't actually plan on telling Brody. It just happened like that." She lifted her eyes up to his. He'd stopped his pacing to lean one shoulder against the fireplace mantel. "He really hit you?"

"Took me by complete surprise. He didn't mention our encounter to you?"

"I haven't seen him since I told him. I think he's mad at me too."

Chase touched his jaw. "Trust me, it's not you he's mad at."

Her eyebrows tugged together. "Why would he be mad at you? It's not like you tied me up and put a gun to my head."

"That's not why he's mad."

She remained in the chair and waited for him to explain.

"He accused me of letting you push me away."

How in the world had Brody gotten that impression? Okay, she'd admitted to Brody she loved Chase and she told him about turning down Chase's marriage proposal. Had Brody come to his own conclusion or had he realized something she didn't realize herself? "That's not what I—"

"He's right." Chase straightened from the mantel and squatted on his heels in front of her. "It took a hit in the face from my little brother to make me realize it. I'm not going to let you keep me at arm's length because you have this instinct to protect yourself from getting hurt." She opened her mouth but he placed a hand on her bare knee to stop her. His palm was warm and sent a tingling sensation to her toes.

"I completely understand why you do that. It's a defense mechanism you built for yourself because everyone in your life who you were supposed to be able to trust has left you in some way. That big heart of yours has some pretty deep scars in it."

Chase's words made something inside her shift. That place deep in her soul she'd kept hidden from people was found by the man she'd fallen in love with. But had she really kept it so hidden? Or had other people in her life simply not bothered to look deeper than necessary? Her own parents or even Ray? Sometime in the past several months, Chase had managed to worm his way inside and get a glimpse of the real Lacy Taylor. When had that happened? How had she not seen that coming? Or maybe Chase was the one person she'd been waiting to show herself to. She felt tears welling in her eyes and trickling, uncontrolled, down her cheeks.

"You may not want to marry me," he continued, "but I'm not going to let you write me off like you have everyone else in your life. I'm not going to abandon you the way your mother did and I won't disappoint you the way your father has. I know that's what you're expecting and that's probably why you didn't want anyone to know about us." He swiped a tear away from her cheek with his thumb. "Like I said before, you don't have to marry me. But I'm not going anywhere."

Another tear followed the one Chase had blotted away with his thumb. How could he be the only person in her life who got her? Lacy wasn't used to people making promises, much less actually keeping them. She'd learned long ago not to hold the people in her life to such high standards. Did this mean he loved her the same way she loved him? While they were certainly nice words, nicer than anything she'd ever heard, they didn't exactly hint at a declaration of love. Oh, she knew he cared about her. But how deep that caring went, Lacy could only guess.

What if he didn't really love her and someday he went on to marry someone else? And have kids with them? Lacy didn't think she'd survive that.

You're doing it again. Always expecting the worst to happen.

For once in her life, Lacy forced the worst-case scenario out of her mind.

"Just think about that for a little while before you respond. And I thought of a way you can thank me."

She narrowed her eyes at him when the corners of his mouth turned up. "No sex."

His smirk turned into a full-blown, melt-your-bones grin. "Although that would be nice, that's not what I'm talking about. You see, what I really want is—"

TWENTY

THINK I WOULD RATHER have sex."

Chase wrapped one large, rough hand around hers and guided her toward the bed. With a gentle nudge, he sat her down and placed her mother's letter in her hand. "Nice try, but you're not getting out of this."

Her name scrawled in loopy ink on the white envelope stared back at her. "Do I have to do this now?"

"Yes. You've been putting this off long enough. You'll thank me later."

She lifted her eyes to his. "I don't think I will."

He crossed his arms over his wide chest. "You will." When she only stared at him, he took the letter from her, opened it up, and placed it back in her hands. "Here."

Her eyes ran down the page filled with words. "You'll stay with me?"

His blue eyes softened. "I'm not going anywhere."

Okay, it's only one page. Just do it, like ripping off a Band-Aid.

She scooted herself to the top of the bed and rested her shoulders against the headboard. The words *My darling Lacy* jumped out at her first.

With her heart in her throat, Lacy read her mother's last words to her:

In a box with my old belongings, I have a picture of you swaddled in a hospital blanket just after you were born. Your skin was bluish purple and your hair was so fair it almost looked nonexistent. As far as babies go, you weren't the most attractive thing in the world, and you had a set of lungs on you that could have put Pavarotti to shame. But moments after laying eyes on you, I knew I held the most beautiful part of me in my hands.

You're an adult now and I can only speculate how beautiful a woman you've grown into. Were you blessed with my lean body and cursed with my boring, straight hair? These are things I will never know the answers to and I only have my own shortcomings to blame for that. I can also only wonder as to what you must think of me.

This isn't a letter of apology or explanation. My guess is you have such little memory of me or your life before I left that you've gotten to the point where "sorry" is pretty much useless. The only explanation I can offer is this: when you were born, I was in a very bad place in my life. This had nothing to do with your arrival in the world. At that point, I didn't have the common sense to make good life choices, with the exception of giving birth to you. You most likely don't remember this, but by the time you were three years old I had slipped far past any recognizable form of myself. In any event, I felt leaving Trouble and my loved ones was the best decision for everyone.

As for your father, Dennis isn't the most responsible person in the world but he loves you. Despite the behavior I know he will no doubt display in the years to come, he does love you. And you have a grandfather who worships the ground you walk on. You are Ray's only grandchild and the apple of his eye. I'm sure he took good care of you in a way neither your father nor I could.

I'm sending Megan to meet you and deliver a few things to you. When she was a child, she reminded me so much of you, it hurt my heart to look at her. She's grown into a wonderful young woman. But she will be confused and hurt when she learns of your existence. Go easy on her, Lacy. It's not her fault. One day the two of you will be the only family each other has left. I want to leave this world knowing my two girls have grown to love each other.

This seems a little premature, but if I should pass away, I want you to have something of me. I know money is impersonal, but right now, it's all I have to give. This is your money and you're free to do whatever you want with it. I don't blame you if your anger toward me prevents you from taking it. Donate the money if you would like. Or take it and do something nice for yourself. Buy a house, go on a vacation, save it for your children, if you have them. Either way, the money is yours and I want you to have it without feeling any sort of attachment or obligation.

I love you, my dear Lacy. I'm sorry I wasn't a better mother.

Lacy's trembling fingers crumpled the letter into a tight, wrinkled ball. Why did she have to care so much?

Why did those words have to slice her heart in two so that she bled dry? Why couldn't this be an insignificant piece of paper from a meaningless person?

Her teeth ground together as her eyes filled with unwanted, damnable tears. Her eyelids pressed tightly together to prevent the moisture from leaking over. So many tears had formed from years of wondering, speculating, always asking why that they finally trickled over and ran down her cheeks. She hiccuped once, then again as a never-ending stream flowed down her face and fell to the bed beneath her. Chase's shoes scuffed along the carpet as he moved toward the bed. Lacy forced her eyes open and looked at him through distorted, blurry vision.

When he reached the edge of the bed, she chucked the wadded-up paper at him and it bounced off his chest. "Why did you make me read that? I was doing just fine."

"No, you weren't."

She crawled clumsily on her knees until he was within reaching distance. Her weak hands curled into angry fists again and came down hard on his chest. She pounded on his thick muscles once, then again. "How do you know? How the hell has anyone ever known?" Her fingers dug into his crisp white work shirt. "I don't care about this anymore. She's nothing to me. She's *never* been anything to me."

He wrapped both warm, comforting hands around her face. "We both know that's not true." His thumbs stroked back and forth over her wet cheeks. "You don't have to be iron-clad all the time, Lace."

"It hurts too much if I'm not."

His arms came around her like an old, comforting security blanket. They surrounded her in the strength and love that had always been missing in her life. Her head dropped down to his shoulder and her arms went around his torso. He held her while she emptied everything she had inside her. All the hurt, loneliness, and confusion that had plagued her for the better part of her adult life poured out of her. Chase, bless his big, mushy heart, remained silent and maneuvered the two of them back on the bed. He somehow got them into a vertical position with her head resting on his chest and his arms cocooning her. The tears eventually subsided to a point where she had some semblance of control again. When was the last time she'd allowed herself that kind of release? More importantly, when was the last time she'd allowed anyone else to see that precious vulnerability?

When the last tear had leaked out, Lacy took in a shuddering breath and allowed the sweet arms of sleep to take her.

Sometime later, when even the moon had retired for the night and left her room in inky blackness, Lacy blinked her gritty eyes open. While she'd slept, Chase had pulled the bedsheets up over both of them. Her left leg was tossed over both of his. One of his hands rested on her hip and the other was folded up behind his head. Only when his thumb glided back and forth over the exposed skin above her cotton shorts did she realize he was awake.

"Why did you do all that for me?" she asked him in the dark.

"Other than the fact that you're carrying my child?"

"Yes."

"Because you needed it."

She floated her fingers across his bare stomach. "That's not why."

His flat belly moved up and down in the even rhythm

of breathing while he waited to answer. "Because I'm in love with you."

Lacy drifted to sleep with a smile on her lips.

The vast nothingness of dreamless sleep Chase had slipped into was interrupted by a muted sound coming from far away. Degree by slow degree, he sifted through the layers of unconsciousness and found his way back to reality. He forced one heavy eyelid open and found his surroundings as black as his empty mind. Then the same sound that woke him kept him from dropping his eye closed. He rolled onto his back and dug the heel of his hand into his eye sockets. He blinked several times until the red glowing numbers of the clock came into focus. Almost four-thirty. Had almost the entire night really passed?

This time the vibrating of his phone was unmistakable. Who in the world would want to talk to him at this hour? The device jittered across the nightstand again. Chase pulled his left arm from underneath Lacy, grabbed the phone, and held it up to his ear.

"What?" he asked in a voice gravelly with sleep.

"The restaurant's been broken into. Get down here." Even at four-thirty in the morning, the harsh, demanding tone of his father's voice grated on Chase's tired nerves.

He lifted his head off the pillow. "What?" he asked again.

"Just get down here." The call ended without any further pertinent information from his old man.

He took the phone away from his ear and stared at the screen. Had he heard his father correctly or had Chase never really woken up? He dropped the phone back to the nightstand and rubbed his eyes one more time. Moving slowly so as not to wake Lacy, Chase swung his legs over the side of the bed and stood. His clothes lay in a pile where he'd discarded them after Lacy drifted off to sleep. He dressed quickly, grabbed his phone, and walked out the front door.

A familiar and comforting calm hovered in Lacy's aging neighborhood. Black iron lightposts highlighted the cracks and lumps in the concrete sidewalk. Chase tossed his keys from hand to hand as he lumbered toward his truck. He probably should have left Lacy a note. They were at that point in their relationship that was beyond the early morning slip-out. The thought of confusion or hurt clouding those stunning green eyes made something sharp twist in his gut. On second thought, he spun on his heel, slipped back into the house, and scrawled a brief explanatory note. He was better than that, better than leaving her with a wham-bam, thank-you-ma'am feeling. Especially after his admission last night.

Chase let himself out of the house once again, then climbed into his truck. After turning the key, he backed out of the driveway and headed toward the restaurant.

Did he regret admitting he was in love with her? Absolutely not. Not even her silence could damper his confidence. She loved him. She might not be comfortable enough to say the words to him, but the small tilt of her mouth as her eyes had drifted shut told him what he needed to know. His words hadn't left her unaffected. All he needed to do was give her the time she needed to make the same declaration. And she would. She'd changed too much in the past several months for her not to. He didn't want to toot his own horn or anything but Chase liked to think he played a small part in her shift. She'd jumped the largest hurdle last night by finally letting go of her most burdening demon. If he hadn't all but shoved the letter into her hands, the thing probably would have ended up in the garbage.

Lacy had been too wrapped up in the past to admit she needed that release. Lynette Taylor had held shackles around her daughter for long enough. Chase had needed to see those restraints fall off Lacy for good. True, he'd exposed a very raw wound that would no doubt bleed for a while. But Lacy was the strongest person he knew. She'd bounce back from this and be a better person for it. And he intended to be by her side while she worked on patching up that part of herself.

Not ten minutes later, he maneuvered his truck into the smooth parking lot of McDermott's. Flashing red and blue lights spun in the dark night and bounced off the neighboring buildings. He pulled his car next to his father's and entered the building. Chase braced himself for Martin's thunderous temper. A volcano lurked just beneath the surface that tended to erupt when pushed far enough. Nine times out of ten, Chase had been the one to force the steam to come flying out of his father's ears. Now Martin had a legitimate reason for blowing a gasket. Nobody but nobody messed with his business. The restaurants were the old man's ultimate pride and joy, a reward for all the years of sweat, money, and stress he'd poured into the establishments.

A handful of uniformed officers mingled about the dining area. His father stood with his arms tightly crossed over his barrel chest, speaking in low tones to a man in a wrinkled suit. Chase approached them and waited for them to finish their conversation.

"This is my son Chase," his father introduced him to the other man. "He runs things here. Would you mind giving us a minute before you take her away?" he asked the suit.

Take her away?

The man slid a silver pen into a pocket on the inside of his jacket. "I'll give you three minutes."

Chase turned to his father when the officer left them alone. "What happened here?"

"She stole Henry's keys. The new alarm system went off when she came in. Because it's a silent alarm, she had no idea she'd triggered anything. But the Trouble police were immediately alerted, and they contacted me."

Nothing made sense. "Who stole Henry's keys? What the hell is going on?"

Martin jerked his head to the left. Chase's eyes danced over the officers and empty tables until landing on an occupied chair. Slumped over like a dejected, scolded child was Diane. Her dark choppy hair stood up in a frizzy, uncombed manner. Giant holes in her faded blue jeans revealed thick, pale knees. Shiny, silver handcuffs circled her round wrists, which were tucked between her stocky legs.

Chase whipped his gaze back to his father. Deep lines of tension bracketed the old man's thin mouth. "Tell me I'm seeing things."

"You try talking to her. She won't say a word to me."

Chase's eyebrows twitched. "What did she say when you caught her?"

Martin lifted one shoulder. "She just kept apologizing. She didn't even put up a fight when I called the cops. It was almost like she wanted to get caught."

Diane hadn't so much as lifted her head since Chase walked in the doors. He scrubbed a hand down his scratchy chin and slowly ate up the space between them.

When he stopped in front of her, she still didn't look up. Her head stayed bowed and her chest gently expanded and fell. Without saying a word, Chase pulled up a nearby chair and straddled it. He folded his hands across the top and stared at Diane's unruly hair.

What in the world could he say to her? *How could you? What were you thinking?* Such things were moot now and a waste of everyone's time. Plus, Chase already knew the answers to that. Someone who had fallen on such desperate times as Diane would not be thinking clearly. Most likely her only thoughts were putting food in her children's mouths. Of course, there were other ways of accomplishing this. If she'd approached him from the beginning, they could have worked something out. Maybe a raise or…what? Hell, there was nothing Chase could have done. The only raise he could have offered would have been pennies more compared to what she needed to replace her husband's lost income.

"This doesn't seem to be your night, does it?" Not a very sensitive way to start this sort of conversation. But hey, cut him some slack. He didn't have very much experience in arresting an employee. Dealing with Becky-Lynn was the closest he'd come to this.

An exhausted sigh escaped him. "Diane, look at me."

Thick, dark lashes swept up over brown eyes when she lifted her head.

"I like you," he said gently. "You're a good waitress. But it shouldn't have come to this."

Perspiration glistened on Diane's wide forehead. "I'm sorry, Chase," she replied in a hoarse whisper. "I didn't mean to betray you."

No explanation. Not that he expected one. It wouldn't have mattered anyway. Her reasons why didn't change what she'd done.

With a shake of his head, Chase stood and approached his father again. "What's going to happen to her? You're not pressing charges, are you?"

Martin's gray eyes darkened. "She's in handcuffs, Chase."

"I saw that but"—he tossed a glance at Diane—"don't you think she's learned her lesson already? Come on, Dad. Her husband's unemployed. What'll happen to her kids if she goes to jail?"

"She can't go unpunished. Besides, I doubt she'll spend that much time in jail anyway."

"The amount of time she spends is irrelevant. How do you think she'll find a job after she has a criminal record?"

Martin wrapped thick fingers over Chase's shoulder. "This business is my livelihood, son. I have to protect it."

Chase shook his head. A heavy weight had settled over his shoulders. "There has to be a way to resolve this that doesn't end up with her in jail."

Both Martin's white brows flew up his forehead. "Such as?"

"Suspend her for a little while and garnish her wages." He tossed a glance around the dining room. "I don't have the heart to watch Diane walk away in handcuffs."

"Chase..." Martin led them near a wall so they could continue their disagreement in semiprivate. "I know you like Diane and have a soft spot for her, but she deceived both of us. One of these days if you ever end up owning your own restaurant, you can do whatever you want with your employees. But I built this place from the ground up. I won't take this kind of risk with it. I'm sorry." A softness settled over his father's faded gray eyes. "This is the way it has to be."

Of course, Chase understood that. Never would he intentionally ask his father to risk his own business. If he'd been in the old man's shoes, Chase no doubt would have done the same thing. The shock and disbelief that had washed over him after seeing Diane had thrown his sensible thinking for a loop. No matter how much he liked her, Diane had broken the law and lied to them.

Chase threw one more glance at the waitress. One of the officers grasped her elbow and lifted her to her feet. "You're right," he said to his father. "I'll tell Anita when she comes in."

"I'll leave it up to you two to explain this to the staff. In the meantime, go home and get some more sleep."

Chase didn't stick around to watch Diane being taken away. Seeing her in handcuffs was wrenching enough. How had he not seen this? How could one of his best waitresses have been stealing right under his nose? He'd been so convinced of his father's paranoia and keeping him placated that Chase ignored all the signs. Of course, now it made sense. Woman's husband loses job. Woman falls on hard times. Woman gets desperate. Maybe the possibility of getting caught never even occurred to Diane. The woman had five mouths to feed. She probably thought if she could sneak one or two pieces of steak, maybe some bread and a little extra cash, she'd be able to float her family through until they got back on their feet.

They say money, or lack of it, has a way of changing a person. Diane must have gotten to the point where the hopelessness was too much to handle. Maybe in her mind she didn't have any other choice. She was just a mother who didn't want to see her children starve. While Chase couldn't relate, he could see how that would push a person to do something stupid. But should she be arrested for it?

Chase pushed through the restaurant's front doors and walked across the parking lot to his car. The sky was still black as midnight. Would Lacy have woken up by now and found his note? No, he'd bet she was still sound asleep, not even aware that he'd slipped out. She'd been so emotionally drained after her outburst she'd probably doze for the next two days. The rest would do her some good. Lacy was one of those people who rarely took time for herself. Over the next several months, before the baby came, Chase would see that Lacy got plenty of rest.

He started up his truck and exited the parking lot. A shower and change of clothes was absolute music to his ears. So why was he headed back to Lacy's so he could crawl back into bed with her?

TWENTY-ONE

*B*ECAUSE *I'M IN LOVE WITH YOU.*

Had Chase really said that to her? Or had her over-worked mind conjured it up as she'd drifted off to sleep? Of course, she hoped it was the former but she had no idea for sure. It also could have been a really, really good dream. One where Chase was hopelessly in love with her and wanted to marry her for real and not because he'd impregnated her. She wanted something more than him showing up after work and dragging her off to bed.

All the pretending and keeping their affair secret had taken its toll on her and probably hadn't been the best decision to begin with. Her interaction with Brody last week made her realize that. In her roundabout way of protecting herself, she'd hurt her closest friend and come between two brothers. How had it gotten so out of hand?

She rolled onto her back on the mattress and ran her eyes down Chase's note again. *Something came up at the restaurant. I'll explain later.* What could possibly have happened at the restaurant at this hour?

Lacy gave up trying to sleep and rolled out of bed. Sometime after she slipped into slumber, Chase had removed most of her clothes and pulled the sheets up over her. The fact that he'd tucked her into bed and hadn't tried to make love to her had her heart turning over even more. A few occasions in the past, they'd hadn't even made it to the bedroom before he all but pounced on her. What was so different about last night? Is that what men did when they were in love? Chase had shown an endearing side of himself last night, one she'd never seen before. Their picnic by the Green River came close but that wasn't really the same. Was that when she'd fallen for him? In the months past, Chase had done a damn good job of showing that animalistic side of himself. The one that practically trembled while he peeled her clothes off, then gave her no reprieve before taking her again. Not that she was complaining. Lacy certainly enjoyed that side of him. But the part of him that refused to let her put up her walls and dug deep enough into her psyche to see the real her was what she cherished more than anything else.

Lacy pulled on a soft cotton robe and padded barefoot down the hallway. She flipped on the kitchen light and brewed some of the decaffeinated coffee she'd purchased last week. Coffee was the crux of her life but the last thing she wanted was to pump her baby full of caffeine. She figured a good compromise was to settle for some decaf.

She'd inhaled half the cup when the front door slowly opened and Chase stepped through.

"You're up early," he said in that rich baritone of his.

"I couldn't go back to sleep." She set the mug on the table. "What happened?"

He shook his head and trudged across the wood floor. "Trust me, you won't want to hear about it."

"That's decaf," she announced just before he poured some coffee into a mug.

He paused with the cup below his mouth. "Whatever," he muttered, and then his throat muscles worked up and down as he took a long sip.

"Tell me." Whatever happened had been more than just a routine check-in at work. The deep worry lines stretching across Chase's forehead and the hard set of his square jaw spoke of an unpleasant experience to say the least.

The rickety dining chair creaked under Chase's weight when he lowered himself. "Diane was the one stealing."

The hot liquid she'd just sipped got caught in her throat. A few coughs and swallows managed to keep the coffee from coming out her nose. After regaining her composure, Lacy set the cup down and looked at Chase. "Tell me you're joking."

His blue eyes stared into hers. "I wish I was."

So why did he have to go down there this early in the morning? "She got caught breaking into the restaurant, didn't she?" Lacy asked as the realization hit her.

"My father caught her. She'd stolen Henry's keys."

Diane? The same rosy-cheeked, always-smiling woman was the one who'd been stealing food and money? Never would Lacy have guessed that Diane of all people was the one Chase had been looking for this whole time.

"I don't understand," was all she could say.

"Who knows what was going through her head. She didn't have very much to say."

Lacy lifted her gaze to Chase's again. "You saw her?"

Chase nodded. "She was in handcuffs waiting to be taken away." He paused to take a sip of coffee. "For the life of me, I couldn't figure out what to say to her. I kept getting the feeling that words would be useless."

Lacy lifted a shoulder. "In some situations they are."

"How could I have not seen it?"

She placed a hand on his forearm. "You did everything you could. Who in the world would have suspected Diane anyway?"

A snort popped out of his mouth. "Henry did."

"You said when you talked to Diane she seemed just as unlikely as everyone else."

Chase shook his head. "If I would have talked to Henry sooner, I might have been able to get to Diane sooner."

"And done what? Chase, stop beating yourself up. Things like this happen all the time. Diane was obviously very good at covering her tracks." Even after talking about it, picturing Diane stealing was like picturing Santa Claus stealing. "The only thing you can do is be glad that it's over and move on." Then a disturbing thought occurred to her. "What if she goes to jail? Her family won't have any income coming in."

Chase ran a hand over his scruffy face. "That's what bothers me the most. I know it's my father's restaurant and it's his decision to make. But I don't think Diane deserves to go to jail."

"She doesn't." There had to be something Lacy could do, some way to help this poor family who couldn't seem to catch a break. She knew firsthand what it was like to grow up with practically nothing. "I think I'm going to give some of my mother's money to them."

Chase set down his coffee cup and glanced at her. "Diane's family?"

"Yeah. She was just trying to take care of her kids. I can't stand the thought of keeping all that money for myself when there are others who need it more."

Chase's warm, calloused palm settled on her cheek. The contact heated her from the inside out. "You have such a soft heart."

"I can't stand the thought of kids having nothing."

They gazed at each other for a few intense moments. Then he removed his hand from her face. "To be honest, I don't want to talk or think about Diane. Are you feeling a little better about last night?"

You mean when you said you were in love with me? Did she dare bring that up in case he really meant it?

She tucked some free hair behind her ear. "I'm okay."

He leaned back in his chair. "I don't want to say I told you so or anything."

She narrowed her eyes at him, then twirled her mug around. "At the risk of making your ego any bigger, you were right. I needed that."

One corner of his mouth kicked up. "I knew it wasn't something you'd do without being forced."

She ran her gaze over the dented and chipped dining table. "I kept telling myself I should read it, but I don't think I ever had any intention of doing so. Now I feel like a huge weight has been lifted off my shoulders, like I can finally let her go."

The back of his index finger drifted down her cheek. "You should have let her go a long time ago."

The delicate caress of his finger had her heart dancing inside her chest. He trailed it along her jawline and her mouth where he'd dropped his attention. "Did you mean what you said last night?"

He cupped her chin and traced his thumb along her lower lip. "You mean about being in love with you?"

The feel of his rough hand on her soft skin made the words tumble over in her brain, so she nodded.

"Of course."

The words were said so matter-of-factly, like she should have known without having to ask him.

"I know you love me, so you might as well say it," he said without giving her a chance to reply. He grinned.

How was it he was always so sure of himself? For as long as she'd known him, Chase always seemed to know what would come out of her mouth before she even said the words. Like last night, he knew she needed that release from her mother before she knew she needed it. And now he was so sure she loved him when she hadn't told him.

"You already know I do."

He pinched her chin. "Just waiting to hear you say it."

Her tongue darted out and touched the corner of her mouth. "I love you, Chase."

With a smile creating shallow lines around his mouth, he leaned forward and brushed his lips along hers. Her eyes dropped closed as his large palm curved around the back of her neck and pressed her mouth harder against his. His warm tongue slipped between her lips, forcing them open so he could sweep inside her mouth. The kiss was delicious and torturous all at the same time. Fantastic ribbons of pleasure weaved their way through all parts of her body. Her toes curled against the cold floor. Her stomach quivered and a euphoric light-headedness settled over her.

When Lacy expected to be dragged back to bed and ravished like a randy teenager, Chase pulled away and stood from the table. Was he really going to leave after setting her on fire like that? The man didn't play fair!

"I have to go home and get ready for work." Her eyes strayed to his amazing glutes when he walked to the kitchen and put his empty cup in the dishwasher. When returning to her, he lifted her out of the chair and pulled her flush against him. His warm palm tunneled beneath the curtain of her hair and gently squeezed until her lips fell against his. She opened beneath him, because the temptation to feel his tongue swirling around hers again was too great.

"I'll see you later," he said when he broke contact. Without another word, he left her standing by the table with her head still spinning.

Lacy was no longer surprised by how deeply Chase always affected her. It was like he'd found that special place inside her and knew how to stroke it *just* right. The man had an absolute impeccable talent for making her feel all... Heck, there wasn't even a name for it. She picked up her empty mug and placed it in the dishwasher next to Chase's. There was something so endearingly domestic about seeing their two mugs side by side. The only person Lacy had shared dishwasher space with was Ray. What a trivial and simple thing to cross her mind.

When she turned, her eyes landed on the baby picture on the fridge. She removed it from under the magnet and ran her gaze over the black-and-white image. Lacy had a hard time making a connection between the picture and what was going on inside her body. While Chase had accepted the pregnancy and seemed to be okay with it, they still hadn't really talked about it. How would their arrangement work? Would they share joint custody? Sure, they loved each other but Chase hadn't mentioned marriage again. Okay, so one step at a time. An admission of love was a major hurdle the two of them finally crossed. Maybe she was being a tad impatient.

She placed the picture back on the fridge and thought of Brody. The two of them had never fought like this before. And it wasn't even really fighting. She knew he wasn't too happy with her right now, but neither of them had done anything wrong. There was a chance he'd been hurt after he found out about her affair with Chase. Lacy fully accepted responsibility for that and admitted she needed to make amends.

A heavy cloud of fatigue settled on her shoulders. Lacy dragged herself out of the kitchen and shuffled down the hallway. She slithered back into bed, inhaled Chase's comforting and orgasmic scent, and slipped back to sleep.

Lacy had just popped her third muffin into her mouth when Brody pushed through the double doors of the coffee shop. Her mouth automatically turned up in a grin when she saw him.

"You're glowing," he said with a wink as he pulled out the chair across from her.

"That's because I just stuffed my face," she said after her last bite.

He leaned back in his chair with a chuckle. "You still look good."

She lifted a brow as her smile fell. "Don't be too nice to me, Brody."

"Because you don't deserve it?" The light in his gray eyes kept his words from being too harsh.

One of her shoulders lifted in a negligent shrug. "I wouldn't go that far. But most likely, yes."

A thick silence fell between them as Lacy dropped her gaze to the smooth tabletop. Brody placed one palm over hers until she looked at him again. "You deserve the world, Lace. Don't ever let anyone tell you differently."

Her heart cracked open a little at his words. Brody always knew how to lift her spirits. A single tear leaked out the corner of her eye.

He flicked her nose with his index finger. "Don't do that."

"I can't help it." She picked up a napkin from the table and dabbed her eye. "My emotions have been all over the place lately."

"It only gets worse. Kelly was a basket case by the time Tyler came out."

Her lips pulled up at the corners. "I'm sorry about lying to you."

Brody lifted one hand. "I don't want to hear sorry. You're allowed to get involved with whoever you want." His head tilted to one side. "It just came as a surprise that you chose my brother."

Lacy studied his handsome features for a moment. "Were you really that surprised?"

He drummed his fingers on the tabletop. "No, I guess not. I was more shocked about the pregnancy than anything else."

"Trust me, you weren't the only one."

"Have you two worked things out?"

What did that mean exactly? Lacy had yet to figure out where the two of them stood. Oh sure, she had a general idea. She was mildly sure the two of them had a future together. But guesses had never come comfortably to her. There were still a few things she and Chase needed to lay on the table.

"For now," was all she could offer her friend. "Speaking of working things out," she added before Brody could prod some more. "You and your brother need to have a talk."

Brody shrugged. "About what?"

She gave him a droll look. "What do you mean, about what? You punched him."

"Left a mark on him, did I?" he asked with a shit-eating grin. "That was a heat-of-the-moment thing. Chase knows I'm not mad at him."

Lacy pushed crumbs around the table with her index finger. "I don't think he does."

Brody leaned forward and rested his forearms on the table. "Lace, this is what brothers do. We get pissed at each other, sometimes we throw punches, and then we're cool. Trust me, there's no heat between us."

"I still think you should talk to him."

His brows lifted. "Would it make you feel better?"

"Yes."

"Consider it done."

Lacy leaned back in her chair and crossed her arms. "As long as we're on the subject of you, how's dating life?"

He snorted. "What dating life?"

"What happened to the summer school teacher?"

Brody's eyes skipped around their surroundings. "She didn't make it past the second date."

Her stomach erupted in a low growl. Maybe she ought to shove a fourth muffin down her throat. "Big shoes to fill?" she asked Brody.

He shook his head slowly. "Don't start that."

She held her hands up in defense. "I'm just saying. And for the record, I wasn't referring to Kelly specifically. I'm talking about the whole wife thing."

His brows flattened over his eyes. "What do you mean?"

"That last time you were single was in college, right? I think your standards are too high."

"You have no idea how much I've lowered my standards over the past two years."

She shook her head. "Please tell me you're not sleeping with these women, then ditching them."

He narrowed his eyes at her. "What kind of guy do you think I am?"

"You're a guy. That's enough."

"Oh, Miss Twiggy. How little you know me." His eyes dropped to her midsection. "Although I have to say you're not as twiggy as you were a few weeks ago."

Leave it to a man to point out something like that. No one knew more than her how tight her clothes were these days. "Thank you very much," she said with a tight smile.

"That wasn't an insult, Lace. Pregnancy is a beautiful thing."

Beautiful? Lacy had yet to see that side of it. "How often did Kelly tell you that?"

"Never," he replied with a smile. "But she had a rough pregnancy." He held up his index finger. "What counts is that I always told her how beautiful she was even when she was all big and swollen."

She leaned forward in her chair and drew circles on the table with her fingernail. "I bet you were one of those husbands who rubbed her feet and went to the store in the middle of the night."

Her friend actually looked embarrassed. "There's nothing wrong with doing stuff like that. Besides, men have it easy compared to what you women have to go through."

Her face broke into a grin. "Did you actually rub Kelly's feet?"

He shrugged. "When I wasn't studying."

She watched him a moment before responding. Brody was one of those people who would give you his last dollar if he were broke. The sacrifices he'd made for Kelly and their son was probably something he didn't even think twice about. The good-guy streak ran strong in him and was something Lacy always admired most about him. Not often did men like Brody McDermott come along.

Kelly probably had no idea how lucky she'd been to have a husband like Brody. True, one never knew what went on behind closed doors. Maybe Brody wasn't half the husband as he was a friend. The fact that he'd put Lacy up on a pedestal had caused her to have hero worship for him. It was very possible Kelly had an entirely different view of her ex-husband. Lacy had a hard time imagining any woman not being able to fall in love with Brody. Luckily for her, she'd never had anything but platonic feelings for him. By the time she'd met him years ago, she'd already been head over heels in lust with his older brother. Maybe her intense attraction for Chase prevented any such feelings for Brody. In any event, that was all moot now. The bottom line was, Brody was one of her dearest friends and she only wanted him to be happy.

"What's going on in that head of yours?" he asked after a few moments of silence.

She ran her gaze over his face. "Just thinking about what a great guy you are."

His eyes softened. "You think too highly of me, Lacy."

"No, you're definitely worthy of it."

"Why did we never get involved?"

"Because we're too much alike."

"Hmm." He tapped his fingers on the table again. "I suppose you're right."

"But I still love you."

His face broke into a disarming smile. "I know."

TWENTY-TWO

FALL HAD FINALLY DESCENDED over Wyoming and in the process lifted the suffocating heat of summer. Crisp bursts of wind routinely swept through the town, often pulling thick white clouds in their wake. The previous day, the weatherman had predicted a high in the low sixties with a possible chance of rain the following day. Lacy didn't mind the rain. It had a way of dropping the air temperature to a point where she wasn't sweating bullets anymore. She'd read on the Internet that pregnant women suffered from bouts of hot flashes as early as their second trimester. Lacy was well into that particular stage and been spending as much time as she could opening the refrigerator door and allowing the cool air to brush along her heated body. So when the first cool front of the year swept through their valley, she practically wept with relief.

The only drawback was the possible negative effect on the art festival. The entire event lasted Friday through Sunday. Although the first day was beautiful, Saturday and Sunday were both question marks.

Over the past few weeks, she'd worked furiously to

get as many drawings ready as she could. By last week, she'd had enough to last her all three days. Not too shabby considering that several months ago she couldn't think of even one drawing worthy enough to display in public. Thursday night, Chase had come out to the festival grounds with her and helped her arrange her booth, dragging tables from one spot to another. A few nights earlier, as they shared a dinner on his living room floor, she tried to reassure him that one little art booth wasn't too much for her to handle. Chase, being the stubborn man that he was, practically balked at the idea of her lifting so much as a number two pencil. Because she had no willpower around him, she had no choice but to agree when he started digging his thumbs into the arches of her feet.

After setting up her booth for her, he drove them back to his place where he drew her a warm bath, and then when she was warm and drowsy, he settled into bed next to her. In the weeks leading up to the festival, the two of them had enjoyed dinners, taken rides on his motorcycle, and torn each other's clothes off whenever they were near a bed. But in all that time neither of them mentioned marriage or any kind of long-term future. He told her he loved her every opportunity he got but always stopped short of anything beyond that. It was almost like they'd fallen back into the honeymoon stage of dating.

He'd followed up on his promise of being involved with the pregnancy. When she had her five-month checkup with her OB/GYN, Chase had been right there next to her. He'd taken her hand in his while the doctor squeezed that cold, slimy gel on Lacy's belly. When their baby's rapid heartbeat filled the exam room, he'd pressed his lips to her knuckles.

All these were endearing sentiments that told Lacy

Chase's feelings for her were genuine. She knew he loved her. But she needed to know she was in a relationship that had some sort of grown-up future and was not just dating.

As the sun fought its way through relentless clouds, Lacy lowered her aching feet to a chair and watched a minimal amount of people stroll by her booth. In the two hours since the festival officially started, she'd had some curious glances, even some questions about her work. However, she'd yet to actually sell anything. Did that worry her? Not exactly. Of course, she didn't expect to be bombarded with admirers the second people started arriving. The reality was, it would probably take her a few years to get her name out there in the art community. That was all right. Lacy enjoyed what she did and was willing to put forth a little effort to get her career started. After all, success wasn't built overnight.

Luckily for her, she had a great support system of friends who were doing everything they could to spread the word for her. Courtney and Avery both passed out flyers where they worked to let people know Lacy would be here. R.J. had hung notices of the festival around the bar and Brody mentioned it to Kelly, who'd said she'd tell her friends. At the end of the day, all she could do was her best and hope her work paid off.

Candlelight-blond hair flashed in the corner of Lacy's eye. She craned her head around one of the easels holding a drawing and spotted Megan.

"I'm sorry I'm late," Megan said in a rush as she plopped her black and white Chanel purse on a table. "My layover in Albuquerque was extended by an hour." She slid her oversized sunglasses off her face. "This looks really good. I had no idea you could draw like this."

Lacy smiled as she tried to force away the heat that

crept into her cheeks. "I've always enjoyed drawing and I decided it was time to get my stuff out there. Brody convinced me."

Megan's eyes strayed back to Lacy. "Brody? Was he the shirtless hunk I met before?"

"No, that was Chase," Lacy said with a grin. "Brody was the one who was at my house the first time we met. They're brothers."

"Ah. The attractive gene must run in their family."

Oh, the McDermott men definitely came from good stock.

The younger girl meandered around the displays. "You know, Mom liked to draw."

Lacy shifted in her chair. This time when her mother was mentioned, the pain around her heart wasn't so deep. "Did she?"

Megan nodded and ran her finger along the edge of a blown-up picture. "She wasn't nearly this good, but it was a hobby of hers." She shifted her attention to Lacy. "I'll send you some of her stuff."

"I'd appreciate that." Lacy pushed herself out of the folding chair and shifted one of the easels. When she turned, Megan's eyes dropped to Lacy's midsection.

"Okay, either you've gotten really out of shape since the last time I saw you, or you're having a baby."

Megan's wide emerald-colored eyes reminded Lacy her half sister didn't know about the pregnancy. Lacy pulled at the too-tight shirt that was practically shrink-wrapped over her round belly. Maybe she ought to go shopping for maternity clothes. "I guess you could say both. It's kind of shocking, I know," Lacy went on when Megan's eyes remained fixed on Lacy's stomach. "I'm still not used to all this stuff up front."

Megan shook her head. "Sorry, I didn't mean to stare. It's just that you've gotten big really fast."

"Tell me about it. I barely had enough time for the idea to sink in before I started getting too big for my clothes." Lacy lowered herself back to the chair.

Megan sat down next to her. "When are you due?"

"February."

Megan placed a soft, manicured hand on Lacy's arm. "Congratulations."

"Thanks. I still feel bad you had to miss school to come here."

"I'm not really missing school," she said with a shrug. "It's only one class and I can easily make it up. Besides, we had a deal."

That's right, they did. And it was one Lacy had been glad she made.

Two women carrying cloth bags wandered over to Lacy's booth. One woman, with thinning black hair, wobbled on stumpy legs to one of the easels. She scanned the drawing with her deep-brown eyes. The other woman, who already lugged several sacks full of stuff, flipped through copies of drawings Lacy had placed in a box. She sifted through one box, then started on another.

The woman aimed a pair of sharp blue eyes at Lacy. "Are you the artist?"

"Yes, I am," Lacy said with a nod.

"This is beautiful stuff." The woman lifted a drawing of the old courthouse out of the box. "My grandfather helped build this. How much for one of the small ones?"

Lacy rattled off the price Chase had helped her to determine. The woman paid for the drawing, along with another one she chose off the table. After the transaction was over, the two women ambled off toward other booths.

A small zing of exhilaration coursed through her blood. In her hand, she held bills from her first sale. Okay, so it wasn't enough for her to go out and buy a new car, but it was better than nothing, right? And this was also better than missing another year and another chance to make a name for herself.

She tucked the money away in a tin box and was just about to reseat herself next to Megan when an audible gasp came from behind her. Lacy spun around and connected gazes with Courtney. The younger girl, who now sported a spunky yet odd shade of blue hair, approached Lacy and placed both her palms on Lacy's stomach. "Oh my gosh, look at your belly. I can't believe how much you're showing."

"How did you—"

"Brody told me," Courtney announced while she ran her hands in circles over Lacy's stomach like she was some kind of magic lamp.

Lacy threw a glare at Brody when he appeared behind Courtney. "You have such a big mouth."

Brody lifted his hands. "She practically forced it out of me. What was I supposed to do?"

Courtney stepped back from Lacy. "What, you think you're going to be able to hide this? Look at you. Where is the idiotic man who did this to you, by the way?"

Lacy tugged on her shirt again. "He'll be by later. By the way, do you know Megan?"

Courtney's eyes, which always reminded Lacy of blue topaz, landed on Megan, who'd remained in her chair. "You're the sister from California?"

Lacy stepped around Courtney while the two girls introduced themselves. The people meandering by, as if they had no destination in mind, had thickened by slow degrees. Several people slowed their pace and tossed curious glances her way, but none of them stopped. Lacy grabbed one of the easels and pushed it farther out of the booth.

A warm, thick arm wound around her shoulders. "This looks really great." Brody pressed a soft kiss to her forehead. "I'm proud of you."

"Tell me that when I've sold some more stuff."

His gray eyes softened as he looked down at her. "It'll happen. Just give it some time."

"I know. That's my impatient side coming out."

Brody stepped back and slid his hands into his jeans pockets. "Where's Chase?"

Lacy absentmindedly placed a hand on her stomach. "He had to stop by the restaurant this morning. He'll be by soon." She narrowed her eyes at him. "You never talked to him, did you?"

"Lacy, I told you, we're fine. And I'm very happy for both of you." One of his palms cupped her cheek. "My brother is a lucky bastard."

"The two of you look a little too cozy for my comfort." The same deep timbre that whispered to her at night and sent delicious shivers down to her toes came from behind Brody. A pair of dark sunglasses covered Chase's eyes when he approached them. As always, her gaze danced over him and appreciated the way his black T-shirt hugged his wide torso like a lover. The shirt was tucked into a pair of soft-looking faded jeans that cupped his world-class ass like he just stepped out of a Levi Strauss commercial. Her stomach dipped and her heart turned over in a thousand somersaults when his freshly showered, unbelievably masculine scent swirled around her head.

"You're not jealous, are you, bro?" Brody asked as

his arm around her shoulder tightened. Ah, her big sweet Brody was such a gem.

"Not in the least." He tugged on Lacy's hand and pulled her out from under Brody. "But go find your own woman. Quit trying to make out with mine."

Brody kissed Lacy's cheek and whispered in her ear, "Just the reaction I was hoping for." He slugged his older brother in the shoulder and whistled as he strutted away.

God bless Brody McDermott. Someday some woman would be lucky enough to snag him.

"He did that on purpose," Chase said as he glared at his brother's backside.

"You know he enjoys getting a rise out of you."

He circled his arms around her thick middle. "Yeah, he's good at it." He nuzzled his nose just underneath her ear. "Pretty soon I won't be able to get my arms around you."

She let her head fall back so he could drop light kisses down her neck. "That's not very flattering."

"Are you kidding?" His hands roamed to her front where he flattened his palms over her round belly. "This is all mine."

"All right, already," Courtney groaned from behind them. "You're all hot for each other, we get it."

Chase kept his attention on Lacy. "Take a hike, Court." He pressed his hips against hers and dropped light kisses on her mouth.

"You know what? I think Megan and I will take a stroll around."

Lacy paid scarce attention to the two young women exiting the booth. She was too busy allowing Chase's tongue to slide into her mouth. His hand tunneled in the curtain of her hair and tipped her head back. After kissing like a couple of obsessed teenagers for several minutes, Chase stepped back and swiped his thumb across her bottom lip.

Lacy inhaled a steadying breath. "We ran everybody off."

"That was my intention. I wanted to be alone with you."

Lacy glanced around at the people walking by. "I wouldn't really say we're alone."

He pinched her rear. "Alone enough." A mousy squeak propelled out of her when she dodged another one of his grabs. "I came by to purchase some of this fine art before it's all gone." When she lifted a brow at him, he said, "You think I'm kidding?"

How could she take him seriously when he was just all over her? Or her heart had yet to come down from his kisses? Lacy shook her head. "Don't feel like you have to buy something."

Chase's long legs took him around the booth while his bottomless blue eyes darted from one drawing to the next. "This one's my favorite."

Lacy's gaze focused on the pink-blossomed tree she did several months ago. At first, she hadn't wanted to display that particular piece. Something about the tree had struck a chord within her, something deep and personal she hadn't been able to put a label on. She'd selfishly wanted to hoard it for herself so only she could enjoy the angelic beauty of it. Then one day, while walking past her drawing room, she caught sight of the piece. Her eyes landed on the tree, illuminated by the morning sun. There was something about the way the light captured the strokes of her pencil that almost moved her to tears. No other drawing had affected her on such a personal level before. And in that very brief moment she thought of her mother. Not the "how could she leave me?" bitter thoughts that had consumed her for so many years. This had been something entirely different. It was of times Lacy had had with her mother before the woman left.

Epiphanies or hallelujah moments didn't happen to her much. Lacy supposed what had happened to her that day had been as close to that as any other person could feel. In a hasty move, she gathered the drawing, took it to be enlarged, and set it with her other pieces for sale.

"I want this one," Chase said, pulling Lacy out of her memories. "And I want you to frame it for me."

Lacy swallowed the tennis ball–sized lump that formed in her throat. "But I don't have any frames."

"I know." He retrieved his wallet from his back pocket and withdrew a wad of cash. "Frame it for me. I want to hang it above my fireplace."

The stack of bills fluttered in his hand from the relentless wind. Her bargain-store flats remained rooted on the concrete.

"Look at you," he said with a tilt of his delicious lips. "You want to protest, don't you?"

She shook her head again. "It's not that. It's just—"

"You can't stand the idea of someone doing you a favor or giving you a handout." The picture remained in his grasp when he took a step toward her. "This isn't a handout, Lacy, or a favor. The picture reminds me of my mother."

Okay, *that* she wasn't expecting. Julianne McDermott was a vulnerable spot for all three of her sons and one they rarely spoke of. Lacy knew next to nothing about the woman other than what she looked like and that she had given birth to three outstanding men.

Lacy tilted her head up when Chase stopped a breath away from her. "How's that?"

He held up the drawing. "The house this tree sits in front of? She grew up there."

Lacy blinked. "You mean the house at the end of the street? Like, right down the street from me?" Chase nodded when Lacy paused. "Your mother lived in that house?"

"She lived there her whole life."

"I never knew that."

He glanced down at the picture. "She once told me a story about how she fell out of this tree and broke her arm. The second I saw this, I knew I had to have it. She would have loved this."

On an impulse, Lacy stood on her tiptoes and brushed a soft kiss on Chase's rough cheek. Oh, how she did love him. Never would she have guessed that Chase McDermott would have been the one to capture her heart. He'd always been the antithesis of everything she looked for in a man. However, she'd been half in love with him not long after moving back to Trouble. Her steady and dominate stubborn streak refused to allow her to acknowledge such feelings. In order to protect her vulnerable heart, she'd played it safe by keeping him at arm's length. Sparring with him had seemed like the best way of accomplishing that. After an interminable amount of time, she'd been unable to hold him at bay. Her defenses had grown too weak. His knowing looks and imposing presence had been more than her hormones could handle. Sometime after that, her heart had succumbed to him and there had been no looking back from that.

"Are you okay?" he asked after she'd been staring at him for too long.

She swept her lashes down in a slow blink. "I'm fine. This baby has a way of sucking all the energy out of me."

"Well, you're in luck because I have a treat for you tonight."

Both her brows lifted. "What sort of treat?"

"You'll just have to stop by and find out." He hefted the picture up. "Are you going to let me buy this or not?"

Lacy took the money from Chase, tucked it away in the tin box, and glued her eyes to his phenomenal backside when he tucked the drawing under one arm and waltzed away.

Several hours went by with slow but steady traffic. At the end of the first day, Lacy had sold about a dozen drawings. Not outstanding numbers, but still not half bad considering her current status in the art community. Brody, Courtney, and Megan came back and each purchased one drawing. Then they stayed to help her clean everything and load it all in Brody's truck. Chase had to go back to the restaurant but told Brody he'd be the one helping Lacy from now on. Lacy couldn't help the smile that appeared at Chase's caveman-like possessiveness. Completely offensive, yes, but unbelievably sweet.

Brody hauled her, along with all her stuff, to Chase's house, then left her standing by the front door with another smooch on the cheek.

Chase swung the door open before she had a chance to knock. "I heard you pull up," he explained when she only stared at him.

She stepped over the threshold. "You weren't by any chance waiting for me, were you?"

He shut the door with a provocative tilt of his mouth. "Now, why would I do that?"

"I can't imagine." She turned to face him. His untucked work shirt was a wrinkled mess and carried the distinct aroma of grease, sweat, and cooked food. His brown slacks were far from pressed perfection and had an odd dark stain on one side. All-day stubble shadowed his square jaw and made him look like some disreputable hellion. Overall, he looked like he'd just spent eight grueling hours going through the restaurant ringer.

Lacy had never seen anything sexier in her life.

For the second time that day, she gave in to her impulse and kissed him. She kissed him like her very life force depended on getting as physically close to him as possible. His tongue did a slow glide into her mouth and sent waves of quivers through her belly.

"Boy, you can't keep your hands off me today," Chase said when they separated.

Lacy shook her head. "Always looking for a way to stroke your ego."

"Are you feeling okay? Do you need to sit down?"

Would she ever get used to having someone love her as much as Chase did? "I'm a little tired. But other than that, I'm good."

He took her hand in his and led her upstairs. "Well, before I start pampering you, I need to show you something."

They went past his bedroom and stopped at the room at the end of the hallway. Lacy had never been in this room; Chase had been using it for storage and said he was going to turn it into an exercise room.

When Lacy got a peek inside, all the breath expelled from her lungs. The walls of the room had been painted a pale blue. A dark cherrywood crib with blue and brown bedding sat along one wall. A plushy recliner with stuffed animals was angled in the corner of the room. Next to that was a changing table.

She took a step inside and ran her eyes over the

infant-themed decorations. "It's darling," she whispered. "Did you do all this yourself?"

Chase leaned against the door frame. "Courtney and Avery helped me. They objected to me making everything blue. But I'm hopeful."

The room could have been painted lime green and she wouldn't have cared. She walked to the crib and ran her fingers along the top edge. "Tell them they can do one at my house for me."

"You won't need one at your house. This is for both of us."

His words tumbled over in her head. Did he mean what she thought he meant? Or was she reading more into it? She turned to face him just as he pushed away from the door.

He stopped just a hair away from her. "I want you to live here with me. As my wife."

What was left of her breath emptied out of her in a dizzying whoosh. As his wife? He wanted to marry her?

"I shouldn't have asked you to marry me the way I did before. It was impulsive and hasty." He gathered her clammy hands in his. "I'm not asking you now out of obligation. I'm asking because I want to wake up next to you every day for the rest of my life. I love you and I know you love me." He paused and touched her cheek. "Say you'll marry me."

Lacy had dreamed of this moment for months. Even though she'd tried terribly to push Chase away, she'd needed him. Maybe she'd always needed him but had been too stubborn to admit it to herself. Her desire to be with him now went way beyond need. She loved him with every follicle of her being.

"Yes, I'll marry you," she said through tears that had

pooled in her eyes. Several trickled over and Chase blotted them away with his fingers.

"Are you ready to be pampered now?"

She grinned and kissed him full on the lips. "Absolutely."

See the next page

for a preview of

ALONG CAME

TROUBLE.

ONE

SETTING ASIDE THE RESTAURANT'S OVERLY cluttered, sport-themed decor, the waitstaff was efficient, friendly, and brought the entrée in a *very* timely manner. However, I can only assume the reason the food was mediocre is in no small part due to the fact that it arrived in less than ten minutes. I'd like to be able to say the appearance made up for the bland, overcooked hamburger and sweet-potato fries with enough seasoning to set my mouth on fire…' "

Brody leaned back against his desk as his assistant manager, Charlene, lifted her eyes to his. "And?" he prompted.

Her tongue darted out along her bare lower lip before she continued reading. " 'But, unfortunately, the dish looked just as unsatisfying as it tasted. The hamburger was large enough to feed a small horse, yet sat on a bun much more suited for a silver dollar. Only about a dozen French fries accompanied my burger, and while most French fries tend to please my palate, these weren't worth eating more than one.' " Charlene dropped the magazine down to her lap and sent him a desperate look. He knew the feeling. "Do I have to keep reading this?"

He pinched the bridge of his nose to ward off a bitch of a headache. "Yes."

The magazine trembled when her fingers grasped the pages once again. " 'I forced myself to eat as much as I could, hoping to find some redemption, only to get my twenty-five ninety-nine's worth out of the meal. The only pleasant part was my waitress, who seemed to sense my disdain as she shot me a look of sympathy before carting away my half-eaten meal. The Golden Glove has been a staple of the small town of Trouble, Wyoming, for more than ten years now, but it's hardly worth the price. On the upside, I was able to catch the game from one of the dozen televisions mounted on the walls. Maybe the owner should have taken the money he spent on forty-six-inch LCD televisions and hired a better chef instead.' "

Charlene placed the magazine down with great care on his immaculate desk so as not to add yet another blow to poor Brody's day. "This is the second bad review we've had in six months, Brody."

"Yeah, no shit." He pushed away from the desk and tried to walk the agitation out of his bones. One bad review was enough to send a restaurant into restaurant hell, but two? He kept reminding himself that these kinds of restaurant reviewers were just freelance writers who couldn't make it as chefs, so they spent their time dogging every restaurant they could. But what were the chances of two different reviewers giving his restaurant such a similarly poor report?

When the Golden Glove had opened ten years ago, the place had had a line wrapped around the building just to get a seat at the bar. Even though he'd known next to nothing about restaurants, his father had placed him in charge. Brody had stepped in and done the best he could, which had been damn good if he did say so himself. The Golden Glove had thrived under his leadership for several years. So much so that Martin had eventually backed off and had given Brody free rein. Unfortunately, a series of simultaneous events, including losing their chef and R.J., had caused their numbers to dwindle. Despite his efforts, the Golden Glove was on a downward slide in terms of diners and profits.

In fact, the situation was so dire, if they kept up like this, they'd have to close their doors in six months. The thought created a sick feeling in the pit of his stomach, something he'd been dealing with a lot lately. And not only would all their employees be without jobs, but also Brody would lose his meal ticket and his means for taking care of Tyler.

Saving the Golden Glove was crucial to his and Tyler's futures.

"Well, the only good thing is this was written when we had Gary. Now we have Travis."

"That doesn't make me feel better." Brody eased into his chair and leaned his head back. Travis was their third executive chef this year. The man had come highly recommended by a manager of another restaurant in town. The fact that said restaurant recently announced its closing had sent tremors of uncertainty through Brody. Michael, the man who'd been the Golden Glove's original chef and a freakin' miracle worker, had left them for greener pastures. Greener pastures that had included the title of executive chef of a major five-star hotel in Los Angeles. Now, Brody wasn't going to lie to himself; Michael's departure had rubbed him the wrong way and left a sour taste in his mouth. After the sting had worn off, Brody admitted that Michael needed to do what was best for him and his three kids. Then Gary had come strolling in, promising to outshine Michael and put the Golden Glove on the map of great restaurants. After three short months, Brody had shown his incompetent ass the door.

Charlene stood from the chair, grabbed the magazine, and tossed it into the trash can. "That guy doesn't know what he's talking about. He's probably some loser who has nothing better to do with his time."

"He's right, though. Gary was a terrible chef. That's why I fired him."

She placed her hands on her narrow hips. "I'm trying to make you feel better, here. Tell me it's helping a little."

Brody stared back at her. "It's not helping."

She plowed fingers through her chin-length black hair. "Okay, here's what we're going to do. We're going to ignore this stupid review, go forward with the photo shoot today, and pray this relaunch will put this place back on its feet. Then we'll show people like that idiot reviewer we're worth coming back to."

Charlene's legs ate up the expanse of his office. "You're awfully confident."

"Why wouldn't I be? This place has been completely redecorated and looks way better than it did when it first opened, and we have a new chef." Then she added, "With a new menu."

"Are you saying you think Travis can turn this place around?"

"Don't you think he can?" Charlene's thin brows shot up her forehead.

Brody swiveled back and forth in his chair and ran a

hand along the edge of his desk. "I'm not sure yet. To be honest, I'm not all that impressed with him."

"He's a hell of a lot better than Gary."

A snort popped out of him. "My eleven-year-old son can cook better than that guy."

The corners of Charlene's lips turned up in a smile. She inhaled a deep breath and sat back down in the chair. "Look, I know you're still kind of pissed about Michael leaving and you think you won't find anyone as good as him. But you will. And I'd hate to be a killjoy or anything, but it could be a while before we get back to those days."

If they ever got back to those days. "Trust me, I know."

She leaned forward in her chair and propped an elbow on the edge of his desk. "I think we're taking a step in the right direction today. The place looks great and we've got an official photographer coming in to take the pictures. I know Travis is young, but I think he shows a lot of promise."

One of Charlene's best assets was her positive attitude. At times when Brody found himself moping like a moody teenager, Charlene would come in with her Julie Andrews–like persona and pep talk him into straightening up his act. Brody would be the first one to tell anyone he'd been an unbearable hard-ass since his divorce four years ago. Something about separating from Kelly had opened up a side of him even he hadn't known existed. Charlene had never let a moment escape without telling him to "get his shit together." Being spoken to like that wasn't something he appreciated, but from Charlene he tolerated it. She didn't put up with his crap anyway, so telling her to stuff it would only be speaking to air.

His assistant manager was four years younger than him and a force to be reckoned with. She also had a tender streak that ran deep in her, which wasn't something she allowed a lot of people to see. Shortly after his divorce, she'd allowed him to see that side of her when she showed up at his house with a bottle of wine and told him he needed to shave. For one weak moment, he indulged himself and broke one of his own cardinal rules by sleeping with her. Almost immediately following, he'd relented that he'd made a huge mistake. Granted, the release had been much needed, but its inappropriateness weighed on him. His employees knew full well the boundaries that management had set about professional relationships. Things like that only made for sticky, unfortunate situations. Luckily for him, Charlene had been professional and told him she had no intention of jumping into a relationship with him. Neither of them had mentioned that night since. Both were happy to pretend it had never happened.

"Tell me again why we're publishing pictures in the same magazine that just gave us a bad review?" he asked Charlene.

She lifted a finger. "First of all, that reviewer isn't employed by this magazine. Second of all, they're the only ones who agreed to do this spread. We could use the good publicity."

At this point Brody wasn't sure the restaurant was capable of generating good publicity. "Are you sure this photographer is any good?"

She narrowed her deep brown eyes at him. "You saw some of her work. She's been published in several food magazines and blogs."

"Forgive me if I'm a little paranoid." He leaned back in his chair and rubbed his hands over his weary eyes.

An exasperated sigh came from Charlene. "What happened to the Brody who never let anything bother him? I miss that guy."

"So do I," he muttered to the ceiling. "You said you know this girl?" he asked after lifting his head.

Charlene shrugged a slender shoulder. "I told you she's a friend of mine. When you said you wanted to do this, her name immediately popped into my head. Do you really think I'd ask her to do this if she didn't know what she was doing?" she asked after Brody had begun staring her down.

"I suppose you have a point."

A sneaky grin crept along her mouth. "And I'm sure that was so hard for you to admit."

Brody found himself smiling for the first time during their conversation. Yes, Charlene knew when to call his bullshit. The creak of his office door had him taking his attention off the woman in front of him.

Travis poked his head in the door. "The photographer's here."

Ah, yes. The photo shoot that was probably a waste of time to begin with. A spread in a magazine that had already trashed them? Would those same readers even give a damn about the Golden Glove's new, toned-down decor? Or the new chef who had introduced inventive, unique items? In his experience, once a diner had a bad meal at a restaurant, they were likely not to return. Not only that, but they'd also probably tell everyone within earshot to stay the hell away from the place. His father had already pitched a fit about the first bad review. Once he read the latest one, Brody was likely to be excommunicated. His earlier fear of his and Tyler's futures returned with a wicked vengeance. How would he pay for his son's college, or even his house, if he was unemployed?

"Brody?" Charlene asked after he'd failed to move from his chair. "You're on board with this, right?"

He blinked at her. "On board, right. Yeah." He pushed himself out of the chair and followed Charlene and Travis downstairs.

Okay, he'd be on board with this. As the restaurant's manager, he set the tone for the whole staff's morale. If he went around dragging his hands on the floor and grumbling like an ape, he'd be a pretty piss-poor leader. And Travis was a pretty good chef. Yes, the man had times where he was inconsistent, but for the most part he was good. Youth played a major part in his inability to perform on a steady level. With time, he'd be a valuable asset. Brody only hoped that the time he would need wouldn't be long. He didn't have the patience nor could he afford to be Travis's learning experience. The man needed to start showing some serious skill. Like, now. Maybe today would be that opportunity.

The dining room, recently redone to be more appealing to families and less to rowdy college students, had been mostly cleared for today's shoot. The tables and chairs had been pushed aside to make room for the "shooting area," as Charlene had described it. The restaurant had never done anything like this before, so he knew next to nothing about what to expect. Charlene told him the photographer would come in, set up her equipment and the food Travis had prepared, and snap pictures. Sounded short and simple to him.

Except it wasn't. The area that used to be the dining room now looked like a professional photographer's studio. In the middle of the room, surrounded by several tall lights and mirrors, were tables draped in dark brown tablecloths. Travis walked ahead of them and disappeared into the kitchen. Several seconds later, he reappeared with plates on each hand. He lowered them carefully to the tables, added garnishes, wiped the rims, and spun them around until satisfied they looked presentable.

After his inspection, he went back into the kitchen.

"Is all this really necessary?" Brody asked Charlene.

Charlene shot him a narrow-eyed look. "You can't just come in and take a few pictures of the food the way we would normally serve it. You have to doll it up and make it look attractive."

He lifted a hand toward the shoot area. "But we don't serve our dishes on brown tablecloths with wineglasses on the tables. Isn't that a bit misleading?"

They stopped next to one of the tall light things. "Brody, do you trust me?"

His eyebrows pulled together at her question. "I'm not sure."

She patted him on the arm like one would a small child. "Well, you're going to have to this time. Besides, this is the way food is photographed. And Elisa knows what she's doing."

He shot her a glance. "Elisa?"

"The photographer."

Bright morning sunshine glanced over them when the doors to the restaurant opened. A tall woman with hair the color of a moonless night hanging halfway down her back floated across the parquet wood floor. Her attention was on a spiral notebook, which was cradled in long, thin arms. Her fingers thumbed back and forth through the pages and her eyes darted from one page to the next. A loose-fitting, flower-printed blouse covered petite shoulders and disappeared beneath the waistband of wide-legged, light gray slacks. She was as professionally dressed as any person in a corporate office, yet the gentle sway of her hips exuded a magnetic sexuality that had blood rushing to his groin.

The woman set the notebook down on a table, and then her long legs took her to a bag on the floor.

Brody's eyes followed her every move. "Did we hire a model for this shoot?"

Charlene had started to walk toward the woman. She glanced back at him. "What?"

He jerked his head in the Amazon's direction.

One corner of Charlene's mouth curled up. "She's the photographer."

"Are you sure?" The woman who looked like she should be posing in front of the camera was behind it instead?

"Quite sure." Always-present amusement lit up Charlene's eyes.

Brody sauntered over to focus on the tables with the food only because he didn't want to stand around looking like he had his thumb up his ass. This whole thing had been Charlene's gig. Right after the last reviewer came in, she'd expressed her concern about getting a decent review from him. To quickly clean up the mess, she'd suggested redecorating the place and having some of their dishes showcased in the same magazine. Because he didn't know jack about decorating, Charlene had taken the reins on that as well. With his father's approval, she'd replaced the carpeting with concrete flooring. At first Brody had frowned at the choice, but after seeing it he'd realized how much more fitting it was, because it gave a more casual look. The walls, once covered in wood paneling, which Brody had never liked, had been completely refurbished with paint and collages of sports pictures. Even the lighting had been changed. Once dim, and not fitting for a family restaurant, they now had bright overhead lights that made the place feel so much more open. The result was a revamped, fresher, family-friendly atmosphere.

His father had only shown mild enthusiasm, which was typical for the man. Brody could have shown his father an article stating all three of his restaurants were voted best in the country, and the news would earn Brody nothing more than a tight-lipped smile. Not that his father was that much of a hard-ass. He was just a serious and competitive business-man who never took his restaurants' success for granted.

Travis had prepared a wide variety of dishes and ones that were more favored among their diners. Chinese chicken salad, minestrone soup, a bar-b-queue-bacon-cheddar burger and a grilled chicken penne pasta with a garlic bread stick sat on pristine white plates. Charlene may have organized this, but Brody had handpicked the dishes. Two of them were Travis's signature meals and had proven to be very popular with the diners.

"You're in my light."

The let-me-seduce-you, husky voice came from directly behind him and danced over his skin. Brody glanced over his shoulder and locked gazes with the willowy Amazon who already had certain parts below his belt stirring. The woman either found time to visit a tanning salon on a regular basis or had a natural olive complexion. Almond-shaped eyes accented by thick, black lashes gazed back at him. The corners of her full, pillowy mouth were turned up ever so slightly.

"Sorry," he managed. For hell's sake, he ran a successful business, dealt with servers, chefs, and customers on a daily basis and he barely managed a two-syllable word. He'd really been out of the dating game too long.

When he stepped aside, she continued adjusting the

mirror her ring-adorned fingers were wrapped around. The smooth skin of her forehead furrowed as she concentrated on her task.

"Is this going to be enough light?" he asked her.

Her attention remained on the food as she tried to achieve the right angle with the mirror. "Windows are best, but I can make do with the skylights. Plus I have lights." She extended her hand to his. "I'm Elisa, by the way."

Brody allowed his eyes to drop down to her mouth one more time before wrapping his hand around hers. Her fingers were long and thin and the silver rings she wore were cool against his palm. His hand lingered in hers, probably longer than necessary, but what the hell. Her hand felt good in his, a perfect fit. And he liked the way her hand felt wrapped up in his, small and feminine. A sudden image of them on his skin, exploring intimate parts of his body, slammed into him and assaulted his senses.

"Brody." Another two-syllable word he had trouble forcing out of his mouth. What was wrong with him today? He'd always been able to hold a semi-intelligent conversation with an attractive woman before. Then, in comes this exotic beauty and his brain ceases to function.

"Nice to meet you," she replied with a playful gleam in her dark brown eyes. Before he was ready to let go, she slipped her hand from his and continued adjusting all her lights, mirrors, and other props.

Thirty minutes went before she actually started snapping pictures. The first dish was arranged on the brown cloth-covered table with silverware and napkins placed casually about as if an actual diner had been sitting there. The wineglasses had been picked up and moved half a dozen times before Elisa was satisfied they were in just the right spot. After giving the setup one final glance, she took an expensive-looking camera out of a bag and dropped to her knees directly in front of the table. With her elbows resting on the table, Elisa cradled the camera in her hands and started snapping rapid pictures, one after the other.

"She sure is thorough," Brody muttered to Charlene.

"I told you she was good."

Not only was she good with the camera, but also her ass looked damn fine in those slacks of hers—round but petite at the same time. The same image of her hands roaming over him continued, only this time her derriere took a front-and-center role. He bet it would feel damn good cradled in his lap rubbing against his thighs...

Okay, you're supposed to be saving your restaurant here, and all you can do is admire the photographer's ass?

Time to be professional.

"You might want to keep your eyes on a place that won't get you sued for sexual harassment." Charlene had the nerve to actually smirk.

He tossed her a narrowed-eyed look. "You're not funny."

As usual, Charlene ignored his surly remarks. "She could be a while. I'm going to work on next week's schedule." And with that, Charlene left him alone with the woman who made him stumble over two-syllable words. And had a great ass. *And* had soft hands.

Over an hour passed and Elisa had only done two dishes. Her camera would rattle off, and then she'd stop to make an adjustment with one of the mirrors or point the lights in a different direction. Call him ignorant, but Brody had no idea so much went into taking pictures of food. He'd thought Travis would cook some dishes, place them on a table, and he would take some pictures with his digital camera. Charlene had rolled her eyes like a teenage girl when he'd told her this. "Why don't you let me take care of this?" was what she'd said to him.

Gladly. He'd had enough on his plate at the time, including having to decide which employees had to take fewer hours in order to cut back on costs.

Elisa lowered her camera and rolled her head from side to side.

"Do you need a break?" he asked her.

She craned her head over her neck and then stood. "No, I'm fine. If I stop, I might lose momentum."

"I was thinking the soup would look better with some steam coming out of it."

Elisa set her camera down, then pulled her hair back in a high ponytail, revealing a long neck. One that was perfect for dropping light kisses onto. "I always digitally add steam in later. If you want it."

His eyes danced over her neck. He'd never paid such attention to a woman's neck before, so why was he starting now? "Won't digital steam look fake?"

"Charlene said you'd never done this before," she said with an alluring smile. "Digital steam looks just as good as the real stuff. Besides, real steam is too much of a variable. The slightest breeze can make it curl in an unattractive shape."

Suddenly he found himself interested in the art of photographing food. Who knew? "And all the mirrors? What are those for?"

She planted her hands on her slim hips and ran her tongue along her lower lip. It was full and looked good enough to nibble. "They deflect the light in different directions. Different foods need light coming from different angles." She gestured to the table. "Like with the salad, I had the light coming from behind so you can see the veins in the lettuce. But the soup needed light coming from above so you can see the reflection on the surface of the liquid. With the hamburger, I'll probably have the light coming from behind so we'll have some cool reflections on the plate and also have some translucency in the tomato…" Her deep eyes lit on his. "Sorry. I tend to get carried away when people ask me about taking pictures. Most people don't realize how technical this all is." Her laugh was melodious and blood rushed down to his groin.

He barely managed not to adjust himself around her, glanced at the staging area. "Very technical, I can tell."

Her teeth nibbled her lower lip.

If she didn't stop that, he'd do something to seriously embarrass himself.

"I'm boring you, aren't I?" she said. "It's just that you're the first client to ask me questions. Most don't care about the process, only the end result."

His eyes stayed on her white teeth, which were still worrying that delectable lower lip. "It's not boring at all." Well, he wouldn't go that far. It was a little boring. The light in her eyes alone was reason enough to keep asking her questions. "This is all new to me. I just thought I'd be able to take pictures with my camera and send them to the magazine."

"That's what most people think. But you would have ended up with yellow food." When he lifted a brow, she continued. "Light is very important to photographing food. If you don't have enough, the food in the picture will look yellow. Not very attractive to potential customers."

He nodded his understanding even though the science of it still eluded him. "That makes sense."

Elisa's eyes roamed down to his mouth before she cleared her throat and picked up her camera again. Was she checking him out? Could he possibly be having the same effect on her that she was having on him? Couldn't be because he hadn't been this attracted to a woman in a long time.

"After you're done, you should stay for something to eat." *Now, why would you go and say that? Isn't it bad enough you've been staring at her ass, and now you have to come on to her?* "You're taking pictures for us. The least you could let me do is feed you." *Okay, that sounded much more reasonable, not like you're trying to hit on her while she's doing a job for you.*

She gazed at him over her slender shoulder. "I'll have a Caesar salad with grilled chicken."

THE DISH

Where Authors Give You the Inside Scoop

♥ ♥ ♥ ♥ ♥ ♥ ♥ ♥ ♥ ♥ ♥ ♥ ♥ ♥ ♥ ♥ ♥

From the desk of Jennifer Delamere

Dear Reader,

One reason I love writing historical fiction is that I find fascinating facts during my research that I can use to add spice to my novels.

For Tom Poole's story in A LADY MOST LOVELY, I was particularly inspired by an intriguing tidbit I found while researching shipwrecks off the southern coast of Australia. In describing the wreck of a steamer called *Champion* in the 1850s, the article included this one line: "A racehorse aboard *Champion* broke loose, swam seven miles to the shore, and raced again in the Western District." Isn't that amazing!? Not only that the horse could make it to land, but that it remained healthy enough to continue racing.

Although I was unable to find out any more details about the racehorse, as a writer this little piece of information was really all I needed. I knew it would be a wonderful way to introduce the animal that would come to mean so much to Tom Poole. Tom and the stallion are the only survivors of a terrible shipwreck that left them washed up on the coast near Melbourne, Australia, in early 1851. Tom was aboard that ship in the first place because he was chasing after the man who had murdered his best friend. By the time he meets Margaret Vaughn in A LADY MOST LOVELY, Tom has been involved in two other real-life events as well: a massive wildfire near Melbourne, and the gold rush that would ultimately make him a wealthy man.

As you may have guessed by now, Tom Poole is a man of action. This aspect of his nature certainly leads him into some interesting adventures! However, when he arrives in London and meets the beguiling but elusive Miss Margaret Vaughn, he's going to discover that affairs of the heart require an entirely different set of skills, but no less determination.

Jennifer Delamere

♥ ♥ ♥ ♥ ♥ ♥ ♥ ♥ ♥ ♥ ♥ ♥ ♥ ♥ ♥ ♥ ♥

From the desk of Erin Kern

Dear Reader,

There are two things in this world that I love almost as much as dark chocolate. One of them is a striking pair of blue eyes framed by thick black lashes, with equally dark hair just long enough for a woman's fingers to run through...Excuse me for a moment while I compose myself.

And the other is fried pie.

Okay, I just threw that last part in as an FYI. But what I'm really doing is tucking that useless tidbit away for a future project. That's just how my weird mind works, folks.

But in all seriousness, while I really do love a blue-eyed man, even more than that I love a wounded soul. Because I love to fix things. In my books. In real life I kind of suck at it.

Way back when I first started writing the Trouble series, as was kicked off with *Looking for Trouble*, I had an atypical wounded soul already forming in the cavernous recesses of my mind. I just needed to find a home for her.

Yes, I'm talking about a wounded heroine. I know that sounds kind of strange. Most romance readers love a scarred hero who gets his butt kicked into shape by some head-strong Miss Fix-It. Not that I don't love that also. But I also knew *Looking for Trouble* wasn't the place for her.

Lacy Taylor needed her own story with her own hero. And not only her own hero, but one with an extra tough brand of love that could break through her well-built defense mechanisms.

But make no mistake. Lacy Taylor isn't as much of a tough cookie as she'd like everyone to think. Oh, no. She has a much softer side that only Chase McDermott could bring to the surface. Of course, she tries to keep Chase at arm's length like everyone else in her life. But he's too good for her defenses. Too good-looking. Too loose-hipped. Too quick with his melt-your-bones smile. Not to mention his blue eyes. Gotta have those baby blues.

But Chase underestimates Lacy's power. And I'm not talking about her tough-girl attitude. Never in Chase's years as an adult would he have expected Lacy Taylor to get under his skin so quickly. Not only that, but nothing could have prepared him for his reaction to it.

Or to her.

You see, Chase and Lacy have known each other for a long time. And that's another one of my weaknesses—childhood crushes turned steamy love stories. And Chase and Lacy can cook up steam faster than a drop of water on hot pavement. But it wasn't always like that for these two. You see, Lacy blew out of Trouble years earlier, and after that Chase hardly gave the tough blonde a second thought.

But then she comes back. Now *that's* when things get interesting.

Mostly because Lacy had to all but beg Chase for a job, which, in Lacy's opinion, was almost as painful as a bikini wax. So then they're working together. Seeing each other often. Subtle brushes here and there…you get the picture.

It gets hot. *Real* hot.

But the most fun part is seeing how these two wear each other down. Lacy thinks she's so tough, and Chase thinks he can charm the habit off a nun. Well, actually he probably could.

Needless to say, heads butt, tempers flare, and the clothes, they go a-flying.

But which of these comes first? It's all in HERE COMES TROUBLE. Because every woman needs some Trouble in her life.

Especially the blue-eyed kind.

Steamy readin',

Erin Kern

♥ ♥ ♥ ♥ ♥ ♥ ♥ ♥ ♥ ♥ ♥ ♥ ♥ ♥ ♥

From the desk of Lily Dalton

Dear Reader,

History has always been my thing.

Boring? Never! I've always viewed the subject as a colorful, dynamic puzzle of moving pieces, fascinating to analyze and relive, in whatever way possible. I used to have a history professor who often raised the question, "What if?"

For example, what if Ragnar Lodbrok and his naughty horde of Vikings had decided that they adored farming, so instead of setting off to maraud the coast of England in search adventure and riches, they had just stayed home? How might that omission from history have changed the face of England?

And jumping forward a few centuries: What if historical bad boy Henry VIII had not had such poor impulse control, and had instead just behaved himself? What if he'd tried harder to be faithful to Catherine? What if he'd never taken a shine to Anne Boleyn? There wouldn't have been an Elizabeth I. How might this have changed the path of history?

At the heart of history, of course, are people and personalities and motivations. *Characters.* They weren't flat, dusty words in black and white on the pages of a textbook. Instead, they lived in a vivid, colorful, and dangerous world. They had hearts and feelings and suffered agonies and joy.

Just like Vane Barwick, the Duke of Claxton, and his

estranged wife, the duchess Sophia, who stand on the precipice of a forever sort of good-bye. Though the earlier days of their marriage were marked by passion and bliss, so much has happened since, and on this cold, dark night, understanding and forgiveness seem impossible.

Of course, in NEVER DESIRE A DUKE, the "what if?" is a much simpler question, in that the outcome will not change the course of nations.

What if there hadn't been a snow storm that night?

Hmm. Now that I've forced that difficult question upon us, I realize I don't want to imagine such an alternate ending to Vane and Sophia's love story. Being snowbound with someone gorgeous and intriguing and desirable and, yes, provoking, is such a delicious fantasy.

If there hadn't been a snow storm that night. . .

Well . . . thankfully, dear reader, there was!

Hugs and Happy Reading,

Lily Dalton

www.lilydalton.com
Twitter@LilyDalton
Facebook.com

♥ ♥ ♥ ♥ ♥ ♥ ♥ ♥ ♥ ♥ ♥ ♥ ♥ ♥ ♥

From the desk of Debbie Mason

Dear Reader,

So there I was, sitting in my office in the middle of a heat wave, staring at a blank page waiting for inspiration to strike. I typed Chapter One. Nothing. Nada.

And the problem wasn't that I was writing a Christmas story in the middle of July. I had the air conditioner cranked up, holiday music playing in the background, a pine-scented candle burning, and a supply of Hammond's chocolate-filled peppermint candy canes on my desk. FYI, best candy canes ever!

No, the problem was my heroine, Madison Lane. I didn't get her, and honestly, I was afraid I wasn't going to like her very much. Because really, who doesn't love Christmas and small towns? At that point, I was thinking of changing the title from *The Trouble with Christmas* to *The Trouble with Madison Lane*.

It took a couple of hours of staring at her picture on my wall before Madison finally opened up to me. Okay, so I may have thrown a few darts at her, drawn devil horns on her head, and given her an impressive mustache before she did. But she won me over. Once I found out what had happened to her in that small Southern town all those years ago, I fell in love with Madison. She's strong, incredibly smart, and loyal, and after what she suffered as a little girl, she deserves a happily-ever-after more than most.

Now all I needed was a man who was up for the challenge. Enter Gage McBride, the gorgeous small-town sheriff and single father of two young girls. A born protector, Gage is strong enough to deal with Madison and smart enough to see the sweet and vulnerable woman beneath her tough, take-no-prisoners attitude. But just because these two are a perfect match doesn't mean their journey to a happily-ever-after is an easy one. The title of the book is THE TROUBLE WITH CHRISTMAS, after all.

I hope you have as much fun reading Gage and Madison's story as I did writing it. And I hope, like Gage and Madison, that this holiday season finds you surrounded by the love of family and friends.

Wishing you much joy and laughter!